STAR REQUIEM

BOOK 3

WARLORD OF HEAVEN

A D R I A N   C O L E

AVON BOOKS • NEW YORK

W9-CUI-179

Other Avon Books in the
STAR REQUIEM *Series*

BOOK ONE
MOTHER OF STORMS

BOOK TWO
THIEF OF DREAMS

Coming Soon

BOOK FOUR
LABYRINTH OF WORLDS

AVON BOOKS
A division of
The Hearst Corporation
1350 Avenue of the Americas
New York, New York 10019

Copyright © 1990 by Adrian Cole
Cover illustration by Lee Gibbons
Published by arrangement with the author
Library of Congress Catalog Card Number: 92-93579
ISBN: 0-380-76769-4

First AvoNova Printing: April 1993

AVONOVA TRADEMARK REG. U.S. PAT. OFF. AND IN OTHER COUNTRIES, MARCA REGISTRADA, HECHO EN U.S.A.

Printed in the U.S.A.

RA 10 9 8 7 6 5 4 3 2 1

CONTENTS

PREFACE

THE LAST DAYS OF MAN

Man once ruled over an empire that stretched throughout countless worlds, worlds that formed a complex cycle, a self-contained chain.

In his hunger for knowledge, Man unlocked the door to another realm, that of the alien race, the Csendook, and thus began a thousand-year war in which these ferocious aliens, faster and stronger than Man, began the inexorable conquest of his empire.

In desperation, facing extinction, Man's Imperator Elect and his Consulate sought to escape the Csendook tide. On the world of Eannor, the Imperator's Prime Consul and principal scientist, Zellorian, used dark and forbidden powers to create a gate into a separate cycle of worlds, a feat thought to be impossible. Zellorian brought the Imperator Elect, his remaining Consulate and the last of Man's army through to the world of Innasmorn, the Mother of Storms.

Innasmorn is a world of elemental forces, where the storms are worshipped as gods by its inhabitants. They, who are themselves partly elemental, have no use for technology and have almost completely outlawed the use of metals. When they learn of the arrival of the intruders, the Men of the Imperator, they begin preparations for a war.

However, a small group of Innasmornians under Ussemitus, a woodsman, question the decision of the Shamen, the Windmasters, to carry war to the intruders, about whom little is known. Ussemitus meets Aru Casruel, a girl who flees the Sculpted City, where the Imperator has built a base in the mountains. Aru warns Ussemitus that Zellorian is prompting the Imperator to subdue the people of Innasmorn. Those in the Sculpted City who would prefer an alliance and peace with the races of Innasmorn are being eliminated by the ruthless Zellorian.

Ussemitus and Aru begin a search for a forbidden land far in the west of Innasmorn, which is said to contain ancient powers. They fear that Zellorian will seek out these powers and attempt to harness them in his new thirst for control. With the help of a renegade Windmaster, Quareem, Zellorian attempts to release the storm-of-the-dark, terrible destructive forces chained by the gods of Innasmorn, but Ussemitus and his companions enlist the help of the Windmasters and thwart Zellorian's ambitions.

As the shadow of a new war threatens to embroil Man on Innasmorn, the victorious Csendook declare their own Crusade against Mankind ended. A Supreme Sanguinary is appointed, Auganzar, and he is given the task of subduing the last surviving Men in the original world cycle. Auganzar creates gladiatorial schools, where Men are trained as *moillum*, human gladiators who have exchanged their freedom for service to the Csendook. They perform in the Games and are used to hunt down fellow Men who will not capitulate, for which the *moillum* are well rewarded.

But Auganzar is obsessed with the belief that the Imperator Elect is still alive and that somehow he has evaded the Csendook and achieved the unthinkable, breaking through the very fabric of the world cycle to whatever lies beyond. When the Csendook military rulers, the Garazenda, learn that Auganzar may be seeking the Imperator Elect, some of them, led by Zuldamar, embark on a secret plot to assassinate him as they have no desire to renew the costly Crusade.

Auganzar sends one of his loyal commanders, Vorenzar, to the world of Eannor, where it is believed by most Csendook that the Imperator Elect perished along with Zellorian and his principal supporters. But Vorenzar has been charged by Auganzar with searching for any trail that might lead to the Imperator: he has been told to find him at any cost.

Using an Opener, one of the Csendook sub-races bred for the creating of gates between worlds, Vorenzar finds a way through to Innasmorn, aided by a strange, ghost-like guide that promises him power. With a handful of survivors from the carnage of the Crossing, Vorenzar hears of and searches for a land in the far west of Innasmorn that is said to contain absolute power – the World Splinter.

Meanwhile, Ussemitus and his companions also journey to the lands of the west in search of the fabulous land, knowing that Zellorian will be seeking its powers for his own ends. The gliderboat of Ussemitus is pursued by another similar craft, the quasi-human death machine, a black gliderboat, created by Zellorian.

Ultimately Ussemitus and his companions reach the World Splinter, an immense fragment of a lost world of power, and in a grim struggle defeat Vorenzar and his minions and turn aside the corrupt power of the black gliderboat. The dark powers that Innasmorn once chained are now embroiled in the conflict, using the evil in Vorenzar and in Zellorian's terrible servant to release a Malefic, a nightmare force that prepares to unleash the old powers of the night.

As Ussemitus and his companions make ready to carry the war to Zellorian, Auganzar renews his determined hunt for the key to Innasmorn, while his enemies devise the scheme that will destroy him and ensure Man's freedom.

PROLOGUE

Vittargattus stirred in his sleep, but it was no dream that troubled him. Once he had been cursed with nightmares, the sendings of his enemies, rebel Windmasters. But something in the tent had disturbed his sleep. He swung round, arm coming up from under thick pelts, knife flashing in the early light of dawn. He was one of the few men of the Vaza who carried metal.

The warrior who stood in the opening to the tent of the clan chief smiled wryly. Vittargattus was sharper than ever these days, as alert and deadly as he had ever been. Perhaps it was the smell of war in the air, injecting new youth into his veins.

'Sire, there is something you should see. The watchers on the hill report a shadow coming from the north west.'

'A storm?'

'They think not.'

Vittargattus grunted, slipping easily from the bed and wrapping a fur about him. The day would be hot, but the air in the forests was yet cool at this early hour.

'Ondrabal is awake also,' said the warrior. 'He is coming.'

Vittargattus nodded, strapping on a belt and clipping the broadsword in its scabbard to it. He strode out into the light. Below him in the forest the tents were pitched right to the edge of the trees and he could hear the stirring of the horses, hundreds of them. His own tent and those of his chiefs were pitched on this hill above the army, while those of Ondrabal were to his right on the adjoining hill. The two armies had met less than three weeks previously, both having been on the march for what seemed like months. It was difficult to maintain order: the warriors were eager for a taste of battle.

Figures moved in the last wisps of early morning mist

and Vittargattus recognised Ondrabal, King of the southern nations and his newest ally. Ondrabal was a man as large as Vittargattus, though less unkempt : he wore his hair short, cropped, and had no beard, just a thin black line of moustache. He was several years younger than the Vaza warlord but his eyes spoke of the power that had commanded armies as large as any amassed by the Vaza nation. Once he and Vittargattus might have been enemies but in these troubled days they had been glad to put aside their differences. Such meetings as they had had recently augured well for their alliance.

Ondrabal inclined his head as he came up to the Vaza clan chief. 'Our scouts have seen something,' he said.

'Have the Windmasters been told?' Vittargattus asked his guard.

'Azrand is awake.'

'My Seers are also alert to this strange thing,' said Ondrabal. He had noticed that Vittargattus did not seem unduly perturbed.

Behind them they heard soft movement in the grass. It was Azrand, his long hair flowing over his shoulders, gleaming in the light. 'We have seen this craft before,' he said.

Ondrabal's eyes narrowed. 'Is this the flying creature you spoke of? The *machine*?'

Azrand answered for his ruler. 'Sire, it is the gliderboat.'

'Come to warn us away from the north-eastern mountains, I'll warrant,' snorted the clan chief.

'You trust them?' said Ondrabal, who had heard several unsettling tales of the mysterious allies of the Vaza, the ones who had fought against a rebel Windmaster in the Dhumvald and who had, it was spoken, prevented the unleashing of the deathstorm there. If this were true, these would be allies indeed.

Azrand again answered for his clan chief. 'We have to, sire.'

Vittargattus looked up at the skies. He could discern distant movement. A craft, little bigger than a speck over the horizon, but coming nearer. 'I told them I would not be turned from war. Let them beware the consequences of suing for peace.'

Ondrabal also watched the skies, but he did not yet voice an opinion.

In the gliderboat, Jubaia studied the forests below them. In the far distance he had caught sight of something on the low hills: the camp, he was sure, of Vittargattus, now swelled by the tents of his southern ally, King Ondrabal. A formidable army.

Aru squeezed up beside him in the prow of the craft. 'You have seen them?' The little thief nodded. He turned, his lock of hair trailing in the wind, his eyes lidded against the cool flow of air. 'It is the army. Vittargattus has been as good as his word. He and Ondrabal march on the Sculpted City.'

Aru called back to the others, Fomond and Armestor. 'How far to the mountains in the north-east?'

Fomond grinned. 'It will take them a month. The southerners aren't used to these forests. They prefer their grasslands!'

Armestor had unslung his bow and was testing its string. 'Spoken like a true forester. But quite so. At least a month.'

'Neither of them will travel quickly in the mountains,' said Aru. 'I know that terrain.'

'Whatever,' said Jubaia, 'we don't have much time. So who will talk to Vittargattus?'

'I see no reason to alter our plan,' said Aru as the hills flashed closer.

Don't ask me to land among them, came the voice of Circu, the gliderboat, gentle in the minds of both Aru and Jubaia.

The little thief chuckled. 'Have no fear. We will not tempt disaster. I recall well enough my last moments in the city of the clan chief.'

'Azrand is with them,' said Aru. 'I can feel his mind upon us.'

Fomond and Armestor could not help but shiver at the thought of the powerful Windmaster. They wondered if Aru could speak to his mind as Ussemitus had. Their journey to the far west, to the World Splinter, had wrought changes in all of them. 'Are you ready?' said Aru, cutting into his own thoughts.

Fomond nodded, watching the speeding forests, the land of his birth. 'Yes. And you, Armestor? We act as agreed?'

Armestor's face contorted in a grimace that brought smiles from his companions. 'I still think they'll hang us up for the crows.'

'Nonsense!' said Aru. 'They know we're allies.'

'Of course,' rejoined Jubaia. 'And they must be eager to hear of our journey to the west.'

'Yet you won't land,' snorted Armestor.

Jubaia looked away, muttering something and pretending to study the ground, the oncoming hills. Aru laughed softly. 'These are your lands, your people. They have no reason to harm you.'

Fomond looked more serious. 'We'll do what we have planned. Though I must be honest and say that our chances of halting this march on your city are slim, Aru. Such an alliance as you see below is a rare thing. Only the threat of a powerful mutual enemy could have brought the Vaza nations and those of Ondrabal together. Unless they get an opportunity to release their war-lust on Zellorian's stronghold, they'll begin quarrelling among themselves.'

'We need time,' said Aru. 'Time to warn my allies in the city. I have to get word to Pyramors. He is the only hope for my people. If he can be persuaded to abandon the city, to bring his own supporters out with him, then your people can attack it. They can unleash their storms.'

'If only Ussemitus had come back with us,' grumbled Armestor. 'He was the most persuasive, the most powerful of us. Vittargattus would have listened to him.'

Aru's face clouded in anger. 'He has more vital work! We cannot rely on one man, Armestor. He gave us all responsibilities. Now that it's time to exercise them, you carp! We follow the plan. You and Fomond – '

'*Peace*,' said Fomond, holding up his hand. He understood Aru's sadness at Ussemitus's decision not to come with them.

'Armestor and I will go down to them. You and Jubaia fly on to the Sculpted City. With all haste.'

Aru began to cool down, nodding slowly. 'I'm sorry,' she murmured. Armestor also nodded. The tension in the craft had stretched them all out like the strings of his bows. It had been a long flight from the World Splinter. Like the warriors below, they needed action.

Jubaia guided the craft downwards and they made out the faces of countless warriors in the trees, gazing up with amazement. They watched this craft above them, like a huge bird, arms sweeping out from its sides, gliding in silence over the trees, gleaming in the sunlight as if cast in metal and not made of flesh at all.

On the hills above the armies, Vittargattus prepared to receive the ambassadors he had once been eager to execute.

Far across the world, from the mouth of an immense cavern, a single figure stared up at the skies of Innasmorn, where darkness writhed and unseen storms swirled, as if hesitating to unleash themselves on the stark landscape below. Night held sway, blotting out the stars, a blanket that smothered the land, shutting off its life from the eyes and thoughts of the solitary figure.

Aru and the others had gone beyond his reach. He had listened to their passage back through the skies to the eastern continent for a while, but no longer. The night had claimed them, though by now they would likely be in a new dawn.

Ussemitus already felt an ache at their parting. He had known that they would part, and even though they must come together again in time if they were to avert the chaos that threatened Innasmorn, he understood that Aru could never be his, not now. It had been a shock to know this, to realise that his need for her, his love, was far deeper than he had admitted to himself. He had wavered, here in the World Splinter, with its powers roaring in his ears. Knowing that she read his love, that she would have returned it, made it all the harder.

But he had been brought here. The Mother shaped him, his destiny. He belonged to her. And it was not for him to deny her.

He looked for the last time that night at the skies, listening to the wind as it hurled itself in useless fury at the immensity of the World Splinter, source of so much power. Something was loose in those skies now, a horror beyond knowing.

Ussemitus turned. Somewhere in this vast reservoir of power he must find what he needed to prepare himself, and his world, for the coming of endless night.

BOOK ONE

PYRAMORS

1

ULDENZAR

'He will be here tomorrow.'

The Csendook Zarull spoke softly, as though the shadows would steal his words and carry them like a threat beyond the stone walls and out to waiting enemies. Uldenzar did not feel secure away from the barracks of his warhall, even here in the castle of the Keeper. He was a huge Csendook, his muscled arms and stony face scarred, a warrior who had been involved in many fierce campaigns and who now trained his Zemoi hard, using them to make gladiators out of the human slaves, the *moillum*, who the wars had subjugated and cast into the schools, the warhalls. But Uldenzar understood fear.

Beyond him, at the edge of the torchlight, Cmizen sat stiffly, his mind on the promised arrival. His own unease was far more evident than Uldenzar's.

'Tomorrow,' he repeated. 'What does he want this time?'

'The Supreme Sanguinary will review the land beyond the towers, once again. He will never tire of it.'

'Since my reinstatement on Eannor,' said Cmizen tiredly, 'he has been here repeatedly. The Garazenda assume he is merely trying to ensure that there are no more accidents, tightening the security of this world.'

'Our master, Zuldamar, knows better,' smiled Uldenzar, though it took none of the fierceness from his face. He watched Cmizen closely, reading the fresh terror in the Csendook. Cmizen was smaller than most of his kind, though fatter, and did not have the look of a warrior who trained much. Had he ever seen battle, true battle? Uldenzar doubted it. It seemed to him as though Cmizen had been put here on Eannor merely as a puppet, easily controlled, but Uldenzar would not have been content to have such a cowardly warrior as an agent. It meant relying on his fears to control him, and although Cmizen was undoubtedly afraid to disappoint the

3

Marozul, Zuldamar, he was also terrified of Auganzar, the Supreme Sanguinary.

'He will be looking for a sign of Vorenzar's return,' said Uldenzar.

Cmizen's face twisted with distaste. 'He will search until the world breaks apart. Neither Vorenzar nor his Zemoks will ever return.'

Uldenzar nodded slowly. He was almost convinced: Cmizen seemed sure of it. He would never speak in detail of the ritual that had sent Vorenzar through the forbidden gate to a realm beyond the cycle of worlds, but Uldenzar did not press him on the matter. He had his strict orders from Zuldamar, whom he served faithfully. He was here on Eannor to train *moillum*, and for a specific purpose.

Since the mysterious disaster in which Vorenzar and a large company of Zemoks and *moillum* had been, so the reports said, destroyed, there had been a number of developments on Eannor. At first there had been heated discussion among the Garazenda as to what the future of Eannor should be. Some felt that it should be properly sealed, as there were certain terrible dangers in parts of the world. However, the debates concluded with an agreement that Eannor should continue to be used as a training ground for *moillum* but that the dangerous areas should be strictly forbidden to all Csendook, on pain of death. This was a rule that excluded a handful of warriors, those who watched over the areas where so many had died.

Cmizen, Keeper during the last disaster, had been restored to his post, as had his Opener, Etrascu. Both were weak, but they were unambitious and unlikely to desire to tamper with the danger zones, as Vorenzar clearly had. It was recognised that the zones were safe provided no one interfered with them. Whereas Auganzar had previously controlled the movements of all Csendook on Eannor, he now had less control. There were a number of gladiatorial schools here and various members of the Garazenda had an interest in them. Eannor had become the centre for the development of the *moillum*.

Auganzar's passionate desire to understand the mysteries

4

of the forbidden areas was known to very few of his colleagues. And the Supreme Sanguinary had become even more guarded about it. But Zuldamar knew his intentions. He had ensured that the Garazenda's representatives were placed in all installations on Eannor. Auganzar no longer had control of the warhalls nor of the sentinel forces that watched over the forbidden regions.

Uldenzar suddenly chuckled. Cmizen's eyes widened, his whole manner one of unease. 'What amuses you?'

'I laugh at us. Our fear. We crouch in shadows. But the truth is Auganzar dare not lift a finger to harm us. We are Zuldamar's, and it is a well known fact. The Supreme Sanguinary is very limited in what he can do here.'

'I've heard that he has had Csendook murdered, on the very Warhive.'

Uldenzar shrugged. 'I'm sure he has. But he's drawn a lot of suspicion on himself. There are a good many of the Garazenda who admire him and who would doubtless turn a blind eye to his killings. But our own master has him pinned. Eannor is closely watched, Cmizen. You're safer than you've ever been.'

'Yes,' nodded Cmizen, though his expression betrayed his lack of conviction.

'Which is why we have been able to pursue Zuldamar's plan.'

Cmizen again nodded. 'There are developments?'

Uldenzar's mild amusement faded. He rose and paced the dark chamber, speaking half the time from its shadows. 'My warhall contains hundreds of potentially excellent *moillum*. Whatever one thinks of the Supreme Sanguinary and his ambitions, one has to admire his mind. The concept of *moillum* was quite brilliant. Man will eventually be subjugated, there's no question in my mind of that. *Moillum* are the means to the eventual victory. And they respond so well. Most of the gladiators that my warhall trains have accepted their lot, almost eagerly. They're worked hard but they have their pleasures. Some of them die but most of them accept the risks. It's up to them to survive.'

5

'You say most of them,' repeated Cmizen, leaning forward. 'Have you found anyone to suit our master's purpose?'

Uldenzar stopped pacing and snorted. 'There are a few rebels. They have great spirit. We never underestimate Men, Cmizen. Those of us who've fought in the wars know better. On a one to one basis they find it hard to match us, but as a military machine, they are powerful.'

'These rebels,' said Cmizen. 'They hate us?'

'All Men hate us. Inside,' Uldenzar grunted. 'But most of them hide their hate. They know it is sterile.'

'And those who do not?'

'I've had a few of them singled out and sent on to the island of Skellunda, where the recalcitrants are kept. So far I've not been able to shape their hatred.'

'I know what Zuldamar wants. But so far the Men who hate us enough would never help us. They let their emotions blind their reasoning. Skellunda! May as well send a Man to his death than that hell-hole.'

'Zuldamar must have an assassin.' Uldenzar sat down heavily. It was unusual for him to show his frustration at being unable to find a way around a problem. 'The difficulty is getting one of them to listen. As soon as one is found who would rather starve himself than become a *moillum*, or who would sooner put a sword to his neck than train with it, you take him aside. You hint that there would be a better life if he cooperated. You tell him that he could kill selected Csendook − aid in the assassination of high officials who persecute his kind.'

'It does not fire them?'

'They do not trust us!' Uldenzar said again. 'Twice I have found excellent warriors. Men who I thought might develop into the killers Zuldamar wants. I went as far as to tell them precisely what was expected of them, the *assassination* of Auganzar.'

Cmizen's eyes took in every shadow of the room, as though he expected to see their enemy rise up from the very stones. 'And?'

'Both Men assumed it was a test, a trap for them. They would not bite on the bait. And I could not let them live with such knowledge. Ironically I had to have them put to the sword.'

'Must it be a Man who hates us?'

Uldenzar nodded. 'If we are to get an assassin to Auganzar, we must be sure of his loyalty to *us*. If we send in a Man who has merely capitulated with us, and who has no more than his own personal needs at heart, then he'll be susceptible to bribes, to the lure of betraying us. How easily such a Man would become Auganzar's puppet! No, we need a Man who hates the Csendook so intensely that he would stop at nothing to kill our Supreme Sanguinary. Zuldamar is right and very shrewd: hatred is the fire that will drive that Man. But so far, it has blinded him.'

Cmizen looked even less comfortable. 'This is not the news I prefer to take to Zuldamar when I report.'

'Auganzar's warhall here on Eannor is strictly controlled. And I've no doubt the *moillum* he trains there are as loyal to him as his Thousand. It simply is not possible to get an agent in there, never mind an assassin.'

'And Skellunda?'

Uldenzar growled. 'I'm not sure if I shall pursue it again. They fight among themselves and there are many deaths. The island is little better than a prison. Auganzar created it because he thought it would ultimately produce the best of the *moillum*. But that is not how it seems to be working, not from what I hear. Haven't you visited it? As Keeper, you have every right to do so.'

Cmizen ignored the challenge in Uldenzar's tone, the hint of mockery. 'Not for some time. There seems little point. Like you, Uldenzar, I cannot see it being anything other than a cage for wild beasts. The hatred you seek is there, but it could never be channelled.'

Uldenzar rose. 'No. Perhaps not. Very well. I have nothing more to report. I will, of course, continue with my efforts.'

Cmizen rose and nodded. 'I will tell Zuldamar.'

Uldenzar nodded and left him to his thoughts. The shadows closed in. Cmizen sat at his table, his mind roving

7

back over the events of the past months. He had hoped to be free of Eannor once but his destiny seemed to have chained him to it. And Auganzar would be here again tomorrow. Would he seek Cmizen out? Attempt to trap him, betray himself?

They had spoken a number of times since the events surrounding the disappearance of Vorenzar. Auganzar wanted information but, as Uldenzar had said, he dared not be too open on the matter. If Auganzar could be implicated in any way with Vorenzar's interference with the forbidden area, he would be withdrawn from Eannor, and probably stripped of his title. If the Marozul could prove that Auganzar actively sought a gate out of the world cycle, in search of the Imperator Elect, they would have him dismissed from office. Auganzar knew it and trod the ground very carefully. Meanwhile, Cmizen knew that his testimony alone would never be enough to trap Auganzar, and Zuldamar knew it as well. Thus the elaborate dance of treachery continued, and the nights grew darker for the Keeper.

The knock on the door was gentle but it startled Cmizen. However, he gathered himself and went to the door. He guessed who it would be.

Etrascu stood in the open doorway for only a moment before entering. The Opener looked as though he had been listening to every word that had passed between his master and Uldenzar.

'Has he gone?' said Cmizen.

Etrascu nodded. 'He does not stay in this place any longer than he has to.'

'I wonder sometimes if he trusts me,' mused Cmizen, though he did not find the thought amusing.

'Has he any reason not to?'

Cmizen met the round-eyed challenge, though it was an empty one. He closed the door and motioned Etrascu in. 'You and I are inextricably bound up in this matter. I've told you that often enough.'

'Yet it might serve you better to betray Zuldamar,' said the Opener as he took the liberty of seating himself. He had grown more obese with every passing month; his huge face was like a moon in the torchlight, his mouth slack and wet.

Cmizen looked away from the disturbing visage. 'Our position is precarious. Auganzar is bound to attempt to intimidate me. Does he know about the Paths?'

Etrascu shuddered at the very mention of the Paths that had been opened beyond the world cycle. He and Cmizen knew well enough that it was possible to break through what had once been considered an impassable barrier. But the Marozul, and in particular, Zuldamar, had not wanted the secret known. He had once instructed Etrascu to attempt an Opening in pursuit of the Imperator Elect, knowing that he did not have the power to succeed. Zuldamar had not wanted the Path opened. It would have meant the pursuit of the Imperator Elect, the prolonging of the war. Etrascu wondered if there were other reasons, terrible prices that had to be paid for tampering with the very fabric of the worlds. Vorenzar had learned that Zuldamar had tried to use Etrascu, prior to his own opening of the Path through his own Opener, Ipsellin who had been an Ultimate, high in the order of his kind and far more powerful than Etrascu. But one thing about the opening of the Path was not certain: had Vorenzar communicated with Auganzar since he had gone through, if he had survived at all?

'If Auganzar knows that Zuldamar deliberately failed to open a Path,' said Etrascu, 'surely he would have used the knowledge against the Marozul by now. Would he not have brought the matter to the attention of the Garazenda, thus discrediting Zuldamar?'

Cmizen shrugged.

'If he had done so,' Etrascu went on, emboldened by his own logic, 'the Garazenda would have given Auganzar exactly what he wants: the right to bring another Opener, another Ultimate.'

'We must assume that Vorenzar has not communicated with Auganzar since he went through. As we have said before, he may well be dead.' The Keeper looked exhausted, his face pale, his eyes ringed with darkness, misery.

'It must be why Auganzar waits.'

'My feelings on the matter have not changed. I am sure Auganzar is waiting for word from Vorenzar. He seems certain that he was successful and will at least get a message through. Which is why he returns again and again to Eannor.'

'If Vorenzar does return, or one of his Zemoks comes through,' said Etrascu, 'Auganzar will destroy Zuldamar. The Garazenda would have no choice but to dismiss him from office. The pursuit of the Imperator Elect would begin afresh, with Auganzar even more firmly established. It might even lead to his promotion to the Garazenda, even to the Marozul.'

Cmizen swore. 'Yes, yes. I'm sure that is what Auganzar plans.'

'If that happens,' breathed Etrascu, lowering his voice 'you and I are dead. Our loyalty to Zuldamar is understood. Especially by Auganzar.'

Cmizen banged a fist down on the table. 'Why torment me with this! We have discussed it many times. Always we come back to the same argument. A simple choice – Zuldamar or Auganzar.'

'At first only I, Etrascu, was permitted by the Garazenda to open Paths to and from Eannor. That has changed. Auganzar has convinced them that in order to control events here thoroughly he needs to have a team of Openers. Admittedly Zuldamar and other Csendook who have warhalls here can use these Openers. But it is yet another gain for the Supreme Sanguinary.'

'What do you suggest?'

Etrascu drew in a deep breath, his bulk quivering. He had little respect for the Keeper, but he recognised in Cmizen the same fear that was in himself, and the understanding that both of them were minor characters on a wide stage. They both desired freedom, a place far from the events of history. Etrascu wanted to protect himself as much as Cmizen. They were indeed inextricably bound together.

'Auganzar gains in strength. He may prove the stronger,' said Etrascu at last.

'We agreed to choose Zuldamar.'

'Only because his servants spoke to us of his plans. This assassination attempt,' Etrascu added, a hint of impatience in his voice.

'When Auganzar falls, many of his loyal servants will fall with him. If we side with him – '

'When he falls,' echoed Etrascu. 'But who will hold the knife? Where is the Man who will be won over to our cause?'

Cmizen looked at him sharply. He did not relish the idea of Etrascu listening in to conversations, though he knew the Opener had certain skills. 'You were listening to Uldenzar.'

'I did not need to. His concern is easily seen.'

Cmizen rubbed at his eyes, sitting back. 'Well, it's true – The plan to find a human assassin is not proving easy. Zuldamar is patient, just as Auganzar is. They both seem capable of amazing self-control. But I'm certain that Zuldamar cannot wait indefinitely.'

'Then what will he do?'

'How can I predict – '

'I can imagine what he will do. He will arrange for a choice to be made. It will be forced upon us. Uldenzar will be made to select the Man most suitable. Whether the Man is ideal or not.'

'And risk failure?'

'I don't care if Zuldamar wishes to risk his own life. But it would put our lives at risk, too.'

'If the plot fails – '

'I would suggest,' said Etrascu, leaning forward so that his grotesque eyes seemed even more huge, 'that if we are given such an instruction, we consider our position.'

'Betray Zuldamar?'

'To Auganzar.'

'And if Uldenzar finds his assassin first? One in whom he has confidence?'

'If he is ever that sure,' smiled Etrascu unpleasantly, 'then we remain as we are.'

Cmizen thought long on this, but eventually he was nodding. 'Very well. I agree. If Zuldamar forces Uldenzar to act against his better judgement, we betray him.'

11

Etrascu seemed content but he did not rise as Cmizen thought he would. He merely put his hands on the table and stared at his thick, pudgy fingers. They interwove like huge, white worms.

'There is something else?' said Cmizen uneasily.

'The area of sacrifice,' said Etrascu, his eyes avoiding those of his master. They did not often speak of the place, of the horrors they had seen there.

'What about it? Have you news?'

Etrascu shook his head. 'I have not ventured close to it. Nor will I go near it again. But Auganzar will want to inspect its perimeter at the very least.'

'There is nothing to see,' said Cmizen, relieved that the Opener had not been about to reveal something. He dreaded the possibility that Vorenzar or one of his servants would return. Surely the entire party had perished.

'If Vorenzar should return – '

'You cannot believe that he will?' The perspiration beaded Cmizen's brow.

'How can we know? But if he should – '

'We'd be finished. Our loyalty is known.'

'Should we not consider some other plan, in case this disaster occurs?'

Cmizen again rubbed his eyes. He was tired. These discussions made him dizzy. They seemed to lead nowhere, merely pave the way for his worst dreams. 'Such as?'

'If word comes back from Vorenzar that the Imperator Elect is alive Auganzar will waste no time at all in denouncing Zuldamar. If that happens, I suggest we move very swiftly.'

'Leave Eannor? There is nowhere that would be safe.'

Etrascu shook his head. 'I agree. Flight would merely delay the inevitable. No, we would have to go straight to Auganzar's agents, here on Eannor. In his warhall. Tell them at once of the plot to assassinate Auganzar. Armed with the news of Vorenzar's success and Zuldamar's assassination plot, Auganzar's triumph would be assured.' Cmizen sat forward slowly, thinking over his Opener's words. He nodded. 'Yes, that is sound. Zuldamar would be hopelessly implicated. We would be exonerated, victims of his schemes.'

'Forced to obey the Marozul.'

Cmizen brightened, 'Yes, that seems to me an excellent plan.'

'The matter will be decided for us, I think.'

'Oh?'

'We have to see which occurs first: the return of Vorenzar or his Zemoks, or Uldenzar's success in finding an assassin.'

'Or Zuldamar forcing one upon him.'

'As you say.'

Cmizen studied the table as though he would find the answer to other questions in the knots of its surface. 'There are other matters that would have to be resolved, if we should go over to Auganzar. Our own future. I would not wish to remain on Eannor.'

'I can imagine what Auganzar would do with us,' said Etrascu coldly, and for once during the conversation his calm assurance seemed to desert him.

'He would not kill us,' insisted Cmizen. 'There'd be no need. Not if we gave him his assassin. He'd have us sent to some remote place where we could have nothing more to do with his plans.'

'Yes. I'm sure that is so. Which is what I fear.'

'There are other worlds as pleasant as Eannor –'

'And with the Path open to another world cycle Auganzar could send all those through he would rather isolate. To, where was the place, Innasmorn? Why not cast us adrift there?'

Cmizen shuddered. He knew Auganzar's mind would already have thought of such a thing.

'We had better find the assassin,' breathed Etrascu.

It concluded their discussion, as it had before. They would, without question, prefer Auganzar dead.

Vittargattus and Ondrabal watched as the gliderboat swooped over the treetops, both secretly marvelling at its grace. It had come almost to the ground at the crest of the hill, allowing two of its occupants to alight. Ondrabal was surprised to see

13

that they were both Vaza, even though they were from the northern forests and slightly built and unlike some of the more muscular of Vittargattus's warriors.

Azrand waited as they approached. He recognised them both. They had been with Ussemitus. Vittargattus also recognised them: he glanced sternly at his Windmaster but did not speak until the two foresters were close. Several warriors had lowered their spears defensively in case this was an attack.

'Have your aerial companions abandoned you?' said Ondrabal, overcome by curiosity.

Fomond bowed and Armestor quickly followed. 'My lords, we can only apologise for the unexpected nature of our visit.' He gestured to the gliderboat, which was swinging about in a wide circle as if it would return to the hill. 'Our companions cannot remain with us. Will you allow us to explain where we have been and why we have come to you?'

'Where's Ussemitus?' growled Vittargattus. He had not seen him in the strange flying craft.

'In the far west,' said Fomond.

'In the forbidden lands?' gasped Azrand. 'Did he find what he sought?'

Fomond nodded.

'Powers that can overturn the evils from beyond our world?' said Vittargattus. 'Powers that will help us?' Again Fomond nodded.

'And them?' said Ondrabal, glancing at the circling gliderboat.

'There are a few people in the city who must be spared. They are not all our enemies,' Fomond told him. Beside him, Armestor felt his stomach churn as the southern King screwed up his face in distaste.

'You had better come to the war tent,' said Vittargattus. 'We will hear your tale of the west. But we march on this alien city, we will spare no one that we find in or near it. I made that clear to your friend once before.'

Fomond glanced at Azrand. The Windmaster said nothing but there was, in his eyes at least, no hostility.

14

In the gliderboat, Aru and Jubaia watched. Fomond turned and waved twice, his bow held high. It was an agreed signal, it meant that the march on the Sculpted City would not be interrupted. If Pyramors and his allies were to be spared they would have to be met swiftly. She nodded to Jubaia and he spoke to Circu, who climbed into the sky, delighting in the speed of the flight.

2

THE BONE WATCH

The air was still — utterly silent. The land seemed frozen in an instant of time, events suspended. But in the folds of darkness, fear was a tangible, crawling thing, something that could be touched, awakened. In this forbidden place, even the air seemed reluctant to stir.

A tall serpent of stone wove through the forest, a black band that separated the dark zone from the rest of Eannor, enclosing it in its valley of silence, of grim memory. Above the wall, as dark and brooding as the wall itself, a single sombre tower rose up. It had few windows and on its heights no lights burned. But the warriors who paced its upper turrets were vigilant, eyes fixed on the land contained by the wall, with its serenity, its unnatural coldness, its menace. They were Zemoks, fierce fighting warriors without gods and without superstitions, but not one of them failed to sense the oppressiveness of the dark land, the place of death, of sacrifice. They could see very little in the night and the shadows smothered what sunlight often revealed beyond them: the field of bones where the grisly reminders of the past snared the attention by day.

Dagrazem, one of the guards for the night, paused in his round to speak to a watchful colleague. 'Nothing?' The single word echoed hollowly along the battlements.

Xinnac, whose eyes had been fixed on the wide plaza far below, shook his head. 'I'll be glad when this spell of watch ends. The place is truly dead.'

Dagrazem grunted, sympathetic. 'Your tour of duty ends at dawn. But try and stay alert. We are to have a visitor.' Xinnac's eyes widened briefly. He nodded. 'Then the rumours were true? He's back?'

'Aye. The Supreme Sanguinary. And he'll be up here. Never misses when he visits. He, at least, expects something.'

Xinnac glanced at the zone of sacrifice. 'An attack? By what forces? Nothing could hide in that place. The dead cannot rise. Surely Auganzar does not believe in such things.'

'Many Csendook have died out there,' said Dagrazem calmly, leaning on the stone wall. He eyed the plaza with distaste. 'They tampered with that place. I sometimes wonder – '

'What do you wonder?' came a voice from the darkness behind him.

Both Dagrazem and Xinnac twisted quickly round, their long swords flashing from scabbards in a flowing movement. Beyond them, almost entirely hidden in the shadows, a huge Csendook observed them, his own hands resting on a sword as he leaned gently on it.

'A sensible Zemok always guards his back as well as his front,' said the warrior.

Dagrazem took a step forward, sword still raised. 'What business do you have here? Identify yourself quickly, or – ' He nodded to the shadows, where a number of other Zemoks had materialised, weapons ready.

The figure opened his cloak. On his breastplate were embossed two scarlet circles: they were known as the Eyes of Auganzar. Behind him another Csendook stepped forward. It was Kurduzar, commander of the tower, the Bone Watch. 'Put away your blades. This is Auganzar.'

Dagrazem almost gasped but recovered himself, sheathing his sword and bowing. Beside him he felt Xinnac stiffen.

Auganzar stepped forward, a head taller than the Zemoks, who themselves had been chosen for their size. 'You were saying? You sometimes wonder what?'

Dagrazem swallowed, but kept as calm as he could. 'Zaru, I was merely saying that it was a wonder to me that anyone should desire to enter the place of death beyond the wall.'

'You fear the dead?' said Auganzar, a faint smile crossing his features. His eyes, however, were cold, too cold to look into for more than a moment. Everything about him, his immense build, his huge hands, spoke of physical power and of authority. This was the warrior that countless Csendook

17

throughout the cycle of worlds cried out to serve, a warlord, some said, who did not want to see an end to the Crusade against Man and who would have gladly taken up a fresh banner against him.

'Of course not, Zaru,' said Dagrazem. 'But something in that place killed our warriors. We have seen their bones – '

'Then note them,' said Auganzar, the smile fading. He stood by the wall, lowering his voice. 'You are here to watch, no more than that. Do not let your curiosity get the better of you. Csendook have paid the penalty for that, as you observe. And if others are tempted to visit that place, they will reap another grim reward.'

Dagrazem was perfectly aware that unauthorised entry into the zone was punishable by instant execution.

'No more accidents,' said Auganzar.

'We remain vigilant, Zaru,' said Dagrazem with another bow.

'I'm sure you do. Who do you serve?'

The question threw the Zemok for a moment and he looked unsure of himself. Auganzar turned his full gaze on him. 'Your own Zaru? Is it Kurduzar?'

Dagrazem glanced briefly across at the keeper of the tower, whose expression was far colder than the Supreme Sanguinary's. 'I am seconded to him, of course, Zaru. But otherwise my unit is with Gadruzar.'

'Ah yes, a fine warrior. One of Marozul Zuldamar's commanders.'

'Yes, Zaru.'

Auganzar again looked out at the silent lands. He nodded abruptly, straightened, and turned back to where Kurduzar was waiting. 'Very well. Keep watching. It's dull work, I'm sure. But all the more reason to be observant. Eannor now has a large population. Our Zemoks rely on your protection.'

Dagrazem and Xinnac bowed a final time, waiting until they knew Auganzar and Kurduzar had left the battlements before they were able to relax.

'There are whispers,' said Dagrazem very softly, 'that it

is not an attack he fears. He waits for ghosts.'

'Ghosts?' said Xinnac, equally softly.

'Vorenzar, one of his commanders. They say he may not be dead.'

Xinnac stared out at the fields of death. 'How could he survive such a place?'

'Yes, how?'

Silently they waited, until Dagrazem moved on down the wall, visiting other Zemoks of this night's watch.

Deep in the tower, Auganzar and Kurduzar sat in one of the keeper's private chambers where they knew they could speak without being overheard. Auganzar had stripped off the armour that he almost always wore and he sipped at the wine his host had given him.

'Everywhere that I look,' said the Supreme Sanguinary with a wry smile, 'I seem to see the warriors of Zuldamar, or Horzumar. They are anxious to ensure that they're well informed.'

Kurduzar, himself a large warrior, veteran of numerous campaigns, as all of Auganzar's loyalest supporters were, grimaced. His short hair was iron grey, his face and eyes dark. 'They're no trouble to me, Zaru. I've had no dissent among them.'

Auganzar smiled. 'No. Zuldamar is as cunning an adversary as one could expect. He dare not raise a hand against me until he is certain he has evidence that I am in some way betraying the Garazenda. Just as I cannot raise a hand against him without proof that he is attempting to bring me down. But the impasse suits me better than it suits Zuldamar.'

Kurduzar relaxed. He had known Auganzar for many years, and had fought with him, but he knew the power that Auganzar possessed now was greater than it had ever been. It distanced them, but that was as it should be. No Csendook should be close to Auganzar. He was a warrior with his own private mission and no other would truly know it. Even so, it was a pleasure to be able to relax a little in his company, to know that one was trusted.

'You are wondering by now why I am on Eannor yet again,' said Auganzar.

Kurduzar shrugged. 'You are always welcome, Zaru. I know your basic purpose in coming, and you shall have full reports. Is there any other, more specific reason?'

'I'm reviewing the *moillum*. I want to spend a little time in my warhall, and perhaps I'll look at some of the others.'

'Zuldamar's?'

Auganzar again smiled. 'Why not? If only to make his Zarull uncomfortable. Who does he have there? Uldenzar, isn't it?'

'Yes, Uldenzar. His loyalty to Zuldamar is strong. No amount of coercion could win him over to us.'

'I'm sure you're right. His father was a remarkable warrior, too. Zuldamar has made quite sure that only his most trusted followers are here on Eannor.'

'Does he know your real purpose?'

'I suspect he has been told. But nothing can be proved.'

'Does Zuldamar know that Vorenzar went through?'

Auganzar's brows knitted. 'He may have guessed. Much depends on what he has been told by Cmizen and that loathsome Opener of his. I am amazed that Eannor's Keeper fears Zuldamar more than he does me!' He laughed. 'What possible hold could Zuldamar have over those two?'

'I have tried, discreetly, to infiltrate Cmizen's network, but without much success.'

'It does not matter,' said Auganzar. 'The Bone Watch was built for a number of reasons. It ensures that Zuldamar cannot pry into the zone of sacrifice himself. If he does believe Vorenzar to be alive, he dare not attempt to find him. He knows that would lead to other truths.'

'The Imperator Elect is alive.'

'And can be reached.'

Kurduzar nodded, eyes flashing. The thought that Vorenzar had had the courage, the staggering audacity, to attempt to break through the very walls of the system into a realm of probable nightmare, still amazed him. There had been so much violent death in the zone, and there was frightful evidence of that, and yet Vorenzar had persisted. There was even a name to go on – Innasmorn. The world beyond.

'So, what news do you have?' Auganzar asked him, his face more serious.

Kurduzar sighed. 'The Bone Watch is fully manned at all times, at every hour of the night and day. I am careful not to leave the Zemoks on long spells of watch. They're changed each night. You have already seen how restless they become, how their concentration wavers – '

'Tomorrow you will have to be very hard with them. Tell them I was not pleased. Vigilance must be absolute.'

'Rest assured, Zaru. Zemoks will be punished.'

'Nothing has been observed?'

'Nothing, Zaru. Not as much as a change in the air, not a breeze. No movement. Nothing lives there and all life shuns the valley. There has been no need to warn our Zemoks away, though they are told repeatedly.'

'And the patrols?'

'I exercise the strictest of controls over them. They go out regularly, no more than a dozen Zemoks. They report back to me personally as soon as they return.'

'What have they found?' said Auganzar, calmly lifting his glass, though his eyes narrowed, his interest intense. Kurduzar knew how important this was, how badly Auganzar wanted news. But he shook his head. 'They have been over as much of the valley as is possible. It sweeps back far into the mountains that enclose it. Everywhere it is the same. No life. The trees are rotten – blasted. No grass, not even seed. There are no birds, no insects. Not even the vipers, which thrive in the forests on the other side of the wall, have ventured into the zone.'

'And no evidence of Vorenzar, or his Zemoks?'

Kurduzar shook his head. 'I have instructed the patrols to search for life. My own loyal Zemoks have particular orders. Those who have been seconded to me from Zuldamar and others of the Garazenda I tell merely to be careful. I cannot say what Zuldamar has told his Zemoks.'

21

'We must assume they are looking for Vorenzar. But if they find him, or get word of him, it will be to my benefit!'

'Yes, Zaru. But so far, nothing.'

'Are all Zuldamar's warriors as loyal to him as Uldenzar?'

'Again, I have been discreet in testing them. But yes, I would not expect to win them over to us. Zuldamar has chosen carefully. Of course, I could exclude them from the patrols, but should I do so, it would raise suspicions.'

'Excellent. Much as I dislike Zuldamar's interference, I have to accept it. At least for now. The weight of the Garazenda falls to my side of the balance, but the scales could so easily be tipped the other way. I must accommodate my rival.'

'If Vorenzar returns – '

'He will. Believe me, Zellorian survived. And Vorenzar will find him. When he returns with word, it will not matter who meets him. Zuldamar's warriors will not be able to suppress the news.'

Kurduzar nodded. It was interesting, but he had noticed that Auganzar rarely spoke of the Imperator Elect. It was Zellorian who really interested him. For some reason, the Supreme Sanguinary hunted Zellorian above all. It was almost as though he had no real interest in the rest of Mankind, the toppled Imperator. But Zellorian was of paramount interest. Kurduzar did not remark on this. He knew enough of his master not to pry.

'You patrol the zone daily?' said Auganzar suddenly.

'Three times during daylight hours – '

'But never by night?'

Kurduzar made no attempt to mask his surprise. 'You think I should, Zaru?'

'I do. Have the Zemoks on the tower doubled during night patrols, but send out at least two patrols each night. We should take every precaution.'

'I will begin tonight. It will be unpopular, but those who murmur about being bored will have something more positive to do.'

Auganzar smiled. 'Boredom can be cured. Fear is something else.'

Kurduzar said nothing. He wondered if there were fears rooted somewhere in the huge warrior opposite him. If so, they were well hidden.

Dagrazem came off watch and wound his way down into the bowels of the Bone Watch. Usually he felt tired and irritable after a long spell on the battlements: the nights were long up there, and boring. Nothing of interest had been seen out in the valley. He would have preferred life in a warhall, where there would at least be some action. But after his meeting with Auganzar earlier, tonight he had remained alert. He was intensely annoyed with himself for having been embarrassed by the Supreme Sanguinary. But at least he had not incurred his wrath; even his own masters could not have protected him from that.

He plunged himself into a warm pool, bathing and taking greater pleasure than usual in the waters. Afterwards he drew on a robe and exercised gently. He would not sleep, instead trying to relax on a couch. His rooms were small, shared with other warriors, but they were all asleep, their snores resounding around the stone walls.

He was about to settle himself when he heard the clank of accoutrements beyond the door to the corridor. Puzzled, he got up and slipped his sword from its sheath where he had left it hung up. There was no real reason to suppose treachery, not in such a building as the tower, but he had been trained as a Zemok. He crept to the door, edging it open. Beyond it he saw Vulporzol, his immediate captain. He was adjusting his war gear, preparing to leave the chambers. Dagrazem opened the door.

'Is everything in order, Zolutar?' he asked. Vulporzol should be asleep. He had been on duty until after the last meal.

Vulporzol grunted non-commitally. He was a swarthy warrior, his face thin, pinched for a Csendook, his hair sparse, his ears small. But he was known for his speed, his quickness of hand. Many of his Zemoks wondered why he had not been promoted from Zolutar to Zaru, though he never complained about this. Dagrazem wondered if, secretly, Vulporzol did hold a higher rank, and went about his present work for specific reasons known only to Zuldamar.

'So Auganzar is here once more,' said Vulporzol, his voice a whisper. He guided Dagrazem gently back into his chambers, looking this way and that to see that they were alone.

'Yes,' said Dagrazem, also lowering his voice to a whisper as the door closed. He explained about the meeting above the tower. Vulporzol nodded attentively. 'You can do no more. Keep your Zemoks alert. There will be fresh work soon.'

'There is news?'

'Not from the zone. But Auganzar has just ordered night patrols. Kurduzar called some of the Zolutars together after Auganzar had retired for the night. I am to go out into the zone.'

'By night, Zolutar? What possible purpose can this serve?'

'I cannot believe treachery. Auganzar is far too cautious. But he is relentless in his policing of the zone.'

'Do you need Zemoks? I can have as many as you require – '

Vulporzol shook his head. 'No. The patrol is to be limited to a dozen of us. All Zolutars.'

Dagrazem took this in. Patrolling of the zone was usually done with Zemoks under Zolutar command. Now at night, Zolutars only. Without protection?

'You think Auganzar came here to eliminate those who are not loyal to him?' said Vulporzol wryly.

'An accident could easily be arranged at night. There are stories of accidents on the Warhive, Zolutar. Opponents of Auganzar have died.'

'I know the stories,' nodded Vulporzol. 'So I am wary.'

'Zolutar, allow me to prepare Zemoks.'

'They cannot be taken on patrol.'

'No, but I will have them ready to enter the zone if you find yourself in danger. I have Zemoks up on the walls of the tower. You have only to get a signal to them and I'll release them to you.'

Vulporzol stroked his jaw, weighing the situation carefully. 'This is a dangerous game, Dagrazem. If Auganzar finds Zemoks in the zone at night, he'll use the incident against us.'

'I have Zemoks I can trust. Say six of them. As loyal to you as I am.'

Vulporzol nodded slowly. 'Loyal enough, then. But what of the watch?' He nodded upwards.

'Xinnac is still up there, due to remain until dawn. He could see to it that I receive any message.'

Vulporzol grinned unexpectedly. 'Yes, but how am I to alert him without alerting other guards on the tower?'

Dagrazem considered this. A signal. But what?

'Wait, I have it,' said Vulporzol. 'If this patrol is truly to be an act of treachery, then Kurduzar will be a party to it. He will brief his own Zemoks on watch above. No doubt they'll be told to *ignore* anything they see among the patrols. So if I were to give a signal of distress, they would ignore it. If we are being too cautious and there is no treachery, it will not matter.'

Dagrazem considered slowly. 'Yes, but what of Xinnac and my other guards up there? They'd see any distress signals, and report them – '

'You think Kurduzar will have them ordered off the wall when the patrols go out?'

'If he does, no one will be watching for me. If you are under attack, I will not know it.'

'Then you will have to try and station at least one warrior somewhere above. There must be somewhere that you could discreetly place one of your Zemoks.'

Dagrazem frowned. 'It might be difficult. But it will have to be done. I'll see to it. I'll go at once, before my Zemoks are relieved.'

Vulporzol touched his arm, a grim smile on his thin face. 'This may all be nonsense. The patrols may be no

25

more than another extension of Auganzar's determination to find something. In which case, your Zemoks will be up there anyway.'

'But why night, Zolutar?'

Vulporzol grunted. Even the shadows could not be trusted in these times. 'Get your warriors ready.'

Kurduzar sat alone. He, too, found sleep difficult. He had made the necessary arrangements for a night patrol, beginning at once. Auganzar liked to know that his orders were being carried out swiftly and precisely. Kurduzar finished his wine and gazed into the glass as if it would reveal something of interest.

Why should Auganzar want night patrols? The zone of sacrifice was like pitch at night. Had some pre-arranged plan been made with Vorenzar? Was he to attempt to slip back to Eannor by night? Did it have something to do with conjunctions? Some of the Openers, Kurduzar knew, attached significance to such things. Opening a Path to the darkness beyond the world cycle might have something to do with this. But if Auganzar were intending to open a Path himself, how would he achieve this? He had not brought an Opener with him, although he must have used one other than Etrascu, Cmizen's servant. Vorenzar had also eschewed the use of Etrascu, using Ipsellin, an Ultimate. Perhaps Ipsellin was to arrange the return.

Kurduzar concluded that Auganzar could not be thinking of opening a path, even in the secrecy of night. It made the idea of night patrols even more curious.

'What do you think?' said Armestor nervously.

Fomond pulled a face. They sat together in a small tent they had been given on the edge of the camp, below the hill of Vittargattus. The army was restless, eager to be on the march again. It had been delayed by the arrival of the strangers and many of the warriors, both Vaza and southern tribesmen, glanced up to the tent where the two strangers were sitting. Since dawn, over two hours ago, these foresters had been in the war tent with Vittargattus, Ondrabal and their advisers, and the latter were still holding talks. The word was already spreading that dark powers were to be used during the coming siege.

'They listened, I thought,' Armestor went on. 'Azrand was again attentive. He, at least, trusts us.'

'I'm not so sure of Ondrabal. Or his Seers. They have always been rivals of the Windmasters. Anything Azrand says in our defence, they seem to question. And there is something else that worries me.'

Armestor's frown deepened.

'Kuraal is here. He saw us. His eyes told me clearly that he has not forgotten how we escaped him in our own lands. We have not won his trust. He may yet try to poison Azrand and the other Windmasters against us.'

Armestor paled. Kuraal! He had not forgotten the spite of the Blue Hair.

Fomond grinned. 'Never mind! We have a concession. They will not begin the attack on the city until they hear from Ussemitus. Let us hope it gives Aru time to contact Pyramors.'

3

REBELLION

Zellorian, Prime Consul of the Imperator Elect, stared into the flame of the candle as though it could burn away the darkness in his mind. Around his chambers there were other candles burning: he never slept in darkness as once he had been able to. There were guards pacing the corridors softly outside and occasionally he heard the pad of their feet as they walked up and down. It was a reassuring sound. But it was not assassins he feared, though he knew there were men in the Sculpted City who would have gladly have put him to the sword had they been given an opportunity. No, his fears stemmed from the darkness, the darkness within him. He had been through horror, had even engineered it, for the good of the Empire. And he would drive his people on through deeper nightmares yet if they were to reach salvation. But the darkness that probed at him from within was something he could not understand. It had nothing to do with conscience, or guilt. He had every belief in what he had done, however cruel.

This cloud, this presence, was connected with the world outside the walls of the city, a world where the elementals ruled and where storms writhed like living entities. He had mocked all that once, until he had tasted their power. And they had turned their attention to him. They whispered to him through the superficial barriers of the city walls. Whenever he was resting, or trying to sleep, the darkness rose up.

It had begun with Vymark, the warrior he had rebuilt as a gliderboat. Their minds had linked and he had controlled the craft from afar. Until something else had interfered, blanketing Vymark's will. If Vymark was still conscious of himself in any way, Zellorian had no way of knowing. For, just as the warrior had changed from man to gliderboat, now he had been transformed into something else, something dark and inconceivable. Something that Zellorian could not contemplate and from which his own mind veered.

But it probed. It hungered. For knowledge?

Zellorian grimaced, turning from the candle, telling himself that the shadows dancing on his walls were not alive. Innasmorn could not send her agents into his citadel. There were other powers he possessed. He would use them. When the time was ripe, he would go out and take the war to this accursed world. Far below him, deep in the secret places of the city, his servants worked incessantly to perfect new machines, new methods of conquering this world. They dug back into the past of their race, hunting for the lost sciences, for powers older than history itself.

But the darkness slipped back to the far recesses of his mind. It would not exercise these powers. Not yet.

Onando entered the chamber and gazed about him nervously, his white face the face of a frightened man, though it was his natural pallor. His hands, soft and pale, fidgeted with each other and his eyes turned this way and that as though he might see a dozen accusers leap from behind pillars to confront him with his illegal acts. But the chamber was empty. It was an annex to the Prime Consul's apartments, a place he had visited a number of times in recent weeks on the business he enjoyed most, intrigue.

He wore, as ever, the white robes of his office as Consul: they were barely paler than his flesh, as if he never exposed himself to sunlight. Softly he walked over to one of the couches, but he thought better of sitting.

The guards had not entered with him. He had been surprised to see so many. Zellorian must be concerned about his safety. Once the Prime Consul had moved about the city without such concern, with haughtiness. But recently he was a changed man. Something disturbed him.

As Onando speculated on this curtains at the side of the room parted and Zellorian entered. His eyes were the first thing that Onando noticed: they seemed to have sunk back into the Prime Consul's skull, their sockets smudged with lack of sleep. Or was it drugs? Was that what had turned Zellorian? Something ate at him but Onando could not believe it was fear.

'Sit down,' said the Prime Consul, waving at the couch, and his voice was sharp, edgy.

Onando bowed and did as bidden. He waited while Zellorian poured himself a glass of water and drank swiftly.

'If I may say so, sire, you do not look well,' ventured the Consul. 'Is there anything – '

'I am a little tired,' said Zellorian, with an effort of will. He seemed to be holding his emotions in check, possibly controlling anger, as if Onando's words had annoyed him.

'I would not have disturbed you at such an early hour – '

Zellorian ran a hand through his hair, then waved the Consul's apology aside. It was an hour after dawn. 'No matter. It was I who called this meeting.'

Onando did not argue. It was true. But he had become used to dealing with Zellorian at strange hours. It seemed to be part of the secret way in which he operated. Much of what they had to say to each other was strictly between them.

'There have been developments,' said Onando, knowing that this would at least brighten the Prime Consul. Zellorian looked directly at him. He saw a short, pudgy creature, face crawling with deceit, eyes sunk in a fatty mask. This was a Consul? From such men leaders were chosen in this city? But Onando was needed, his greed for power was useful, vital. 'Well?'

'My spies have at last come up with the information that confirms my, that is your, beliefs that Consul Pyramors is behind the defections from the city.'

'You have infiltrated his system?'

Onando nodded. 'I have. It was bound to happen eventually. Pyramors spreads his net wider and wider. At first he was able to contain his rebellion amongst his friends and those close to people he could trust. But as his plot grows more ambitious, he has been forced into taking more and more risks.'

Zellorian had not sat down. He nodded slowly, eyes narrowing. 'Go on.'

'I have several men working in the lower city. They are part of the teams that service the drains. As you know, Sire, we are improving certain areas, particularly where more houses are being constructed. There are a number of outlets and although there are guards on patrol, things are a little lax. Attacks from outside are not really expected.'

Zellorian scowled. 'That is a matter which will have to be attended to. But at another time. Continue.'

'Pyramors evidently understands the system and its weakness. He has prepared to have a large number of soldiers drafted into the team of workers in the new drainage system. It is quite a complex system and there are over two hundred men employed at various parts of the wall.'

'How many men?' said Zellorian coldly, and for a moment Onando saw a darkness behind those eyes, cold and violent. But it moved away as quickly as it had come.

'He intends to release fifty at least.'

'Fifty! Fifty of our knights in one defection. To where?'

'There's no word of their exact destination. But it is in the mountains, further to the north and east. They will join with others who have left us.'

'Gannatyne is behind this,' Zellorian growled. 'In his exile, he plans rebellion. But I have him secured. In a fortress. No matter how many defect, they'll never prize him out of it. But he is behind this, I swear it.'

'With respect, sire, I think not. Oh, he is not at all as exhausted and tired with affairs of state as he would have everyone think. But it is Consul Pyramors who calls the tune. Gannatyne is the figurehead, but Pyramors masters the rebellion.'

Zellorian might have reprimanded Onando for contradicting him, but he did not. The fat Consul had been most helpful in uncovering details of the rebellion. He was the only one who had achieved any success. Zellorian's other spies had come up against a wall of silence. Onando was known, trusted by no one. But his connections were extraordinary. The lower city. Onando knew every thief that slipped through its gutters. He had built his own tiny empire on such people.

'When is this latest defection to take place?'

'Tomorrow night, Sire. The workers involved have been paid handsomely for their part in it. Fifty of them will change places with Pyramors's knights long enough for them to get away into the mountains.'

'Pyramors will not go with them?'

'No, Sire. He will remain in the city, preparing others for the flight.'

Zellorian straightened. 'You know where on the wall? The names of those involved?'

'I have every name, sire.'

'Very well. We shall outmanoeuvre these traitors. And we shall rid ourselves of this meddling Consul.'

For another hour, Onando gave up the detail of the plot as he had learned it, and as he did so, Zellorian began to prepare his net, taking from its cabinet his own detailed map of the city with the areas where construction had been approved. No one moved a stone in the Sculpted City without him knowing it.

Like a black ghost between two peaks, the gliderboat hovered. Both Aru and Jubaia could feel Circu's discomfort, the coldness the craft felt here in the mountains. But it was not just the height that made them all shiver. They felt something else, a kind of brooding, as though Innasmorn herself studied the city that nestled among the peaks below them. The Sculpted City, home of Men.

Aru closed from her mind her last view of the place, the day she had fled, when her father, Mannaston, plunged to his death. Sensing her sorrow, Jubaia was quick to speak to her. 'I can see no other gliderboats in the air above the city. But there must be guardians. How do you intend to get into the city without being seen?'

'By night, I suppose.'

I still think it's ridiculously dangerous, came Circu's soft voice.

'I have to get to Pyramors. Somehow I have to get him out of the city before the Windmasters begin their workings. Ussemitus told us that Innasmorn will not spare the City.'

Jubaia watched the swirling skies. 'Innasmorn may help us. But there are other forces at work. Something has been following us, watching our own movements.'

'You can't mean the black gliderboat?' said Aru with undisguised horror.

'It could not have survived at Shung Nang. But out of its death may have come life of a different nature. I am afraid to try and read it.'

'What is its purpose? Revenge?'

Jubaia shook his head. 'It is not that simple. It may have been summoned here by Zellorian. When the storm breaks and Vittargattus attacks, who knows what will be waiting for him?'

Consul Pyramors waited in silence. The room was a narrow one in a poor quarter of the city. It always amazed him how quickly these areas sprang up. The Sculpted City was young and yet in no time at all it had produced its depressed areas, where people struggled to survive on their wits. In a way it was as though the city had been ripped from its foundations on one of the old worlds of the Empire, and transported here wholesale. Even so, he was glad of it, for it was this which had enabled him to plot his rebellion, and he was dependent on these insalubrious places for cover.

He was alone in the room. In such a room he had seen Gannatyne betrayed, and the girl, Aru Casruel, trapped by the cleverness of Zellorian. It had broken Gannatyne's spirit. Pyramors had subsequently used Gannatyne's exile to fuel his rebellion but he wondered just how much enthusiasm the older Consul would have for it. Certainly Pyramors told his followers that Gannatyne was behind it, but for all he really knew, Gannatyne languished in exile, the fortress that was, in effect, his prison.

Pyramors steeled himself for the coming meeting. How hopeful could he be? He told himself not to despair, although it was an emotion that clung to him, cloaking him sometimes now. So much had gone wrong, so far had that once-glorious Empire tumbled. Too many friends had died, in war, in treachery, in confusion. There were times when it became impossible to see an end to Zellorian's stranglehold on the new empire. Empire! It was a mockery. A rabble of Consuls, trying to protect an Imperator Elect who was no more than a step away from madness. Was it worth the struggle to hold it together? Should he himself leave, go out into this new world and abandon the Sculpted City, release the men who were waiting for him? Again and again the thought came to him. You have lost everything, there is nothing here for you. Your family is in ruins about you, and Jannovar –

There was a soft knock at the door. Once more he steeled himself, forcing back hopelessness. There were men yet willing to fight, men who relied on his leadership.

He opened the door, ushering in the two men. They had cloaks wrapped about them and underneath were the ordinary clothes of street workers. But they were knights. Pyramors had seen them train; they kept themselves in battle-readiness, as though the war with the Csendook had never ended. While he took in their eager faces, their determination, the spirit that burned brightly in their eyes, he had to check himself again. This is how I should be, he thought. Fired, like them. I, too, am a young man, not yet thirty, and yet at times I feel as though I have been at war for half a century.

He held out his hand and shook those of both men firmly. 'Celsius, Morias! It's good to see you looking so well prepared.'

'Everything's set for tomorrow night, Sire,' said Celsius. He was tall and muscular, with a face that looked as if it had been cut from rock. Pyramors had seen him throw many a strong warrior in training. He was a captain that other knights were proud to follow. His hair was dark, longer than usual for a knight, and a scar ran down the edge of his chin, a reminder of harder days before the Crossing from Eannor and the death struggle with the Csendook. Celsius was at least three years younger than the Consul, but what he lacked in years he more than made up for in experience.

'Excellent,' nodded Pyramors, turning to Morias. He was the elder of the three by ten years, a grizzled sergeant with arms that could snap the back of a lesser man, but who was known for his power with the double-edged sword. There were stories in the barracks about him having stood toe to toe with a Csendook once and having got the better of it. Pyramors did not mock the story, but wondered if it could be true. Whatever, such tales were fuel for the spirit of the men who stood by Morias and his rebels.

'You know our pact of silence,' Pyramors said to Celsius, locking eyes with him.

The young captain nodded. Pyramors, he knew, was as capable a knight as any of them. It was unlikely that any other Consul could match him in speed, in tactics and in loyalty to Gannatyne. He looked every inch a warrior, a general who men would gladly follow, though there was a hint of tiredness about his mouth. There must be a strain on such a man, living as he did in the palace and seeing so much that he abhorred. Pyramors smiled but in the smile there was almost an element of regret. His hair was iron grey, as if the events of the wars had turned it, but there was yet a resolve in him that his men responded to without question. Even the hard-bitten old sergeants like Morias, true veterans, looked up to this Consul, whereas they had little more than contempt for many others.

Morias answered for his captain. He knew that the agreement was one that Pyramors found distasteful. 'Sire, we exercise every caution in this rebellion. If any of us are caught, we will do nothing to implicate you, or Gannatyne.'

Celsius grinned, eager to dispel the tension. 'You, above all, must be protected, Sire.'

'There are over a thousand of us out there now,' said

Pyramors. 'And believe me, there are members of the Consulate who would come over to us if they knew. So secrecy is vital. Without it, our cause falls apart. Don't think I'm hiding behind this – '

'If any of us doubted your commitment, Sire, the risks you take, we would have abandoned you long since,' growled Morias, though he grinned, his beard bristling.

Pyramors sighed. '*Pah*, all this deceit and duplicity,' he said, turning to where a flagon of wine sat on the rough table. He poured them all a goblet. 'It is hardly the way to fight a war.'

Celsius grimaced. 'It won't always be this way, Sire.'

Pyramors handed them their glasses, annoyed that he had tried to justify his need for secrecy. 'I hope not.'

'This time there'll be fifty of us,' said Morias, finishing his wine in one gulp. He was a man who much preferred his beer, but Pyramors had been unable to smuggle any down with him from the upper city.

'Jorissimal will meet you up in the mountains. Your men will be watched as they leave the drainage works. As soon as it's safe, Jorissimal will meet you and take you to where the others are in hiding.'

'How soon, Sire?' said Celsius.

Pyramors sipped his wine, eyes distant for a moment. 'How soon?'

'Can we think of freeing Gannatyne?'

Pyramors put down his goblet thoughtfully. He had not seen the fortress, but he had had reports of it. The place had been built as a fort shortly after construction of the Sculpted City had begun, a lookout to the north-eastern fastnesses, where it was thought a possible invasion might come. It overlooked the only pass there that could penetrate the mountains. To storm it would be extremely hazardous, almost unthinkable.

'I have yet to devise a way of getting into his prison.'

'Can it be taken by force?' said Morias.

'If we had gliderboats, we could contemplate it, Morias,' Pyramors told him with a grin. 'But a better weapon would be stealth.'

Morias wrinkled up his nose. 'Ah, then maybe they'll need their drains attending to?'

In spite of his mood, Pyramors chuckled. He spent far too much time away from such men. 'Perhaps.'

'Sire, can I speak freely?' went on Morias. He was not normally a garrulous man, preferring to use his strength and speed rather than his tongue, but he had a lively mind, as many of his rivals had found to their cost.

'Of course. What's on your mind?'

Morias sniffed. 'This subterfuge. Why must it be so elaborate?'

Celsius would have interrupted but Pyramors nodded. 'That's all right. I understand the frustrations of our campaign. Sometimes I would rather take up my sword, climb out on to the highest battlements of the city and shout out for the head of Zellorian.'

'There's a good many who'd rally to that!' avowed Morias.

Pyramors laughed gently. 'I hope they would. But we'd be crushed in a day. Morias, I saw Gannatyne humbled before the court. And I saw the fear in the eyes of those who should have been his friends. The truth is, fear rules this city of ours.

'Zellorian holds the Imperator Elect in the palm of his hand. He jerks his muscles as if pulling strings. Zellorian also commands the gliderboat fleet, which he is personally having rebuilt and redesigned. The craft may not yet respond to the skies of Innasmorn, but they will. The engineers toil for Zellorian. He also controls the army, having all the key commanders under his sway. But most of all, he holds the balance of power among the Consulate. Most of them owe their being here on Innasmorn to him. He selected them. They remain in his thrall as do their families, their knights.

'And yet, many of them would rebel. I say would. *If* they knew that there was a sufficiently large force to take up arms. Many of them are sympathetic to Gannatyne. Just as our Imperator Elect is a figurehead to Mankind across surviving worlds, so Gannatyne is a banner which the rebellion needs. Free him and we have power.

'Now, I don't say we should gather our troops, amass, and attack Zellorian. I want to free all those in this city who want to begin a life elsewhere. I envisage us building another city, smaller than the Sculpted City, possibly in the mountains, somewhere that we could easily defend. Zellorian would then have to come to us, assault us. But he would tire. And there may be other allies.'

'The Innasmornians?' said Celsius.

'Gannatyne told me, before his exile, that the future of Man would depend on an alliance with them. They are an intriguing people. They may not have technology but Gannatyne was convinced that they have other strengths.'

'Enough to defy Zellorian?' said Morias.

'Perhaps. But this is a large world, with huge land masses. There should be room enough for us to abandon the Imperator altogether, once we have broken free of this city.'

'Why does Zellorian refuse us our freedom?' said Morias.

Pyramors's smile faded. 'If you heard the man as he stands before the Consulate, you'd know. Power, Morias. It is like an illness with some of us. Zellorian holds it all at the moment. And there are other powers he has, powers that most men would be averse to touch. To him, we are servants, almost slaves. He brought us here, we are in his debt, and he will never relinquish his hold on us willingly.'

'But why?' said Celsius. 'We have broken free of the Csendook. It's a miracle that we've come beyond the world cycle. What else is there for Zellorian to achieve?'

'If you tell a man with absolute power that there is no longer a reason for the existence of such power, you poke at a serpent with your bare hand.'

Morias laughed. 'Give me a sword, Sire! I'll prod this serpent for you. Aye, and take off it's head!'

'I've thought of it many times, believe me. But no man is better protected than Zellorian. No assassin would ever cut him down. Thus we are left with subterfuge, duplicity, secrets. So – what of tomorrow night? Are the arrangements complete? What about the men who work in the drains?'

'They have been paid handsomely,' said Celsius, 'one of our agents has seen to that. At the given time tomorrow night, they are to put down their tools and go to a yard where others are waiting for them. They will wait while our knights take up post in the drains, feigning work for a while. Then the knights will file out in groups. As each group moves away, so a group of drain workers will be brought back into line.'

Morias grunted. 'Aye, and none of the workers will know who it is that has left the city. They'll not have seen faces, only money! They'll not blab, not for a long time, being glad of the money. Maybe some of them can be used again.'

'The fifty knights have taken the oath of silence,' said Celsius. 'If any should be caught, he will not implicate his companions, neither those who wait for them out in the mountains, nor those who are left behind. They'll die rather than give up names.'

Again Morias grunted. 'They will. And they'll kill if they have to, Sire. We are taking the strongest of them. Those who have no ties.'

'We must get whole families freed before we begin the rebellion in earnest,' said Pyramors, though secretly he wondered how this could possibly be managed.

'And you, Sire?' said Celsius, a look of concern on his face.

Pyramors's jaw tightened. 'I'm watched. Constantly. Zellorian knows where my loyalties lie. We fence with each other politically. But he contemplates my death.'

'How long will you remain here?'

'Not much longer. Once you've met up with Jorissimal and word gets back to me, I'll think of coming out myself. We need to free Gannatyne.'

Both Celsius and Morias beamed at this. 'The men will delight — '

Pyramors shook his head. 'No. Keep it to yourselves. Say nothing of my intent. The less that's known about me, the better. But I'll get word out to you.' He shook their hands again. 'Keep your wits about you tomorrow night.'

'We will,' nodded Celsius.

'My life on it,' said Morias.

After they had gone, Pyramors sat down and sipped at the wine. Yes, after this he would quit the city. He was tired of its shadows, its ghosts. It would be hard on the run, in the mountains. But perhaps such a life would sharpen him, give him the edge that he once had. It could not possibly be as dull and as unfulfilled as his life here in this doomed place.

4

THE SPECTRAL

Celsius pretended interest in the tiles before him, moving them as though carefully setting them in place on the wall. But he watched the line of men on either side of him. Morias had taken the last group but this one. Everyone was away except the last handful under Celsius. Over fifty men were busy on the wide drains that were being constructed, digging under the wall of this part of the city, beyond which was a narrow valley that dropped sharply down to an even wider valley, an open gorge that led northwards.

The teams of workers toiled through days and nights, working in shifts, for there was an urgent need to have the new drains finished so that the houses could be occupied. The city was growing quickly. Once this project was over, there would be others to start. Around Celsius, the drainage workers laughed, some singing as they dug at the earth and rock: the state paid them well for their labours, particularly when they worked by night. And there was the bonus given to them by the agents of these other men, who slipped out of the city past the curfew like ghosts.

Hamritkar, a huge fellow, brow gleaming with sweat, beamed at Celsius, his eyes white in the glow of the torches. 'Time for you to move, friend. My boys and I will see the guards on the wall are distracted for the last time. You'll hear me shout when you're clear to go. Got your last team together?'

Celsius nodded. His face was smeared with dirt, his hair darkened with soil and powder, so that few who knew him would recognise him. He and the last group would not have been easily recognisable as anything other than drainage workers.

'Get down into the bottom of the drain,' said Hamritkar. He had no idea why these men wanted to flee the city. Life in it was good as far as he could see. No wars to worry about, plenty of work, and a life that was a marvellous contrast to the last days of the Empire, when death had closed in on Mankind, always no more than a step away. But Celsius knew he was dependable.

Hamritkar walked up the line of workers. Beyond, on the wall, a group of soldiers were talking idly, some of them watching the valley beyond the city, others looking down at the men. They were very relaxed, not expecting trouble of any kind; after all, the men working were not slaves. He nodded to a companion and the fellow produced from under a robe a large flagon. The bigger man took it and climbed the steps up to the soldiers. He called out cheerfully.

'Come to tempt us again?' one of them laughed.

'Get on with your work, Hamritkar – '

'Ignore him! Bring the beer – '

'Have you no women smuggled under your cloaks?'

Hamritkar laughed with them, passing round the flagon. The guards were content. Like him, they were glad of an end to the Csendook wars. There were few families among men who had not lost someone.

Celsius waited until the men up on the wall were immersed in conversation, laughing softly. Hamritkar and his workers had been surprisingly inventive in distracting the guards while the groups of knights wriggled away through the new construction. There had been card games, dice and now the beer. Hamritkar had taken the enterprise seriously.

Celsius nodded to the men on each side of him. They pulled up their hoods, ducked down into the wide tunnel and made for the opening that led under the wall. As they filed out, a runner fetched the last of the workers who were waiting in the yard beyond another wall. They quickly slotted into the missing places in the line of workers. When Hamritkar idly leaned over the edge of the wall and shouted a few instructions, he received a number of rude replies, but everything had been rehearsed. The fugitives were away.

'You'd better get back to your workers before they rebel,' one of the guards laughed. Hamritkar belched. He nodded, leaving the flagon, and went down the steps. It had been a good night's work and the money would be most useful. A few more jobs like this and he could retire.

Under the shadow of the outer wall, Celsius watched as his own men slipped through the gully, well hidden from any eyes that might have been watching from above, although it was unlikely that the guards would be watching. The escape route had been well chosen – the only place along the entire city wall where anyone could get outside without being noticed. There were strict rules about leaving the city, imposed by the Consulate at Zellorian's prompting, as contact with the Innasmornians had not yet been approved. But here, with the new drainage channels opening out into the land beyond, men could get away. The guards who watched this place were not vigilant, thinking it most unlikely that enemies would attack in force. They did not take the watch seriously, Celsius knew. As he slipped into the shadows, following the last of his escaping men, he was watched from above by two others. One, a guard, held aloft a torch. Beside him, wrapped in a black cloak that had obscured him even from the watchful eyes of Hamritkar, a smaller figure gloated.

'The last of them, I think,' he said.

The guard nodded. 'Aye, Consul.'

Onando smirked. 'Give the signal.'

The guard made sure that he was not seen by any of the workers within the city. Hamritkar was busy at the rock face, as though nothing out of the ordinary had occurred. The guard walked to the outer edge of the wall and made circling motions with the torch. Onando stayed a few moments longer, then himself slipped away into the darkness.

Down in the gully, Celsius caught up with the last of his group. Morias was with them.

'All safely out?' called the sergeant.

Celsius thumped him on the arm. 'Yes! Let's move off quickly, to the rendezvous. We've several miles to cover before dawn.'

They followed the knights up another gully, knowing

that the entire company would be assembled and ready to leave. When they came to them, the company had already taken off their backpacks and removed their harness. They quickly stripped off the workers' clothes, although Celsius wondered if they ought to be more careful until they got far from the city. But Morias had warned of the dangers of the open country, especially at night. They knew little about the predators of Innasmorn.

Armed, gathered in ranks, the company was ready to go north east in search of allies. Celsius nodded, satisfied, and led them up the gully.

They had not gone more than a hundred yards when torches flared on the upper ridges of the gully. There were scores of them. Swords rang from scabbards and heads turned this way and that as the knights strained to see into the ring of flames.

'These cannot be our allies,' said Morias hoarsely.

A voice rang down from the rocks. 'Celsius! We know you are down there! This is Gavraland, Commander of the night watch. We know you are armed. Throw down your weapons and give yourselves up to my men. I warn you, you are surrounded and greatly outnumbered.'

Morias swore vehemently, and there were gasps from the men. But as they looked at the circular ridge, they could see the soldiers. There were far too many of them to resist. Celsius shouted, 'This is preposterous, Gavraland! How dare you draw weapons against us! There is no dispute between us.'

'On the contrary, Celsius,' came the harsh reply, 'you and your knights are in breach of the curfew laws of the city. No one is permitted outside without the express permission of the Imperator Elect.'

'We are no longer in his jurisdiction,' said Celsius. 'We forfeit our right to citizenship. We are free men.'

Gavraland laughed but it was a contemptuous sound that filled the men below him with apprehension. 'Your own words are against you, Celsius. Since you are not loyal to the Imperator, you are traitors.'

'That's ridiculous! We – '

'I'm not out here to argue with you. I have two hundred soldiers with me. If you don't throw down your arms and march back to the city at once, I have instructions to ride you all down. Every last one of you! Is that quite clear?'

Celsius turned to Morias. The burly sergeant scowled, but he shook his head. 'We'd make a good fight of it, Sir, but they'd hack us to pieces if it came to it. Gavraland will have chosen his bullies well. They'll be bloody bastards, every one of them.'

'Then we've been betrayed,' hissed Celsius. 'Hamritkar?'

'I think not. But we'll never know.'

'They dare not kill us, not if we give ourselves up. It would only add fuel to the rebellion.'

Morias nodded. 'Aye. I hate to agree but we may get the chance to use our swords on another field. But not here, Celsius.'

Celsius drove the point of his sword into the earth, walking away from it angrily. He gestured to his knights to do the same, and as they saw Morias toss away his weapon, they began the surrender.

'What does it mean?' whispered Jubaia.

Aru's face was clouded with puzzlement. They had been watching events below them on the city wall and beyond it, the gliderboat circling in absolute silence, high enough above the city not to be observed, under the cover of night. Aru's plan had been to get as close to the walls as possible and then to try and probe the workings of the city with the powers of their minds, and in particular the palace, but as they had drifted in, they had seen the movements below, the flickering of numerous torches.

'They are knights, loyal to Pyramors,' Aru finally said. 'I don't know them but I can feel his name in the air.'

Jubaia nodded. 'Their minds are full of fear for him. He planned this escape. But he's not with them.'

Aru watched as the torches moved back towards the city wall, where a narrow gate opened like a well of darkness.

'There'll be no bloodshed.'

But it endangers Pyramors, came Circu's voice, laden with concern. *Zellorian will punish him for this.* Jubaia could feel Circu's horror, his mind recoiling from the strength of her reaction. 'We may have to risk flying into the city and finding him. Snatching him from them,' he said.

Whenever you're ready, said Circu.

'It isn't going to be that easy,' said Aru. 'They'll kill us without question if they get the slightest chance.'

There's no time to deliberate! Pyramors is in danger. Zellorian will use this defeat of his knights to betray him. He'll suffer just as Gannatyne did. Act quickly! Let us go in! Aru was surprised at the assertiveness of the gliderboat. She was about to argue when Jubaia suddenly took the craft upwards in a dramatic sweeping arc so that Aru thought he had decided to take matters into his own hands, but he was nodding down at the city. Several shapes were hovering over the towers. Aru recognised them as gliderboats.

'Patrols,' said Jubaia, taking Circu even higher. 'They are clumsy things compared to Circu, but we'd better keep out of their range while we plan.'

Then plan quickly! snapped Circu. *Before Zellorian's men get to Pyramors.*

Circu rose at Jubaia's bidding. He knew she could ignore his control if she wanted to, but in spite of her impatience to go into the city, she listened to reason.

'If it is possible to contact Ussemitus,' said Aru, 'we must try. We need his advice.'

Jubaia nodded in silence. They rose high up beyond the peaks until the air about them swirled like the chilling waves of an ocean, biting into their bones. The city was like a star far below them, and silence closed in.

'Ready?' Jubaia asked Aru, and both she and Circu indicated for him to go ahead. Using the combined strength of their minds, Jubaia sent out a call, as Ussemitus had told him he must in time of dire need. He directed the call to the west, to where the World Splinter would receive it like a listening giant. Somewhere within it Ussemitus must hear.

The cold receded. A nothingness took over and Jubaia saw only a dark wall. Then something stirred at its far edge, a brief glow of light, blue. It swept to and fro like a beam, searching. Then it had found the gliderboat and it moved forward from the horizon, incredibly fast, until it swirled around the vessel, coalescing into a figure at last, a vague human-like shape.

'A spectral,' breathed Aru. They had seen such creatures hovering about the World Splinter, its ghostly servants.

'I must speak to Ussemitus,' said Jubaia.

The spectral spoke, its voice soft but clear. 'He hears you, little thief, but he is deep within the World Splinter, learning its mysteries, preparing for what is to come. But he has sent me. What do you wish?'

'Pyramors is in danger, down in the city. We must help him.'

It listened, as though contemplating the words and relaying them on to its distant master. After what seemed an age, it spoke. 'The Mother has brought Man to Innasmorn, to enhance his powers, to ready him for the new war with the Csendook. To invest him with powers. Pyramors is vital to this. Only he has the qualities that the Mother needs. If he is given power, Man will turn to him. He must be protected, brought from the city.'

'How?' said Aru.

Again the spectral was silent. Then it spoke. 'I will go down and search. You must wait for me. I will be your eyes, your senses. We must secure Pyramors. The fate of both our races hangs on his.'

Pyramors rubbed at his eyes. He had been deeply asleep, the bed enveloping him so that it took minutes for him to come to properly. One of his guards stood over him.

'Your pardon, Sire,' said the armed man, his face creased in concern. Pyramors could see at once that something was badly wrong. 'What is it?' he said getting from the bed and pulling on his clothes. Already he was beginning to guess what must have happened.

'You have been summoned to the palace. An escort is waiting.'

'Summoned by whom?'

'Sire, the Prime Consul. His men say it is a matter of urgency and also of some secrecy.'

'Are other members of the Consulate involved?'

'I think not, Sire. But the guards who have come for you have mentioned the name of Celsius.'

Pyramors stiffened. His face paled, but he shrugged as if it was a light matter. 'I'll be with them at once. Say nothing of this to anyone.'

The guard bowed, surprised that his master had not told him to send the men packing at this hour. Something clearly troubled Pyramors about their visit.

In the corridor, the two guards from Zellorian waited impatiently. They saw the sword at Pyramors's side. The Consul rarely went anywhere in the citadel without it, a fact that other Consuls had commented on. 'This had better be urgent,' said Pyramors.

'We are assured it is, Sire,' said one of the guards, saluting rigidly. It was all either of them did say as they went into the courtyard, mounted their horses and escorted Pyramors on the brief ride to the palace.

The Prime Consul was waiting, a spider at the heart of the citadel's web. He dismissed the guards. For once, Pyramors was alone with the Prime Consul.

'I would have avoided dragging you from your bed at so late an hour,' said Zellorian. 'But this matter is both urgent and delicate.'

'I cannot imagine why you should wish to speak to me – '

'It will save time and possibly embarrassment if we dispense with deceit, Consul. I wish to discuss facts with you. That is all. Sit down.'

Pyramors shrugged, feigning bafflement, and casually dropped into a chair. 'If you say so, though this is somewhat irregular.' Zellorian stared at him, measuring him. Yes, a dangerous enemy. Pyramors had strength, determination, and power. But Zellorian could detect the strain of the secret rebellion in the face of his visitor. Since the exile of Gannatyne he had been slowly worn down. He was young, resilient but even so, tired.

'Tonight, beyond the walls of the city, my soldiers apprehended a group of fifty knights. Knights, Consul, though they had disguised themselves as drainage workers so that they could get beyond the walls. They were led by a man called Celsius, a captain in the guard, a very able soldier.'

'What were they doing?' said Pyramors, yawning.

Zellorian shrugged. 'Presumably they were going to join the other rebels in the mountains. There must be quite a few of them by now, these dissidents. Though you'd know more about that than I.'

Pyramors scoffed. 'I? Prime Consul, I have no time for such matters. If a handful of our citizens are dissatisfied and try to find another way of life out in the wilderness, why should it concern me?'

'These knights have implicated you fully in their escape.'

Pyramors remained unmoved. 'That's ludicrous. This is just some attempt to dishonour me. The Consulate would laugh at any such suggestion.'

Zellorian turned and walked slowly about the room. Pyramors eyed his back, preparing to continue the façade as long as he had to. He felt his resolve slipping but he gritted his teeth. If Celsius and Morias had been taken, they would never have involved him, even under torture.

'Gannatyne is gathering a following, even though he is in exile,' said Zellorian, turning. 'These knights say they were sent by you to join him. But the rebellion puzzles me. Gannatyne is well secured. He is not officially a prisoner but believe me, Consul, he can never hope to get out of the fortress in which he is kept. And any rebellion would depend entirely on his freedom. These defections seem to me to be a complete waste of time and energy. What can you gain?'

Pyramors shook his head. 'I grant you I was Gannatyne's friend, but as you say, what could I gain by sending a few men out into the wilds? Why should I waste my efforts?'

Zellorian smiled. 'Then you have no intention of admitting your part in the rebellion.'

Pyramors said nothing, watching his enemy closely.

'I could have the entire plot exposed,' Zellorian went on, his own emotions completely in check. 'I could bring enough witnesses forward, enough men who would implicate you, and others. Gannatyne would be executed. So would you, Consul. The Imperator would gladly sign the warrants. We could argue about it all night, but you know that *I could bring the evidence forward.*' He pointed at Pyramors, his eyes narrowing, his hatred of the young Consul exposed, naked and ugly. 'Yes, you know it. I could have scores of your supporters executed, hung out on the walls of the city for your rebels to see.'

Still Pyramors said nothing.

'But, and this will surprise you, I would prefer to handle the rebellion another way. I would rather not resort to more killings; I merely wish to restore order. We are a young nation here on Innasmorn and rebellion will weaken our growth. Executions will fire the rebellion. The more brutal the force used against your followers, the more they will grow in number. It is an old game.'

Pyramors watched, but again, said nothing. Everything Zellorian said was quite true. Blood would be the fuel. Executions created martyrs.

'If I have to use force, I will do so. As I have done before,' Zellorian went on. He held his anger in check well, Pyramors thought. He stopped pacing and sat opposite the young Consul. 'Now, I propose a better way forward.'

'You are offering me a bargain?'

'If you like. I have fifty of your knights in my cells. No one knows they are there, apart from my guards. As far as your own agents are concerned, the men escaped. I'll free the knights. Nothing more will be said about their attempt to join the rebels. Gannatyne will not be hounded, and your own name will not be dragged through the mire.'

Pyramors smiled, but it was an expression of contempt. 'If these men were my allies, do you think I would accept any bribe you offered me? Why should I trust you? You want the rebellion crushed!'

'Without blood. Without needless death.'

'And your price? The names of all those who oppose you?'

'The price would be cheap.'

'I find that difficult to believe.'

'The Imperator Elect will not be made aware of this latest rebellion, and no one will be implicated. But in return, Consul, you must leave Innasmorn.'

Pyramors kept very still. The trap had opened up before him; he could look down into its maw and see his death waiting for him.

'Without you, Consul, the rebellion will collapse. You are the last hope of the rebels. If you go, there will be no more struggle. No more deaths. A potential civil war would be averted.'

Pyramors sat back slowly. It was probably true, he realised with a tremor of shock. If he renounced the rebels, gave his support to the Imperator, albeit verbally, then the last embers of the rebellion would go out. There was no one else strong enough, or stubborn enough, to fight on to rally the men. Who else could hope to win over enough of the Consulate? Zellorian knew it, but surely he was not stupid enough to imagine that Pyramors would agree to give up just so that fifty knights could be spared? Those knights knew the price of failure. They were prepared to die. Pyramors swallowed hard. How easy it was to dismiss them. But if he had to, he must.

'Prime Consul, if I were the focal point of this rebellion, what makes you think I would leave Innasmorn? Besides, where would I go?'

'Perhaps there is somewhere. Where you could be reunited with those you care most about.'

Pyramors frowned. What was the Prime Consul talking about?

Zellorian leaned forward, assured and smug. 'When we left Eannor, not everyone was able to come with us. Many loved ones were left behind.' He saw Pyramors's hands clench on the chair arms, the veins standing out in fury.

51

'What do you mean?' he hissed.

'*She is alive.*'

Very slowly, like a disturbed serpent, Pyramors got to his feet, his face at last betraying emotion. His teeth gritted. 'I have nothing more to say – '

'I tell you, she is alive. And there is a way back to her.'

'You expect me to believe this?'

'Not without proof. But I have it.'

Pyramors stared at him for a long moment, then turned away. He should have known Zellorian would attempt to bring him down by probing every weakness, every source of pain. 'You underestimate me. I would never betray my friends.'

'You will be betraying no one. You will be sparing us all from a bloody conflict that will split the city, possibly for years. Thousands may die in the battles. It may even lead to open war.' Zellorian crossed the room and opened a door. He called softly and another figure entered the room. Pyramors's head snapped up and he met the wide eyes of Onando, the fat Consul. Was this odious creature his lackey? It was no surprise.

Onando carried scrolls with him. He looked nervously at the young Consul.

'You know Consul Onando,' said Zellorian.

Pyramors nodded, unable to keep the contempt from his face.

'I said I had proof,' Zellorian went on calmly. 'The woman, Jannovar, wife of Fromhal Djorganist. Onando has records of her fate on Eannor.' Onando looked apprehensively at Zellorian, but he nodded.

'Well?' said Zellorian, suddenly a challenge in his voice. 'Do you want to hear this?'

Pyramors clenched his fists against an outburst, he knew it would be pointless. He nodded.

Onando began to read from the records. 'Fromhal was favoured by the Imperator Elect, and during preparations for the Crossing from Eannor – '

Pyramors said something under his breath and Onando stopped, his face white. Zellorian motioned the fat Consul to silence. 'She was your mistress, Consul. It had become common knowledge more than you thought, though you and Jannovar were remarkably discreet. But you are a discreet man. You allow your opponents few opportunities to undermine your authority.'

Pyramors would not permit himself to react. He watched in cold silence, feeling the trap closing.

'Everything is in these reports,' Zellorian went on, knowing that he had his victim at swordpoint. Now he would draw blood. 'For all your carefulness, Fromhal found out about his wife's infidelity. A few more weeks and it would not have mattered. You would all have taken part in the Crossing. Fromhal and Jannovar had been on the lists drawn up.'

Pyramors hardly heard Zellorian's voice, his mind going back over those terrible days that had led up to the final confusion, the days of terror as the Csendook had closed in on the beleaguered city of Rannor Tarul, and as Fromhal had uncovered the secret that had been kept from him. In his fury, he had cast out his wife and other members of his family, shutting them off from the flight that would take the Imperator Elect and the chosen ones out of the world cycle to the unknown oblivion beyond, the sanctuary Zellorian had promised. Pyramors had learned of it too late. By the time he was preparing to leave, to submit with the countless troops to Zellorian's rituals, there was no hope of finding Jannovar. For all he knew she had been slaughtered. As a final irony, Fromhal was killed in one of the last battles fought on Eannor, victim of a Csendook assault. With him went the secret of his wife's fate. Pyramors had come to Innasmorn certain that his lover had been left behind, a victim of war and almost certainly killed.

'You know all this,' said Zellorian, pointing to Onando's scrolls. 'But the Consulate does not. They have no idea that one of their most respected members caused so much distress to the noble house of Djorganist, a house that is now little more than a whisper from the past. A great name from the days when the Empire was strong. Or are there relatives of the Djorganists surviving yet? Here on Innasmorn, perhaps? Part of the rebel force? It would do their morale no good to learn of Fromhal's dishonour.'

'The Csendook killed him,' said Pyramors softly.

'Word may be that he threw himself needlessly into the last battle on Eannor, that he died rather than face dishonour.'

Pyramors almost cursed aloud. 'He never loved Jannovar.'

'So I understand. But the people of the Sculpted City do not.'

Pyramors could see how well Zellorian had prepared this trap. He would use whatever means at his disposal to bring Pyramors down.

'But none of this matters,' said Zellorian. 'The past is dead. It can remain so, as far as the people and the Consulate understand it.'

'If I agree to leave Innasmorn.'

Zellorian nodded. 'You want proof that she's alive? I know that the Csendook did not automatically destroy all those we left behind. They were never known to slaughter our women. They may have had other uses for them. Onando. Show him what else you have.'

Nervously Onando brought out from his robe an object. He passed it to Pyramors, who took it and held it up to the light. It was a metal bracelet, with writing etched into it. He recognised the script, that of the Csendook.

'A slave bracelet,' said Zellorian. 'Placed on those of our women that were singled out by our own slavers before Rannor Tarul fell. The name on that bracelet should be familiar to you. It is that of Jannovar.'

Pyramors knew that it was no trick. If he had the writing checked, he would find the name just as Zellorian said. Could she be alive? Somewhere on Eannor? But where? And how could he possibly get back to her?

'You may think the way back to Eannor is sealed up,' said Zellorian, reading the hope in the young man's eyes.

'To prevent the Csendook from following, to make us think we were annihilated. You have said so many times.'

'I could send one man back, alone. I have that power,' said Zellorian. 'There must be rebels on Eannor and on many other of our worlds. You'd do better to plot the fall of the Csendook rather than the downfall of our own Imperator.'

Pyramors looked at him in disgust.

'Decide, Consul. Go back to Eannor. Search for the woman. And spare the lives of thousands here.'

'If I agree to this, how will I know that you have not betrayed them?'

'Because you will end the rebellion before you leave. You will go to your leaders, tell them of your decision. That it is hopeless to follow Gannatyne, that you yourself are going back to Eannor. You will order the rebels to disband, follow the Imperator, unite under him.'

Pyramors tuned away, his blood cold, his heart thundering in his chest. The stress of the last months, the despair, all rose up like a wall. As darkness, it covered him, and there was no avenue of escape from it, no relief. He had thought earlier of his fifty knights, expendable for the cause. But were they? Why should any of them die? He could end it all, just as Zellorian said. And go back to Eannor? To what? Another impossible quest? What could he possibly achieve there? There was no answer from the darkness.

5

THE ACCRUAL

The old man sat wearily, shaking his head over and over again. He began speaking a number of times, but then hesitated, fingers stroking his long beard.

'I know how you must feel, Uncle,' said Pyramors, sitting opposite him. 'But it's done. I have already spoken to the others.'

'But why? Why?' said the old man, his eyes gleaming.

'It's for the best,' said Pyramors. 'I've thought it over many times. What Zellorian says is right. The longer the rebellion goes on, the more it fosters war. Our people have had enough of it. As a race, we edge towards extinction. Is that the way our light will go out, with us tearing at each others' throats?'

The old man looked at him hard. 'There's another reason.'

Pyramors looked away from the accusing eyes. 'No.'

His uncle shook his head again. 'And you trust Zellorian? To send you back to Eannor? *Pah*, he'll send you into oblivion. It's a trap.'

'That's a risk I'll take.'

The old man's anger finally got the better of him. He stood up, one gnarled fist banging down on the table. '*Risk!* You talk of risk! Ridiculous! You – '

'I have spoken to my fellow Consuls. The word is out. I am to go.' Pyramors rose and pulled on his cloak.

His uncle would have argued further but he seemed to lose strength, sitting slowly, gazing emptily ahead of him. He sat like that for a long time. When Pyramors put a hand on his shoulder in a final gesture of farewell, he hardly noticed. Moments later he was alone with his disillusion.

Zellorian smiled, but without mirth. He looked haggard,

his eyes lined, his mouth a thin, bitter streak. 'You are satisfied that you have spoken to all those to whom you wish to speak?'

Pyramors stood stiffly before him, cloak drawn about him as if it were cold in the stone chamber. Beneath it he wore his thin mail, at his side his battle sword. He nodded.

'Very well. I am satisfied.'

'You will release the men?'

'Of course. Do you wish to see them?'

Pyramors shook his head. Zellorian knew the answer. He smiled again. 'I thought perhaps not, under the circumstances. Come with me. I have prepared everything carefully.' He turned and led the way through a narrow doorway and on down a winding flight of stone steps. Guards flanked Pyramors silently but he was hardly aware of them, his thoughts straying to his uncle, the others he had told of his departure. He had said nothing of Jannovar. Those who had known about the affair had never approved. Now they would be even more appalled if they knew. But he no longer had the heart for rebellion, not with this latest disaster. How had Celsius and Morias been betrayed? How had their system been infiltrated? It seemed impossible to keep trust in this city, it was every bit as corrupt and rotten as Gannatyne had said. Listen to its voices, he had told Pyramors. The despair that sings a requiem for mankind.

When they finally reached the bottom of the stairs, Pyramors knew they must be deep under the mountains. His memories of this place, like that of other citizens, were like a dream. It was the place where men had first emerged after the Crossing from Eannor.

Zellorian nodded to more of his guards and another door opened, this time into a huge chamber. Its detail was obscured by a haze but Pyramors was struck at once by its atmosphere. It was warm, clammy, as though there were hot underground springs here. And there were curious sounds, contorted by the curves of wall and ceiling. Sounds which mimicked pain, though Pyramors told himself this was illusion. Through the haze he could discern wide steps going upwards, and beyond them massive pillars that looked as though they supported the weight of the mountain. Beside them, two enormous steel dishes filled with oil blazed, adding to the temperature.

Zellorian pointed to the top of the steps, a wide area that suggested a gate to infinite depths, although nothing could be seen there. 'Take your place between the pillars, Consul. I will open the promised gate.'

'Are you saying the gate is not sealed?'

'No, it is sealed, I assure you. No one beyond can open it, unless I am consulted. The Csendook do not have the means. They would revile the arts used to open such a gate. And they would never give of themselves, least of all to follow Man.'

'I don't understand.'

'Blood opens the gates between worlds, as you know. The Csendook use Openers and we use similar means to go between the worlds of a cycle. But to open a Path between world cycles, that is a different matter. The Csendook call it sorcery. Go up and take your place. I will send you back to Eannor. And take this with you.' The Prime Consul beckoned to one of the guards. He came forward and held out an object to Pyramors. It was the bracelet of steel.

Pyramors took it slowly, without expression, then clipped it on his own wrist.

'You think I'll betray you? Send you to your death?'

Pyramors met his stare with eyes of flint. 'I've given you what you asked,' he said bitterly. 'There'll be an end to rebellion.'

Zellorian nodded. 'Then I'll honour our bargain, Consul. Once you are through, you will never be able to return. I need have no fear of that. So you see, you do not have to die.'

Pyramors eyed the guards. There were a score of them but like statues they held their positions, unmoved by anything they saw or heard. Such men, such slaves, had made Zellorian the power he was. With a final snort of disgust, Pyramors went up on to the flat top of the stairs. He turned to face Zellorian. 'I am ready.'

'It may not be a pleasant journey, but you'll survive it.'

'Where will I emerge?'

'In the place where we congregated before we left. There will still be evidence of death there. So many died.'

Pyramors thought of the Csendook Swarms, the fall of Rannor Tarul, greatest city on Eannor, the clash of ten thousand warriors, the screams of the dying. Behind him he heard a gathering of sound, a roaring like distant wind. He turned. Already the smoke behind him swirled, opening like curtains, tall webs. There was an area of light in their midst, a glow, like sunlight rising through a dawn fog. Something in the mist reached out for him, invisible tendrils that wrapped themselves around his arms. Fear clawed at his innards but he fought it back.

He took his first step down the Path.

Through the corridors of the palace, moving as fast as the wind, the spectral hunted. It fed on the complex tangle of dreams and waking thoughts of the inhabitants of the city, sifting them, sorting those strands that wove the pattern that would lead it to Pyramors. If guards caught a glimpse of the being, they put it down to a trick of the night, a distortion of light, and it moved on undisturbed. But it reached a barrier deep below the city, a wall through which it could not pass. Yet it understood what was beyond it. The place of limbo, the vault that hung between worlds. Pyramors was in there but he and his enemies were enclosed as though in a sealed egg. The spectral could not crack that shell. It knew what the fate of Pyramors was to be.

An arrow of light, it rose up through the layers of the city, out into the night, where it sensed the darkness gathering, the probes of another shrouded mind. Veering from this, it sought out the gliderboat.

'Have you found him?' called Jubaia, his shadow moving against a backdrop of brewing storm.

'I have,' the spectral told him. 'But he is lost to you. He is going back through the gate to Eannor. He has abandoned Innasmorn.'

Aru's strained features glowed in the light of the spectral.

'We must prevent him! If he leaves Innasmorn, no one will rally my people against Zellorian. When Vittargattus comes, the City will be razed.'

The spectral's halo of light dimmed for a moment, as if its thoughts drained it of power. It seemed to be in communion with other forces, distant Ussemitus perhaps. At last it spoke again. 'There is a way for me to follow Pyramors. But there will be no contact between us, nor between me and the new Ipsissimus. But I will be his eyes.'

'Ussemitus?' said Jubaia.

Aru nodded. 'It must be. He's gathering deeper knowledge by the hour. What are we to do?'

'We must leave these skies,' Jubaia answered her. 'Something evils lowers itself from above us. And we can only hide and wait for the spectral to return with news of Pyramors.' He turned to it. 'Can he be brought back?'

'If he is willing, possibly,' it replied. 'I must leave you and find my own way to Eannor. I must gather power from the World Splinter.'

As it whirled away, the skies above it echoed to the sound of oncoming thunder, the first breakers of the storm.

Pyramors heard sudden shrieks from either side of him; he thought he saw figures in the mist, shadows that fought each other. He looked down, recoiling at what he saw, for something ran down into the slope of the stones, something dark and viscous. Blood!

Behind him he heard Zellorian laugh harshly. 'I told you it would take blood to open a Path. But you can see, your destiny summons you. Walk down the Path, Pyramors. You cannot turn back now.'

Pyramors was forced onward, pulled by the sudden strength of the mist, his arms dragged. He tested them against this power, but he could not resist. He was committed. His feet slopped through the blood. It thickened and there were more cries beyond the circle of vision.

'The Path demands life,' said Zellorian. His voice was close to Pyramors, as though he had come with him, though Pyramors knew this was illusion. 'For a single man to cross, a few lives will suffice. In your case, shall we say, fifty.'

Pyramors jerked as the implication struck him. Then it was a betrayal! He tried to speak, but his throat was clogged. Again he fought the powers that were pulling at him. But the winds rose down in the tunnel of mist, swirling upward, strengthening. Like a cork caught in a whirlpool, he was being sucked onwards. Now nothing could prevent his being drawn in.

'Fifty men, Consul. A small price to pay for your passage back to Jannovar. No, I'll not send you to your death. You'll suffer, though. You'll *live*, Pyramors. Live, knowing that your rebels gave up their lives to send you back. You hear them? Their screams? Look before you. The offering in the Path that runs on to unlock the way for you.'

Pyramors tore his eyes from the slick of blood, but he could do nothing to prevent himself walking onward. The mists closed in, themselves changing hue, lit by the fires, their swirls clouded in pink, further reminder of Zellorian's triumph. He stood far behind, watching as his figure was absorbed by the mist. As he looked, something within him shifted, a darkness, the same darkness that lurked behind his thoughts, stealing through his sleep, probing at him. He shook his head to rid himself of the notion but the inner dark fought him, strengthened by something beyond the city, out in the night, the gloating storm.

He gasped but he could not take his eyes from the Path. Whatever it was that used his eyes was devouring the vision before it. He felt the abrupt shudder of recognition. Innasmorn! Quareem's power. The storms. They had lodged in him like a splinter of the night. The mists closed in, swallowing the far shape of Pyramors. Darkness slammed to like a door. The portal was closed. Zellorian stumbled back. He shut his own mind.

Below him, swords dripping, his guards waited. 'It is done,' he nodded, lurching down the steps. 'Burn the corpses.'

Indifferently, the guards bowed and left him to his darkness.

Pyramors found himself stretched out, cold and stiff. He was in a bed of mud, or so his bemused mind told him. He struggled to his knees, gasping for air. This was not Eannor. It was the first thought that hit him. He peered about him. The pink glow of the Path was here yet. He was in some kind of tunnel, the walls slick and dark, the floor slippery with mud, or something that felt like it.

He stood, holding on to the wall to steady himself. Again he thought, this is not Eannor. His cloak, weighed with muck, tried to pull him down. He undid its clasp and dropped it, wading on, unsure of his direction. The tunnel led downward to another that joined it. He gazed at the intersection, amazed by it.

The Path. This was the Path between worlds, between world cycles. Like an artery, it ran away to his left and right, its walls scarlet, gently pulsing, banks of flesh. It must be an illusion. But the effect was real. He dropped down into the wider tunnel, moving along it. It was three times his height. Somewhere beyond he could hear the whine of the wind, a remote storm. It was the only guide he had. He slipped his sword from its sheath. The floor here was dry but pulpy, making progress awkward and slow. He moved on, listening. The dizziness left him and he shook off the last of the effects of the Crossing.

As he moved onward, searching for the source of the light far beyond him, he became aware of other sounds. There were a number of smaller tunnels running off the main one, scarlet tubes that led into darkness. From them he heard sounds emerging, as though another large tunnel must run parallel to this one, and something moved within it, dragging itself, slithering through this soft womb.

Fear rose like bile in his throat. He moved as quickly as he could, but there seemed to be no escaping the sounds. They closed on him, coming from every direction, like the wind of the Path, formed from the air. He looked behind him only to see an obscuring darkness.

Eventually he came to an opening into what appeared to be a wide chamber, its ceiling lost in a mist that was similar to that in the chamber where Zellorian had prepared him. Had he returned? Yet he could see nothing in the bright light, no pillars, no braziers. Surely this could not be the same place. Behind him he heard the sounds gathering, the shifting of a vast weight, the pounding of blood through the walls, as though he had dropped down into the gut of an unimaginably large being. He shook his head, trying to free himself of this grotesque image.

Cautiously he stepped out on to the flat area of the chamber. After he had taken a few steps, he lost sight of the walls, and there was still no sign of a ceiling above him. But he was convinced this was not Eannor: this was neither earth nor rock beneath him. He could feel it tremble, vibrate.

Pyramors.

He grunted with shock. His name had been spoken, but he had heard it inside his head.

Pyramors.

He turned, peering into the haze on all sides. Something was moving, a shadow, a stain on the golden mist. It was huge. He felt himself shaking, his skin crawling with fear.

'Who are you?' he said softly, but his voice was as clear in the air as that other voice had been in his mind. It was deep, guttural, not a human voice.

I read you, Pyramors, it came again. The shadow-thing moved, the ground shuddering as it did so. Pyramors stepped back, clutching his sword with both hands, hands that were slick with perspiration.

Put down your fear. And your sword is useless here.

Pyramors automatically lowered his blade, wanting to see this thing that could put words into his mind, yet not wanting to see it. But he could not turn away. The mists shredded and he saw the thing that had followed him. He cried out in shock.

It was huge, deep red, a hunched mound that crawled on thick limbs, bloated legs that ended in knuckles of flesh. Its arms were short but massively thick, the hands large enough to grasp a man, the fingers an exaggerated length, nailless. It had no neck, its head almost as wide as its thick body, though its eyes were tiny in comparison, twin beads, obsidian black. But they were fixed on Pyramors. Its mouth, a long, wet slash, twin flaps of skin, hung slackly, a huge open darkness, like a great wound. Ropes of saliva hung from it, flecked with scarlet. Pyramors was instantly reminded of a leech, one that had recently been draining its victim. But on what could such a monstrous being feed?

It looked slow and cumbersome, and Pyramors searched for a way to evade it, certain that it would attack him.

You are of no use to me dead, came its deep voice.

Staring up into that awesome face, Pyramors found it almost impossible to believe that it was this thing that spoke to him.

I do not use my mouth to speak with, it said, understanding his confusion.

'Who are you?' he asked it once more.

I am an Accrual.

It meant nothing to him. 'Where is this place?'

You are on a Path. Between worlds. Between world cycles in fact, where very few of your race ever come. But I sense you search for Eannor.

Pyramors nodded. Something must have gone wrong with the Crossing. Or was this Zellorian's doing?

Zellorian? He sent you here?

'You know him?'

Something that could have been a snort or a sigh flushed through Pyramors's mind, as though the Accrual had found this question amusing. *I have had dealings with Zellorian.*

'Dealings?'

You are mystified. I will explain, if you wish.

Pyramors nodded.

No being may cross between world cycles without recourse to certain powers. Zellorian confuses his enemies, the Csendook, by disguising his actions as sorcery. But he learned of the means to

64

contact the Accruals, my own species. There are not many of us, mutations that we are, but we travel the Paths at will. We are jealous guardians of them. They are the key to our own survival.

'The sacrifices!' murmured Pyramors, but he could just as easily have shouted.

Life sustains us. We can open Paths, but it needs great power. What we use, we must replace.

'With blood?'

With blood. Just as blood sustains Man, so it sustains the Csendook, the Accruals. All life. It flows through the veins of the world cycles just as it flows through your own body.

'Then when Zellorian took us through the gate from Eannor to Innasmorn, the power he used – '

Was the power of blood, yes. Life, sacrifice.

'But whose? The Csendook that attacked us? The Swarms?'

A little. But mostly it was human sacrifice.

Pyramors had sloughed off his fears, his mind racing back to the days of the Crossing, the darkness and confusion that had seemed at the time to be little more than a nightmare.

Accruals can open Paths. We can permit as many Men through the openings as we wish to cross. Zellorian sought to bring thousands. Thus the cost was high, the toll in human life great.

Pyramors felt his chest constricting as the words echoed inside him. The slaughter! Only now did he realise the true nature of Zellorian's betrayal, the reason for so much secrecy. 'The battle. Our rearguard – '

On Eannor? A deceit.

'But there must have been thousands in Rannor Tarul, called to protect the Imperator as we prepared for the Crossing.'

Zellorian did not tell you how they were used, their real purpose.

'Sacrificed! Destroyed?'

To bring your ruler through. With as many of his people as possible.

Pyramors shook with anger. 'What happened to them?'

The voice that replied was devoid of feeling, of remorse. *They fed the walls around you. It is how the Accruals survive.*

65

Pyramors shook his head, sickened. For a long time he could not speak. Something else came to him and he swung round to face the monstrous bulk of the Accrual. 'And my own men? The fifty who died back on Innasmorn to send me here now – '

They, too, have become part of the Path. It is the order of things.

Pyramors put his hands to his eyes, stunned.

I will release you to Eannor. Your toll is paid.

Pyramors hardly heard the words, his mind still struggling with the horrifying concept of the ritual slaughters that Zellorian had performed in order to preserve the Imperator. If the Consulate should discover the truth –

Before I send you to your destination, I would speak with you.

Pyramors looked up, his mind still fogged.

Do you understand me?

'What is it you want?'

Your thoughts speak to me of your purpose. You go to Eannor in search of a woman.

Pyramors nodded.

What will you do when you find her?

Pyramors shrugged helplessly. 'I can't be sure that she's alive. Even if she is, she will be held by the Csendook. To prize her from them – ' He lifted an arm in a gesture of defeat.

But even so, if you succeed. What then?

'Flight. We'll be hunted.'

You will wish to return to Innasmorn?

Pyramors again studied the extraordinary face but he could read no emotion in its alienness, in those dead eyes. 'Innasmorn?'

I could open a Path for you.

'You think I would betray my people just as Zellorian did? Lead them to you for slaughter? You think I could live with that?'

I understand Human sentiments, loyalty. You have a very different way of thinking, unlike Zellorian's. He had thrust aside his emotions, put them deep within himself. But I do not ask you to consider betraying your own people.

'What then?'

What of your enemies? The Csendook. Does blood not course just as hotly through their veins as it does through yours? I can assure you that it does. I have tasted it.

Pyramors was taken aback. He had not thought of the possibilities of this. 'Csendook?'

Can you not engineer a sacrifice?

But Pyramors was derisive. 'How could I possibly deceive them into a trap – '

Do they not crave Innasmorn?

Pyramors felt himself going cold. 'They know nothing of Innasmorn. The Path was sealed. They think us dead, destroyed on Eannor.'

You are certain of this?

Again Pyramors felt the fear closing around him. The Accrual said it had tasted Csendook blood. What did that mean? 'They know?'

There are those who seek you yet. Those among your enemies who would make great sacrifices to find the way to your Imperator Elect and his Consulate.

'But if they succeed – '

You fear for your race.

'The Csendook are bent on our destruction. They will not rest until they have eliminated us all. And you ask me to lead Csendook to you, to help them achieve their end!'

I am interested only in the survival of the Accruals. I have no interest in the Csendook, other than to feed on them, as I feed on others. Blood is blood.

'If I lead Csendook to you, will you send them to Innasmorn?'

Others have gone before them.

'To Innasmorn? Csendook?'

A few. The price was high. They gave up the lives of many of their Zemoks, and of many human slaves. But a few reached Innasmorn.

'Where are they now?'

As they have not returned to Eannor, they must still be on Innasmorn. No doubt they are hunting your ruler.

Pyramors shrank from the thought: he knew that none

of his people would be safe, that the Csendook would be indiscriminate.

You can control the flow of Csendook to Innasmorn, if it is your wish.

'How?'

Through me.

'I must prevent this thing!'

You wish to return to Innasmorn?

'I must go to Eannor first. I must find Jannovar, if she is alive.'

And then return, through the Path I will open for you?

'There is no other way.'

That is so. But I will create this Path for you. And after you have passed through, I will seal it up. Your world will then be closed to the Csendook.

'Why should you do this? What do you expect in return?'

Sacrifices. They are ever the price. But Paths between world cycles are rare things. They are tenuous, dangerous to create, even for an Accrual. Those who have power over us, they who control the Great Circles, are not pleased with our interference, our hungers. I can do this thing between Eannor and Innasmorn perhaps twice more. I wish to enjoy the full pleasures of such a working.

'You want Csendook? As many as I can bring?'

A Swarm, if you can achieve it. Pretend to betray your people on Innasmorn. Trick the Csendook. Offer them the greatest prize that they can imagine. But bring them to me. And you and your woman will go back to Innasmorn. There was a sudden swelling of desire in the mental voice of the Accrual, the longing for success, for appeasement.

Pyramors felt it and turned away, appalled, but lured by the plan. Bring Csendook to this hell? Was such a thing possible?

Decide quickly, Pyramors. Go to Eannor on my mission, or you will know what it is to feed the hunger of my kind.

BOOK TWO

THE GLADIATORS

6

VULPORZOL

Shadows drifted apart like wraiths, fanning out across the stones of the huge plaza where once the sacrifices had been made. Bones and skulls littered the place even now: no instructions had ever been given for them to be removed. They were a powerful reminder of the past. No one was allowed into this region now unless given express permission by Kurduzar. He had addressed the night patrol, a dozen or so Zolutars, and they spread out from the central area of the plaza, each having chosen a vector of the land beyond to study. They would have hunted in pairs but Auganzar had insisted that the patrols be limited in numbers; the only way to cover most of the land was singly. They carried no torches so that they could move secretly but their night vision was excellent, sharper than that of a Man.

The command to work alone had sharpened Vulporzol's belief that the Supreme Sanguinary planned treachery. On the high walls of the Bone Watch, the guards would turn away. If Vulporzol was wrong, and they were watching, he could do his work without anxiety. He looked at the Bone Watch: it was a stain against the night, dark and obscure.

He moved up into the valley. There were broken slabs jutting from the land and what might have been columns, parts of buildings, that Man had once erected here. It was conjectured that this entire area had been a small city, a temple to strange gods. Man was known to worship a variety of these, their nature varying from world to world. Perhaps, Vulporzol mused cynically, Man had tried to elicit their aid in dragging him away from Eannor to freedom. He himself had no great desire to see the Crusade begin anew. There were far more important things to be done in the worlds of the Csendook inheritance. Though he knew that most of his race would prefer the chaos of war. Yet to seek a way beyond the cycle of worlds was madness. Zuldamar, finest of all the Garazenda, was correct in his beliefs, worthy of loyalty. He, of all Csendook, possessed real vision.

Kurduzar was discreet, however, in his treachery. He had the measure of every Csendook on Eannor, and knew exactly how loyal they were to either Zuldamar or Auganzar, his own master. Even so, Kurduzar would be taking a great risk if he intended to eliminate any of Zuldamar's warriors tonight.

Vulporzol climbed one of the heaps of stone. He was over a mile from the Bone Watch and had no intention of getting away from its eyes. From the top of the stones he could see the tower. He scanned the land about him, which rose gently to where he stood and beyond up to the foot of the mountains in a steep bowl. There were no sounds from the land; his fellow warriors were well practised in keeping silent, going about this night's work with infinite care and patience. Seven of them were Kurduzar's Zolutars. If they were planning murder, there was nothing to indicate that they had followed Vulporzol.

He was about to climb down from the stones when he heard a sound. It was faint, so that at first he assumed it must be distant, but it came once more and he realised that it was close to him, merely very subdued. It had sounded like the moan of the wind. But no wind ever disturbed this region. The very air seemed to avoid the place.

A trap?

He circled the area where he thought the sound might have come from, pausing to listen. But there was no other sound. He waited for a long time. If warriors were waiting for him, they were extraordinarily quiet. Carefully he moved in, circling the place where he felt the sound had come from, fixing it in his mind. For an hour he closed in and all that time he heard nothing. If this was a trap, the warriors were unique. Even Csendook could hardly be so silent, as silent as death.

At last there was another sound, a groan it seemed. A suggestion of muted suffering.

The place ahead was ideal for treachery: more tumbled rocks, jutting slabs, stark against the night sky. Vulporzol glanced over his shoulder. The Bone Watch was still in view, but once he entered those rocks, he would be out of sight of it if he attempted a signal. If Xinnac was watching, he would not see.

Again Vulporzol moved in. The sound did not come again. He made his way up over the rocks, keeping the Bone Watch in view. They would not use arrows, not in this poor light. It would have to be swords and they would need to be very quick. He paused to look down into the broken shadows. There was little night light, the moon of Eannor mostly obscured by cloud cover, but among the rocks he thought he saw a pale flutter of movement. A creature, trapped or dying? But what creature could have groaned?

He moulded himself to the rocks. If Csendook were there, waiting, they would not have seen him. He waited, ears cocked. The silence was almost painful in its intensity. Overhead the clouds shifted. The moon was a third full. For a few moments its light brightened fractionally. Something was trapped down in the rocks, a twisted form, too small to be Csendook. Vulporzol was certain it was no animal.

The light faded, darkness flowed in anew. Vulporzol tugged the short brand from his belt. He had made it before leaving the Bone Watch. It was cut from an old, narrow branch, the end of the wood soaked in the oil used in the lamps in the tower. Ignited, it would burn long enough to alert anyone in the tower.

Vulporzol gripped his curved blade in his teeth. He needed both hands for the torch and the flints that would ignite it. But he did not light it yet. With great care he began to go down towards what he thought he had seen. He knew he would be going out of sight of the Bone Watch. Even if he lit the torch he would have to fling it up to the top of the stones if he were attacked. Xinnac would have to ensure that Dagrazem's Zemoks got out here very quickly. If this were to be an assault.

As he went down among the rocks Vulporzol wondered. Still the night was eerily silent. Because of the peculiar silence of the zone of sacrifice any sounds were magnified, and even the best of the Csendook warriors would be bound to make some small sound if they were here. Vulporzol himself scraped a heel on rock, the sound of it loud in his ears. He cursed inwardly. But nothing moved.

Below him there was no movement. Again a blotch of moonlight touched the rocks. Part of a body was revealed. An arm, a chest. There was blood, and now that Vulporzol saw it, he could smell it. *Human* blood.

He crouched down, edging forward, the taste of metal strong in his mouth. He was upon the body before he knew it. Again he looked about him, readying his torch for ignition. But nothing stirred. He looked down. It was a Man. Crumpled among the rocks as if he had been tossed here, an arm flung out. It was the hand that he had seen move, like the broken wing of a bird. He touched it. Warm. *Alive.*

But where had the Man come from? He was dressed in light armour, and there was a sword, a dagger. Blood seemed to smear him, but on his breastplate were the embossed royal arms of -

Vulporzol drew in a sharp breath. The Imperator Elect! This Man was one of his warriors. One of the fugitives. *Returned?*

The Csendook rose, again studying the rocks about him. This could not be a trap, not if this Man was really what he seemed to be. If the others had found him, they would have sped back to their master with him, wallowing in their success.

Vulporzol climbed the rocks, scanning the land as best he could. Still he saw no movement. His fellow warriors were busy with their own vectors. It seemed unlikely, after all, that they would disturb him. He went back down to the body, slipping his sword back into its scabbard, the torch into his waistband. He examined it. The Man was alive, unconscious. Neither his arms nor his legs were broken. It was difficult to say if there were any internal injuries but there was no bleeding from mouth or nose. Otherwise there was much blood but Vulporzol wondered if it would turn out to be the Man's at all. It had a strange smell to it, an unfamiliar alienness. As he wiped at some of it with his fingers, Vulporzol noticed the bracelet on the Man's right wrist. He could not unclasp it, but the slickness of the blood enabled him to work it over the hand and off. He held it up, seeing the single word carved on it. The name of a human woman, Jannovar. He squatted in the rocks, thinking hard. If this was indeed one of the Imperator's warriors, Auganzar must not find him. If he did, he would insist on an attempt to open a Path beyond Eannor.

Vulporzol soon reached his decision. In his mind he had already wondered what would happen if he should ever find anything in the zone, any clue to the survival of the last of the Men. The wounded Man would have to be hidden. Where better than among the *moillum*? But how to get him among them? If he could revive him, it would be possible. But as he was, it would be almost impossible.

In spite of all his attempts the Man remained unconscious. Vulporzol sat back, confused. He must get the Man away before daylight, when other patrols would begin their daily search. Somehow he must enlist the help of Dagrazem's Zemoks. As he considered his possible moves, Vulporzol lifted the Man and began carrying him over the rocks. Below, further down the slope, the ground evened out into a flat, earthen trail, leading up towards the foothills. There were no living trees there but there were broken trunks, snapped and rotted, a tangle of wooden columns. Vulporzol entered their maze, again checking around him to see that he was not observed. He felt sure that if he had been seen carrying the Man, he would have been instantly accosted by the other warriors. But the night remained still and empty.

He carried his burden deep among the maze of broken trunks, turning at last from the twisted path. He counted out trees to his left, seven of them that made a rough line at an angle to the path. At the seventh trunk he stopped, searching for the former glen. He found what he sought: a hollow, scooped out under one of the trees there, under its roots. He put the body down and used his sword to enlarge the natural hole. When it was twice as large as the Man, he pushed him into it. He was certain the Man would not revive until the morning at the earliest, if he were to revive at all. Carefully he pushed the earth back around the body, using snapped branches to distribute the waste evenly, covering tracks. The Man was now completely hidden from view, with barely enough of an air hole to breathe. Again Vulporzol counted the trees as he went back to the path. He listened to the surrounding trees. They were as dead as the air. Nothing stirred.

Among the trunks, he found a fallen one. It was partly rotted but its roots still clung to the earth. However, Vulporzol dragged at it, exerting great strength, tearing it from its bed. He stretched it over the path, again careful to ensure that his tracks were obliterated. The trunk looked as though it had fallen here by chance. Then, satisfied that he had not left anything to suggest he had been here, he began the trek back.

After a short walk, he angled away from the wood, knowing that he was now about to cross into the next zone, where one of the other Zolutars would be patrolling. He had to find high ground, far from the wood. As he crossed the zone, another broken band of land where the stones were like teeth, treacherous and eager to snap a leg, he was again careful to be silent. Once he thought he saw movement below him but he climbed away from it, circling a bare hill, moving further across the land until he was in a third patrol zone. This should be far enough away from his own zone for his purpose.

Climbing still further up into the foothills, he turned. He could just discern the far outline of the Bone Watch. He was high enough. Taking the brand from his belt, he ignited it, ramming its grip into the soft earth. Flames licked up at the night. Drawing his sword, he leapt down from the hill, no longer careful to avoid making a noise. He turned back once to see the brand burning, a bright pennant in the night. It would undoubtedly be seen from the Bone Watch. Warriors would be sent, almost certainly riding xillatraal, the fierce quadrupeds of the Csendook. And Dagrazem's Zemoks would also come. They would already have an excuse to hand.

Vulporzol knew he would come across his colleagues quickly. He was right. One of them, Ukrazol, came crashing through the dried undergrowth beyond him, having seen the firebrand. This was his zone and his face showed his fury at having an intruder enter his area of watch. But the anger died a little when he saw that it was Vulporzol.

'Vulporzol!' he gasped, his sword raised before him as though he meant to attack with it. 'What is happening?'

'I raised the alarm.'

'Why are you in this zone?'

'I followed something from my own.'

'What?' Ukrazol was looking all about him, raking every patch of darkness with his scowl, expecting an attack.

'I saw only dimly. But creatures moved towards those foothills.' Vulporzol pointed to the slopes opposite the wood where he had hidden the wounded Man. 'At first I thought I could catch one of them,' he said, pausing for breath as though he had been running hard. 'But they eluded me.'

'Were they Men?'

'I couldn't tell. Darkness covered them.'

'Runaway *moillum*?'

'Possibly. It may only have been creatures down from the mountainside. I lit a torch. We were told to report anything here. Any sign of life.'

'Aye,' Ukrazol nodded. 'You did the right thing. Especially with the Supreme Sanguinary here on Eannor. If we miss anything, he'll have us hung up by the heels. Even those of you seconded from outside of the Thousand.'

Vulporzol grunted. 'That's what I thought.' He knew Ukrazol to be one of Kurduzar's most eminent warriors.

'Do we follow, or wait for help?' said Ukrazol.

'I suggest we make for my brand. It will guide the others, and bring warriors from the tower.'

'Aye, that's the best course.' Ukrazol nodded and together they trotted back up the path to the crest of the hill. It was not long before the first of the other night patrols arrived, equally as alerted as Ukrazol had been. Vulporzol repeated his story, careful not to over-elaborate.

'It may just have been creatures from the mountains,' he said again. 'But if so, it would be the first time they had come down here to this zone.'

'We should report everything,' said another of the Zolutars. 'And I agree, we must begin the hunt as soon as the tower sends warriors. That brand was a sensible idea.'

'Vulporzol was the only one with that foresight,' said Ukrazol. 'Though we were told not to bring torches.'

Vulporzol snorted. 'I had no intention of slipping on any of these rocks and breaking a leg and then bleeding to death because no one heard or saw me! The brand was a precaution.'

'It's a dangerous place and that's the truth,' agreed another of them.

They heard the drumming of hooves beyond and behind them. Other torches shimmered and a company of Csendook pounded through the night. The xillatraal screeched, eyes wide, maddened by the wild ride and the fire of the brands, but the warriors held them in check.

When they reached the hill, Vulporzol again explained what had happened and at once the warriors began preparing to spread out in a hunt that would take them up into the foothills. The xillatraal were excellent tracking beasts; they would soon pick up the trail of any intruders. Word was also sent back to the Bone Watch. Vulporzol waited for as long as he dared, knowing that Dagrazem's Zemoks would come to the firebrand on foot. When they did appear, slipping from cover, swords raised, they were challenged by Ukrazol, who had taken charge of the search party, this being his vector of the search.

'What are you doing out in the zone at night?' he shouted at them. There were a dozen of them and Vulporzol knew every face. They were Dagrazem's chosen, and all were to be trusted. He stepped up beside Ukrazol.

'Your pardon, Zolutar,' said the Zemoks' leader. 'We saw the firebrand. Dagrazem, our sergeant, sent us out at once. We assumed something was amiss.'

'Then Dagrazem should be congratulated on his quick thinking,' said Vulporzol before Ukrazol could question the Zemoks further. 'I know these Zemoks. I can vouch for every one of them.'

'Then let's move!' snapped Ukrazol, annoyed that events

were moving on more quickly than he would have wished. 'Let's get up into the hills.'

Two of the Zemoks from the tower had given up their xillatraal to Ukrazol and Vulporzol, and the former shouted out instructions to the Zemoks and other Zolutars who had been patrolling the zones.

Vulporzol spoke quietly to Dagrazem's Zemoks. He told two of them what he had found and where he had hidden the Man, giving them careful instructions. 'Get him up into the valley as far as you can. We must get him out of this area as soon as possible. We dare not leave him here beyond dawn. You *must* get him out. High up, over the hills. Hide him for a few days if you have to, but do everything you can to get him out of the zone. Alive if possible.'

'Zolutar, what if we are found?'

'The Man must not be seen. If he is, you must kill any Csendook not loyal to Marozul Zuldamar. Be very clear on that. None of Auganzar's spies must know that a Man has been found in the zone of sacrifice. At all costs, the Man must not be seen. If all else fails, kill him and bury him, or have him dropped into one of the deep ravines in the mountains. If he's found, we are all dead.'

The Zemok, Huurzem, nodded. 'We'll go at once.' He and another of the Zemoks darted off into the night, away up into the hills, not veering off on the route given to them by Vulporzol until they knew they were well out of sight of the rest of the search party.

'Shall I lead us?' Vulporzol called to Ukrazol as he mounted the bucking xillatraal. 'These beasts are anxious to hunt.'

'Maybe they smell something,' said Ukrazol. 'Have you deployed your Zemoks?'

'I have.'

They raced up the slopes, those who were on foot fanning out behind them, breaking into the steady trot of the Csendook, a loping run that they could keep up hour after. Vulporzol led the party further and further up into the hills, angling away from the dead wood and the Man hidden there.

Some miles to the west of them, Huurzem and his fellow Zemok, Thagran, dropped down a hollow towards the wood that their master had told them of. They scanned it carefully but it was motionless, as though sculpted out of stone. Neither of them spoke. There were many things they would like to have discussed, but these could wait. They went about their business with efficiency.

Thagran guarded Huurzem's back as they went along the path that had been taken earlier by Vulporzol but the Zolutar had covered his tracks exceptionally well. There was nothing to suggest that a Csendook had been here. Perhaps a xillatraal would have scented the tracks but by the time any xillatraal ever came here, the trail would be cold.

'There's the fallen trunk,' said Huurzem.

Again Thagran took station, positioning himself carefully, watching the trail. Huurzem left him and began counting tree stumps in a diagonal line to the left of the path. A hundred yards into the wood he found what he sought. Using his sword as Vulporzol had, he worked at the earth that had been levelled against the lower trunk of the tree the Zolutar had specified. He had not been working long when he came to the Man. He checked carefully: the Man was alive but still unconscious. Huurzem tugged him free of his temporary grave. The soil clung to him and to the excessive congealed blood. Was it his own? If so it was amazing that he was yet alive.

Huurzem stretched the Man out at the foot of another tree, well hidden in its shadow. He returned to Thagran.

'I've found him. He must be carried.'

Thagran looked northwards. 'To the mountains?'

'If there is another way out of this zone of sacrifice, we have to find it. Let us go.'

They said nothing more, asking no questions, merely carrying out the instructions given to them by Vulporzol. Whatever the wishes of Auganzar, those of Vulporzol came first to these Zemoks. He was the voice of Zuldamar. It was enough.

Huurzem picked up the man, shouldering him easily. Not many months ago they had been fighting such Men, caught up in the bloody mayhem of front line battle on a remote world where Man still resisted Csendook overlordship. But they did not think of that now. If Vulporzol wanted the Man kept from the sight of Auganzar, they would see to those orders, or die attempting to fulfil them.

They ran on into the night, northward up into the steep slopes of the lower mountains, then veering westward, climbing all the time. They took turns to carry the unconscious Man, who never showed a sign of coming round, but he was an easy burden for them. Both were extremely fit, hardy warriors who had trained every day of their lives, and the eccentricities of this terrain, the steepness of the climb, were nothing to them.

As dawn spread its uncertain glow they were high up on a ridge, overlooking the upper reaches of the zone of sacrifice. The mountains made a natural amphitheatre of it and there seemed to be no natural gorges or passes to the west that would enable them to cut through and back to the safety of the outside. They rested briefly, assuring themselves that they were not being pursued. Where possible, they had entered streams, ensuring that any trail they left was spoiled and broken. No xillatraal could follow here and it was unlikely they would be found. Across the valley they could make out the crags of the eastern range, but there were no signs of the others, the false hunt that Vulporzol was leading.

Thagran went on ahead while Huurzem used fresh spring water to wash both himself and the Man. Once he had cleaned the muck and dried blood off him, he found that he was not wounded at all, just bruised. The blood had not been his. And he was a warrior: his muscles, hardened and well used, attested to that. He wore light armour and carried a battle sword. But the shock of wiping clean the breastplate and seeing the royal arms of the Imperator Elect made Huurzem gasp. No wonder Vulporzol did not want the Man seen. Had he returned from beyond Eannor? It was whispered that some of the Imperator's Men had used sorcery to avoid the trap set for them.

Thagran reappeared. He, too, saw the breastplate. 'What does it mean?'

Huurzem shook his head. But he stripped the armour from the Man and took away the sword. 'I will see that these are never found. We never saw them, you understand?'

'The Imperator – '

'We must say nothing. We do our duty by our Zolutar. This Man is an escaped *moillum*, no more.'

Thagran took a deep breath. 'Very well.' He pointed up ahead. 'I have seen a ridge. A difficult climb, especially with our burden. But it is our way over the mountains.'

Huurzem was already wrapping the armour and sword in a sheet he had taken from his backpack. He nodded. 'I'll strap the Man to my back.'

'I studied the land behind us. I saw no pursuit.'

'A rider!' hissed Thagran, and Huurzem immediately dropped down into the deep grass, flattening himself. He untied his burden, the Man who as yet remained unconscious. As his face neared the ground, Huurzem could hear the drumming of hooves: a xillatraal.

It was almost midday. They had crossed the precarious saddle high in the mountains, clambering down like flies on the wall beyond. But they had come safely out of the zone of sacrifice. Here on the west-facing slopes of the mountains, they were in a different terrain, where low trees clung to the mountainside, and the grass grew rich and deep. The air hummed with birds, and the sound of insects droned loudly, filling the silence they had become so used to in the dreary land beyond the mountains.

'Safe,' said Thagran. 'I recognise him.'

As Huurzem rose slowly to his knees, he saw Thagran go down the slope to converge on the single rider. A road ran to the south, back towards the Bone Watch, which must be several miles away.

On the road, the xillatraal lifted its head and showed its rows of yellow fangs, snarling as it caught the scent of the Csendook in the trees. Vulporzol lifted his sword, making a pass in the air with it as he spurred the beast along the road. If the Zemoks he sought were in the trees, they would know the signal. He was cloaked, his hood thrown over his head in spite of the heat. It had been a long night.

Huurzem concealed himself well, but the xillatraal found Thagran.

Vulporzol pulled the beast up, striking its neck to quieten it. He turned, looking back behind him, but no one was following him. 'You got across in safety?'

'We became spiders, Zolutar,' said Thagran. 'And we brought – '

Vulporzol eyes signalled him to silence. 'Excellent.'

'You are alone, Zolutar?' said Thagran, watching the road.

'We got back to the Bone Watch at dawn. I kept the hunt going as long as I could, but when it was evident we would find nothing, not even a scent, the hunt gave up. Some of them muttered about my being in need of a rest and talked of my imagination falling prey to sorcery. I took the jibes. They suited my purpose well enough. When we got back to the tower, I was relieved. Awaiting a summons, no doubt, but I slipped away.'

'Where will you go now, Zolutar?'

'Quickly to Uldenzar and the warhall. Go with Huurzem, back to the Bone Watch. Report to Dagrazem.'

'Have we been missed, Zolutar?'

Vulporzol grinned. 'You will not be the only Zemoks to arrive late. But be careful. They must not know that you found a way out of the zone. Enter the tower cautiously, through one of the camps, I suggest. A few are still scouring the hills, anxious to impress the Supreme Sanguinary.'

'And . . . our burden?'

'Mine from now on.'

Thagran led him through the low trees to where Huurzem waited. He bowed as the Zolutar rode up.

Vulporzol glanced only briefly at the unconscious Man. 'Secure him behind me.'

Huurzem did so at once. 'I've stripped him, Zolutar. His things are in the mountains. Even an eagle would never find them.'

'Excellent. Go with Thagran. I will return to the tower tonight. Be watchful.'

Moments later the two Zemoks watched as the Zolutar spurred the xillatraal northwards, skirting the road, his burden strapped tightly behind him like an escaped slave that was being returned to its pens. 'Strange days, these,' muttered Thagran.

Huurzem clapped him on the shoulder. 'Let's get back. Have you thought of a good story to tell when we're grilled? Kurduzar himself will want full reports from everyone who was out there last night.'

For once Thagran's severe face broke out in a grin. 'No one would believe us if we told them we'd been over the mountains.'

'No, but we'll give them something far duller, eh?'

Thagran shrugged, his grin slowly dissolving as he thought of the tower and of the Csendook who waited there.

7

THE *MOILLUM*

Pyramors opened his eyes, but closed them again. There was not much light but his eyes ached, as though they had been dazzled. He was stretched out on something hard, his whole body aching. Somewhere in the distance he could hear birdsong, and then a voice shouting, others. It sounded like a fight, the curses of effort, the clash of staffs, or something wooden. Slowly he opened his eyes again. It took a while for him to get accustomed to the poor light but when he did, he found himself in a small room. It smelled of earth and dried leaves.

He was naked except for a loin cloth. Gone was his armour, his weapons. His arms were bare. The bracelet was gone! Angered by its loss more than the loss of anything else, he sat up. It made his head swim but he steadied himself. He was on a stone bench, a single pelt stretched over it. The light entered the room from a small window eight feet from the floor. He could see thick wooden bars set into it. So this was a cell.

Eannor? Had he come through as the Accrual had promised? He closed his mind to thoughts of the strange being as if it had been the inhabitant of a nightmare, with its gross hunger, its sibilant promises.

Who had found him? His own kind? But they would not have imprisoned him. He looked around the room, getting to his feet unsteadily and walking about. It was empty except for the bench. The floor was earthen. More shouts came from outside and he recognised what it must be. Men, undoubtedly, and fighting. But it was not a battle. They were training! This must be an outpost, a pocket of resistance, even though by now the Csendook would have taken Eannor.

After a time, when he felt a little stronger, he leapt up

for the sill of the window, clung on, and hauled himself up, gripping the bars for support. His view of the outside was restricted but it told him what he had suspected.

He could see a score of warriors, men dressed as he was, in almost nothing, engaged in combat with one another, using long staves. There were two or three sergeants strutting about in the training circle, calling out instructions, or bawling crudely when someone made a poor move. But these men were physically strong, evidently well trained and used to rigorous exercise. They were fast, skilful, and from the type of tactics they used on one another they looked experienced. Front liners? Pyramors wondered.

Beyond them in the morning light he could see a line of wooden huts, unmistakably barracks, and beyond them a green wall of forest that rose up in a steep sided valley. He craned his neck in an attempt to widen his view of this place, but could see little more. His arms grew tired and he dropped to the ground, stumbling, but he sat on the bed to steady himself. After a moment he went to the door and tried to open it, but it was locked. Why should he be a prisoner? They should have recognised the insignia on his breastplate. But perhaps the bracelet, with its Csendook wording, had made them suspicious. Maybe they thought he was a spy for their enemies. He should have been more discreet with the bracelet but it was too late to worry about that.

He thought of calling to the men through the window but discarded the idea. He would wait. Sooner or later they would come for him.

It was over an hour before he heard movement outside his door, by which time he had exercised lightly enough to rid himself of the last of the stiffness in his joints. His head no longer rang. The Accrual seemed even more like a dream, a product of the mind.

The door swung inward and two men stood beyond, one holding a short staff, a rounded knot at its end, and the other a crude tray on which there was a clay pitcher and food. The man with the food entered and the other closed the door, waiting outside as if on guard. Pyramors was sitting on the bed. He had the advantage of his visitor for a moment, as the latter had to squint in the darkness.

'Awake then,' he grunted, putting the tray down on the floor. Pyramors nodded but said nothing. He did not move.

'Better eat this. And drink. You'll have to earn your next meal.'

'Whose unit is this?'

The man flinched at the sharpness of the question. 'Unit?'

'Who commands here?'

'We answer to Dacramal. But this warhall is under Uldenzar.'

'Warhall? I don't understand you.' He slipped easily off the bed and reached for the food, watching the man in case he did something unexpected. It seemed unlikely that he would be hostile, but he was clearly uneasy.

'Don't you know where you are?' he grunted, backing to the door.

'I presume this is Eannor.'

'You're with the *moillum*.'

Pyramors did not know the word, and that much showed in his face. 'Gladiators. This is a warhall, a school. The best. So they tell us. When you've eaten, you'll be shown. Dacramal will want to see what you can do.'

'You said this place was run by a Zaru? A Csendook?' Pyramors went on, picking up the tray and starting to eat the meat. It was excellent and evidently there was plenty available. He sipped at the water, which was cool and fresh.

'Of course. All warhalls are.'

Pyramors stopped chewing. 'Men train under Csendook? For what reason?'

'Why else do gladiators train? To fight.'

'Fight who?'

'Other gladiators.'

'Men fight men?' He found it impossible to conceal his growing horror. He put down the tray and stood up.

The man backed off. 'Where've you been, soldier?'

'What of the war?'

'Over. The Csendook took the last of our worlds months

87

ago. They rule now. And if you want to live, soldier, then look to your battle skills. You'll need them in this warhall. The weak ones are soon weeded out.' The man moved surprisingly fast, opening the door and backing out before Pyramors could call him back. Again the door was locked.

He sat on the bench, staggered. Men were slaves to the Csendook? Fighting slaves? He considered the appalling prospect as he finished the remainder of his meal. But he began to glimpse what must be behind this. Survival. Either the men who had put up the final resistance capitulated or they would be executed. They would have been fighting men, soldiers used to combat. It would not have been easy for them to give up their lives, even in a suicidal last stand. But slavery!

Again Pyramors touched his arm where the bracelet should have been. If men had been spared and were used, then the women, too, might be alive. But who had taken the bracelet? Presumably the commander of this camp.

Pyramors was forced to bide his time in the cell. It was late in the afternoon when the door was opened again. This time a group of four warriors stood outside. One of them called him out. Pyramors stood in the doorway, blinking in the sunlight. The training had either stopped or moved to another part of the grounds. Beyond was a wide circle, dusty and bare where many feet had scuffed it up over the months, and around it more of the wooden huts, crude dwellings such as would be used by fighting men in the field. Pyramors had been used to such conditions during much of the action he had seen before the Crossing to Innasmorn.

The four warriors who had fetched him studied him with interest, their eyes appraising him, his build, his stance, assessing his potential as a warrior, he could see that. They would be men who judged others by their own standards, and they traded in one coin only, fighting merit. They would have spent most of their lives in the front line. They knew about survival, about killing, about being faster than the man next to them. They would scorn any weakness. Pyramors knew all this: he had trained such men and had relied on them during numerous battles. These, he knew without reservation, would be utterly reliable.

They exchanged glances, briefly, but even in this fleeting moment, Pyramors could read their respect. They had seen the warrior in him. It was something bred deep, a way of being that could never be eradicated. Pyramors wondered if Man could truly be Man without it, even though history showed how he fought to end war.

'You're- to come with us,' said one of the warriors. He carried one of the light staffs with the knobbed end. None of the men wore swords and Pyramors saw no evidence of steel anywhere in the camp. The warriors all wore the minimum of clothing, although Eannor was warm enough. He glanced about, wondering if he would catch a glimpse of the Csendook, but he did not. The camp could have been a forward unit behind enemy lines.

Pyramors was escorted across the training circle. No one spoke. The warriors moved easily, their eyes on the forest, which Pyramors could now see completely enclosed the warhall, offering it protection from the outside world. But how far was it from the zone of sacrifice? Where, precisely, had he emerged? It should have been somewhere very close to the place where Zellorian had performed the rituals. If so, Rannor Tarul could not be far away.

As he walked with these silent men, Pyramors thought again of the things the Accrual had told him. Of how Zellorian had betrayed Mankind, had used countless thousands to make the Path to freedom. Did these survivors *know*? Did they understand that the Imperator's freedom had been bought with an ocean of blood? He himself had been a party to that sacrifice, that betrayal. Unwitting, yes, but his own life had been bought with blood. The thought made him cold. If these warriors learned who he was, they would tear him limb from limb. And who could blame them for that?

They came to a larger hut which had been raised slightly on thick trunks, steps leading up to an open door. Pyramors was led up the steps and the leading warrior motioned for him to go inside. It was cool within, and there was a minimum of furniture – a crude table, some seats. It was typical of a war zone command post. Behind him the four warriors lined up, arms folded, silent as statues. Pyramors was impressed with the discipline. He always expected high standards from his own troops in the field. So far he had seen many signs in this warhall to suggest that these were men who would have served him well. The despondency that he was prone to, the ailing spirit, was not reflected in these men.

A hanging at the back of the room swung aside and another man entered. He was stocky, neck as thick as an ape's, his shoulders disproportionately wide, though not so wide as those of a Csendook. His beard was thick and black, his chest matted with the same coarse hair down to his belly. His arms were scarred, the veins like wires. and everything about the man spoke of force, of physical strength. He looked directly at Pyramors, eyes sunken in a huge face, chips of cold stone.

The man moved easily in spite of his size, standing before Pyramors without arrogance but in a manner intended to intimidate. His eyes held those of his prisoner for a long time but Pyramors did not flinch, his own face a mask. There were laws at work here and he understood them well enough.

'You have a name?' growled the man, his voice rumbling up from his chest like the growl of a hound.

'Pyras, sire.'

The man reached out with his hand, the fingers spreading wide, and put them lightly on Pyramors's chest. 'You don't call anyone sire. Not here. We're *moillum*. I'm Dacramal, and I run this warhall. You can think 'sire' when you address me, but you don't say it.'

Pyramors nodded.

Dacramal grunted, walking slowly around his prisoner, studying every muscle, every scar. He found it interesting that the man had a relatively pale skin, unlike the warriors here, who had become bronzed and weatherbeaten, skins like parchment. Yet this warrior had clearly been a fighting man. It would take very little to unlock those skills. He came before him again and looked into his face. 'You've seen battle, I think. Front line?'

'Front line.'

'Under?'

Pyramors had already considered what he would say. 'Karr Philostron.' It was the name of the head of a house that had been almost entirely destroyed on a neighbouring world shortly before the withdrawal to Innasmorn.

Dacramal grunted. It was impossible to tell whether he was impressed. The Philostrons had been reputable warriors.

'We've none of them here,' said Dacramal after a moment's thought. 'But you're under me now. Clear?' Pyramors nodded.

'They didn't tell me where you came from. Lost on Eannor like a good many others, no doubt?'

Pyramors frowned. 'I think so,' he said hesitantly.

Dacramal had not read the lie, though it did not seem to matter to him. 'Since the last of the fighting with the Csendook a number of your kind have been found in the outer regions. Even a few units putting up resistance. But the Csendook pull most of them in.'

'I seem to recall a fight. Csendook – '

The big man moved away. 'Forget it. You've had a rough time. But it'll get rougher.' He laughed softly, his back to Pyramors. 'Can you still fight?'

'I would hope so – '

Dacramal whirled, his fist suddenly shooting out with blurring speed. The punch would have landed in Pyramors's midriff, but Pyramors reacted instinctively, his right hand chopping down, deflecting the blow harmlessly along his side. He stepped aside, riding the blow, ready to follow up with another chop, but Dacramal had pulled back with deceptive speed for such a big man. He was grinning.

'Well, well. Very good, Pyras. If you took a bang on the head that slowed you, your recovery is quick. You'll be put to good use here. What weapons do you favour?'

'I am a swordsman first – '

Dacramal shook his head. 'Not in this warhall. Here we use only the short-staff. Swords are not permitted. But if we graduate to higher things, perhaps.' He glanced over to the four warriors, none of whom had flinched. 'You can go, Troidan. I'll summon you.'

The leader of the warriors bowed and the others left with him. Dacramal went to the table, turning and sitting on its edge. He folded his huge arms and again studied Pyramors. 'Most of the men here are a mystery, Pyras. We like it that way. No one will probe your past. If you've secrets, keep them. This will be a new life. That's the first thing you've got to understand. In this warhall, Troidan is my right hand. When he says jump, you do it. You don't argue. You know about military discipline, I can see that.'

Pyramors nodded.

'Fine. No titles. What we were doesn't matter. But we have a system. The warriors, Troidan, and me. Simple enough.'

'And you?'

'You want to ask questions, then get them off your chest now. After that it's time to get to work. This place is all work. It never stops, even when you're asleep. It's hard here, hard as any front line ever was. Men die. You won't, I think. You're too tough. I can see it in you, Pyras. You adapt, survive.'

'I hope so.'

'I'm sure. You want to know who I answer to? The Zarull who runs this warhall is called Uldenzar. Like all Csendook, he's a huge, ugly bastard and he could squeeze the shit out of the best of us with one hand. You won't see him. I rarely do. I just give him what he wants and it keeps us all alive.'

'And what does he want?'

'Gladiators. *Moillum*. He wants the best. Just as his rivals do.'

Pyramors frowned. 'His rivals?'

Dacramal nodded. 'I know. Why aren't we out there, using our skills to harass them, perpetuate the war?' He shook his head. 'No use. We're beaten, Pyras. Get used to that. Man as he was perished along with the Imperator. Right here on Eannor. Any dream of victory, of turning the tide, smashing the Swarms, is dead. So we bend. And *that's* how we *survive*.

'We bend. We train and we work hard. They keep us alive if we give them what they want.'

'Men kill each other for sport? For the Csendook?' breathed Pyramors, the full impact of it suddenly striking him.

Dacramal shrugged. 'That's the fact of it. You don't like it. None of us did. Some of us will never like it. But we do it. We bend. You want to eat, to be as free as is possible. Then you'd better become one of us. Excel and you may even enjoy the sort of life you never had as a warrior under the Imperator.'

Pyramors stood by the door and looked out at the circle. A few *moillum* were exercising, not engaged in combat, merely going through easy moves, exercises of balance, of suppleness. 'Men have given up their freedom?'

'They have.' Dacramal stood close behind him. 'There is no other choice.'

'The Imperator – '

'No one believes he survived. There was talk of Zellorian, the Prime Consul, busying himself with his science, the lost arts. But it was for morale. The Swarms closed in on Rannor Tarul. There was word of a place where they made a final stand, where today the bones and skulls are piled in hillocks. The Csendook are ruthless. But serve them well and you'll find life is far from over.'

Pyramors shook his head in amazement. 'Serve them. It seems incredible.'

Dacramal laughed. 'You don't have to love them. Who does? But you'd better put aside your hate. You're a warrior. Emotion undoes a fighting man. Hate feeds you, but too much of it gives strength to your enemy.' Pyramors nodded. He would have to convince Dacramal that he would be a model gladiator. But he could not stay here. He had to get away. But what hope did he have of finding Jannovar? What hope, though, had there been at the outset?

'Let me ask something,' he said, turning to the big man.

Dacramal again shrugged. 'Ask what you like. You may not get other opportunities.'

'What happened to the women?'

Dacramal's mouth split in a wide grin. 'They all ask that! Where are the women slaves? Are you hungry for a woman so soon?'

Pyramors hook his head. 'Since we are slaves, I wondered what the Csendook had done with our women. Surely they have not killed them.'

'No. If you have heard stories of how the Csendook are murderous killers bent on the utter destruction of mankind, they are mostly propaganda, left over from the war. True, some of the Garazenda would have wiped us out entirely. But others are less ruthless and are no less merciful than we might be. No, many of the women have survived and are treated well enough. You had a wife, children? No, don't answer me. But you'd do well to put them from your mind, Pyras. You can never see any family you had, not again. In answer to your question, yes, there are women. Like us, they are slaves. Sometimes they are brought here to the warhall. Men who train hard and please Uldenzar are permitted time with the women. Others of us are sometimes permitted to leave the camp and go to others that are part of the warhall and spend time with the women there. But it is controlled. Everything is controlled. All our moves are watched. Everything we do is scrutinised. Remember that. You no longer have privacy.'

'Then we are prisoners.'

'In a way. But we are permitted aspirations.'

'Oh?'

'The best of the moillum go on from here. Those who represent Uldenzar in the games, the Testaments – '

'Games?' repeated Pyramors, his distaste clear.

Dacramal scowled at his displeasure. 'Testaments, they call them. On the Warhive. The best of us end up there.'

'Dying before the Garazenda?'

'Those who triumph are promised better than that.'

'Freedom?'

'Of a sort. I have never been beyond Eannor. Nor do I expect to. If I have any value, it is as a trainer of *moillum*. Only the very best get to the Testaments. I know my capabilities.'

'What is the highest prize at these – games?'

Dacramal looked away into the forests, as if seeing in the trees his own fleeting freedom, always a short distance beyond him. 'I hear rumours, no more. Rumours that men serve in select companies under the Zemoks.'

'In what way serve?'

'As warriors.'

Pyramors scowled. 'But the war is over – '

'There is resistance on some of the worlds yet. Where belief in an Imperator, a saviour, persists. Idle dreams – '

'You are saying that men fight *with* Csendook? Against free men?'

Dacramal grunted, annoyed with himself. He turned away. 'Rumours! You'll hear plenty of them. Ignore them. Unless you find strength in any of them. Strength to help you survive for the games. That had better be your target, Pyras. That, or go mad.'

'The Warhive?'

Dacramal faced him again, his face devoid of emotion, as though he had shown something of himself that would now be locked away from Pyras, a secret not to be shared again. 'You may have to kill other men. Men who become your friends. It may be a choice of their life or yours. Even here, in this warhall. Already those men out there will have marked you, weighed you. Guard yourself, your back. The place is full of potential enemies. All of them your brothers.'

Pyramors nodded slowly.

'There's nothing more I can tell you,' said Dacramal. 'Go back to the hut in which you woke. It will no longer be locked. You're not my prisoner. Your training begins soon.'

Pyramors walked down the steps, aware that he was being observed by a number of warriors, but none of them spoke to him. They went about their business quietly and efficiently. He went back to the open hut, sitting on the bench, thinking over the things he had been told.

Man as slave, his mind repeated, over and over. Belief in the Imperator Elect restricted to a few small outposts. And man hunting man, used by the Csendook.

He stretched out on the bed, feeling tired. How was he to pursue his quest? Where would she be? On the Warhive? Or here on Eannor? The only way to begin his search would be to talk to other women. He would have to win the right to access. Perform like an animal for his new masters.

95

Another thought worried at him. Who had found him? What had they done with his armour? Why had Dacramal so obviously not been told that this was one of the Imperator's men? So that he would not spread the word of the possible survival of the Imperator? That must be it. Then could it have been Csendook who found him, in the zone of sacrifice? They would not tell their enemies but they would tell their superiors. He had no recollection of what had happened to him after his conversation with the Accrual, if that had indeed been a real event.

A shadow crossed the doorway. It was Troidan.

'You're very fast,' he said, his voice no less harsh than it had been when he had first collected Pyramors.

Pyramors sat up. 'I'm out of practice.'

'We'll change that. Beginning now.'

8

BATTLE CIRCLE

The two warriors stalked each other slowly, circling, slightly bent forward, perfectly balanced, searching for an opportunity to get beyond each others' defences. They were naked save for their loin cloths and carried only the short lengths of wood with the rounded ends. Both these men had already landed blows, raising blotches on their opponent's skin, bruises that they would carry for days. Around them, at the edge of the circle of earth, the other *moillum* watched in silence. Encouragement was neither asked for nor given.

Dacramal also watched, though he stood on a narrow dais, hands on his hips, face screwed up in a scowl as though he did not approve of what he saw: it was how he always watched his fighting men. In his belt were thrust two thick wooden clubs, and he was known to use them freely when the men displeased him. He was no bully, however, and his own skill in the ring was well respected.

One of the gladiators sprang forward and to the side, offering himself as a target, but the other feinted an attack. The first warrior followed up but his opponent was not where he expected him to be. Instead his club came down hard on his shoulder, numbing his arm. He tried to lift it to counter-attack but the next blow caught him in the stomach and doubled him. A steely hand gripped the back of his neck. Above him the club was raised in a blow that would have split his skull.

Dacramal raised his hand. 'Enough.' He got off the dais and walked to the two warriors. They remained as they were, one as a captive, the other as executioner. Dacramal nodded and the latter released his man, who coughed violently, trying to regain his composure. He massaged his bruised shoulder, though without bad grace. 'Too ambitious,' Dacramal told him. 'And still too impatient. Your opponents

97

read such eagerness. They will use it against you, as Hoyrens has.'

The defeated warrior stood up stiffly, face pale. But he bowed to his opponent. Hoyrens bowed in return, his face blank, no flush of victory there. Both men bowed to Dacramal and returned to the ranks of men around the circle. Dacramal again put his hands on his hips and walked around, looking at the men. They had trained hard for some weeks, and only now was he beginning to bring them into the ring for battle testing. Many of them had been warriors and knew as much as they could learn about combat, but here they had an opportunity to tighten up and to pass on their own particular skills to others. It was early yet, Dacramal thought, but he had the core of a fine warhall.

His finger stabbed out, pointing at a burly figure in the front ranks, one who was keen to get into the circle and show off his prowess. His name was Brabazuk, and although he was relatively young, he was known to be a veteran of several campaigns. He walked out into the circle with a hint of arrogance, his pride undisguised. His chest curved like a shield, his skin browned by the sun, his muscles hard as stone. Across his back he bore a long scar, the mark of a Csendook blade that had almost taken his life, and in his resilience his fellow warriors recognised survival, their own strength of purpose.

Dacramal walked around again. Some of the warriors would not be keen to take on Brabazuk, knowing he would best them, but others were ready, defeat or not. Some would not meet Dacramal's gaze and he made a point of noting them: they must learn not to show fear. But he would not put them in the ring today, not with Brabazuk. He had already made his mind up who he would match with the steel warrior.

He pointed to the new man, Pyras, who had shown agility and strength in training, and whose fitness was beyond question. How much was he holding in reserve? 'Pyras, step into the circle.'

Pyramors bowed and did as bidden. He had wasted little time since coming here in bringing himself back into the peak of condition, his muscles aching for the first few days as he accustomed himself to the fierce sessions, a way of life that he had not forgotten but had been away from in the sanctuary of a Consul's office. No one here knew who he was, and he kept himself apart as much as he could. The word in the warhall was that he had been found wandering Eannor, dazed after a battle, brought here as others had been, last survivors of the final thrust of the Csendook, the end of the wars.

He faced Brabazuk, who bowed, and bowed back. Dacramal went to his dais.

'You both understand the rules,' called the latter. 'You're not here to kill each other or break each others' bones. Save all that for a better arena than this. You understand, Brabazuk?'

'Yes, Dacramal,' replied the swarthy warrior, without a smile, though his manner implied that he could do these things easily enough.

'Anyone who disobeys this rule,' Dacramal went on, 'will be punished. Must I elaborate?'

Brabazuk shook his head.

'Pyras?'

'I understand,' said Pyramors. Without discipline of self, no warrior would survive for very long.

'Then let's see what you can do,' nodded Dacramal.

Both warriors tensed, but neither dropped into the more obvious bent position of the former two warriors. Pyramors did not move. He watched his opponent's eyes, which were studying him, his weight, the length of his arm, waiting to see him move so that he could judge his balance, the detail of his movements. But Pyramors remained still.

Someone shouted something from the ranks but a furious look from Dacramal silenced them.

Brabazuk began to circle Pyramors, walking slowly, still studying him. He tapped the knob of his club in his free palm; the slapping sound carried on the otherwise silent air.

Pyramors turned, allowing his opponent to walk round him, turning to face him, making no special effort to swivel with grace, or ease. Nothing in his movements said anything. The way that he held his own club, at his side, almost limply, told his opponent nothing about him, how he would use it.

Brabazuk stopped walking. His face did not show it but he was puzzled by the man Pyras. He was either totally ignorant of how to prepare for such a contest, or he was very dangerous. There was no fear in him: Brabazuk could usually smell fear, could almost touch it. Pyras was like ice, unemotional, as though either bored or unaware that he was going to be tested hard.

Dacramal was also puzzled. He had expected Pyras to be good. He showed no fear, and that was no ignorance, that was experience. But this apparent indifference would fall apart when Brabazuk went for him. Dacramal had had Pyras watched carefully for the last few weeks, noting his fitness, his speed, his strength. Speed and strength, the two deadliest weapons that the Csendook possessed, that had undone men. And Pyras was very strong. That was something he had been born with, but where had he forged it into the art that it was? Who was he?

Brabazuk decided that it was time to move in, and he did so. He made two preliminary sweeps with his club, the air humming. Pyras merely moved aside, the club inches away from him. He lifted his own a little, whether in defence or in preparation for an attack, no one could tell. Brabazuk watched closely, trying to learn. But so far he had gleaned nothing. Everything his opponent did was vague, as if the man knew nothing about combat.

He tried a more ambitious pass, darting in, swerving, again sweeping his club sideways. Pyras turned away from it, agile, effortless. Still he kept his own weapon in a neutral grip. Brabazuk forced him to give ground, stepping up the assault, the air alive with the sound of the club. It blurred, high above the two men, then swept to shin level. Pyras was forced to use his own weapon to block, but did so effectively. As he did so, he twisted aside, moving back towards the centre of the ring.

Brabazuk knew now that the man had fought before, and at a high level. His speed was very deceptive. Somehow he knew that Pyras had not exerted it yet. And always he brought the fight back to the very centre of the circle! Whatever attack Brabazuk engineered, Pyras not only turned it aside, but with his footwork returned to the centre of the circle.

Brabazuk determined to break this pattern. Perhaps by doing so, he reasoned, he could break the confidence of his opponent. He set up a fresh series of attacks, designed to put Pyras on the defensive and to drive him towards the ring of warriors. This was immediately successful, for Pyras had to duck and weave to avoid being struck. Slowly he was driven back towards the *moillum*. Twice he tried to sidestep and swing round so that he could work his way back towards the centre of the circle, but Brabazuk was ready for that. He blocked him, himself very fast on his feet. Again he pushed his attack, and now Pyramors was no more than a few yards from the line of watchers. Brabazuk prepared to complete his success, his arm raised for an instant, but abruptly Pyramors was at him, using not his club but his left arm, the fist rising up in a blow that wwould have exploded in Brabazuk's stomach. Instantly the latter altered the angle of his own strike, the club coming down to meet the fist, but as it did so, Pyramors used his own weapon to meet it.

His timing was perfection. As the two clubs met, that of Brabazuk split in half, rendered useless.

Pyramors landed his punch, though not on its target. It did not matter. He moved back. Brabazuk glanced once at his ruined club, released it and rushed in, hoping to grip his opponent and fling him to the ground. But he was having to improvise very quickly, whereas Pyramors had already planned his moves. His right foot shot out and took Brabazuk on the instep. He tumbled, arms clutching at air. As he fell, Pyramors used a quick chop of his club to strike at his right wrist.

By the time Brabazuk hit the ground, Pyramors was out of reach. The men behind him gasped, staggered by the speed of the manoeuvre they had seen. Brabazuk's hand felt numb, nerveless. He got to his feet, face dark with suppressed fury.

Pyramors went to him and put his right arm on his left shoulder in a familiar gladiatorial salute. 'You're not without skill,' he told him, locking eyes with him.

For a moment Brabazuk looked as though he might renew his attack, wounded though he was, but instead he grinned, recognising the skill of a master. He lifted his damaged hand and put it on Pyramors's shoulder. 'You'll have to teach me that move.'

Dacramal was beside them, though he looked annoyed. 'If that wrist is broken, Pyras, I'll have you emptying latrines for a week – '

But Pyramors smiled at him. 'It'll be numb for an hour or two. But it'll heal soon enough. You said no breaks.'

Dacramal dismissed Brabazuk, who went back to the ranks, but there was no dishonour in this defeat, and none that he showed. The men knew his skill, but Pyras was exceptional.

Dacramal leaned close to Pyramors. 'Where did you learn such tactics? Who did you serve under?'

Pyramors straightened. 'You told me the first rule of this place was that no one had a past. We keep our secrets. My past doesn't matter to you.'

'Don't mock me, Pyras. You'll do all that you're told to do here, and if I tell you to – '

To his amazement Pyramors stepped aside and turned to the *moillum*. 'You think yourself the master of these men?'

Troidan and two others were at the edge of the circle, both wearing harnesses and carrying twin clubs. They watched Dacramal, waiting for a nod from him. Pyramors saw them, knowing what might be coming.

Dacramal smiled, but cold fury gleamed in his eyes. 'Think carefully, Pyras. Don't cross me. You may be a fine warrior, but discipline runs this camp, under me – '

'For whom?' said Pyramors, turning a cold glare upon him.

Something in that look made Dacramal flinch, but he took in a deep breath. 'For – '

'A Zarull! A Csendook! You fight each other, for their pleasure.'

Troidan and the other two were coming across the circle. The *moillum* sensed trouble but they would not get involved. The outcome of these matters was always the same: someone rebelled against the system but there was nothing to replace it with. The newer warriors took time to learn, and in some ways it was the hardest lesson of all.

'You should be arming yourselves against the Csendook,' said Pyramors. 'You have enough men here to – '

'Be silent!' snapped Dacramal. 'I thought you had more sense. Do you want to be beaten in front of the entire camp?'

Troidan stood ready, an eager smile on his face. Pyramors backed away from Dacramal. 'How many other warhalls are there on Eannor? How many thousand men now serve the Csendook? As slaves? Have you given up your freedom so easily?'

Dacramal nodded to Troidan, who waved his two guards forward. The three of them prepared to subdue Pyramors.

This time he did not play the waiting game, using their mistakes to snare them. He moved with dazzling speed and efficiency, knocking Troidan senseless with his first thrust, and turning back on the other two with equal rapidity. They were good, he knew that, probably chosen as the best of Dacramal's warriors, but even so they could not match the extraordinary ability of their opponent. They, too, were sent reeling, heads bleeding.

Dacramal swore and lifted his own twin clubs.

'If I have to, I'll open your skull,' Pyramors told him softly.

'Stop this lunacy,' Dacramal hissed as they circled. 'Will you take on the entire warhall?'

'We should be fighting Csendook, not each other,' said Pyramors. Then, as abruptly as his assault had started, he ended it. He flung his weapon down in the earth, shaking his head like a man stepping from a dream.

Dacramal approached him carefully, putting his hand on his shoulder. 'All men resent what has happened. But we are survivors. Perhaps we will have an opportunity to change things one day,' he said very softly. 'But not today. Today we are *moillum*. We train and we fight, for them.'

Pyramors grunted assent, looking around him as if seeing the arena for the first time. His demonstration had been useless, a waste. Dacramal was right. Man had nothing here but his despair, a new way. His chances of finding Jannovar, of fleeing with her back to Innasmorn, were as remote as they had ever been. These men were as doomed to their fate as were those in the Sculpted City. It was better to die here, among these warriors. But not against each other. There was no shred of glory in that.

Uldenzar sat beside a small fountain in the gardens. These were full of bright blooms, plants that had been nurtured by Man when this city had been built on Eannor, many years previously. For all their bellicose traits, the Csendook loved things of beauty, and here in Rannor Tarul they had inherited many fine things, not least of all the exceptional gardens. Since the defeat of the Imperator Elect and the setting up of the warhalls, the city had been taken over by the Csendook, and Men were no longer permitted to come here unless expressly ordered to do so by their masters. There were a few small arenas in some of the larger Csendook households, where personal *moillum* exercised and entertained, but otherwise Rannor Tarul had become a centre of Csendook culture.

A Zemoi entered, bowing. 'Zarull, the Man, Dacramal, has been brought.'

Uldenzar yawned, stretching his huge arms. He had put aside his war gear and donned simpler robes. He nodded. 'Have him brought in.'

Dacramal entered the garden with a feeling of regret. He had known this part of the city once; it had been a stronghold, both of the Imperator's forces and of Man's culture, a city filled with fine treasures, a centre of wealth and splendour. The Csendook had not debased it, for they were lovers of the arts. But such places were no longer for Man, unless, through good service, they earned a small place here. Dacramal knew he would never be chosen to go to the Warhive, but someone like Uldenzar might take him into his private estate in time.

The Csendook did not rise, but he dismissed his Zemoi with a wave so that he could be alone with Dacramal.

'I am told there are problems at the warhall,' said Uldenzar. He had no fear of being attacked by a Man like Dacramal. He knew him well enough. The Man was resigned to his station, and indeed, had filled it well. He produced excellent *moillum*. At the next Testament, those who had once been under Dacramal would do well.

Dacramal eyed the huge warrior, so typical of his race. The face of the Csendook was in essence human, though bigger boned, the jaw more square. The eyes were not a man's eyes though, the brows chiselled, the forehead sweeping back, hair cut close, more like wire. There was more than a hint of the beast in the Csendook, the hunting animal.

Dacramal cleared his throat. 'Zarull, you have told me before that if a certain type of warrior should emerge, a rebel with particular feelings about slavery – '

'Few of your race would prefer it to the freedom they once enjoyed. But they adapt well, Dacramal. An attitude that will ensure the survival of your species.'

Dacramal nodded. He had spoken many times to the veteran and knew the futility of resistance. He knew the Zarull was not a cruel warrior and not one who enjoyed inflicting suffering on his enemies without good cause. He was loyal to the members of the Garazenda who had promoted an end to the wars, and was a Csendook who could be reasoned with. Others were less patient, harbouring only hatred for Men.

'I have a new warrior at my warhall. He has been with me for only a few weeks.'

Uldenzar turned his gaze from the fountain to his guest. His interest was clear. 'His name?'

'Pyras. Two things distinguish him from other warriors. Firstly, his skill. He has the qualities of a commander. I have not seen his equal since the last days of the wars. It has not been fully tested, but I do not have the men to do it. Besides, Pyras does not enjoy fighting his own kind. That is

105

the second point, Zarull. His hatred of the Csendook. There is a total lack of compromise. He would rather be put in an arena – '

'With Csendook?' Uldenzar smiled. 'Many Men have rashly made that boast.'

Dacramal looked away. 'You may wish to remove him from my warhall, Zarull. Perhaps he would be better on Skellunda. It may be that his spirit effects my *moillum*, raises false hopes among them.'

'You doubt your own ability to control them?'

'Zarull, they progress excellently. But this Pyras is a threat. And he is of that breed that you mentioned to me once before.'

Uldenzar rose and looked down at the gladiator. 'Very well. I'll have him tested. In front of your *moillum*. I have no wish to break their spirits. It is what makes warriors of them. But their hopes for a rebellion I must crush. You understand these things, Dacramal. You are a warrior.'

'As you say, Zarull.'

Uldenzar nodded. He waved one of his Zemoi to him and Dacramal was escorted away. Once he was gone, Uldenzar went into the house, to his room of books and paintings where he sat at a huge, carved desk. He opened a drawer and took out the single object that had been in it; he placed it thoughtfully on the table.

It was a bracelet, carved with Csendook letters. They spelled a name. Jannovar. For a while he contemplated it, the riddle that went with it, then he placed it back in the drawer.

Pyramors had been confined in his hut, the prison hut, for three days. He had been allowed out to train, to keep himself as fit as he could, but always under guard, and always away from the battle circle and the other *moillum*. Dacramal had hinted that he would have an opportunity to show the *moillum* just how viable rebellion was, but no one else had been permitted to speak to him. He himself was past caring.

He went through the routine of exercise, pushing himself as hard as he could, but he endured it all like a man in prison, a man with a life sentence. He understood the dilemma of his people, and their position, but he himself could never come to terms with it. He wondered about telling them the true fate of the Imperator. Would knowing that they had bought his freedom with their own turn them? But against what? The Csendook, who now controlled the empire effortlessly?

On the fourth day, he was taken up into the forest, away from the camp. He knew that its limits were fenced off and were patrolled, probably by Csendook. None of the *moillum* had ever attempted to escape. He wondered if an opportunity would present itself to him. But Dacramal had come, with several of his strongest guards. No one said anything, they just marched Pyramors up through the trees. He wondered if this was to be an execution.

There was a hollow among the trees, a flattened area of grass that looked familiar. Yet another battle circle, he mused. Around it had gathered a score of the *moillum*, Dacramal's finest warriors. Brabazuk was among them. In the centre of the battle circle was a light suit of armour. Dacramal pointed to it.

'Put that on, Pyras. Today you put your strength to the test, the way you desire it. You have rejected what this warhall offers you.'

Pyramors went to the armour. It was of good quality and with it there was a sword, which was also of the finest craftmanship. He weighed it, testing its balance. Around him the warriors watched, intrigued, knowing that he would be expert in the use of this blade.

A movement on the ridge beyond the trees caught his eye and he looked up casually, seeing other shapes there. For a moment his composure was briefly shaken: he knew the silhouette of a Csendook well enough. There were several above. The masters of this warhall? Slowly they came down into the trees. The central figure was typically huge, his armour dark, a sword belted at his waist. He stood with his arms folded and looked down on the gathering, his power and confidence in it absolute.

The *moillum* had fallen silent, including Dacramal. They all watched. On either side of the Csendook, a Zarull by his insignia, three Zemoi in full battle gear stood to attention, hands clasping long steel pikes, murderous barbed weapons. All were masked, wearing the familiar war helms of their kind.

'I am your Zarull, Uldenzar,' came the voice of the central Csendook. He spoke in the language of Pyramors's people, the words coming easily to him, though his voice was deep and sonorous. It carried the weight of command.

Around Pyramors, the *moillum* bowed. He did not. Was he to give this creature a show?

Dacramal answered his unspoken question, stepping forward. 'This is the Man, Pyras, Zarull.'

Uldenzar's helm turned to Pyramors and for a moment the Zarull was silent. 'The Man with spirit. I like that. I wish to see such spirit in my *moillum*. All of you, learn something from this Man!'

'I am not one of your slaves,' said Pyramors clearly. 'I do not fight my own kind.'

Uldenzar did not move. 'So I am told. Very well. Since you insist on exercising your rebellion, for such it is, let us give it its head. Let the *moillum* know what it is to challenge my rule.' He turned, barking a command in his own tongue. From behind the trees a fifth Csendook emerged.

It was not particularly tall, but perfectly muscled, wearing a thin mesh of armour and carrying a short, flat sword. It had no war helm, its hair like a black down, tight to its skull, its neck as thick as its head, its eyes small, arrogant.

Uldenzar pointed to the armour that Pyramors had been inspecting. 'Don your protection, *moillum*. Here is a chance to show your fellows how you prefer to fight.'

Pyramors hesitated only briefly. He could not avoid this fight; he had brought it upon himself as surely as if he had begged for it. The Csendook would be too powerful, too fast for him, he knew that. In hand to hand combat, Men rarely bettered Csendook. But there was no question of seeking mercy. Should he force the Zemoi into killing him? It would resolve his hopeless position. But it would utterly destroy all hope these Men had: he knew this to be the Zarull's intention.

The armour in place, Pyramors took up the sword and stood in the centre of the grass circle. In a moment the Zemoi stepped into the ring, face leering, teeth gleaming like those of a beast. Some of them killed with their teeth, taking a bestial pleasure in the act. It stood a foot taller than Pyramors, and at the shoulder it was many inches wider. But he knew there was nothing in the least cumbersome about it.

'Begin!' called Uldenzar, seating himself comfortably, chin on hands, watching as though he had no idea how this fight would resolve itself.

Pyramors did not waste time studying the strengths of his opponent. He knew his best chance would lie in keeping away from the sword, which would slice the air in its avid hunt for him, relentless, impossibly fast.

It was pointless to stand ground or close in. He backed, twisting skilfully. At once the Zemoi was looking for a blow that would cripple him, possibly having been ordered to cut this insolent rebel to shreds in front of the *moillum*, to make his death as bloody and humiliating as possible. But Pyramors would not permit that. Again and again he ducked and dodged the onslaught, never following up with a strike. Around him the *moillum* watched hungrily, in their hearts praying for a mistake, something that would bring the Zemoi down, giving the man a chance to thrust home his blade.

Pyramors felt the flat of the blade catch his breastplate, the Zemoi changing a strike so quickly he could not avoid it. But he read the strike and turned into it, preventing the Zemoi from getting another blow home, crowding him and using the flat of his own sword to drive down at the Zemoi's knee. His blow rang out against the armour, but it broke the stride of the Zemoi, and as the warrior adjusted, Pyramors sprang aside and kicked backwards into its other knee. Only its phenomenal speed saved it from disaster. Many Zemoi would have been injured but this one had been carefully picked. Uldenzar wanted no errors. Even so, he called out in praise of Pyramors's move. Pyramors hardly heard: he was again having to wheel away from a fresh onslaught. The Zemoi was angered, but it knew how to control such anger in combat. It persisted doggedly in its assault and Pyramors knew that it would wear him down, exhausting him.

Twice he tried to trick it into thinking he was weak enough to be taken, but at the last moment it read the trick and avoided his own fatal lunges that would have split a man in two.

Then the Zemoi struck, fast and with irresistible strength, driving hard at the Man, who took its full weight, chopping at it, even drawing Csendook blood. But the Zemoi used its blade to smack Pyramors down, kicking out with steel heels. Its sword came down once, twice, crashing aside the blade of its opponent, which tumbled out of reach.

Pyramors felt the fury of the *moillum*, for an instant hanging, ready to be unleashed on the Zemoi, but it subsided almost at once. They had tasted defeat before and it had an all too familiar flavour.

The wide blade was at Pyramors's throat. He could not move. Above him the face of the Zemoi glared, the face of a predator about to enjoy the blood of the hunt. It raised its head, howling in a way that had turned human blood cold on many a battle front. Pyramors merely waited.

But the death blow did not come. Instead the Zemoi kicked at him, brutally, doubling him up, then bent down and dragged him to his feet. Through tears of pain, Pyramors saw that Uldenzar had stepped into the battle circle. None of the *moillum* had moved.

'Hardly a contest,' said the Zarull.

'Spare me your contempt,' muttered Pyramors, blood running from his mouth. 'You have your prize. Take it.'

'Your life?' said Uldenzar, leaning closer. 'I give it back to you.' He dismissed his Zemoi, who sheathed his weapon, bowed, and trotted easily back up to the other Zemoi guards.

Uldenzar waved Dacramal to him. 'This Man is wounded. Have him attended to.'

Dacramal nodded to two of his *moillum*. They assisted Pyramors, who could do nothing to prevent them taking him away. He only turned his gaze from Uldenzar when it was no longer possible to direct it at him.

Uldenzar waited while Dacramal dismissed the *moillum*. As one they bowed to the Zarull, then formed into a neat unit, marching away, back through the forest. 'The discipline of this company is superb, Dacramal,' observed Uldenzar.

'You did not want the Man, Pyras, killed, Zarull?'

'I was intrigued by his hatred. Did you mark it?'

'Did you think to cleanse him of it, Zarull?'

Uldenzar nodded. 'To be truthful, I did. But you saw the way his eyes fell on me as he was taken from here? I think I have deepened his hatred for the Csendook.'

Dacramal did not understand. It was as though the Zarull took pleasure from this. 'But, Zarull, this may lead to more trouble with the *moillum* – '

Uldenzar shook his head. 'No. As I said, the discipline is superb. They have seen the pointlessness of resistance. We work as one, Man and Csendook. We have an understanding. Is it not so?'

Dacramal nodded. 'Indeed, Zarull.'

Uldenzar grunted, turning. 'Perhaps I will speak to this Man again. Keep me informed of his movements. I have it in mind that he will make a superlative gladiator.'

Dacramal watched as the Csendook rejoined his Zemoi. They did not turn back, but went up into the trees, disappearing. A cold fury simmered within Dacramal, the fury of impotence, of defeat, of knowing resistance was truly useless. But his men were survivors. Pyras would not be permitted to disrupt them, fill them with false dreams. Uldenzar, damn him, was right.

Uldenzar nodded to his Zemoi, who was cleaning his blade. 'Only one with your degree of skill could have avoided the worst of that kick. The Man is dangerous. He has killed Csendook, I swear it.'

'As you warned me, Zarull, he was no ordinary *moillum*. And if hatred was a sword, I would even now be opened up, stretched out on the grass!'

Uldenzar grinned at the Zemoi's blunt humour. 'He wanted your blood that much, eh?'

9

CMIZEN

Uldenzar sipped at the dry wine. It was passable but of a poor quality. He much preferred the rose wine in the city where he had made his base, but he did not say so to his host. Cmizen had other things on his mind.

The Keeper looked no less haggard than he had done the last time the Zarull had visited him. Even with the Supreme Sanguinary returned to the Warhive, Cmizen was on edge, his skin an unhealthy pallor, most unusual for one of his race.

Between them, the table was empty but for a single object, placed there by Uldenzar shortly after his arrival. It was a bracelet.

'Twice before, I found *moillum* who were consumed by their hatred for our kind,' said the Zarull. 'I interviewed them, tried to coax them into my way of thinking, but it was no use. They went to the sword.'

'Tell me again about this new one.'

'He is of special interest. He is the finest fighter I have yet seen in the warhalls. I tell you, he was unlucky not to defeat my Zemoi. Properly conditioned, he would make a superb gladiator, one fit to serve in the front rank of Auganzar's new guard.'

Cmizen glared at the Zarull, but Uldenzar tipped his chin back and laughed softly, though it was more like a growl.

'You think I mock you?' he said.

Cmizen seemed incapable of smiling. 'Explain yourself.'

Uldenzar knew that he was outranked by the Keeper of Eannor, though it was a paper title as far as he was concerned. Anyone who had achieved less than he had in battle was beneath him. Cmizen knew it. 'I am serious,' said Uldenzar. 'Pyras could go to the Testaments and excel. He has an extraordinarily deep hatred of the Csendook. Just

112

as his fighting skill is extreme, so is his hatred. Under normal circumstances, we could never bend him to our plans. Zuldamar would perhaps wish to use him, but I have serious doubts about him.'

'You think he should be transferred to the recalcitrants on Skellunda?'

Uldenzar nodded. 'Whatever happens. Where he is now, he is disruptive. Merely by being in Dacramal's unit, he is a reminder to the *moillum* of what they once were. Take him out and they would go on to perform as we would hope. Dacramal was a fine warrior in his day but he has capitulated. He does not love us. That would be to much to expect. But he is sensible.'

'And this Man, Pyras?'

'He is something of a mystery.' Uldenzar nodded to the bracelet. 'There are other things you should know about him.'

Cmizen again picked up the bracelet. He had examined it earlier but it had meant little to him. He knew about the trafficking of female slaves, about the secret dealings that had gone on here during the final months of the assault on the Imperator Elect. The bracelet was an alloy, its peculiar quality that when snapped on a wrist it moulded itself to it, only able to be removed by a Csendook touch.

'Pyras was found wandering, lost and bemused, having been in a fight of some kind. As you know, a number of Men have been found, even small pockets of them. Eannor is a large world. There may be many others still hidden in its remote parts. Sport for another day.'

Cmizen nodded, setting down the bracelet. He knew from Uldenzar's smug tone that the Zarull had important information that he had not shared before. Uldenzar seemed to take pleasure in annoying him with such things, as though he considered himself to be the true Keeper of Eannor. Perhaps, Cmizen mused, it was what the Zarull aspired to.

'But Pyras was found *within* the zone of sacrifice.' Uldenzar leaned forward, lowering his voice. His eyes bored into Cmizen.

Cmizen's own eyes bulged. His mouth opened, but no sound emerged.

Uldenzar nodded. 'Yes, Cmizen. Within it. The very night that Auganzar's night patrols began, one of my Zolutars found him. Instructions on such matters are very explicit, depending on whom one serves.'

'A Man in the zone,' Cmizen muttered. 'But it means – '

Uldenzar nodded. 'He came through.'

'Can we be sure?'

'He wore the armour of an official of the Imperator Elect. I have had it hidden where it will never be found. All that I have kept is this bracelet.'

'The night of the first patrol,' Cmizen was murmuring, casting his mind back. 'Yes, I recall! One of the patrols raised the alarm. Zemoks were sent out. The entire zone was searched – '

Uldenzar grinned. 'It was my own Zolutar who raised the alarm. To put down a false trail. He had already hidden the Man.' He explained what Vulporzol had done. 'By morning the hunt was over, with nothing to show.'

'Auganzar himself rode into the zone but he found nothing. He spoke to many of the Zemoks and Zolutars.'

'He seemed satisfied that it had been a mistake. A warrior jumping at shadows. Nerves on the first night patrol.'

Cmizen scowled. 'He appeared to be satisfied. But I would not like to say what was in his mind.'

'You think he suspects something?' Uldenzar felt his humour weakening, a shiver of air entering the room.

Cmizen shrugged. 'I don't know. But Auganzar takes nothing for granted. He asks for detailed reports on all sweeps, especially the night ones.'

Uldenzar leaned back. 'Well, Pyras is safe where he is, though he needs to be moved. But there's nothing to trace him to my warhall.'

'Except that,' said Cmizen, pointing to the bracelet. 'Why did you not destroy it with the armour?'

Uldenzar smiled. 'I asked myself an obvious question: why is Pyras here? Why should one Man return to Eannor? Of course, it may have been by accident. He was unconscious, bathed in blood. It was some days before he came to and we thought he would die. But I have a better theory.'

'You think he is from the Imperator? That is known? You saw the armour?'

'Vulporzol saw it. He would not be mistaken.'

'Then the Man cannot be one of those who crossed with Vorenzar. He had only *moillum* with him.'

'Yes, I'm sure Pyras is the Imperator's servant. A spy, perhaps, though he was foolish to come here without at least attempting to disguise himself.' He lifted the bracelet. 'There is a name on this. "Jannovar". Interesting that the Man Pyras was wearing it. Not carrying it in a pouch, hidden inside his shirt. But wearing it on his arm. Like a token.'

'You think this Jannovar is his woman?'

Uldenzar raised his brows. 'Conjecture. But there's a strong likelihood, don't you agree?'

Cmizen grunted. 'You think a warrior would risk his life for a woman?'

'Probably not. But he might try to make it *seem* that way. Pyras is here for a reason. And we need to know what it is. If we can find out, it might give us the hold over him we need.'

'To persuade him to help us?'

'Exactly.'

Cmizen wiped the sweat from his face. 'You do not think. . .that the Man could possibly be an agent of Auganzar? If we reveal our plans to him – '

The Zarull shook his head. 'I find that extremely unlikely.'

'I have never understood why Auganzar wanted night patrols. Perhaps he was expecting something – '

'I still think it unlikely that Pyras is his agent. But we must follow this up. You must come to me and interview the Man privately. If you are not satisfied, then we'll have him put to the sword there and then.'

Cmizen stiffened. Again he dabbed at his face, which streamed with sweat. 'Very well,' he nodded at last.

'Good.' Uldenzar rose. 'Send word when you will come.'

'To the warhall?'

'No. The city. I know a place where the Eyes of Auganzar will not see us.'

They sat in a small, dark chamber, far below the fortress. A single brand burned high above them, its smoke drifting up through a flue that took it outwards beyond the walls. Even in such a secure place as this they kept their voices no higher than a murmur.

'Well, well,' said Etrascu, his gross body quivering as he listened to Cmizen's news. 'This seems to indicate the way we should move.'

Cmizen studied the moon shaped face, the bloodshot eyes. Etrascu had become even more bloated, used to regular travel to and from Eannor now, his body constantly replenishing itself in whatever strange rituals the Openers performed. The features had become stretched, distorted.

'There is no guarantee this Man will become our assassin,' Cmizen told him.

'Quite so. We could simply betray Uldenzar to the Supreme Sanguinary. Under interrogation, he would soon give up the Man.'

Cmizen shook his head. 'Uldenzar is far too cunning. Wherever the Man Pyras is hidden, we would not find him. Not if Uldenzar chose to cover his tracks.'

'Uldenzar does not trust us?'

Cmizen screwed up his face as if in pain. 'I could not guarantee his trust.'

'Then it would be dangerous to betray him and with him, Zuldamar. Not at this stage.'

'We must find out what the Man wants.'

Etrascu snorted. 'You think he'll tell us! When he knows he has been found out – '

'He has no knowledge of how he was found. He was unconscious for days. But he can only surmise Csendook found him and stripped him of the evidence that he is from Innasmorn. He will be forced to tell us why he is here.'

116

'Then if he is not an agent of Auganzar, we can use him. If he will allow himself to be used.'

Cmizen's eyes locked with those of the Opener. 'Uldenzar assures me that Pyras would make a superb warrior. The best. He said he could excel at the Testaments and go on to be one of Auganzar's personal *moillum*.'

Etrascu sat back with an indrawn gulp of air. 'If this were possible – '

'The assassination becomes more than a dream. There is real possibility in it. *If* the Man will cooperate. Apparently he hates us with a ferocity that is rare, even for his kind. If we could channel that hatred, turn it on Auganzar, show him as Man's real enemy – '

'Convince him that the Csendook want peace – '

'That we have no desire to find the Imperator – '

'And give him what he seeks here on Eannor,' Etrascu ended. 'We have to learn what it is.'

Cmizen let out a deep breath. 'So it is our original plan. To support Zuldamar.'

Etrascu looked at the Keeper without pity. Always he came back to it, always he had to state it. To be reassured. Does he trust me? he wondered. Probably not. Fear has conquered him. He hardly sleeps. He clings to Zuldamar, but one twist of the blade by Auganzar, and he would leap the other way. 'Yes, we must stay with Zuldamar.'

'Then go to him. Outline the position.'

Etrascu looked surprised. 'At this stage? Is it not a little premature? If things should go awry – '

'They won't. Not with Uldenzar holding the Man. But we need the highest authority if we are to tempt this Man. We need assurance from Zuldamar that we will be protected. And that whatever path we take in his name, he will support us. If the Man Pyras is to become the assassin, he will need protection wherever he goes. Beyond Eannor, I cannot give it to him. Only Zuldamar can do that.'

'Ah,' said Etrascu, as though something else had fallen into place. 'And it will give us additional protection. Zuldamar dare not let anything threaten our security.'

'Then do as I say. Go to him without delay.'

'As you wish, sire,' nodded the Opener, using the title which he so rarely accorded to his master these days.

Etrascu bowed to the guards who stood aside to admit him to the huge chambers of the Marozul, Zuldamar. They were a dazzling contrast to the gloom of Cmizen's outpost on Eannor, both in size and warmth. Light speared down from on high, the walls decorated with extravagant murals, mostly of scenes from the wars, although Etrascu noticed that Zuldamar had removed a significant number of these and replaced them with more gentle scenes, tapestries of worlds where things were far more tranquil, devoid of conflict, even a hint of it. Strange that a Csendook should so have turned from the natural calling of his kind. The hall itself was more like a vast inner garden than the chamber of a warlord. Zuldamar seemed to be taking the new peace very seriously, and Etrascu wondered what his colleagues made of it.

Once within the hall, the Opener was able to walk through it without being attended by Zemoks. Those who served Zuldamar were outside, although there must surely be a few within, ready to defend their Marozul if for any reason an assassin did attempt to enter, which seemed most unlikely. Another servant, a very young Csendook dressed in a plain robe, materialised from among the huge vases, some of which were shoulder high, overflowing with plants. He bowed and motioned for Etrascu to follow him.

Zuldamar was sitting in the atrium beyond the hall, the open sky above him. There was an even greater profusion of plants here, and a deep pool, half covered with huge, pink blooms. Etrascu was not moved by such things, but he found the atmosphere far more relaxing than the military corridors in the Warhive through which he had travelled to get here.

The Marozul rose. Even dressed informally he was a formidable Csendook. It was said that he had once been as ferocious a warrior as any other, the hero of numerous exploits. Now there was a serenity in his face, a complete

118

contrast to that of Cmizen. But there was power there, and the unmistakable trace of Csendook hardness.

'Etrascu,' he said calmly, gesturing for the Opener to sit on a bench carved from a block of purple marble. 'Be seated.'

Etrascu bowed, doing as bidden, though as always he looked about him with a degree of discomfort. 'Marozul, there are matters that I must report on. Are you satisfied that this place – ?' He shrugged, indicating with his eyes that he thought the atrium far too open.

'Quite satisfied,' said Zuldamar. He had prepared carefully for this meeting, which was not part of the routine reporting he received from Eannor. Etrascu was here prematurely, so there must be news of some kind. Zuldamar's chambers were protected better than any fortress, though his fellows would have been surprised by the extent of his defences. He knew, however, that Auganzar would assume it and therefore not waste energy attempting to infiltrate them. The Supreme Sanguinary had been treading with commendable care in recent weeks. As far as the Garazenda were concerned, he had been a model commander, in no way stepping over the bounds of his duties. He had been discreet in his policing of Eannor.

Zuldamar sat in a large chair, folding his hands comfortably. He seemed, in spite of his position, to be a warrior who felt no pressure, no threat. He nodded for Etrascu to begin.

'A Man has come, Marozul. Through the gate.'

Only a slight nod of the head indicated that Zuldamar had heard, though Etrascu knew the news must have rocked him.

'Uldenzar has had him secreted in his warhall. Only the Zarull and his Zolutar, Vulporzol, who found the Man, two Zemoks, myself and Cmizen know of the Man. Otherwise it is assumed he was found wandering on Eannor, as others have been found.' Etrascu explained how Pyramors had been removed in secrecy from the zone of sacrifice.

Zuldamar smiled at the story. 'And all this while the Supreme Sanguinary was resident on Eannor? The efficiency of the Zolutar greatly impresses me.' He leaned forward, his eyes suddenly becoming hard, the gleam of the days of battle returning to them. 'Are we sure that Auganzar knows nothing?'

Etrascu could not meet the gaze. 'Yes, Marozul. We are sure.'

'Where is the Man, this Pyras?'

Again Etrascu explained, speaking of the armour that had identified the Man as a servant of the Imperator Elect.

Zuldamar listened closely, his emotions completely blank. But his mind raced. Then it is as we feared! They did escape us. He waited until Etrascu had finished. 'As you can imagine, Etrascu, no word of this must get out. If it does, the Supreme Sanguinary will insist on immediately bringing every resource to bear on creating a gate. The Man Pyras is a great danger to us.'

'But, Marozul, he could also be precisely what you have been looking for.'

Once more Zuldamar listened to the words of the Opener, nodding as the assassination plan was given fresh thought.

'Clearly we must establish what mission the Man is on.'

Etrascu shrugged. 'We cannot imagine what it must be. We feared he might be a spy, for the Supreme Sanguinary – '

'Possible, though I doubt it. If he had been able to infiltrate the Imperator's ranks before the flight to Innasmorn, Auganzar would have used any information from him before now. And only a fool would have returned to Eannor in the Imperator's armour.'

'There is one possible clue, Marozul.'

'Which is?'

'Pyras wore a bracelet. The bracelet of a slave woman, one who was to be given to us by slavers. On it is the name, "Jannovar". We did speculate that the Man might have returned to Eannor in an attempt to find her.'

'For what reason?' said Zuldamar, not disguising his puzzlement.

Etrascu looked uncomfortable, sorry that he had brought the subject up. 'She may have been an important member of the Imperator Elect's household. If Pyras is one of his inner guards, or is of high rank, the woman may be of some importance. She may have a significant role that we don't understand.'

'But surely if there is a slave bracelet with her name on it, her own people would have rejected her, bought their freedom with her. Unless that is precisely what we are expected to believe. She may have been planted among the slave women. But why? What possible information could she be expected to find?'

Etrascu said nothing, interested to hear how quickly the Marozul sifted the possibilities, some of which had not occurred to him.

'You said Jannovar? I will have discreet investigations made. If this woman is alive, I will find her.'

'She could be a lever, Marozul. To elicit cooperation.'

'It will depend on what Pyras wants. He has taken an unprecedented risk in coming back to Eannor. He must have known he would be captured. How could he have avoided us?'

Again Etrascu was silent.

Zuldamar considered the situation. 'Intriguing. Very well. Have word sent to Uldenzar that every effort must be made to find out what Pyras seeks. If it is merely the woman, tell him we will do all we can to locate her for him. And if Uldenzar is sure that Pyras is the one we have been searching for, he must be persuaded to our cause, *at any price.* I will ensure that every protection is given to him, and to those of you who are implicated in this plot.'

Etrascu rose sluggishly and bowed. 'It will be done, Marozul.'

'And make absolutely sure that this Man understands that the gate to Innasmorn is to be closed, sealed up so that no Csendook will ever pass through it again. No other Man must ever come through. There must be no contact between our worlds.'

Etrascu left the Marozul with an air of confidence that he had not felt on his arrival. Zuldamar was a remarkable

Csendook, a fine general off the field as well as upon it. His word was not to be taken lightly. If he offered sanctuary to those who served him, he would defend them with all the considerable power at his disposal. And Auganzar, for all his own power, was certainly under threat. If the Man could just be persuaded to do what was necessary! Etrascu smiled. How ironic that the rulers of the Csendook should be relying on a Man to solve the greatest of their disputes!

The Opener entered the chamber which was located at the heart of the citadel where the Garazenda had their headquarters. It was the Chamber of Paths, a large, domed area, where it was possible either to send a single Csendook or an entire Swarm through a gate to one of the worlds of the cycle. Etrascu walked to an area where he could perform the simple ritual, the giving of a little blood, that would open a Path for him, back to Eannor. He was known to be on business here, and he wore on his robe the insignia of Zuldamar, to whom he reported formally. There was no secret in this, the arrangement having been given express approval by the Garazenda. No one came or went to Eannor without such careful consideration, and only a few Openers had access to the world.

As he made for the steps that led to the antechamber he would use, he heard the tread of boots behind him and turned. There were two Zolutars he did not recognise, both dressed in light armour, as though on military duty. On their chests blazed the twin circles that were the Eyes of Auganzar. And with the two Zolutars was the Supreme Sanguinary himself, though he was dressed less formally.

'Etrascu!' he called, as if addressing an old friend. 'This is an unexpected coincidence.'

'Zaru – ' gulped the Opener, unable to move from the steps.

Auganzar smiled at him, coming forward without a hint of malice. 'Are you on your way back to Eannor?'

'I am, Zaru – '

'Then I'll not detain you for more than a moment. You can spare me a short while?'

'Of course, Zaru – '

Auganzar reached out gently, so much so, in fact, that without the Opener realising it, he took him by the arm and guided him back down the steps. 'There is some information I'd like you to take to Cmizen.'

'Naturally, I'm only too glad to be of assistance – '

'I haven't cleared this with the Garazenda yet, but I'm sure it's no more than a formality.'

They were passing through a doorway that led out of the Chamber of Paths and downwards into the citadel. Etrascu felt the icy grip of fear tightening, as though Auganzar could read every thought in his mind, past and present. But he knew he was imagining this. He shook himself free of the notion.

'You've been with Zuldamar?' said Auganzar casually, as though referring to a friend. He towered over the Opener, who was beginning to sweat in spite of the ease of the walk.

'I – yes, Zaru. A routine report.'

'How are things on Eannor? Quiet, I trust?'

'They are, Zaru.'

'No more false alarms? Shadows crossing the zone of silence, getting the Zemoks out of their bunks in the middle of the night?' Auganzar grinned.

'That was unfortunate, Zaru – '

'I make the warriors nervous. My presence on Eannor evidently triggered off that alarm. But it served a useful purpose. It is about the patrols that I want to speak to you. I have something that will improve them. As I said, I will need the permission of the Garazenda, though between you and I, there's no reason why you shouldn't warn Cmizen what I intend. He'll appreciate a little foreknowledge.'

Etrascu tried to swallow, but it had become increasingly more difficult.

They had come a long way down the stairway; at its foot there were several armed Zemoks. All wore the insignia of the Supreme Sanguinary. They opened the steel door at Auganzar's instruction and once the party was inside, bolted it shut. Auganzar led the Opener along another corridor and then through to a high chamber, webbed across with steel girders. They stood on a balcony.

'There,' said Auganzar, pointing down to a number of steel cages. Something within them leapt up, dark-skinned, gleaming as if cast in metal. A wild snarling came from the mouths of the penned creatures. They were enormous hounds, their eyes smouldering, scarlet, their jaws wide, tongues yellowed, teeth like steel. They snarled at one another, clawing at the cage that separated them. In spite of its strength, it looked as though it would be torn apart under the onslaught.

'Tigerhounds,' said Auganzar, his eyes falling on the monstrous creatures with evident pride. 'I've been having them developed for some time. They'll be ready very soon. And Eannor is the perfect place to have them tested.'

'They're – terrifying, Zaru,' said Etrascu.

Auganzar smiled grimly. 'You cannot imagine what they can do. They are quite unique, both as hunters and as killers. Tell Cmizen I will be bringing them soon. They will strengthen the patrols in the zone of sacrifice.'

'Of course, Zaru. An informal word – '

'Excellent. Come, I have delayed you long enough.'

Etrascu was relieved to be out of the chamber, with its sounds of terror, its smells. He thought he would never forget the particular stench of those beasts. As he made his laborious way back up towards the Chamber of Paths, he kept asking himself, over and over, was this a warning? What did Auganzar know?

10

ALLIANCE

Ussemitus drifted in the dark places of the World Splinter, the deep gulfs of its powers. As his body drank in the knowledge, his mind opened on countless vistas, views of a dozen histories, the epics of the eons. Around him in the endless flow of time's voices he felt the shimmering ghosts that were the spectrals, the vivid servants of the powers, now the focus of his own senses as he reached out over the world beyond the Splinter.

As he learned to control them, sift the information they brought to him, the whisperings of the wind, the rumbling of far storms, the groan of stone far under the earth, he listened also to the voices of the World Splinter, the incalculable power housed within it.

Man is the key, it told him. As the forces gather from so many remote places, events can turn around a few lives.

Ussemitus thought of Aru and Jubaia, hovering somewhere near the Sculpted City, thwarted in their attempt to find Pyramors. He thought also of Fomond and Armestor, camped with the armies that moved ever forward to the war that could not be avoided. And he thought of the great darkness that swirled in ever stronger currents about this world, the evils it would unleash.

Pyramors has gone beyond Innasmorn, to Eannor, the powers told him. He must be found and returned. Without him Man is lost. And the Csendook must come. Innasmorn needs both of them.

Ussemitus linked himself to the spectrals, focusing his mind, god-like. He must prepare a way, a gate to Eannor through which the spectral, his eyes and ears, must go. Pyramors must be found.

* * *

Pyramors let the icy water wash over him, leaning back, gasping at its cold bite. Others marvelled discreetly at his resilience, though among themselves the *moillum* muttered that this lone gladiator must be slightly mad, tired of life. Since the fight with the Zemoi, Pyramors had spoken little. He had been housed in the single hut, away from the other men. Those who had tried to strike up a conversation with him during training found him uncommunicative: he remained aloof. Yet he did not stop training, rather working harder than before, as if in some way he looked forward to another opportunity to do battle with the Csendook. He had not compromised.

Here, under the waterfall, the *moillum* were washing after a testing run through miles of woodland. Pyramors had studied the terrain carefully on the run, looking for a possible way out of the long valley, though he suspected it would be guarded at its ends. It would have to be night, he told himself. And up, into the mountains.

One of the younger warriors, Decusis, spoke to him as they bathed in the stream. 'Do you think, one day, it would be possible for one of us to get the better of a Csendook in the arena?' he asked unexpectedly.

Pyramors sensed that a number of the younger gladiators were watching, positioning themselves so that Decusis could speak privately.

'I have to believe it,' said Pyramors softly. 'There is nothing else to believe in.'

Decusis eyed his friends. 'You need not fight alone.'

Pyramors nodded. 'I'll keep it in mind.'

Decusis left him to his thoughts, though the youth would have been disturbed if he could have read them. Pyramors could not rid himself of the darkness from which the faces loomed, the dead friends, the lost ones. And here on Eannor, what future was there for his people? They would become machines, soulless. The young had spirit, but how long would they be permitted to cling to it?

* * *

That night, Pyramors heard movements outside his hut. He had slept lightly, wondering again about Decusis and his friends. He felt he would be able to trust the young men and perhaps even take the risk of using them. If he were to break out, he would stand a better chance with their help. But he did not like the thought of gambling their lives. Too many men had died because of him.

His door, which was now locked at night, was opened quietly. There were several figures beyond. Troidan was the first of them. He held a lamp, its glow confined to a small halo of light, throwing his face into a yellow relief that gave him the appearance of a demon.

'Come with me,' he said. He held his weapon as though ready to use it. Since the incident in the circle, he had been aching for a chance to extract his revenge. But Pyramors had given him no opportunity. Nor would he now. He slid off the bed, nodded once, and walked out of the door. Although he looked to be unwary, a man pulled from deep sleep, he was ready to defend himself, wondering if he would be attacked. This seemed an unlikely place.

They led him to one of the huts at the far end of the camp. Dacramal was inside. Troidan motioned for Pyramors to go in, and when he did so, the door closed. He was alone with the big man.

'We are to ride,' was all Dacramal said. Since the fight with the Zemoi, Dacramal had hardly said a word to Pyramors, as though in some way ashamed that he had brought the fight upon him. If Dacramal felt remorse, or a deep desire for freedom, he would not show it. He was stubborn, fixed. The equal stubbornness of the man Pyras only served to make him more determined to hold to the new way. Rebellion was sterile, full of false hopes and painful reminders of defeat.

Pyramors said nothing, nodding. He had made himself an automaton, doing all that was asked of him, training hard, deliberately keeping himself strong. He holds to his pride, thought Dacramal. But defeat broke him.

They went through the hut and up the sloping woods outside where they were met in the trees by a party of horsemen on sturdy ponies. Pyramors could not see the faces of the men clearly in the dark but he guessed they were not from the camp. Dacramal mounted one of the ponies and gestured for Pyramors to mount the other that had been prepared.

Through the night they rode, beyond the forest lands, through a narrow pass where a number of watchtowers had been erected. They were admitted to the land beyond, Pyramors trying to gauge the strength of the surveillance. Once through the low hills, they reached the gates of the city, Rannor Tarul. It stretched out before them in silence under the starlight, as if only the ghosts patrolled its walls now.

They were met beyond the gates by a party of Csendook. Within moments Dacramal had been dismissed, he and the men riding into some other part of the city. Pyramors was ordered to dismount, led by the Csendook up through the unlit streets, almost stumbling in the darkness. At this hour, it seemed, no one had business abroad. Once, in the days of Man, Rannor Tarul had never slept. Like all cities, it had housed its dens of thieves, cut-throats and whores. If they were here now, they were at one with the stone.

Pyramors knew little about this part of the city, which seemed no more than a slum area. Most of the houses were derelict. The rats had them: no Csendook would dwell here. They were far too proud a race for that. Their own cities knew no such decay.

They went up a long, crumbling stairway and into a tall building, entering a long, dusty chamber. It appeared to be the remains of a vast warehouse, sacks of corn spilled over in isolation, crates smashed and flung aside. There were torches burning in the centre of the long chamber, figures waiting. In the great openness of the warehouse they were grimly conspicuous.

Pyramors recognised the tallest of the figures. It was the Zarull, Uldenzar. Though he had not shown his face in the forest, there was that about him that had marked him in Pyramors's memory. He wore no helm now, and in the weak light his face bore all the marks of a Csendook warrior, the hard lines, the eyes that could shrivel a man's spirit. Shadows danced across the chamber, elongated and monstrous, a dozen Zemoi. Uldenzar had brought his guards in strength.

'We meet again, Pyras,' he said, with the trace of a grin. 'If that is your name.'

Pyramors did not speak. But he wondered why he had been brought here. What had they learned?

'Does your presence in this city surprise you?' Uldenzar asked him.

'You think of me as a threat to Dacramal's warhall. His *moillum* serve you well.'

'And you do not. You hate us.'

'I could deny it. But we are enemies, Zarull.'

'Men who do not capitulate are usually executed.'

Pyramors nodded. 'I understand Csendook ethics.'

'Yet we have failed with you. You do not capitulate. You will never serve us, bury your hatred, curb your pride. I cannot fault you for that. In this you are as the Csendook.'

'You did not bring me here to praise me.'

Uldenzar snorted, a sound which may have been a laugh. 'Perhaps I did. But why I am here is not at issue. It is why you are here that interests me. Here on Eannor.'

Pyramors shrugged. 'Like all Men on this world, I am a slave.'

'You left Eannor once.'

Pyramors glanced at the Zemoi. They were like statues, every one of them wearing a helm that covered its face. Only Uldenzar did not wear one. How much did the Zarull know?

'I fought in the battles, here in this very city,' nodded Pyramors. 'I was here when the Imperator and the last of his defences resisted your Swarms – '

'You went with him.'

'To his death? He perished, along with thousands of others. The rest of us were scattered across Eannor – '

Uldenzar's smile widened. 'Why are you here? What is your mission on Eannor?'

'I have no mission.'

Uldenzar had shown surprising control. Pyramors would have expected anger, fury even, from a Csendook. Uldenzar waved his Zemoi back and they retreated into the darkness at the edge of the hall. Other figures were arriving, one of them a Csendook, though not so large as the Zarull. This one was cloaked, its face hooded as though it hugged secrecy. Beyond it, hovering out of the light, was a smaller figure. It seemed bloated, gross and unnatural, its pale face a blob in the shadows. Pyramors felt himself turning cold as he realised what it must be. An Opener! A maker of Paths. The Csendook had cultivated whole guilds of these bizarre creatures.

The cloaked Csendook positioned himself beside Uldenzar, partially revealing his face. Pyramors did not recognise him. The face was lined, weary, pale and drawn in a way that Pyramors had not seen before in a Csendook. He could smell the being, the faint scent of fear.

'This is Cmizen, the Keeper of Eannor,' said Uldenzar. His intentions were clear: no one else was to hear this conversation.

Pyramors was secretly stunned, though he remained cold. The Keeper? This would be the Csendook with absolute control of Eannor. Only members of the Garazenda would outrank him.

'We know where you are from,' said Cmizen. 'Do not waste our time denying it.' His voice was rasping, as though he had trouble breathing, and his mastery of the language of Men was not good, far less commanding than Uldenzar's. And he found it hard to keep his contempt from his voice. 'You were found in the zone of sacrifice, in the very place where the Imperator Elect performed the rituals that opened a Path out of Eannor.'

'Out of the cycle of worlds,' added Uldenzar.

'You were found,' went on Cmizen, 'wearing the Imperator Elect's insignia. You serve him and are one of his Consulate. What is your name?'

'Pyras.'

'I do not think so,' breathed Cmizen. 'But you are necessarily cautious. You desire to protect your Imperator. You assume that we Csendook desire only to hunt him, wherever he has gone.'

'Why else do you exist?' said Pyramors.

'There are other reasons,' said Cmizen.

'Since the Crusade ended,' said Uldenzar, 'the Garazenda have made new laws. The laws that created the *moillum*. The slaughter of your people has ended. You are slaves, yes, but the Csendook have no desire to commit genocide.'

'Nor do we wish to begin the Crusade again,' said Cmizen. 'If your Imperator has miraculously survived, we do not wish to pursue him. If there is a gate between our world cycle and another, we do not want to go through it. We want it sealed.'

Pyramors frowned. This was unbelievable. Csendook who had given up the hunt for the Imperator? Surely they did not expect him to credit this?

'You do not believe us,' said Cmizen. 'But if we know where you are from, that this gate exists, that your Imperator survived, why have we not followed?'

A trap? But where was the trip wire? They could not open the gate: was that it? Even their Openers could not do so. They had no contact with the Accrual.

'The world you escaped to has a name,' said Cmizen. 'It is Innasmorn.'

Pyramors was very still. The word hovered, the fate of his species encapsulated in it. The Accrual had not lied. Csendook knew of Innasmorn. Then denial would be pointless.

'I say again,' persisted Cmizen, 'we have no desire to follow your Imperator. As far as we are concerned, he is dead. He died here on Eannor, along with Prime Consul Zellorian and all the other high officials of the Consulate. The Crusade is over. The world cycle is at peace. Men who survived will have a new life – '

'As slaves – '

'One day that might change,' said Uldenzar. 'But it will take time.'

'The gate, such as it is,' said Cmizen. 'We want it closed. Closed so that it can never again be opened. We fear no attack from your new world. But we do not want the war perpetuated.'

'You speak for the Garazenda? Then why do you come here in such secrecy?'

Cmizen hissed as if he had been struck. 'We do not speak for all of the Garazenda. There are those who would pursue the war. If they had been the ones to find you, there would have been a very different interrogation.'

'You know of Auganzar, the Supreme Sanguinary?' said Uldenzar.

Pyramors nodded. 'Dacramal told me about his control of the *moillum*. Apparently the greatest honour goes to those of us who win service in his guard.'

'Auganzar has one burning ambition,' said Uldenzar. 'To find your Imperator. To destroy him, Zellorian and all the others.'

'But he does not have the key to Innasmorn,' said Cmizen. 'Nor does he know that you are here. If he did, he would use you to guide him and his Swarms through the gate. And the Garazenda would have to support him.'

'Why?'

'They have denied the gate out of the world cycle. If such a gate were proven to exist, the Garazenda would have to open it. They do not want it found.'

'Then why is Auganzar not removed from office?'

Uldenzar grinned, his teeth flashing in the half light. 'Yes, why not indeed! You understand our position. Auganzar has strengthened himself. He is most cautious. He upholds the law, the new peace. He polices your survivors with the *moillum*. But secretly he seeks the gate to Innasmorn.'

'He must not find it,' said Cmizen. 'Already he has tried to send Csendook through.'

Again Pyramors felt the shiver of dread. How much did they know about the success of that?

Uldenzar's eyes burned into him. 'Did they survive?'

Pyramors shook his head. 'I don't know. If they came to Innasmorn, nothing is yet known of them. Were there many?'

Cmizen looked ashen. 'Many tried. Under a Zaru named Vorenzar. But it is a bloody Path, is it not?'

Pyramors was trying to evaluate his position. He could

deny everything but that now seemed pointless. And if these Csendook seriously wanted the gate closed, he would have to consider whatever proposition they were going to put to him. But how likely was it they were being honest with him?

'Yes, it is a bloody Path,' he agreed softly. 'An unnatural thing. Great sacrifices have to be made for even one man, one warrior, to pass through.'

'You are a warrior, whatever your rank,' said Uldenzar. 'You fought like a commander, a true Consul. You were unlucky not to get the better of my Zemoi.'

'Why are you here?' said Cmizen.

Pyramors looked at him for a moment, reading the fear in him, the many uncertainties. Was he afraid for his position, his life? Did the threat of the Supreme Sanguinary really hang over him?

Uldenzar took something from his belt and held it up near to a torch. By the glow, Pyramors could see what it was. He recognised its inscription. His eyes betrayed him.

'The bangle of a slave woman,' said Uldenzar. 'You wore it on your arm when you came through the gate. It was removed along with your armour.'

'Why are you here?' said Cmizen again.

Pyramors shook his head slowly. 'You would not believe me.'

'Who is Jannovar?' said Uldenzar. 'What importance do you attach to her?'

Pyramors straightened. 'I came here to find her. That is all.'

'She was related to you? Your wife?' said the Zarull.

'She was left behind,' Pyramors told them, his voice falling very low. 'I would have taken her with me. At the end, when we began the Crossing, I could not find her. In the confusion I went through, thinking she must be among the thousands who followed. In the end, she was not.'

'Then she is here on Eannor?' said Cmizen.

'If she is alive.'

Cmizen studied him, nodding, reading the subdued grief in the Man. 'We are searching for her. But it may not be easy for us to find her.'

Pyramors's eyes snapped up, fixing on the Keeper. The hatred that Uldenzar had seen before flared up anew. 'She will not be harmed,' said the Zarull. 'You think we would torture her to weaken you?'

Pyramors did not answer, his control rigid.

'If she is found,' said Cmizen, 'what would be your wish?'

'Would you be capable of returning to Innasmorn with her?' said Uldenzar. 'Well? Would that be your wish? Or do you have some other mission?' There was an edge of impatience in his voice now, a sign that he would know the truth, however he had to get it.

Pyramors's mind was racing. They would find Jannovar for him? In exchange for what? How could they believe he wanted nothing more than to find her? He was a Consul: they knew his rank was high. How could they accept that such an official could come here merely to find a woman! And yet they were asking him to believe something equally preposterous, that they had no wish to pursue the Imperator Elect. They wanted the war ended. It was equally as naive of them.

'If she is found, I would want to take her back with me. I have no other mission. Can you believe that?'

Uldenzar grunted. 'We may have to.'

'As I have to believe you.'

Uldenzar nodded slowly. 'If she is alive, we will find her. We have already had word sent to our Marozul. You understand what that means?'

A Marozul, searching for Jannovar!

'With all the power at his disposal,' said Cmizen, 'he will find the woman. She will be given to you.'

'And if it is possible, you will both return to Innasmorn,' said Uldenzar.

Pyramors drew in his breath, deep and slow. This was the real test. 'And in return?' he said coldly.

Cmizen watched Uldenzar anxiously, perhaps waiting for a signal. How far could they trust this rebellious warrior?

'You have demonstrated your hatred of us,' said the Zarull. 'You hide it well. But it will always burn strongly within you, I think. It is that hatred that we would call on. Properly tempered, it will make a fine weapon. You asked us why Auganzar has not been removed from office. Politically that is impossible. He covers himself too well, and he has many supporters. If the balance of power shifted his way, he would soon be in control of this world cycle.'

'He seeks a place among the Marozul,' said Cmizen.

'And for him, the hunt must go on,' nodded Uldenzar. 'If we cannot remove him politically, then we must find other ways. We have tried to infiltrate his Thousand, his elite corps. And failed. Even the Zemoks that serve the Thousand are beyond reproach. Auganzar commands utter loyalty. He epitomises the traditional Csendook. A warrior first. Many of our race would die for him and give up everything to serve him. No Csendook assassin could breach his defence.'

Pyramors listened to the half whispered words with repressed awe. To be party to this information was staggering. Yet somehow he could not believe it was a lie. The fear of Cmizen was too real, too solid. These Csendook meant to bring down their own Supreme Sanguinary.

'We have come to the conclusion,' ended Uldenzar, 'that we must find a way to Auganzar through another route. Through the *moillum*.'

'At the next Testament on the Warhive,' said Cmizen, 'the best of the *moillum* will be eliminated down to a handful, a picked unit who will serve Auganzar. They will be unique. Further proof of his mastery of Man. Men who will lead the hunt for survivors in the world cycle. Or beyond it. Killers of their own kind.'

Uldenzar leaned closer to Pyramors, a head taller. 'You could become one of this privileged group of warriors. And you could be our weapon.'

Pyramors scowled. 'Assassinate Auganzar? As simply as carrying a sword?'

Uldenzar shook his head. 'No. I admit it will be anything but simple. To become one of the new *moillum* will be difficult, extremely hazardous. But with the will, you could achieve it. And there will be protection. Discreet. Our Marozul will see to it that as much as possible is done to assure your safety, within reason.'

'But if you meet a better warrior in any of the arenas,' said Cmizen, the sweat beading on his forehead, 'we may not be able to help you. We dare not show ourselves to be part of the plot.'

Pyramors smiled wryly. 'If I die, your plot dies with me.'

'You will not die,' said Uldenzar.

Pyramors looked away, thinking about this extraordinary plan. It was a desperate measure, surely. But as it was preposterous, so unlikely, perhaps it had some merit. Would Auganzar imagine that his political enemies would take such a circuitous route to undo him?

'If by some miracle I achieve Auganzar's assassination,' he said eventually, 'how am I to survive the reprisals? How am I to get away? You will not protect me, unless you wish to be implicated in the plot.'

Uldenzar shrugged. 'We have not yet considered the finer details of the plot. We need to move cautiously, gradually. First we must feed you into the system. We will develop a plan slowly. But yes, of course we must bring you out safely, for our own sakes.'

'And we will find the woman,' added Cmizen.

'If we succeed in destroying the Supreme Sanguinary,' said Uldenzar, 'your people on Innasmorn will be secure. The Csendook need never find them.'

'Betray us,' said Cmizen, his own eyes suddenly widening with more than panic, with an anger bred from his fears, 'and we will serve you badly. You will have the woman, piece by piece.'

Pyramors looked away. It was the language he understood, the dialogue of war. But he nodded. He had no other choice.

Ussemitus's mind drifted through the deep innermost gulfs of the World Splinter, an ocean of secrets, of histories, as he sought to strengthen and control the spectral he was creating for his purpose. Instinctively he knew that the World Splinter had sent spectrals beyond Innasmorn before, and with a shock he understood that it was Innasmorn herself who had guided them beyond her, into Eannor. Just as Man One had told him when he had learned something of Innasmorn's past, he knew again that it was the Mother who had engineered the coming of the World Splinter, as well as the coming of the Csendook to Innasmorn. Now she was conveying to him that she would again help: she was eager, hungry almost, to help him recover Pyramors. He sensed in the making of the spectral that she wanted so much more though. Csendook? Was that what she wanted? To bring more of them, to begin the testing of the new race she had created, Innasmornian and Man?

As he shaped the spectral, guided it out of the dark ready for its flight through to Eannor, he felt the thrill of fear, the danger of losing control over the creature, as if at any moment the Mother would wrench from him the power she had given him, through the World Splinter. But he focused his mind.

And he began to see the spectacular, grim voyage of the spectral, as the walls of Innasmorn dissolved.

BOOK THREE

THE RECALCITRANTS

11

THE TIGERHOUNDS

Cmizen stared down into the courtyard, eyes fixed on the open door that led to an area within the Bone Watch that had not been used other than for storage. For the last two nights it had been the home of the beasts that Auganzar had sent. Cmizen had yet to see them but he had heard their snarling, their howling in the night, a sound unlike anything he had ever heard before, a sound of fury, of hate. He tried to convince himself they were nothing to do with his meeting in Rannor Tarul, and that Auganzar had no reason to suspect his treachery. Etrascu had warned him that these monstrous creatures, tigerhounds, were being sent to Eannor, but even his description of them could not match the reality.

Zemaal, warriors especially trained to work with the beasts, brought them out into the early morning light; the tigerhounds lifted their ugly heads and snarled at the skies. They were huge beasts, their heads on a level with their handlers' waists, and they had extended jaws, filled with glittering teeth that were a dull silver. Their eyes also gleamed unnaturally, as if part machine, and their bodies, long and sleek, suggested wolf more than big cat, as did their short tails. But when the Zemaal unstrapped the sheaths to their feet, they were viciously clawed, tearing at the air in readiness for a kill.

Beside Cmizen on the parapet, a single Zemaal stared down at the spectacle, ignoring the snarling tempers of the beasts. He wore unusual mail in that it had been reinforced: his boots sheathed him to the hip, while both arms were similarly sheathed in strong lightweight metal, his right glove huge. From it, two wires ran beneath his arm up to his shoulder and across to the base of his helm. Only his eyes showed in his mask, and they were little different to those

141

of the tigerhound.

'Are they not superb?' growled this Zemaal, his voice grating as though he found speech alien.

'As you say, Zuarzaal. I have not seen fitter, stronger beasts.'

'They have been perfected only recently. Carefully bred. With your permission, I will demonstrate the full range of their skills.'

'Please do.'

They went down to the courtyard, though Cmizen felt himself shuddering at every step. The eyes of the tigerhounds swung towards him and he felt the baleful fires of the five beasts as if they had already found their prey. The Zemaal restraining them were, like Zuarzaal, sheathed in the reinforced metal, protection against an attack if the beasts turned on them.

Cmizen reflected that the tigerhounds must be starving: they had not been fed since they had arrived from the Warhive.

Zuarzaal took from his belt a length of black wire, a long leash. He walked up to the first of the huge tigerhounds, ignoring its snapping fangs and clipped the end of the wire into a connection on the studded collar that circled the beast's neck. He also clipped the other end of the leash to a circle of steel around his right wrist. After making an adjustment to this circle, he stood up, facing the tigerhound. At once it dropped to its belly, eyes lidded, quiescent.

Cmizen gaped at the transformation. The Zemaal had said nothing, yet the beast was absolutely obedient to him.

Zuarzaal nodded to the other handlers and they, too, snapped their leashes into place. Again, the tigerhounds dropped to their bellies, ready for their next command.

Zuarzaal turned to Cmizen, his eyes wide, delighting in his mastery of the creatures. 'I have no need to shout commands to these hounds,' he told the Keeper. 'We work in silence. The leash has been constructed to convey commands, and with it impulses that force the tigerhounds to be obedient. We are one animal.' Again Cmizen gaped. This spoke of sciences that had been lost in the remote past, powers that were little more than myths in Csendook lore. What sources had Auganzar tapped?

'Their eyes scan the land in far more detail than our own,' Zuarzaal went on. 'They pick up differences in light and shadow, in heat and cold. No other creature in all the known worlds has a sense of smell to compare with theirs. In every way, the tigerhounds are unique.'

'So I see,' nodded Cmizen. Though the tigerhounds now watched him lazily, with apparent lack of interest, still he felt his shirt pasting itself to his back where he leaked sweat.

'We have sent them out against the killdreen.' Zuarzaal's eyes sparkled for a moment. 'A tigerhound can pull a killdreen to pieces. Nothing can withstand the attack of a tigerhound. In a pack such as this, they are invincible.'

Cmizen nodded numbly. The thought of a black lion, itself a terrible beast, being ripped apart by one of these creatures chilled his blood.

'Has the zone of sacrifice been cleared?' snapped Zuarzaal. 'If there are any Zolutars out there, or any others for that matter, they had better get into the Bone Watch quickly. Once the hunt begins, no, living thing will be safe. The tigerhounds will be primed to bring anything to ground.'

'Everything is ready for the demonstration.' Cmizen waved to his Zemoks up on the watch above the main gate to the courtyard, and at once the doors began to swing open. The tigerhounds lurched to their feet, each of them straining at their wire leashes, noses pointed to the doors that led out into the zone of sacrifice. Zuarzaal glanced at Cmizen for a last time, his eyes unreadable. He led his small group forward. Again the tigerhounds snarled, as if they had already picked up the scent of an enemy. Cmizen waited until they were out of the gates and then climbed up to the walls once more. Out on the upper parapets, he watched the group of Zemaal and tigerhounds splitting into five units, each going out into a separate part of the zone.

'Powerful beasts, Sire,' said the sergeant of the guard.

Cmizen watched a little longer, nodding, his thoughts deeply disturbed. As he turned to leave, he saw the eyes of the Zemok on him. It was Dagrazem.

'What do you think they'll find, Sire?'

Cmizen knew that there must be Zemoks here who had aided Uldenzar's Zolutar in getting the Man Pyras to safety. He had deliberately avoided trying to find out who they were, though Etrascu had warned him that he ought to know who their own allies were.

'Bones,' muttered Cmizen, turning away. 'And perhaps they'll scent the blood of the long dead.'

Dagrazem turned to watch the disappearing figures below. The Keeper was a fool. He had been chosen for that reason. He knew nothing of the Man's existence.

Zuarzaal felt the beast's sudden leap of excitement. For two hours it had weaved this way and that over the empty wastes of the zone, finding the relics of death, but no smouldering ember of life, no suggestion that anything had been here for a long time. There were traces of Csendook scent, which were to be expected, but the beasts had been programmed to ignore them. They had also been programmed to sift but ignore other trails, information that was already known. They had been given unique memories, in which detailed data could be stored and retrieved; hundreds of varying scents could be compared and analysed in moments. Anything that did not fit the known patterns was immediately picked up.

When the tigerhound raised its head, growling deeply in its chest, Zuarzaal knew it had found something. Something that should not be here.

The ground rose, moving outwards and up from the flat bottom of the valley. Zuarzaal let the beast move as quickly as he could, though it would have raced on if he had let it. Again it snarled eagerly. Its dipped its snout to the ground, then lifted it, ears flat back to its head as though it expected an attack. It did not seem to be following a scent, though it had wind of one, somewhere near. They came to the crest of a ridge, beyond which was a dip, scattered with stones. The tigerhound had found what it was seeking. It circled a

144

place in the rocks, all the time growling. Zuarzaal spoke to it and it sank down, eyes blazing as if it could see its enemy before it. The Zemaal studied the stones.

He grunted when he saw what the beast had found. It was blood. Dried, staining the rocks. He knew from the tigerhound's analysis of the blood that it was not that old. A matter of weeks. And the blood itself was strange. It varied. There were traces of human blood. But most of it was beyond detailed analysis.

Path blood!

The realisation hit Zuarzaal like a blow. The tigerhound raised its head, drawing back its lips, revealing the sharpened teeth, the terrible hunger.

'Something has come *through*,' Zuarzaal said aloud. He looked around for more clues as to what had happened. There were more trails of blood, but they faded towards the north end of the incline.

The tigerhound identified another scent. That of a Csendook. A picture was beginning to emerge as the beast analysed the scents. A Man had come through a world gate: he had been injured, though he himself had not lost much blood. He had been helped, probably carried, by a Csendook. A Zolutar, possibly. But the trail did not lead back to the Bone Watch. It led up into the mountains.

As they followed the trail, Zuarzaal probed the tigerhound's databank memory, analysing the blood scent, comparing it to the blood scent of the World Paths he knew. Nothing matched. Zuarzaal became more and more convinced that this must be a new and unknown blood scent. Auganzar had primed him to hunt for something like it. A clue to the gate that led beyond the world cycle! This Man must have come through such a gate! And he had been met and helped. By a Csendook. Again he searched in the memory of the beast, but the Csendook scent was not recorded. The Csendook who had found the Man had never reported it to the Bone Watch – then it was treachery!

In the dead forest, Zuarzaal and his beast found the place where the Man had been hidden temporarily beneath the tree. Two other Csendook had moved him. He had still been injured. A meticulous inspection of the land, the soil, showed that the Man had been carried. A conspiracy.

The trail led up towards the mountains once more. Zuarzaal grinned. The tigerhound had locked all these scents into its memory now: it would be able to identify the Man, the Zemoks and the Zolutar who had evidently commanded them. It would carry the scents wherever it went. Even if the Man somehow travelled beyond Eannor, to the Warhive itself, his scent was stored. He would be found. The tigerhound bayed its pleasure at the knowledge, the sound ringing out across the desolate zone. Zuarzaal instructed it to call its fellows. The note of its howl altered as it obeyed him instantly.

Less than an hour later the Zemaal and tigerhounds were reunited in the wood. They all committed the Man-scent to memory, together with the scents of the treacherous Csendook.

'Explanations will be sought of the Keeper,' said Guntrazaal.

'No doubt you smelled the fear on him when we arrived?' nodded Zuarzaal.

'You think he knows of this?'

'He serves Marozul Zuldamar. Draw your own conclusions.'

'I shall enjoy seeing the tigerhounds dismember him – ' began Guntrazaal.

Zuarzaal shook his head. 'All of you. Listen to me! No reprisals. This matter must go no further. Not yet. There is a conspiracy here, and we must uncover it all. But when we return to the Bone Watch, we must keep our findings to ourselves. If not, we risk losing the real prize.'

'Which will be what?' grunted another of the handlers.

'The key to the most valuable gate of them all.'

Guntrazaal laughed. 'Then we'll yet be Zolutaals!'

'Zolutaals!' snorted Zuarzaal. 'If we open this gate, we will be made Zaru at least! Each one of us will command his own Swarm. And take it through, no doubt.' They laughed together, and as they did so, the tigerhounds bayed their own triumph.

146

They paused for only a short while before moving on towards the mountains to the west of them, climbing steadily, easily, following the clear trail, a trail which other hounds would have lost. But the tigerhounds could find a trail that was a year old if they had to. The one they scented here was fresh to them.

The climb became difficult, no doubt deliberately picked, but the tigerhounds adapted to the terrain better than the Zemaal, who helped each other over the inclines and precipices. The beasts could leap, or could span rock walls like spiders, their elastic bodies clinging to bare rock as they wriggled upwards.

The party was far up among the peaks when Zuarzaal called a halt, though the tigerhounds, being part machine, needed no rest.

'Do you think we'll find the Man up here?' asked Guntrazaal.

'Not if the Zemoks got him across and out of the zone of sacrifice. That was their aim. Not to hide him. Too dangerous a risk. No, if there is a way over, they'll have got him beyond. I would be surprised if the Man is still on Eannor. But the Zemoks probably are.'

'Zuarzaal!' called one of the others.

At the edge of a chasm, the Zemaal was pointing. 'My tigerhound scents something here. One of the Zemoks came to this place and stood on its lip. Something is down there.'

Zuarzaal looked into the precipitous drop. His own tigerhound sniffed at its edge. 'Nothing alive is down there. And no bodies. But we must be sure. You, Annuzaal. Find out what it is.'

The Zemaal nodded, at once beginning the tortuous climb down that would eventually bring him to the bottom of the precipice. The remainder of the party moved on up towards the last of the heights.

On the lower slopes of the mountains, on their eastern flanks, the trees were healthy, rich in green foliage, a vivid contrast to the dead regions of the zone of sacrifice. Zuarzaal and his three fellow Zemaal rested in the long grass, enjoying the calmness, relaxing after their exertions. The tigerhounds were arranged about them like sentinels, calmly watching for any sign of movement beyond the edge of the forest, where the roadway stretched from north to south, from distant Rannor Tarul to the Bone Watch.

'A reunion, it seems,' said Zuarzaal. 'The same Zolutar.'

'He came here by xillatraal,' nodded Guntrazaal.

'The Man-scent disappears. But I think it is safe to assume that the Zolutar put the Man on his beast and rode northward.'

'It will be difficult to follow the trail of the xillatraal,' Guntrazaal frowned. 'So many of them have travelled this road.'

'Yes, and in Rannor Tarul, it will be worse.'

'A perfect place to confuse the scent completely, even though it is fresh. Thousands of Men have passed through the place – '

'There is another possibility,' said Zuarzaal, his eyes gleaming. 'Some dozen miles or so from Rannor Tarul is a *moillum* warhall.'

Guntrazaal stiffened. 'Belonging to whom?'

'There are no resident Csendook. The Men are well trained, or so it is believed. But the warhall is under the control of Uldenzar, who lives in Rannor Tarul.'

'Uldenzar?'

Zuarzaal nodded. 'Like that pig Cmizen, he is loyal to Marozul Zuldamar.'

'But if he has the Man, surely he would not risk having him in the city – '

'But in the warhall, among the *moillum*, who would notice? The *moillum* would hardly betray one of their own kind.'

Guntrazaal laughed. 'Would they not? *Moillum* covet glory.'

'Everything depends on their own loyalty to Zuldamar. If they wish to serve and honour him, rise in his esteem, to become privileged, they would close ranks. And protect the Man we seek.'

'*But who is he?*' Zuarzaal suddenly snapped. 'What is his mission here on Eannor?'

Nothing they discussed could shed light on the mystery. They waited as the sun began to sink. As its last light faded, the tigerhounds howled at the trail behind them. Another tigerhound was coming.

Annuzaal broke through the grasses, tired, but with a gleam of triumph in his eyes. He undid something at his back and tossed it down into the middle of the clearing where his fellow Zemaal had been waiting for him.

Zuarzaal picked up the objects. Armour. It had belonged to the Man they sought, the scent proved it. Zuarzaal's eyes widened as he saw the chipped insignia.

'You've not seen this,' he told his Zemaal, showing them the markings of the Imperator Elect.

'*Alive*?' gasped Guntrazaal. 'The Imperator Elect *survived*?'

'You know what this means?' said Zuarzaal softly. The Zemaal crowded round him as though eager to smother his words from the listening evening.

'Auganzar will want the Man found. He is the key to much more than we realised. The Crusade may, after all, be far from over.'

'The city?' said Guntrazaal. 'Or the warhall?'

Zuarzaal shook his head. 'We'll begin at the Bone Watch. I want the Zemoks. And the Zolutar, if he's there. Then we'll come north.'

'I heard the tigerhounds,' said Cmizen. He sat uncomfortably at his desk. In the shadows behind him stood the Opener, the silent Etrascu.

Zuarzaal felt uneasy in the presence of the latter, whose kind he considered to be unnatural, not of Csendook blood. The Zemaal sat stiffly, unused to the formal seating of the Keeper's apartments. He preferred the freedom of the outside world, not the claustrophobic shadows of this wretched place. Beside him he had placed his war helm. It was the first time Cmizen had seen the Zemaal without it on. The face was like dark marble, smooth but hard. The mouth was thin-lipped, curved down almost petulantly, nothing in the face expressed weakness. It was the face of a killer, the perfect Csendook warrior, ideal master for the tigerhounds. How much did he have in common with those creatures? Cmizen wondered.

'They found something of interest?' said the Keeper, his voice a little too high.

Zuarzaal looked almost indifferent. 'My orders, direct from the Supreme Sanguinary, are to make as many routine sweeps of the zone of sacrifice as are necessary to cover it all, Sire. The Garazenda approved this as a safety measure against further accidents.'

'I am quite aware of that,' said Cmizen irritably, though he knew this Zemaal would not be intimidated by him in the slightest. He was Auganzar's vassal to the core.

'Such reports as I am required to make, Sire,' Zuarzaal went on dryly, 'have to be confidential. The Garazenda are most concerned about Eannor.'

'Am I to understand that I am not to be a party to your findings?'

'It is not in my brief, sire.'

'I am the Keeper of Eannor!'

'Sire, it is not in my brief.'

Cmizen clenched his fists impotently beneath his desk. What had this impudent Zemaal found? Cmizen had heard his tigerhounds baying, calling the others together, as if in triumph. They had returned to the Bone Watch at twilight, but they had come along the north road, from *outside* the zone. They must have crossed the mountains to reach it.

'And what, precisely, do you require now?' Cmizen added, trying to be terse, though he might have addressed the wall for all the effect his anger had on Zuarzaal.

'With respect, sire, an inspection of the entire garrison. Every Zemok and Zolutar, no matter what duties they have. A complete scan.'

'Scan?' said Cmizen, appalled. 'What do you mean, scan?'

'The tigerhounds, sire. They will scan. It is routine. No more than that.'

* * *

Auganzar considered again the report that had been given to him by the young Zolutar, Immarzol, a warrior he could trust implicitly, and in whom he saw much of Vorenzar, the same fierce will and determination not to be swayed from his beliefs. Immarzol had just arrived from Eannor, brought here by the Opener, Etrascu, and Auganzar was confident that even now the bloated Opener would be delivering Cmizen's verbal report to Zuldamar. He was equally sure that the gist of the report would be much the same as that he had been given by Immarzol.

Immarzol saluted and left the Supreme Sanguinary alone with his thoughts. Few of his warriors were privileged to share his rooms with him, even for a short period. And he could be equally sure of privacy, security. Even so, he knew there would be many who would kill him if they had an opportunity.

He thought about Zuarzaal's report, deeply interested by its implications. Zuldamar would not be party to it and never so foolish as to intercept an envoy of Auganzar's. The Marozul always acted with commendable calmness, apparently aloof from the affairs of Eannor. In reality, Auganzar knew, he was anything but aloof from them.

The report through Immarzol was coded. The Zemaal had found exactly what Auganzar had suspected he might find: someone had come through from Innasmorn. But amazingly it had not been one of Vorenzar's Zemoks or one of the *moillum* he had taken with him through the gate. It had been a Man dressed in the armour of the Imperator Elect. Nothing else was known about him, except that he had been helped out of the zone by two Zemoks and a Zolutar. His present whereabouts was unknown, but Zuarzaal and his team were searching.

An inspection of the staff of the Bone Watch had revealed nothing. Whoever the Zemoks and the Zolutar had been who had assisted the Man's escape, they were no longer in the Bone Watch. The tigerhounds had scanned everyone there and there had been no trace of the scents they had found out in the zone of sacrifice. Auganzar was not surprised at this. Evidently the warriors involved had quickly

151

been transferred elsewhere, probably away from Eannor. Zuldamar had a number of units stationed on Eannor, both in the Bone Watch and in the principal city, Rannor Tarul. It seemed likely that Uldenzar was the Zarull in charge of the abduction exercise. Equally unlikely, Auganzar decided with a wry grin, was that Cmizen was a party to it. Though with hindsight he should not perhaps have warned him that he was sending the tigerhounds. He had not been able to resist terrifying Etrascu, and through him, Cmizen. But Zuldamar would have warned Cmizen of their coming anyway.

He was amused by the terror he knew would be haunting Cmizen's dreams. He was sure the spineless Keeper would be glad to thrust a sword into him. But it would never happen, not by Cmizen's hand.

Auganzar had a list of the Zaru and Zarull whom he knew to be loyal to Zuldamar, as he had a list of the Zolutars who served under them. He took the list from a locked drawer and studied it in light of the report and along with this list he studied also another, that of troop movements.

One particular Zolutar had recently left Eannor, one of Zuldamar's most loyal warriors. His present location was unspecified.

When Auganzar had finished studying the information, he sent again for Immarzol.

'When Etrascu the Opener returns to Eannor, go with him,' he told him. 'Report to Zuarzaal, verbally. Tell him that the tigerhounds are to be placed under the charge of Guntrazaal, who is to continue the search on Eannor. Zuarzaal and his own beast are to return to the Warhive and report to me at once.'

Immarzol saluted stiffly and was gone a moment later.

Auganzar sent for another of his Zolutars, who joined him as swiftly as if he had been outside the door, waiting for a chance to please his master.

'Some information,' said Auganzar. 'I want you to track down the movements of a certain Zolutar for me. He serves under the Zarull, Uldenzar, one of Marozul Zuldamar's warriors. Absolute discretion will be called for.'

'I understand, Zaru,' the Zolutar grinned.

'I'm sure you do, Quenzol. The Zolutar I want you to track was last known to be stationed on Eannor.'

'And his name, Zaru?'

'Vulporzol. Find him and watch his every move. Very carefully. I want daily reports and absolute discretion. He must not know he is under surveillance.'

Quenzol bowed. As with Immarzol, Auganzar had no doubts whatsoever about the young warrior's efficiency. Unquestionably, the Zolutar, Vulporzol, would be found.

12

SWORD

Auganzar watched the Zemoks in the arena below him with interest. It was one of the many that he owned, a small oval where he could test the skills of particular warriors, or where he could put on a show for his guests. At one time he had entertained often but since his elevation to the position of Supreme Sanguinary, he rarely brought any but his closest followers here to his private estate. Even those were not party to some of the developments his technicians worked on here.

As he watched the Zemoks working out, moving with superb skill, demonstrating the highest degree of excellence, unaware that they were being observed from the balcony above them, Auganzar thought of Vorenzar. He had been here, had seen some of the weapons that Auganzar was having designed. Vorenzar had been very much of the old school, a true Csendook who had little time for anything but the sword. Few Csendook would have matched him with it. But in his pursuit of his enemy, Auganzar knew that the sword would not be enough, and that secrets lost to both Man and Csendook would have to be uncovered before true victory could be won.

Auganzar left the Zemoks to their exercise. Ah, but if Vorenzar had been a little less brittle in his love of tradition, perhaps he would be here now. Was he alive? Had he survived the terrible leap from Eannor to Innasmorn? The Man that had been found might know the answer, though it was unlikely that he had been sent by Vorenzar. Auganzar had almost entirely dismissed that idea, although he could not imagine why the Man was here.

He went down into the lower halls of his estate, thinking again of the weapons Vorenzar could have used. The magnetic sword and shield, which Auganzar himself had used

154

to thwart an attempt on his life in the arena. Weapons which were contrary to traditions, a trick to some, and most of the Csendook race, like Vorenzar, would have abjured them. But what was Innasmorn like? What powers lurked there, and what control over them would Zellorian have? He already broached the so-called sorcery of the ancients, though Auganzar knew it was more than that. Whatever it was, he would be properly prepared.

There were private laboratories in this part of his estate. His technicians were housed here permanently. Everything was provided for them: they had access to excellent living conditions and there were spacious grounds for their recreation, for their families. They had no contact with anyone outside the estate. But, as with Auganzar's Thousand, the fighting warriors, these technicians were willing to give up their lives to serve Auganzar. They had no desire to be anywhere else, as it was well known that among the Csendook, technology was not advanced quickly. There were many who thought it should be suppressed altogether. To Auganzar it was part of the muddied thinking that had led to the premature peace. Peace would be fine, but only on the proper terms.

As he entered the private lower zones of the laboratories, he thought of peace, a true end to the war with Mankind. He, too, would welcome it, but not while Zellorian lived. He alone was a danger to the Csendook species, and while he lived, the work in these laboratories would go on.

He was met by Hozermaak, who somehow always managed to be on hand as soon as Auganzar arrived down here. He flitted among his workers like a guardian spirit, seeing everything, tireless. Indeed, Auganzar wondered if the Csendook ever slept. He was no warrior, being diminutive, hardly bigger than an average Man, with an unusual long mane of white hair and huge eyes, his stare almost disarming, punctuating the impassioned way he often spoke about his work. His movements were quick, jerky, seemingly impulsive, though Auganzar knew that he gave detailed thought to everything before committing a view. 'Your Janoks are busier than ever,' Auganzar observed, nodding at the rows of busy technicians.

'We concentrate our efforts on restoration of soils, Zaru. Several worlds are in danger of being closed off for millennia. The ravages of war.'

Auganzar smiled. The worlds that Hozermaak spoke of were just as likely to be worlds that he had helped endanger through his arts. 'Excellent. You work even more closely with other scientists of the Garazenda, I imagine.'

'Yes, Zaru, but not here – '

'No. I assume they are as jealous of their laboratories as we are of ours. But do they make demands on you?'

'Only as they should. In matters such as restoration.'

Auganzar nodded. 'I won't disturb the work. It interests me greatly, but I am very busy at the moment. Let us speak privately.'

Hozermaak's face gave nothing away but he knew precisely what his master had come for. He took him through the rows of Janoks to a private area where the only Zemoks in the laboratories protected stairs to a further area below the level of the laboratories. It was like the crypt of an ancient cathedral, gloomy and cold, lit by the occasional globe.

Inside another chamber only one other Csendook worked, his face masked as he bent over something on a long slab. He did not look up or stop working. Auganzar was always insistent that his presence did not interrupt anything going on in this area.

'I was thinking as I came,' he said quietly to Hozermaak, 'about the sword you developed for me, and the shield.'

Hozermaak made a dismissive gesture. 'Useful perhaps, Zaru. But a part of the process, that is all. Toys, almost.'

'You have something better?'

Hozermaak waited while the Janok finished what he was doing and straightened, pulling the thin mask from his face. It was pale, almost white, suggesting that he never left this area for the sunlight, and his hands were long and tapered like those of a surgeon. He was as unlike a Zemok as the Openers were, a direct opposite to them, being so thin and bloodless. Auganzar guessed he had been bred specifically as a tool, to work in such labs. Hozermaak was also from

156

a very different Csendook bloodline, itself something of a secret. Ximozer bowed elegantly to the Zaru.

'I hope I am not interrupting something vital?'

'Not at all, Zaru,' said the Janok softly, his voice as cold as the air in the room.

'Ximozer, we should demonstrate the sword,' Hozermaak told him. 'Is it ready?'

'Almost. But yes, a demonstration will be possible.' Again the Janok bowed. He indicated another door and they passed through into a wider room. It was bare, the floor earthen, almost as if it could have been a small arena. Auganzar had not been here before; he assumed even the Janoks trained. 'I will fetch the sword,' said Ximozer, disappearing without a sound.

Hozermaak seemed for a moment lost for words, clasping his hands behind his back. Auganzar had never engaged him in conversation other than about his beloved work. Politics did not concern the scientist, nor did anything else.

Ximozer returned, holding the promised weapon. It was sheathed in a dark scabbard, its haft three feet long, bound around with fine steel, and with the thinnest of guards. 'If you will draw out the blade, Zaru,' he whispered.

Auganzar took the proffered haft with one hand and slid the sword easily from its covering. The blade was cast in metal, an alloy he assumed, and was a peculiar dark hue, far darker than the usual Csendook steel. He used both hands to grip the haft and gently moved the weapon to and fro, gradually making faster sweeps with it, turning it, feeling its balance. It was perfection, like a part of him, weighted precisely. He could almost feel his nerves extending into it.

'I took the liberty, Zaru, of using your weight and measurements,' said Hozermaak.

'It will respond to you, Zaru,' added Ximozer, 'as it will respond to no other,'

'Has it the qualities of the magnetic sword?' said Auganzar, marvelling at the beauty of the weapon.

Hozermaak shook his head. 'It is far more powerful, Zaru. If you will permit me.' He went to one of the walls and pressed a small metal plate set in it. At once there was a

157

humming from overhead, and the ceiling, a thin sheet of metal, slid back, revealing a narrow shaft that rose straight up through the laboratory levels and beyond to the sky. The walls of the shaft gleamed as light angled down, splashing the centre of the earthen arena.

Hozermaak turned out the light globes, but the chamber remained well lit. 'If you'll allow the natural light to fall upon the blade, Zaru.'

Auganzar walked slowly to the centre of the arena and held out the weapon so that the sunlight struck the flat of the narrow blade. At once he felt a jolt of energy. The sword vibrated, its blade changing colour, shining like glass. Auganzar's arm throbbed, though not with pain. It was an eerie but pleasant sensation.

Hozermaak was pointing to a block of stone at the side of the arena. He motioned Auganzar to it and the big Csendook walked out of the direct sunlight. The sword was glowing, the pulse still in his arm.

'Touch the rock, Zaru,' said Hozermaak, his eyes like moons in the shadows, his eagerness a living thing.

Auganzar noticed the chunk of rock that had been set upon the bigger slab. He pushed the swordpoint gently towards it and found to his amazement that it would go into the rock as if it were a fruit. The rock, a dark grey mass, flickered internally as if something in the sword had been discharged into it. Then it began to decay, pieces flaking off it, crumbling away like fragments of cake. The heart of the rock was a steaming mass, dripping. Auganzar pulled the blade away. There was no trace of rock on it. Its light began to fade.

'The rock was igneous, Zaru,' said Hozermaak. 'As hard as any known to us.'

Auganzar studied the remains with interest.

'You can imagine, Zaru, the effect the sword would have on a living enemy,' said Ximozer, without emotion.

Auganzar nodded. Had they tested it?

'It draws power from whatever forces act upon it,' said Hozermaak. 'Heat, light, whatever power is to be found in the elements. And it concentrates the power, as you have seen.'

Auganzar slipped the blade back into the sheath that Ximozer held out to him. 'This is dangerous power,' he said quietly.

Hozermaak glanced briefly at Ximozer. They knew the risks they took here. The codes they broke in following their course of experiments. If they ever displeased Auganzar, everything would be destroyed. 'You think I have taken too great a liberty, Zaru?' said Hozermaak, his voice dropping.

Auganzar smiled coldly, nodding. It was a smile that his enemies felt with terror. 'Oh, yes. You have indeed. But it is as I commanded.'

'Some might say,' went on Hozermaak, 'that what I have done is sorcerous.'

'Magic?'

'Zaru, we have merely tapped forces that exist.'

'And used them as our enemies have done. Who knows what forces Zellorian has tapped? If we were to clash again, what would he use against us?'

'It has been said by some that Man once utilised vast powers. Sciences lost to him, technologies on which the Empire was built.'

'Would you find them again, Hozermaak?' Auganzar smiled grimly.

'If you sanctioned it, Zaru.'

Auganzar studied his expression, his own blank. But he pointed to the scabbard. 'Is it ready?'

'A little more work, Zaru,' said Ximozer.

'Are there others?'

Hozermaak shook his head. 'It has taken a year to create this one. I can have others more quickly – '

'No. No more. Perhaps later.'

Hozermaak bowed. 'As you wish, Zaru. No more.'

'Let me know when it is ready.'

'Zaru.'

Auganzar nodded a final time, abruptly leaving them. His Zemoks let him out of the private laboratory and he returned in thoughtful silence to the upper halls. In his rooms he looked out at his lavish gardens. He bunched his huge fists as if steeling himself against some inner decision. Hozermaak had an inevitable thirst for scientific knowledge. What did he know of the histories? Given an opportunity, what would he find? Find and re-create. Auganzar cursed softly. He of all the Csendook knew the answer, the truth.

Hozermaak would have to be stopped. Once the sword was ready. Hozermaak and Ximozer. They would have to be stopped.

The Zolutar stood to attention, eyes fixed ahead of him.

Auganzar studied him closely. These young warriors were the source of true loyalty. But they needed action to perfect themselves. Gladiatorial combat was one thing, but nothing compared to action in the front line.

'Have you fought against Men, Quenzol?' Auganzar asked him.

'Briefly, Zaru.'

'As you know, the war is not over. The Imperator Elect is alive. As are many of his high officials.'

'Yes, Zaru.'

'Never let anyone convince you otherwise.'

'No, Zaru.'

Auganzar tapped the twin circles on the Zolutar's breast-plate. 'These eyes see far. So, what have you to report?'

'I have conducted discreet enquiries, Zaru, as you requested.'

'Troop movements?'

'Just so, Zaru. I have had the movements of the Zemoks and Zemoi of Zarull Uldenzar investigated. It seems that the Zarull operates a routine shift between the various warhalls of *moillum* over which he exercises control. There are five of these. Three are here on the Warhive.'

'One is on Eannor,' Auganzar nodded. 'And the other?'

'On Cyanda. All of the warhalls are Marozul Zuldamar's.'

'Go on.'

'As you know, Zaru, the Zemoks who are stationed on Eannor, at the Bone Watch and at various other places, are drawn from the ranks of a number of the Garazenda's members. Marozul Zuldamar has Zemoks stationed there

160

and some of them are under Uldenzar. His duty is twofold on Eannor.'

Auganzar was perfectly aware of all this, but he had no intention of interrupting the young Zolutar.

'As I said, Zaru, he operates a shift system. His Zemoi move between *moillum* warhalls. Here on the Warhive, there are far more Zemoi present at the warhalls, as they give training. On Eannor there are less Zemoi in evidence and they spend much more of their time in the city of Rannor Tarul, mingling with, and exchanging shifts with some of the Zemoks. Some of them spend a certain amount of time on Skellunda. You will know that the Zemoi who police it are drawn from many warhalls. As with the Bone Watch.'

'I imagine that Uldenzar moves his Zemoks and Zemoi around to keep them fresh. Being stationed at a warhall is particularly boring, especially away from the Warhive.'

'All Uldenzar's staff who were stationed at the Bone Watch at the time of your last visit have been replaced with a new shift, Zaru.'

'Where did they go?'

'I do not have individual details, Zaru,' said Quenzol, swallowing. 'But as far as can be seen, they came back to the Warhive.'

'To Zuldamar's warhalls?'

'About half, Zaru. The rest are stationed with Uldenzar's main force of Zemoks in his central barracks. I understand, Zaru, that a significant number of them are to be transferred to one of the outer worlds of the cycle.'

Auganzar nodded slowly. 'Nyandersul, yes. Zuldamar and a number of the Garazenda are preparing a large force to begin the rebuilding of the cities there. Zemoks are used as labourers. But such duties have to be performed.'

Quenzol waited.

'Then any Zemoks who were at the Bone Watch when I was there and who serve Uldenzar are to be scattered to the deeps of the world cycle. We could spend several lifetimes searching for them.'

'I do have word of the Zolutar, Zaru.'

'Vulporzol?'

161

'Yes, Zaru. I have spoken to our own Zolutars at the Bone Watch. They said that Vulporzol kept very much to himself but that he was clearly Uldenzar's servant. A number of attempts were made to ascertain his thinking about Eannor, the gates, and such things. But he would say little. It was he, Zaru, who raised the night alarm while you were on Eannor.'

Auganzar had guessed as much, but he nodded patiently. 'There was a hunt, with a number of Zolutars and Zemoks involved. But it revealed nothing.'

'And Vulporzol?'

'As with the Zemoks, he was moved shortly after the incident. It was said that Vulporzol had blundered and was accordingly relieved of the responsibility of being at the Bone Watch.'

Auganzar smiled grimly. 'Uldenzar is no fool. I admire his nerve in this matter.'

'Vulporzol came to the Warhive, Zaru. I am trying to have him traced, but I am fairly sure he would be found at Uldenzar's central barracks.'

'Yes, I suspect that is the case. Very well, you've done a fine job, Quenzol. Continue your search, and as ever, be discreet.'

'Zaru.' Quenzol bowed, turning to leave.

'If the Zemaal is outside, send him in.' Auganzar sat back, studying the ceiling for a moment. The control of troop movements had eased up significantly in the last few months. As had the movement of *moillum*. Now that Eannor had again become a centre for the schooling of the gladiators, it was impossible to expect a mere handful of Openers to conduct all movement between Eannor and the other worlds. The Garazenda had debated for a long time on this issue but in the end they were forced to admit that if the scheme for the development of *moillum* was to work as it should, more designated Openers would have to be used. It was this relaxing of the rules that had enabled Uldenzar to move his troops so easily, and legitimately. But where was the Man? And what did he want? That remained the key question.

Auganzar's reflections were cut short by the arrival of Zuarzaal, who was dressed in light mail and not the armour he wore when working with the tigerhounds.

162

'You'll be glad to know that I have more work for you, Zuarzaal.' He knew that the Zemaal had not been pleased at having been pulled off Eannor with the trail so fresh. But Auganzar had known what that outcome would be.

'They tried Rannor Tarul, Zaru,' said the Zemaal. 'But as they feared, it was impossible. So many scents, old trails, new ones − '

'The Man is not there.'

'He may be, Zaru. But not yet found. Zaru, there is something else Guntrazaal has learned.'

'Yes?'

'Uldenzar's warhall. Guntrazaal and the other Zemaal circled its perimeters. There are watches, Zemoi, but with the tigerhounds to alert Guntrazaal, his Zemaal were able to avoid them. They went as close to the warhall as they could. And they found the scent of the Man we are after.'

'He is in the warhall?'

Zuarzaal shook his head. 'Was, Zaru. No longer. Guntrazaal sent one tigerhound in at night. The scent was fresh but if the Man had been in the camp, it would have known.'

'Rannor Tarul would be the obvious alternative. But you've not found him there you say?'

'Your pardon, Zaru. But if the Man was to be hidden in Rannor Tarul, why should he be taken to the warhall first? The *moillum* do not go from the warhall to the city, other than on rare occasions.'

Auganzar's eyes narrowed. 'You have a theory?'

'*Moillum* travel from warhall to warhall, Zaru. The Man may have been brought to the Warhive.'

'To one of Zuldamar's warhalls?'

Zuarzaal shrugged. 'It is possible.'

'Why?'

Again Zuarzaal shrugged. 'Could he be an emissary, Zaru?'

'From the Imperator?'

'I can only guess, Zaru.' Auganzar sat back, silent for a long moment. 'Very well.'

'You have other work for me, Zaru?'

'I do. It will be tedious, Zuarzaal, and it requires even more discretion. And you will need your remarkable beasts.'

163

'A hunt?'

'Here on the Warhive. The Zolutar you scented on Eannor: I think he is here. In one of Uldenzar's camps. Find him. It may take time, but you should be able to eliminate some of the possibilities.'

'If I find him, Zaru?' Zuarzaal leaned forward as though he already had the scent of blood.

'I dare not touch him. He is Zuldamar's. Any move I make against the Marozul will be held against me. Just as he dare not move against me openly. We conduct a combat of shadows. But if you find this Vulporzol, track him. Follow him everywhere. He will lead us to the Man, even if it is only a name he gives us. But the Man must be found. He is the key to Innasmorn.'

'I begin at once, Zaru.'

'It will greatly aid your work, Zuarzaal, if you operate from now on with the freedom accorded a Zolutar.'

Zuarzaal stiffened, as alert and as taut as one of the beasts he commanded. But he smiled faintly, his pride betraying him. Auganzar gave him the twin swords that he had prepared. 'I have already recorded it in my lists. You are now Zuarzol.'

Uldenzar sat in the tiered seats quietly, watching the ferocious battle that was taking place down on the sands below. The *moillum* at this warhall, Zuldamar's finest, were certainly of exceptional calibre. They seemed to have put the wars behind them, able to go at their new tasks with a fresh will. It seemed certain that the coming Testament would rival any that had been held before. He glanced up to see a figure coming down the steep steps towards him, bright cloak flapping behind it in the breeze. A number of Zemoks hovered close at hand. Members of the audience, which included Zemoks and other Csendook who worked in the warhall, stood and saluted. It was Zuldamar.

He took a seat beside his Zarull with a brief nod. 'Fine warriors, these *moillum*,' he commented.

'They'll be a test for our Man.'

'He has agreed?'

'He had no choice, Marozul.'

'You think he will only do as asked as long as it suits him?'

'I cannot be sure of him yet.'

'Perhaps if we locate the woman. Do you think she is the only reason he came here?'

'Again, Marozul, it seems strange. But he is insistent.'

'Where is he now?'

'He has been transferred from Dacramal's warhall to Skellunda. It is a harsh place but his progress will be monitored.'

'If he survives that, he will be a worthy candidate for the Testament. We have chosen a hazardous path for him.'

'He won't be found, Marozul. By the time we bring him to the Warhive, he will have a new identity. He will be absorbed into a company such as that which you see below you.'

'He impresses you as a warrior?'

Uldenzar nodded. 'He was unlucky not to get the better of one of my finest Zemoi. He has fought at the highest level. Skellunda will complete his training. Those bastards will test him, if they don't kill him. But he is formidable.'

'Such a Man,' said Zuldamar, 'would be a dangerous opponent if he ever found himself in a position where he could control an army, as he must once have done. An army that might oppose us. Don't you think?'

Uldenzar considered this in silence for a while. Then he nodded. 'If it came to that, Marozul, yes. Though if Auganzar is to be assassinated, such a unit as we think necessary will need a Man like this one.'

Zuldamar watched the fighting, nodding as he followed the exchanges of blows. 'We will see.'

SKELLUNDA

When Pyramors first saw the plateau where the warhall for the recalcitrant *moillum* had been carved out of the naked rock, he knew that it had been well sited. The Csendook were determined to separate those who would not capitulate and ensure their confinement. They could hardly have chosen a better location. The plateau itself, a dark grey chunk of an island, a seared and lifeless igneous rock, thrust up out of the sea in defiance of the elements. The shores were dangerous: those on the south side of the island faced the full blast of the winds as they tore in from the open ocean, while those that did not were rugged cliffs, plunging down to broken splinters of rock where the swirling tides and currents crashed endlessly against the stone. Twenty miles from the coast, Skellunda was a bleak, merciless prison.

The ship that ferried Pyramors and a handful of other *moillum* across the heaving waters visited the island once a month, taking across supplies. Nothing was grown or made on the island, and apart from a few gnarled shrubs and the hardiest of grass, nothing grew there.

Pyramors and the others, all of them chained during the crossing, had been brought up on to the deck to be given their first view of Skellunda. Several Zemoi were on deck, all armed, though none of the prisoners had any intention of attempting flight. They were all seasoned warriors and they were far too aware of the odds against survival in these seas. The chains made individual action impossible.

Vulporzol, the Csendook who had been given charge of the prisoners, pointed to the rock that now towered up over the craft. When he spoke, it was with the deep, guttural voice of the Csendook, the accent distorting the words as all Csendook did, but Pyramors could tell that this warrior was used to human speech and had mastered it better than most.

How many men had he delivered to this prison? Pyramors knew also that Vulporzol was the agent of the Csendook who had bargained with him, the one who would watch over him, bring him any secret instructions as this strange plot developed.

'Skellunda,' said Vulporzol. 'Never used by the people of Eannor until the Csendook came here. We saw its potential at once, and it has become an effective prison.'

Pyramors wondered if the Csendook intended to bait the men, to attempt to undermine their spirits, though he thought it unlikely. These men were hardened to war: Pyramors had exchanged a few brief words with them, but he recognised the types and their stubborn wills. They would die before they would be broken. Vulporzol would know that. He himself was a shrewd warrior and would understand the nature of his prisoners. Taunts and jibes would be far beneath his dignity, his code.

'A challenge, perhaps,' Vulporzol went on. 'You see its cliffs.' He pointed to them again, casually. 'I would not say no Man has ever scaled them, or that no Man has ever taken to the sea and found a way to the mainland. Those of you who decide to try this for yourself will not find the cliffs guarded. I merely point out the impracticalities of such a venture.

'You are here to train. To forget your differences with my race. There are a number of choices open to you. Capitulate, and join the *moillum* you have left. Train here on Skellunda, and spend the rest of your lives here in isolation. Or attempt escape. You will not be forced into any of these choices. Men have died trying to get off Skellunda. If any have ever succeeded in escaping, we do not know of them.'

Pyramors knew what would be going through the minds of his fellows. If the Csendook had taunted them, they would have strengthened any resolve to escape. But by telling them they were welcome to pit themselves against the cliffs and the sea, without hindrance from the Zemoi, Vulporzol was eroding their spirit far more subtly.

The ship docked at a lone jetty, a finger of stone that swung out from the shore, curving around to a cleft in the

167

cliff face. Vulporzol was met by a party of Zemoi on the jetty and the entire company went along the quay and into the cleft, the sound of waves beating against the rocks drowning out thought as well as speech. A thick wooden portal sealed the cleft behind them, and beyond was another. Neither of these doors could be broken down, Pyramors mused. Even a strong company of Men could not make an escape this way. The cliffs offered more hope of that. But he did not contemplate escape for more than a few moments. There would be other things for him to do here.

They climbed in silence, winding up through the guts of the rock, emerging high up on the plateau, in an area that was walled in like a dead volcanic cone, the grim, forbidding place of stones that was the heart of the prison. It could hardly be called a warhall. There was a central plaza, forty yards across, roughly semi-circular and its walls rose up almost sheer to a series of balconies. Above these were what appeared to be regimented caves, or cells, and Pyramors understood that this would be the accommodation of the *moillum*. Again the cliffs rose smoothly above these cells to a last balcony near their rim – there would be other buildings there, the homes of the Zemoi, watchtowers, armouries.

Vulporzol addressed the prisoners for the last time. There were others up on the balconies, watching with seeming indifference, but there were none in the arena, none training.

'This is your new home. Make of it what you will. There are Zemoi above you. You will sometimes meet them and be given instructions by them. It will be better for you if you obey them. Rebel against them, harm any of them, and you will be executed,' said Vulporzol flatly but with complete conviction. No one doubted his words. He glanced very briefly at Pyramors, turned on his heel and left the plaza. After he had gone, two of the Zemoi that had accompanied the prisoners from below undid their chains, removing them, while the others stood in silence, swords unsheathed, watching. The chains were taken away and a moment later the Zemoi left without another word.

There were calls from above as the prisoners looked about

them, unsure of what they should do next. 'Welcome to Paradise Island!' someone called, a burly man who leaned over a parapet and showed his broken teeth in a hideous grin that brought smiles to some of the prisoners' faces.

'You'll need to rid yourself of that fat if you want to keep up with us here, you scum!' another man shouted, laughing.

The newly arrived warriors were visibly fit, all as tightly muscled as Pyramors, and although they smiled at the jibe, they knew that any training they undertook here would be far more rigorous than any previous training they had known.

'Get back to your troughs, offal eaters!' boomed a voice from the edge of the plaza. A huge warrior had arrived, his black beard almost obscuring his face, his arms and chest matted with hair, his arms like the arms of a great bear. He gazed at the new arrivals as he approached them as though singling out someone for a brawl; as he neared them he crushed his knuckles together like stone, grinding his joints. There were a few jeers from above but the huge man ignored them, his eyes gleaming.

He stood very still, legs apart, fists on his hips. Pyramors would have grinned, for this was not the stance of a general, yet this warrior seemed to have assumed such a role for himself. It was more the stance of a bully, a strong, violent man, mocking all-comers, but whose brain is small, his wits less able than his muscles. But this was Skellunda, and no man would have survived here if he had relied on strength alone. There would be far more to this fellow than met the eye.

'I am Kajello,' he growled. 'Never mind what I once did, who I served, who I've killed. On Skellunda you'd do well to forget all that. Here you're just a name. There are few laws here: we're the lawless, the misfits. No one wants us, not even our own kind. We make too much trouble for them. The Csendook don't trouble us. But they want us. Every now and then someone has a gutful of this stinking rock and goes with them, back to the *moillum*. One of their new toys. Well, piss on them.

'No one rules here. We don't have anything to do with Csendook. We don't work for the bastards, we don't pick quarrels with them, and we don't think about killing them. Hear that? We don't even think it. If you do, then it's a short trip to madness. If you want to keep your mind in one piece on Skellunda, you work at it, hard. Training, using yourself. If you stay fit, you stay alert and you hold on to your self respect. You stay a man. And you resist what they want, warriors for their amusement.'

'What about escape?' someone said.

Kajello swung round to stare at him, his eyes blazing, though not with anger. 'You can try it, any time. There'll be plenty of opportunities. You can die on the cliffs, or below them. You can die in the sea. You can die of exposure. There are a hundred ways to die. Choose your own. But if you want to attempt escape, don't try and involve anyone else. Escaping is like trying to kill Csendook. It's out of reach. But you're new. So try it. No one will stop you.'

He walked up and down the men, punching his fist into his palm as he spoke. 'One thing you don't do while you're here.' He stopped and looked directly at them. 'You don't talk about the Empire. About the Imperator. He left us to rot. Him and his Consulate. They used us as fodder to cover their backs while they scuttled off. The Csendook reckon they're dead. To us they're worse than that. They never existed. Anyone here wants to talk about a revival, or a glorious return to the days of Empire, returning the Imperator to his throne, had better keep his mouth shut. There are a lot of men on this island who would rip the guts out of anyone who tried that.'

Pyramors looked into the bright eyes, reading the power in the man, the bottled fury. 'That's a lot of rules for a place without laws,' he said.

Kajello scowled at him as though about to swing a blow. 'You want to survive, son, you think about it. What's your name?'

'Pyras.'

Kajello's frown deepened. 'I want to talk to you.' He turned, waving others to him. In spite of his address, he seemed to exercise a degree of control. 'Show them to

170

their cells. Get them something to eat.' He turned back to Pyramors. 'They told me about you.'

'Who did?'

'Never mind. I like to know what's going on on this rock. Part of surviving.' He waited as the other prisoners left with their guides. When he was alone with Pyramors, he spoke again. 'You come here with a reputation.'

Pyramors shrugged. 'I don't imagine anyone comes to Skellunda without one.'

'None of us took to being *moillum*. We all hate Csendook. But we don't let it rule us. You need to understand that, son.'

'To survive?'

'That's right.'

'And beyond Skellunda?'

'Nothing exists beyond Skellunda. This is your world now. Cruel and cold. Think of it and nothing else. You're a trouble-maker, a Csendook hater. We all are. But we don't waste energy on that any more. Burn your hate up. Hate the rock. Hate each other. *Fight* each other – '

'Each other?' said Pyramors, surprised.

'It happens. Does the men good. But we don't waste energy running down blind alleys. So sometimes we take it out on each other. Take it out on me if you want to try.' He gestured to the heights, the unseen Zemoi. 'They don't say much, our captors. But they hate it. Sometimes they pull one of us out. But not many. We thrive on their frustration. I suggest you do too.'

Pyramors nodded. 'Who told you about me?' he said softly.

Kajello's eyes narrowed. 'Forget it.' He turned away. 'You'll have a cell. Eat and sleep. Tomorrow you start. And it'll hurt.'

Alone in his cell, a simple, bare rock cave scooped out of the cliff face above the plaza, Pyramors relaxed. He thought over the suggested plan that had been devised for him by the Csendook, Uldenzar, and the strange Keeper of Eannor, Cmizen. Pyramors knew he had to build a team, committed to the assassination of Auganzar. Beginning here, in a place where any kind of resistance to the Csendook was seen as wasteful. And yet he knew that if he were to create a team capable of what he intended, he would need to draw it from the men of Skellunda. Instinct alone told him they were the perfect material. They could be the elite, warriors who could be turned into the only weapon that would stand any chance of penetrating the elaborate defence of the Supreme Sanguinary.

The shadows lengthened outside as the sun began to drop beyond the rim of the upper plateau. There was a cough outside the cell entrance, a deliberate sound. Pyramors was alert at once, sitting up. He could discern two figures. 'Pyras,' called an unfamiliar voice.

'What is it?'

The two figures ducked under the low entrance and leaned against the door, one either side. 'We heard a few things about you,' said one of them, a lean fellow, whose arms were badly scarred. A swordsman, Pyramors decided. But there would be little or no opportunity to use a sword on Skellunda. The other warrior was shorter and stockier, his own muscles tightly banded, weatherbeaten and hard. They were like animals, creatures of the rock. They would be dangerous opponents.

'Such as?' said Pyramors. He did not get up, but he tensed himself in readiness in case they intended to attack him, test him.

'You fought a Csendook Zemoi.'

'I've fought a lot of Csendook. And some I've killed.'

'But not in an arena,' growled the burlier of the men. 'No one kills a Csendook in the arena.'

'There's a first time for everything.'

The two warriors exchanged glances. 'You think that?' said the thin one. 'Maybe you didn't hear what Kajello said?'

'There's nothing wrong with my ears.'

'Good. Then you'll hear us now.'

'Go on.'

172

'You aren't going to lead a rebellion here,' said the burlier one. 'It's been tried. A lot of men have been killed. A waste.'

Pyramors said nothing, but got steadily to his feet. His head almost reached the low ceiling of the cell.

'We mean it,' said the thin one. He nodded to his companion and they came further into the cell.

Pyramors understood their intention. A lesson. They had chosen the cell, not so much for privacy, but because they knew it would restrict his chances of defending himself. They would crowd him. And they would be good. If Kajello had sent them, he would have picked the best.

Pyramors said no more. There was to be no avoiding this fight. He was rested but not as sharp as he would like to have been after the rough crossing on the ship. It would have to be quick, and with these two that would not be easy. He read their attack plan soon enough. The burlier one was the bait, to draw him, while the thin one, who would be slightly quicker, would deliver the blows. Just a lesson. Maybe a broken bone? Not a killing. Nor permanent damage. Discipline. The law of lawless Skellunda.

The burly one made his first play and Pyramors deflected it but kept his attention on the thinner one, who was about to strike but realised his victim had not been fooled, so held off. He would be cautious, Pyramors saw. These men were veterans of many such fights, well synchronised.

Another attack came, on his left, and he had to swing round to block it, his arms moving quickly, chopping at the punches. The thin one darted in like a viper, but his punch only grazed the top of Pyramors's head. He also took a kick on the knee, bending to absorb the strike, dancing back out of range. But he was being backed into a corner. Carefully he moved around the wall of the cell, knowing that they would suspect him of trying to get to the door. He let them think this.

Deftly they manoeuvred for another strike, basing it on the assumption that he would dash for the door if he got an opportunity to flee. They feinted a double move to his right, away from the door, and he knew that if he defended and made for the door, they would pivot and drive into him. For a second he let them believe they had him, but as they attacked, he took three quick steps away from the door. The lunge of the burly one was a shade too late: Pyramors ducked the punch of the thin one, striking upward with his balled fist. It smacked into the naked flesh of the man's belly, hard as a rock, but the blow hurt and the thin man doubled automatically. Pyramors slipped past him and brought his heel up under the man's nose. Blood spurted as the man flung upward, impeding the other.

Pyramors had won the advantage and followed up swiftly, rushing straight at the burly one. He was ready, arms closing round Pyramors and lifting him from the ground, but Pyramors rammed his head into the man's face, cracking his cheek. He was released, but did not pull back, not allowing the man to recover. He stabbed out at the damaged eye, again feeling flesh under his fist. It was a brutal attack, merciless and designed to immobilise. But Pyramors was in no position to compromise.

The thin warrior was coming at him again, blood drenching his chest, shaking his head to clear it of the pain that would be shooting through it. Pyramors backed off through the door, mindful of the balcony and the chance of a third assailant taking him from behind. But it looked clear. The bloody warrior came after him, pride driving him, and again he tried to deliver punches. But without the burly one to help him, his strategy was undone. Again Pyramors caught him with his fist, just below the heart. The man gasped, dropping to one knee, unable to rise for a moment. His companion stood behind him in the doorway, one eye badly bruised.

For a moment they studied each other, but then Pyramors leapt over the thin warrior, dropping into a crouch, a move which again took his opponent by surprise and forced him back against the stone of the doorway. Pyramors sprung up and to one side, lashing out at the man's knee, striking the joint with his heel. The man staggered, groaning, and his hands caught at the balcony. He tried to turn, as if expecting another attack, though Pyramors waited. But as the man swung round, his knee failed him and he fell back. With a grunt of surprise, he was over the balcony, tumbling to the plaza.

Pyramors rushed to the edge but he could see the dark shadow on the stone floor of the plaza below. The man would not have survived such a fall. Around the balconies, heads were beginning to appear. But no one called out, or even spoke.

Pyramors turned back to the thin warrior. He had slumped down, back against the rock. He had lost a lot of blood, his nose ruined. As Pyramors stood up, he cursed himself inwardly. Was this how it ended? Man scrambling in the dust of a remote rock, killing with bare hands? They had brought out of Pyramors the killing drive, the animal fury, reduced him to a barbarian, him, who was supposedly a lord among Men. How easily it comes to me, he thought. How readily murder springs to my hands.

Behind him he heard the growl of the huge warrior, Kajello. 'Is he alive?'

Pyramors faced him, though there was little emotion in the huge face. He gestured vaguely.

Kajello glanced over the balcony to where one of the Zemoi was examining the fallen warrior. Moments later the body was dragged away like a sack.

'You sent them,' said Pyramors.

Kajello was studying him. 'You are a rare warrior. Who were you with?'

Pyramors shook his head. 'On Skellunda, the past is dead. Never mind who I was with, or who I am.' He was conscious that a few other warriors were within earshot.

'Killing each other is one thing,' said Kajello through his teeth. 'But we do not kill Csendook. We do *not* give them the pleasure of humiliating us. Neither here, nor in any other arena.'

'I have not stated my intention to attempt to kill Csendook,' said Pyramors, puzzled. 'Why do you assume I will try?'

'It's why they send us here,' Kajello snorted. 'All of us have spurned the *moillum* warhalls! Their authority. But if we are to go on spitting in the face of Csendook authority, we must be *effective*. If we attack them uselessly and without success, we become pathetic, a mockery. Even the traitorous *moillum* will count above us. Since we cannot be effective, we close out all thoughts of making fools of ourselves.'

'Then in what way do you rebel?' said Pyramors quietly.

Kajello stiffened. 'We show them that there are no better warriors among the ranks of men. That even if they train their *moillum* to be their slaves, superb warriors, they can never surpass us. They cannot defeat us, nor change us. Just as we cannot overcome the Csendook.'

Other warriors were stepping out on to the balcony. One of them pushed past Pyramors, who made no attempt to resist him, and bent down to the thin warrior.

'He's dead.'

'Have both of them taken to the cliffs,' said Kajello. 'We'll give them to the sea and salute them.'

The dead man was carried away. Kajello stood beside Pyramors, looking out over the plaza. There would be no more conflict tonight. 'They were exceptional men,' Kajello breathed.

'You are a warrior,' Pyramors told him. 'There is always the chance of death. Each time we fight, we know that.'

'They did not come here to kill you.'

'Yet they would have done so, had they known it would be the only way to better me. I defended myself, no more.' But as he said it, he wondered if it was the truth.

'Yes, and your principles.'

Pyramors frowned. Kajello was not so dull witted. 'What do you mean?'

The huge man drew in a breath, still studying the plaza. 'What do you want? What do you intend?'

'You think I want rebellion? Here on Skellunda?'

Again Kajello was thoughtful for a while. 'Were you a general? You fight like one. I am sure you must have held a very high office.'

'Who told you such a thing?'

'No one told me,' Kajello hissed. 'Your skill proclaims it.'

'Then I must hide it from the Csendook.' Pyramors looked about him but none of the Csendook seemed to have any interest in the squabble.

'Listen,' Kajello told him. 'Neither I nor the others will respect your old rank, whatever you were. The war is over. We wage a different war here — '

'So do I, Kajello.'

'Then what is it you want?'

'The Csendook on Skellunda are of no interest to me. Neither are the Csendook on Eannor.'

'But you'll never leave Skellunda. Rebellion is futile.'

'There is a way to leave Skellunda.'

Kajello glowered at him. 'As one of their accursed tools? A *moillum*, ready for the Testaments?'

'What is the highest prize the *moillum* can attain?'

Kajello spat. 'No one on this island gives a shit for *prizes*. Slavery is slavery. You can have it, but if you think you can coerce the men of this hell, you'll find us united against you.'

'The ultimate prize,' said Pyramors, ignoring Kajello's seething rage, 'is a place in the elite corps of the Supreme Sanguinary.' He spoke slowly and very quietly. 'Not as his personal bodyguard but as part of his select team. Controlled by his Zemoks, his Thousand.'

'I warn you,' said Kajello through his teeth, 'if you say any more about this to anyone here, I'll have you finished.'

Pyramors was no more than inches from him. 'Part of his team, close to his own Zemoks. Close enough, perhaps, to reach out and touch him, even if it is only once.'

Kajello locked stares with him for a moment, but eventually looked away from those steely, resolute eyes. He muttered something, and Pyramors barely caught the single word.

'Madness,' the big man breathed.

14

THE ENGINEER

They trained hard, as though making the final rigorous
preparations for war, as though each morning they would
be going out on to a field of battle. Pyramors drove himself
as hard as any of them, knowing that if the assassination
plot was to succeed, he must tune himself to absolute fitness,
sharpening his speed, his responses. There were many
bouts in the plaza, both without weapons and with, for
the Csendook allowed their prisoners to train with swords,
pikes and any other weapons they called for. Each evening
these were retrieved, and there was never any argument;
no one secreted a knife or tried to hide away a weapon.
Those who had come to Skellunda with Pyramors quickly
settled into its tough routines: the things they were told by
Kajello and others like him seemed to satisfy them. They
used their exertions to defy any attempts to suborn them.
There were, as promised, many opportunities for the men
to attempt escape from Skellunda, but no one showed any
real inclination to try. Without a craft of some kind, crossing
the seas would be unthinkable. Pyramors studied the terrain
of the island, for there were daily races over its peaks and
rugged valleys, but he could see it had been well chosen. It
had become a self enclosed world.

As the days wore on, Pyramors began to weigh up the
men around him. Without exception they were superlative
warriors, and they had in them a hard, stubborn streak
which had brought them here, a dogged defiance that would
never permit them to compromise with the Csendook. The
word was that a few of them had, succumbing to bribes,
promises of riches, or of power, or other things. The
Csendook sometimes took men aside to some private hall
and coerced them, usually without success. Pyramors knew
that the men here suspected that he would be one of those

178

who succumbed. He wondered what Kajello had told them, or what the huge man actually knew.

Since the death of the two men who had attacked him Pyramors was left very much alone, although during training he was fully tested as a number of the warriors wanted to see just how good he was. But he was careful not to wound any of them, a policy that almost earned him a serious wound. Even so, no one doubted his skill and speed, both of which were even more heightened by the strenuous programme of training. He drove himself almost as mercilessly as the other prisoners.

He knew that Vulporzol, the Csendook who had brought him here and who had evidently been given a specific responsibility to look after him, had returned to the mainland of Eannor, but there were key words he could speak to the Zemoi if he wanted to call upon him. Otherwise he was expected to be here for a number of months, readying himself. It was an ambitious plan, one that could collapse for any number of reasons, but Pyramors had reasoned that if he could not survive the hell of Skellunda, he would never have the skill to pull the plot off anyway.

Many times he thought of Jannovar, wondering if the Csendook were searching for her as they had promised. There were questions he would have asked of the men around him but he was too cautious. One evening, however, an opportunity presented itself.

A group of the men were stretched out on a ledge over the sea, having spent the afternoon testing themselves against the crags. It was dangerous, unnerving work, but they had enjoyed it, forgetting their imprisonment in the thrill of the climb. Now they were resting, finishing the meat and water they had brought with them before setting out along the coastal path that would take them back to the fortress. There were a few Zemoi high on the rocks above but they would not come down. They were quite content to let the men work out their own training and rarely interfered.

One of the men, Bantol, slapped his thigh, laughing softly. 'Once I've scrubbed this sweat off me, I've a mind to enjoy the pleasures of the lower caverns tonight.'

Another of the men, Garrack, nudged him to silence, indicating Pyramors, who sat at the edge of the group. This group of men had all been on Skellunda since its first use by the Csendook, Pyramors being the only one of the latest arrivals to be sent with them today.

'Of course,' grunted Bantol, nodding at Pyramors, 'Pyras hasn't been here long enough to taste such things.'

Pyramors was curious, but waited.

'Perhaps it hasn't got to him yet,' grunted another of the men, wiping grease from his lips with the back of his hand.

Bantol laughed softly again. 'No? It gets to us all in time. How about you, Pyras? You train hard, you push yourself to the edge. A man like you should relax, no?'

Pyramors met his gaze, shrugging. 'Relaxing is part of good training.'

'Stretching out on a rock with the evening sun falling away into the sea is one way of relaxing,' Bantol said, winking at his companions. 'But there are more interesting ways.' He guffawed suddenly as if he had said something hilarious.

Pyramors felt himself tensing. He could guess what was meant. Such things happened among men who were too long confined with one another. 'Perhaps you'll tell me about these ways,' he said, his gaze still level.

Bantol looked to the heavens, face beaming with genuine amusement.

'Depends on your taste,' said Garrack, who had decided to join the conversation as Bantol would clearly not be silenced.

'In what?'

'Why, in flesh!' Bantol laughed.

Pyramors knew they were all watching him, most of them with foolish grins on their faces. Was this a test? A search for weakness in him?

'Were you married?' said Bantol. 'Come, come, we do not discuss our past, we know that. But some things are better said. Were you married?'

Pyramors shook his head. 'I had aspirations.'

Bantol stared at him for a moment, but then threw back his head and laughed again so that the sound must have carried up to the Zemoi on high watch. 'Aspirations! I like that! And who has not had aspirations!'

'A woman?' said Garrack. Pyramors nodded, though he did not smile.

'Well, that's a mercy,' snorted Bantol. 'On Skellunda, men develop strange tastes, or as you aptly put it, Pyras, aspirations. In this group we all aspire to one thing, the embrace of a woman. Unless any of these dogs are keeping something from me,' he added. Again he laughed, and the others joined in.

Pyramors nodded slowly, his sternness fading. 'It is not easy to keep such things out of one's mind.'

Garrack chuckled. 'You have a discreet way with words.'

Bantol stood up, stretching his arms, yawning. On the cliff face, he had been like a fly, and utterly without fear. 'Our captors are a wily race. They understand perfectly the lusts and desires of man. They miss nothing. They use every opening presented to them.'

'Seduction?' said Pyramors.

'Yes, just as the *moillum* have their women, so do we. The Csendook see it as a potential control. In the past some of our number have given in completely to it, like men too fond of wine, a slave to it. Some men are slave to their lusts, is it not so?'

'I have seen it happen,' agreed Pyramors.

'We can have anything we desire on Skellunda,' Bantol went on. 'The Csendook think they can win each of us over in time.'

'And will they?'

They all watched Pyramors, wishing they could read his thoughts, but he was man who gave so little away.

'We must let the Csendook think it,' said Garrack.

'Yes,' laughed Bantol. 'Otherwise they'll cut short our provisions!' Garrack turned again to Pyramors. 'What would you desire most?'

'As I said, there was once someone – '

Bantol held up a hand, shaking his head. 'Better forget

181

her, Pyras. There's no saying where anyone is, who's alive and who's dead. Or worse, enslaved in some hole. If it's a woman you want, a woman it shall be, if the Csendook so approve. But you might have to share her. And she might not be the same one next time!'

'Such things do not matter, not after you have been on Skellunda for a long watch,' said Garrack.

'Better to keep the names of past wives or lovers to oneself,' added Bantol. 'If the Csendook learn of such things, they'll use them against you. I told you, they'll use any weapon.'

Pyramors nodded slowly.

'So I'm for the caverns tonight,' said Bantol. 'I shall convince our masters that I am on the point of breaking down, throwing myself on their mercy – '

'I'm sure your deceit will blind them easily,' said Garrack, and the others laughed.

'Not too soon, I hope,' grinned Bantol. 'I'm in need of special attention.' Again the rocks rang to the sound of laughter.

Garrack turned over in the straw of his cell, sleep drawing closer to him. He yawned. The evenings on Skellunda were short, quickly followed by darkness. He was on the point of slipping under the dark blanket when he heard something at the door. He was awake at once, about to lift himself, but a hand closed over his mouth. The grip was very powerful, but it was the speed of the intruder that appalled him. Only a Csendook could have come in here and taken him like this so swiftly.

Yet he found himself looking up into the steely gaze of Pyras.

The latter removed his hand. 'A talk. Privately,' he said. Garrack nodded, sitting, still amazed at the ability of this warrior. What rank had he held before the war ended? Unquestionably it had been high.

'Are any of the men here from Eannor?'

'Some,' whispered Garrack, eyes narrowing. 'Why?'

'I was here before the Imperator Elect's attempted flight. Never mind what I did. But I want to know about those who survived the assaults of the Swarms.'

Garrack snorted. 'That's simple enough. Many men died, others ended up in warhalls. A few, like us, came here. You know all this – '

'The women?'

'Those who survived were enslaved.'

'Which men here were on Eannor? From Rannor Tarul?'

A look crossed Garrack's face and Pyramors noticed at once. He gripped Garrack's arm.

'The past is better left alone, as Kajello says – '

'You were from Rannor Tarul?'

Garrack looked away. 'What use is it to know such things?' But Pyramors would not let it drop. 'Tell me!' he hissed.

Garrack seemed about to resist, to spit out his anger at this intrusion on his privacy, but he became very still. He was no smaller than Pyramors, his skill in the arena recognised, but he wanted no fight here. 'Why are you here?' he said softly. 'What do you hope to achieve?'

'There are things I must know. Tell me and I will leave you in peace. This will be between us and no other.'

The insistence in the eyes of the warrior made Garrack flinch. He knew that if he chose to, Pyras could find a way of killing him, or tormenting him. Already he had killed with apparent ease. Perhaps it would be better to speak and be done with it. 'What must you know?'

'You were from Rannor Tarul?'

Garrack nodded.

'As what?'

'I was – a soldier – '

'No,' said Pyramors, shaking his head. 'You've become one, and a good one. But I've seen the hands of a tradesman. There are scars that can never be hidden. You worked with metal before you held a sword.'

Garrack closed his eyes. He did not want to remember these things. But he nodded. 'You are very perceptive.'

'Where did you work?'

183

'I was an engineer. I had a team of constructors. We worked on parts for gliderboats. There was a lot of research and development going on.' Garrack's face clouded, his eyes searching the darkness of his past. 'When the Swarms came and the war on Eannor raged, we worked through the nights, preparing craft, as we thought, for the war. Zellorian had commissioned Artificer Wyarne to construct as many of the craft as we could.' He faced Pyramors, eyes suddenly sunken into his face. 'I have no wish to speak of those days, Pyras.'

'I, too, was at Rannor Tarul,' said Pyramors. 'For some of the time. It is of the women I would hear. Is it true that some of them were forced to work in the gliderboat pens?'

'Yes. The pressures on us were unbearable. Everyone raced to and fro, working tirelessly, to the point of exhaustion. For the defence of Eannor, they told us. For the protection of the Imperator Elect and his Consulate, in whom we all had faith.' He cursed under his breath. 'But that bastard Zellorian used us. They all did.'

'You think they found a way off Eannor?'

'You were there, you say. What do you think?'

'I was a warrior. I saw action in the city, when the Swarms closed in.' And when Zellorian betrayed you all, and those he sacrificed. Thousands had been left behind to die, or to be enslaved.

'The word was,' went on Garrack, lips pursed as he let the poison of his resentment flow, 'that Zellorian had a secret list. The names of all those who were to go on this so-called exodus.'

'There was a list,' said Pyramors. 'The Consulate made a decision to attempt flight and only a given number could go. The armies and all other defenders were organised to guard the Imperator Elect and the Consulate while the flight was attempted.'

'Then murder may have been done to ensure that people got on that list,' said Garrack. 'Who would not wish to attempt flight, even risk annihilation in the rituals?'

Pyramors nodded. Jannovar had been on that list, as had

184

her husband, Fromhal Djorganist. But neither had made the crossing.

'Those were evil days, those days of siege,' said Garrack, his voice icy. 'We knew the Csendook would crush us eventually. Rannor Tarul could not withstand the combined might of the Swarms. Who knows what black bargains were struck? A man might sell his own brother.'

Pyramors frowned. 'Bargains? With the Csendook?'

Garrack looked at him. 'You must have seen the panic, the wild attempts people made to save themselves. But if you were in the thick of the fighting, perhaps you didn't know what went on.'

'Tell me.'

Garrack rubbed at his eyes, shaking his head. 'Those who did not try to get themselves on to the list sought other ways to spare themselves the uncertainty defeat would bring. You asked about the women – '

'What of them?'

'The Csendook did not want to lose them. When the siege began, they made it clear they would spare the women, imprison them perhaps. There were certain men, unscrupulous, fired by greed, who worked for the Csendook, their agents. I saw one of them at work. Crasnow, he was called. He promised us freedom, safety, if we helped him. Some of the men were for strangling him with his own guts but others listened to his promises.'

'And what did he promise you?'

Garrack's face twisted with bitterness. 'It's easy to pour scorn on such things now. You think I haven't looked back a thousand times on those days?'

'We all had to survive.'

'Maybe. Or maybe we should have died with all the others. I took what I could get. Crasnow wanted me to mark certain women for him, women who worked in the pens. They were to be taken to the Csendook after the fighting. Prime slaves, he called them.'

Pyramors drew in his breath, face hidden in the darkness. But Garrack had read the shock. 'Curse me if you wish, Pyras. It bought me my life. It got me out of the pens when they should have been my grave. You asked for the truth. Well, you have it. You understand why Skellunda is no more of a hell for me.'

'How did you mark the women?' said Pyramors, though he knew.

'Crasnow had brought bracelets, made by the Csendook with whom he dealt. I stamped each bracelet with the name of the woman who bore it, using Csendook lettering. Crasnow spoke their tongue almost as well as he spoke his own.'

Pyramors dropped his voice so low that Garrack hardly heard him and had to lean forward to catch the words. 'And do you recall the names of the women you marked for Crasnow?'

The implications of the question were not lost on Garrack. He remembered the conversation on the cliffs after the climbing was done. He sat back, running his hand tiredly through his hair. 'There was nothing else I could do.'

'*Do you recall their names?*' The voice cut into him like a knife.

But Garrack shook his head. 'They were just like numbers to me. The coin with which I bought safety.'

Pyramors fell silent. Jannovar had been taken as a slave. But to where? Garrack would have no idea. 'Is Crasnow still alive?'

'He was well paid by the Csendook. He singled out the women with an expert's eye, like a farmer selecting the best meat. No doubt he is still in the pay of the Csendook.'

'How?'

Garrack shrugged. 'The warhalls have their women. On the Warhive, too. Perhaps Crasnow is there, seeing to his herds. You think of revenge? Of settling a debt with him? But there were others. And there were all those who would have cut their mother's throats to get on Zellorian's list. Will you revenge yourself on them all? Forget it, Pyras. Think of Kajello's words. The past is dead. Let it lie. Skellunda will burn it out of you.'

Pyramors considered his words, silent and still. But when he turned back, his eyes were still filled with questions. 'You say people were removed from the list. How?'

'No one would have been safe, once the word was out,' snorted Garrack. 'I don't suppose even the Consulate felt secure.'

'There was concern among the troops about which of the Consulate should remain to defend Eannor. My brother was with Fromhal's troops. They were alerted for duty with the Imperator Elect. They were all listed for flight. Yet neither Fromhal, his family, nor his warriors left Eannor.'

Garrack snorted. 'Fromhal! That scheming bastard of a Consul! He'd wormed his way up the ladder to power. Yes, they say he was on the list, at the Imperator's command. But Zellorian never supported him. Fromhal had the Imperator's ear, so his place should have been secure.'

'What went wrong?'

'Something to do with the family. His wife. She was having an affair with another of the court officials – '

'How could you know that? Surely such an affair would have been conducted with the utmost discretion – '

'It was. But Fromhal found out about it. He had his entire family secretly thrown out, taken down to the lower city. Their names were taken from the list. Probably someone informed on Fromhal's wife and as a reward the informer gained her place on the list.'

Pyramors pictured the betrayal, the confusion in the days leading up to the crossing.

'Fromhal had his family put where they could do nothing to save themselves. Some of them were sent to the gliderboat pens. In which case no amount of bitter complaint would have done them any good. Artificer Wyarne, who was in control, ignored all protests. He worked for Zellorian, no one else. And if any of Fromhal's family were sent to Wyarne's pens Zellorian would have enjoyed their humiliation. He would have endorsed their disgrace.'

Pyramors nodded. The puzzle was almost complete. So Fromhal had found out about the affair, in spite of all their precautions, just as Zellorian had told him. So close to the exodus, a few more days, and they would have crossed to Innasmorn in safety.

'Fromhal's wife would have had the last laugh,' said Garrack, piercing his thoughts.

'Why is that?'

'Zellorian deliberately gave him a difficult defensive position to occupy before his withdrawal to the final stand and the flight. Fromhal and most of his men – '

Pyramors nodded. 'Yes. I fear my brother was with him. Few of them will have escaped. I have met none of them since.'

Garrack seemed to have believed this deceit. After a momentary silence, he put an arm on Pyramors's. 'I've said all I want to about those days, Pyras. They're forgotten. Don't ask me about them again.'

Pyramors nodded.

'And if there was a woman, let it go. She may well be alive, in some slave pen. There are *moillum* warhalls on several worlds I gather. If you did find her, think of her distress.'

Pyramors straightened. Slowly he rose. 'My thanks, Garrack. I will not speak of these things again.'

'Accept your fate. You belong to Skellunda now.'

But Pyramors had already gone.

Later that night, with darkness smothering the island, two figures met among the rocks above the cells. One of them was the huge warrior, Kajello, the other, Garrack.

'Why is he here?' said the former, though the question seemed rhetorical. 'He implied to me that he wants to find a way to get close to the Supreme Sanguinary. To strike at him.'

'Assassinate him?' breathed Garrack. 'We'd all be glad of that chance. But it would be suicide.'

'This man Pyras is a fanatic, I'm sure of it.'

'How practical is such a plan?'

Kajello shook his huge head. 'One man? Impossible.'

'A team then?'

Kajello's face was invisible, but Garrack could feel the eyes on him as if they would dig into his mind for answers. 'From among *us*?'

'Who better?'

Kajello let out a gust of air. 'The Csendook are too wily. They would never allow us to remain together once we left Skellunda. They'd split us up, no matter how well we pretended to bow to their demands and serve them as *moillum*.'

'But if we won through to the Testaments – '

'Separately? The odds against it would be incredible. It's a fanatic's dream.'

'Or a madman's.'

'No, he's not mad,' said Kajello. 'You say he shows interest in a woman? He did not say who she is?'

'No. But his interest was in the fall of Fromhal Djorganist and his house. Pyras claims to have a brother who served with Fromhal's troops.'

'The Djorganists,' repeated Kajello. 'They were disgraced. Something to do with indiscretions.'

'Fromhal's wife, Jannovar.'

Kajello had gone very still. Abruptly he gripped Garrack's arm and the smaller man winced. 'Fromhal's wife!' Kajello hissed. 'She took a lover. A man who would have been of high rank. A Consul, perhaps. A man who would be a powerful warrior, a man trained in all the fighting arts, master of all of them.' He turned to look down into the darkness below, where the cells studded the cliff like nests. 'A warrior such as Pyras.'

'A Consul? But there was none of that name.'

'No,' said Kajello. 'But there was a Pyramors.'

'Pyramors? But he was with the Imperator Elect, one of the inner Consulate. He would have been on the list – '

'Unless he took himself off it. If he had a particular reason for remaining. A lover, for instance.'

Garrack gasped, the implications at last striking him. 'But of course!'

'Pyras, if that is his name, is as brilliant a thinker as he is a warrior. A Consul? He has that skill.'

'What do we do with him?'

'Whatever his personal ambitions, he was a close servant of the Imperator Elect. As such he is one of those who betrayed us and thousands like us. So we kill him, Garrack. We kill him and feed his heart to the gulls, slice by bloody slice.'

15

BETRAYAL

Pyramors was still uncertain whether or not he had done the right thing in agreeing to come up here to such an exposed place. There was hardly any cover in the burning rocks; the sun blazed mercilessly. Skellunda was an oven during the day. Other warriors moved around him in the rocks but they were silent, travelling upwards with all the stealth and cunning they could utilise. Kajello's plan had, at first, seemed foolish, and not without danger. Pyramors would have politely refused to take part in such an escapade, and his reason told him now that it may have been the best course. But he needed to win the respect of these men, or enough of them to form a core group for his team. It may be that here would be an opportunity to work with them, forging the first link. So he had accepted Kajello's invitation to accompany his group.

They were near the summit of one of the ragged peaks of the island, some five hundred feet above the sea. It was often used as a test of the men's skills in climbing, as it had a number of sheer faces and overhangs. The Csendook rarely visited it, although it was known that they occasionally went up to its peak on sentinel duty.

Kajello had had the routine of the Csendook studied. He knew that today a Csendook was up here, for whatever reason. It would almost certainly be alone but it would expect to be ignored by the men. Men and Zemoi had little to do with one another and there was never any trouble between them. But Kajello's plan was to embarrass the Zemoi. To teach it that his men could surround it, get within feet of it, to a position where they could easily kill it.

Pyramors had asked what the value of such an exercise was. Would it not, he had asked, serve to make the Csendook even more watchful, even more suspicious? Kajello had laughed, agreeing.

'They show us nothing but contempt. They have us imprisoned here, but they feel they have no need to take any notice of us. This will be an exercise in pride, Pyras. If we can humiliate the Csendook in any small way, we will be successful.'

Pyramors understood their pride. Without it, without the spirit that kept them training, driving themselves, these men would wither. And he needed them if he was to have any hope of achieving success in his attempt on Auganzar's life. So he had agreed.

The sun beat down on his bare back, which was already tanned dark, his flesh like polished leather. Like a serpent he writhed up through the rocks, which grew smaller the higher up he moved. The cover thinned and the lone Zemoi was able to look out from his perch and survey the island on all sides as well as see across to the distant mainland. A haze of heat misted the shore and the waters gleamed, as still as ice. Faint sounds drifted up from below, echoing as if from miles away, yet very close, the still air deceiving the ear.

None of the men had brought weapons. They were permitted to use many different kinds but these were issued carefully by the Csendook and were always returned and accounted for. Kajello felt that it would add strength to the assault on the hill if they achieved their aim without weapons. The Zemoi would, naturally, be armed. If they could disarm it, said Kajello, they would have a real cause for celebration. Pyramors cautioned extreme care, but the men of this island understood the dangers well enough.

A few yards further upwards, Pyramors was able to squint through the sunlight and see part of the flat top of the peak. At first he saw only a barren area, fairly open, but nothing more. Then the Zemoi came into view. The warrior was of average Csendook build, a head taller than Kajello, with the typical huge chest and bull-like neck. It had removed its helmet, its hair so short as to be more like a dark down over its skull, and it had loosened its armour. But its sword was in its scabbard at its belt. Pyramors could not imagine a

192

Csendook being careless about a weapon: it was almost fused to it, as vital to it as an organ.

Kajello had said he would wait until he was certain that they had got as close to the Zemoi as they could, ringing it, before closing in. Pyramors had warned him that it would scent them, even though the air was very still. Its eyes would be exceedingly keen; no matter how well they merged with the terrain, it would discover at least one of them. If it was unsure of their behaviour, it would simply call out an alarm. Or, if it had a mind to enjoy a bit of sport itself, it might well let the mock assault continue and welcome a brief contest.

'They don't kill us,' Kajello had said to Pyramors. 'The worst that we are risking is to be laughed at in front of our own kind.'

Pyramors moved on. Those who were in the rocks around him had been selected by Kajello and he had chosen his warriors wisely. Pyramors knew that, had they been in a field of war, he would have been glad to have such veterans serving under him.

A gull gave its plaintive cry no more than a few yards to his left. It was the signal, an excellent mimic.

Rising, but keeping low to the ground, Pyramors slipped forward to the lip of the flat area at the top of the peak. Twenty other men had shown themselves. The peak was ringed successfully. The Zemoi had not raised the alarm. It swung round, eyes blazing angrily.

Kajello stood not ten yards from it, hands on his hips, beard bristling.

The Zemoi swung its blade from the scabbard in one flashing movement and the weapon looked huge as it gleamed. The Zemoi said nothing, studying the men around it. Slowly they closed in, forming a circle. If they were to disarm it, Pyramors knew, they would have to be extremely fast. Why had it not bellowed for assistance?

The circle closed to within ten yards but the men did not look as though they were readying for a combined spring. It would be the only way to wrest the sword from the Zemoi. Any individual heroics would be ludicrous: the

Zemoi would simply chop them all down one by one if given the chance.

Pyramors looked to Kajello, who commanded the attack. This hesitation was dangerous. They should move at once, capitalising on their advantage.

The Csendook abruptly lowered his weapon and drove it, point first, into the ground. It was a measure of the creature's strength that the blade sank deep into it. Pyramors did not show his surprise. The action of the Zemoi was incomprehensible.

'Which of you is the fool?' said the creature, gazing about it at the men with contempt. Its voice was deep and harsh, its command of human speech not good.

Kajello stepped forward. 'Allow me to introduce him,' he said with a grin that betrayed his lack of fear and surprise.

The meeting had been planned, Pyramors guessed. The cautious climb to the peak had been a sham. Kajello was pointing to him. 'This is Pyras,' he told the Zemoi.

Pyramors sensed the men about him. They had moved subtly to ensure that he did not attempt to run back down the slope. This, then, had been a trap for him. Kajello had prepared it.

'Or should I say, Pyramors,' added the huge warrior. 'Former Consul of the Imperator Elect. A worthy opponent, wouldn't you say, Torruzem?'

Pyramors kept his fury as under control as his surprise. How had they learned this? Had someone else betrayed him to Kajello? A dozen possibilities flashed through his mind, but none of them seemed rational.

Torruzem strode forward slowly. His eyes took in Pyramors, weighing him, studying his build, his carriage. He would know a warrior, the signs of his skill.

'A Consul?' echoed the Zemoi. 'A prince among fighting Men. Is this what makes you so arrogant?'

'I should explain,' Kajello told Pyramors, with another grin, though there was another emotion behind his eyes. 'Your boast.'

Pyramors glanced at him, but was himself studying Torruzem more closely. The trap was closing.

'Your boast,' said the Zemoi. 'That you could match a Zemoi for speed. That you could disable a *mere* Zemoi without a weapon.'

Again Pyramors did not react. Most Zemoi would have laughed at such a boast. Torruzem must be particularly stupid if he had been stung to respond to it. If his wits were slower than some of his contemporaries, it might impede his speed. But what was intended here? That he should kill Pyramors? Or maim him, as the men of Kajello had failed to do? But if they knew he was a Consul, they would want him dead. Murder, then. He looked about him. Clearly a fight with the Zemoi, without arms, would be lunacy. He could not survive for long. But all avenues of escape were cut off. The men meant him to see this through. They closed in yet further.

'I shall put this boast to the test,' said Torruzem.

'Before you begin,' Kajello told the Zemoi, 'we want your word that no one will interfere.'

'It's been arranged just as I promised,' grunted Torruzem. 'I told my fellow guards not to come up here for another hour at least. By then this contest will have been long decided.'

'My men will not be implicated?'

Torruzem snorted. 'No. Just the fool.'

Pyramors did not waste words trying to explain to the Zemoi that he had been duped. Instead he began a slow circling. The sweat had broken out on his face, dripping on to his chest. He breathed deeply, preparing himself, knowing that when the attack came it would be terribly fast. The Zemoi meant to use its huge hands to subdue him, probably going for blows to the head and neck, blows that would crush his skull like an eggshell.

Torruzem snarled and struck out, just as quickly as Pyramors had expected but he was ready and swerved away. The men closed ranks, shielding his escape route. But Pyramors knew that if he turned and ran, the Zemoi would be on his back like a lion. Flight meant death.

Kajello bent down and from the corner of his eye, Pyramors saw him lift a small rock. Other men were doing the same, out of view of the Zemoi, who concentrated solely on his opponent. He saw no other danger.

Again Pyramors dodged a lunge but it had been an exploratory one, testing his reflexes. Torruzem would not strike until he was sure of landing a telling blow. His feet were encased in thin armour, and he would use the thick leather sandals as violently and as effectively as a hammer if he got within range of using them. A Zemoi could snap a man's spine with one well-timed drive of its heel.

Pyramors knew that the trial blows of his opponent were coming closer each time and that the twisting and turning of his defence was gradually being confined: he was being set up for the kill, but there was little he could do without complete freedom to move. As Torruzem moved in and then sprung back quickly to avoid an unexpected counter-attack from Pyramors, there was movement behind him. His instincts swung him round to find that two of the men were bearing down on him, striking at him with their jagged stones. Caught off guard, Torruzem ducked, his balance for once unsteady. Kajello moved in and delivered a blow to his arm that snapped bone and the Csendook gasped in agony. Pyramors had no time to think about the sudden twist in his fortune. He leapt up and used his own heel to drive hard into the nose of the Zemoi, shattering it.

Two other men rushed in and brought their stones down on the skull of the Zemoi, the sound of the blows sickening in the still air of the hilltop. Torruzem's legs gave way and he collapsed, his body spasming, blood gushing from his nose. Kajello and his warriors leapt back, forming a circle once more.

Pyramors knew that the Zemoi was dead. His execution had been swift and stunningly efficient. He gazed at Kajello, whose eyes narrowed. 'You told me you did not kill Csendook,' Pyramors said.

Kajello tossed away the stone he had used. 'We don't, Consul. We are a lawless breed but we do have certain codes. And we don't kill Csendook, not here on Skellunda.'

Pyramors almost smiled, but he could still not be sure of these men. 'Why this subterfuge? Why have you killed Torruzem?'

Kajello shook his head. 'We have not.'

Pyramors frowned. They were to blame him for this killing, was that it? But it was foolish. The other Zemoi would not believe such a thing.

'The consequences fall on you alone,' said Kajello. He waved an arm at a number of his men and at once they began melting back among the rocks.

'That's ridiculous,' said Pyramors.

Kajello shook his head. 'Not at all. Torruzem warned his colleagues not to disturb him. He was coming up here alone, to meet a single, boastful prisoner, to fight a duel. No weapons, no spectators.'

'A single warrior, without weapons?' said Pyramors. 'The Csendook would have known that no man could win such a duel.'

'Torruzem was the weakest of them,' Kajello smiled. 'Anxious to prove to his fellows that he was as good as any of them. For a Csendook he was slow. You will have noticed that. And we have made a fool of him before. And you, Pyramors, are a full Consul, as fine and as deadly a warrior as our race have produced. I think the Csendook on this island will find the result credible. You won this contest.'

Pyramors did not argue. It had been cleverly planned. After a moment he said, 'You think they'll kill me.'

Kajello shrugged. 'Probably. They know they will never convert you, fine as you are. Either that or they'll remove you. You have undone anything they might have achieved with us, or so they will think.'

The last of the men had gone, slipping silently away as though nothing had happened. Those who carried bloodied rocks took them with them, flinging them out over the cliff edge into the sea below.

'We could have killed you,' said Kajello. 'It was my first intention, when I guessed who you were – '

'I understand your contempt,' Pyramors told him curtly. 'But there are many things you don't understand.'

'About the betrayal? How you and your bastard Consulate left us and thousands like us to *rot*. To be carved up by the Csendook vermin – '

Pyramors stood very close to the huge warrior, their eyes locking as if they, too, must fight like dogs here on the hilltop. 'I promise you, Kajello, that there will be a reckoning for that act of betrayal. If any of the traitors live, *I will find them.*'

Kajello studied him for a moment, surprised by the intensity in the man's voice. But he snorted derisively. 'And you think you can reach the Supreme Sanguinary? It would take his life to assuage your guilt – '

'If I am guilty, perhaps. But not all the Consulate were loyal to that fool of an Imperator – '

'Pah! It's too late for that now! The Csendook have it all, world upon world.'

'Perhaps not all.'

'If by some miracle the Imperator is alive, the Csendook will find him and raise his head on a pole! You talk of revenge. Well, *Consul*, I wish you luck.' Kajello spat, turning on his heel.

Pyramors would have called him back but he knew that nothing he could say would convince the huge warrior. His mind was fixed, as were the minds of all these wolves of Skellunda. They would never serve him. They were the best chance he had of building a team of assassins, and yet he could never hope to win them. He looked down at the body of Torruzem. The face was contorted in death but it seemed to mock him, silently grinning at his hopelessness.

They came for him in the early evening, just before the sun fell and darkness closed in with its familiar suddenness. He had no way of knowing whether or not Vulporzol had put someone among the Csendook to protect him. He had been told to wait until he was contacted by a nameless Zemoi. He dare not speak to any of them about Vulporzol without compromising whatever plans were in existence.

Two Zemoi snapped commands at him, pushing him out of his cell and along the balcony to stairs that led upward, through steel gates to the balconies that overlooked the cells. Below him, Pyramors could feel the eyes of the warriors.

Kajello would be among them, not gloating, but secure in the knowledge that Pyramors would never be a threat to him here. And in the eyes of the prisoners a blow had been struck, however small, at the ones who had betrayed them.

Pyramors was thrust into a cold stone room, little better than the cell he had become used to. His incarceration lasted for many days, and though his captors fed him, they did not speak to him. He began to console himself with the thought that perhaps they would not kill him. But if they kept him in this cell, nothing he could say or do would further his cause.

He thought of Jannovar often but she seemed far beyond his reach, like someone he had once dreamed of. How foolish it seemed now, this attempt to find her, to avoid the countless traps of a world, a score of worlds, that were in the complete grip of the Csendook. The darkness closed in and he needed the last of his reserves to prevent it from smothering him completely.

When the Zemoi came for him again, he had no way of knowing how long he had been in the cell. He would have guessed that it was a number of weeks. He had been careful to exercise, to eat properly and to use his mind in an attempt to remain as sharp as he could. The long months of training he had had as a youth helped him to sustain his powers. He refused to let the darkness swallow him, blotting out the despair that could so easily have broken him. But it was always close at hand, eager to lure him.

The light confused him, even though it was dim. He was taken into the inner chambers of the Csendook fortress of the island. He hardly had time to assess his whereabouts before he found himself in a huge room, scooped out of the bare rock, but lavishly furnished. There were a number of windows cut into the walls, high up near the roof, and light filtered down dramatically. The room was cool, there were two pools in it, where women sat and Pyramors guessed they were slaves. They did not look at him.

199

Two Csendook were waiting at the centre of the room, sitting on throne-like seats. They had been eating but pushed away their plates, mopping at their mouths as Pyramors was brought before them. One of them stood, saying something Pyramors did not understand to the women. They rose and left immediately. There were no guards in the chamber, and a deep silence fell, as though the rest of Skellunda was as remote from the chamber as the mainland.

The Csendook who had dismissed the women was a Zolutull, and Pyramors assumed him to be the commander of the island. He had never met him before, but he recognised the other figure at once. It was Cmizen, Keeper of Eannor, though he showed more of himself today than he had done on the night of his first meeting with Pyramors in the shadows of Rannor Tarul.

'You know why you are here,' said the Zolutull, his face twisted in an ugly grimace, his seething anger scarcely under control. His voice was oddly pitched for a Csendook, as if he found human speech difficult, and his face was narrow, a scar running over his brow, white in the light of the chamber, a badge of war.

Pyramors looked at him, standing stiffly. He assumed this Zolutull knew nothing of Cmizen's plot.

'Murder,' said the Zolutull, almost spitting the word out. 'Your own kind have condemned you. They found you and the body of the Zemoi, Torruzem. Your own kind! Man is an unworthy animal! Beneath the contempt of the Csendook.'

Cmizen coughed gently. He wore the robes of his rank, no armour, and again Pyramors could see that he did not have the build of a fighting Csendook. He was a little taller than a Man, but his physique was slight compared to that of the Zolutull. Such Csendook did not normally fight among the ranks of the Zemoks or Zemoi.

'I think, Zolutull Karanzol, that we are aware of the position of our erstwhile opponents. Let us dispense with any dispute here. Unless this Man wishes to deny the charge against him?' He raised his thin brows at Pyramors as though he had never set eyes on him before.

200

Pyramors had decided, days before, that he would not implicate Kajello and the others. He understood their hatred of him, their distrust. But they must be protected. He shook his head.

'I would be interested to know how you killed Torruzem,' snapped Karanzol.

'I was fortunate. It was a combination of skill and luck. The sun tricked him, I think,' said Pyramors. 'Though only for an instant.'

Karanzol drew in his breath slowly, his mouth twisting again. He spoke to Cmizen in his own tongue. 'As I thought. Chance.'

'Let us not dwell on the Zemoi's death,' said the Keeper.

'No,' agreed Karanzol. 'I trust we can execute this Man as soon as possible? I have had him in a cell for over a month.' He would have taken Pyramors out and beheaded him in front of the entire island the night of the incident if it had been any other Man, but Karanzol had been given express orders by Vulporzol to isolate him if he gave any trouble. Vulporzol had explained that it was feared that Pyras, as the Man was called, might be a problem, a dissident who would try and unite the prisoners against the Csendook. They were all troublemakers, these Men of Skellunda, but this Man, Vulporzol had said, was utterly uncompromising. And so it had proved.

'Make an example of him?' said Cmizen, showing his uneven teeth. 'So that you would break the spirit of the Men here?' He shook his head. 'On the contrary, it would undo all the work we have done. The Men would make a martyr of him. Perhaps that's what he wanted. Is that so, Pyras?'

Pyramors scowled, feigning agreement.

'Fanatics make the most dangerous opponents of all,' said Cmizen.

'Which is why we should show them no mercy, cut them up before their supporters!' snapped Karanzol.

'Which is why you are the keeper of a rock, Karanzol. And may be so for many years to come.'

Karanzol's eyes widened with fury at the rebuff, but he did not retort.

'Leave me alone with the prisoner,' said Cmizen. 'I will send for you when I've done.'

Karanzol glared at him. 'Is that sensible?'

'He won't harm me,' said Cmizen, with an indifferent wave of his hand. 'He is not that stupid.'

With evident bad grace, Karanzol marched from the chamber, ignoring Pyramors as he passed him, though he made some crude comment as he went through the door and slammed it. Cmizen rose and went to Pyramors. All calmness left him. Suddenly he had become the nervous, pale creature that Pyramors remembered. Deceit and intrigue did not, after all, suit him.

'What really happened here?' he asked.

'It was a trap. Perhaps I should have expected treachery. But I did not know they had uncovered my identity,' Pyramors told him. He explained how the Zemoi, Torruzem, had been duped.

'If the Men of Skellunda know who you are,' said Cmizen, the sweat standing out in tiny beads above his brow, 'do they realise the Imperator Elect is alive? On Innasmorn?'

Pyramors could see how this possibility frightened the Keeper. His own safety would be seriously threatened by such a breach in security. 'No, they don't realise I went with the Imperator. They think I was left behind, as they were. But they hate all of the Consulate. They felt their revenge on me was a fitting one.'

'You must be removed from Eannor at once. I will have Vulporzol take you to the Warhive. To one of Zuldamar's warhalls.'

'The men of Skellunda would have made a team of assassins that would have stood a chance,' said Pyramors, gritting his teeth on his frustration. 'If I could have persuaded them to my thinking — '

'There's no time for that. Skellunda has become too dangerous for you. Besides, there is other news.'

Pyramors frowned. 'News?'

'We think the woman you seek is on the Warhive.'

* * *

After the darkness there was a scarlet light, a whirling chaos of red, pulsing with energies, the life force of the world cycles. Ussemitus felt the shaping of the spectral, part of his mind travelling with it as it breached the boundaries of Innasmorn, spearing beyond on its quest, its remarkable journey.

Monstrous shapes moved within the deep places, the scarlet oceans, but he guided the spectral away from them, concentrating instead on finding a way through other barriers, other living walls of energy that would allow him ingress to worlds that he had previously only imagined. Until at last the spectral slipped out from the chaos into the sunlight of Eannor. Invisibly it began its movements, flashing like the thought it was.

And the search for Pyramors began.

BOOK FOUR

JANNOVAR

16

DESSUL

At first the Warhive seemed like any other world with which Pyramors was familiar. The sky was little different to that of Eannor, less changeable than that of Innasmorn, and the immediate terrain of the warhall in which he had been placed had no unusual features. Not much had been known by Man about the Warhive during the wars and there had been numerous reports and tales about it, many of which suggested an artificial world, created long in the past by a Csendook technology as ancient and forgotten as Man's own.

Zuldamar's warhall, one of a number he owned, was itself very different from the warhall Pyramors had first been sent to on Eannor. The buildings were not graceful by architectural standards, but were superbly functional. They were a combination of stone and steel, and while the *moillum* here were in no way permitted a life of luxury, they were housed in the best accommodation, and were given the opportunity to spend a certain amount of leisure time in gardens and lawn areas away from the series of arenas where the majority of their training took place. Zuldamar encouraged this, as did his staff. The *moillum* who had been selected from the other worlds to come here were the pick of the warriors and it was clear that Zuldamar wanted the very best from them.

There were Zemoi in evidence, as there had been on Skellunda, but again they did not interfere with the work of the *moillum*. They studied the progress of the warriors, and if they thought any of them were not putting enough into their work, they would take them aside and drill them hard. Very few of the *moillum* were ejected from the warhall: the weak-willed ones who spent too much time taking what pleasures a warhall offered had usually been discovered long before getting this far.

Pyramors was given his own rooms and by the standards he had seen so far, they were lavish. He had a bathroom, a small courtyard where he could relax and exercise areas that were equipped with various items that would enable him to work at his fitness here if he desired. He understood perfectly how some of the warriors would welcome this existence. Everything they needed was provided, and although they were a kind of slave, their real slavery was to a military life. Most had known no other. Pyramors could not bring himself to criticise them but it would make his task of building a team of assassins even more difficult.

He came out of one of the pools in the courtyard one afternoon, shortly after his installation by Vulporzol, the Csendook who seemed to have been given a specific responsibility for him. He towelled himself vigorously. He was naked, his body gleaming, every muscle as taut as cable; he had brought himself to a new peak in fitness, a battle-sharpness that he intended to maintain throughout the coming weeks. He looked up to find that he was not alone. The apartments of the *moillum* had no locks, although privacy was respected. The Csendook, of course, had access at all times, and the other gladiators could enter an apartment if they wanted to, but usually did so by appointment or at least by announcing themselves.

The warrior who stood before Pyramors now was of medium height, lightly armoured, his build that of another practised fighting man. He appraised Pyramors openly, devoid of any embarrassment at his nakedness, his expression one of indifference, as if studying a thoroughbred horse or a warhound.

At first Pyramors said nothing. It was the first of his own kind he had seen other than distantly since being brought here. He slipped into his light clothes, then approached the intruder.

'They told me you were here,' said the latter, hands neutrally at his sides. 'I am Dessul Mynak. Formerly I served under the Consul, Tarabas Ekubal.'

Pyramors bowed slightly. The Ekubals had been a renowned family among men. The wars had all but wiped

208

them out. 'I knew the son of Tarabas,' he said.

'Our status has changed since we became *moillum*,' Dessul went on. He had a handsome, tanned face, his hair thick and dark, and though his smile had warmth in it, the eyes betrayed him for a hardened veteran of the wars. If he had fought with the Ekubals, he would have seen terrible fighting, and it would have left scars inside him that were never likely to heal. Pyramors wondered if the Csendook had sent him here deliberately.

'I fought under the Djorganists,' said Pyramors. 'My name is Pyras.'

Dessul bowed, and if he knew that Pyramors was lying, he did not show it. Vulporzol had told Pyramors to assume his false identity for the time being, since his true name had caused such reaction on Skellunda.

'I have been given orders to instruct you in the ways of this warhall. Now that you have settled in.'

Pyramors detected a gleam, possibly of mischief or sarcasm, in Dessul's frank gaze, but he was content to let the man do the talking for now. He nodded.

'Since you've been brought to the Warhive, you'll know that the Csendook think highly of you as a warrior. Certain stories have preceded you, Pyras. You'd be amazed how news travels between warhalls.'

'Not really. Gossip is like any other disease. It can be contained but not eradicated.'

Dessul laughed softly. 'I'm glad that you have retained a sense of humour. You may need it here. Though if you've come from Skellunda, you'll find this warhall an improvement.'

'My initial impression is that this warhall is a little more salubrious.'

Again Dessul laughed. 'Well, don't be fooled. This is where we are made or broken. Only the very best go forward to the Testaments.'

'What of those who fail?'

For once Dessul looked away. 'When we test each other here, Pyras, it is sometimes to the death. Those who fail have no need to think of anything else.'

209

Pyramors nodded coldly. 'I understand.'

Dessul looked at him once more, his gaze as open and unflinching as it had first been. 'Whatever we think of the system here, however we see ourselves, we have only one option: win through to the Testaments and become one of the honoured victors. That is what drives the *moillum*.'

Pyramors smiled wryly. 'Of course. What else is there now?'

'Vulporzol chose me to be your mentor.'

Pyramors considered this slowly. 'What did he tell you about me?'

'There are two versions. One was the truth, which only I am party to. The other is the history of Pyras, the rebel from Eannor who killed a Zemoi on Skellunda. Too dangerous to leave among the trouble-makers on that island, too fine a warrior to kill, you have been brought here to be shaped. You would make an excellent *moillum*, and have every chance of winning honour at the coming Testament and becoming one of the Supreme Sanguinary's own.

'Rumours have spread already. The men here are eager to meet you, to hear about your exploits. They will want to test you, severely. Those who have a reputation are always targets.'

'One of the Supreme Sanguinary's own. Much honour would attach to such a position.'

'And much freedom.'

'Tell me something, Dessul. Who do you serve?'

Dessul folded his arms, his smile widening. 'You want the truth?'

'You know nothing about me other than what you have been told – '

'I know your true name, Sire. And there are many men who would yet praise your valour, your defence of the Empire – '

Pyramors shook his head. 'I am Pyras. The rest must be wiped away.'

'I know the truth. And I'll give you the same. I serve the Marozul, Zuldamar. He is one of the most respected of the Csendook powers. I am not ashamed to tell you that I am

210

loyal to him and what he believes is best for the Empire we once held.'

Pyramors frowned. 'That is interesting. But go on. I welcome your honesty.'

'Why have I seemingly betrayed my own people? Two reasons, Sire – '

'Pyras. Always Pyras, Dessul.'

Dessul nodded. 'Of course. Pyras. What I do is no betrayal. Zuldamar was instrumental in ending the Crusade. He and Horzumar, his close friend and fellow Marozul, led the drive to bring the Crusade to an end. If they had not done so, Mankind would not have survived.'

'Zuldamar brought the Crusade to an end because he did not want us exterminated? That seems to be contrary to Csendook thinking. Surely they had some other motive.'

'Oh yes. The wars have been costly and too many worlds have been ravaged. War had to end.'

'What else?'

'Zuldamar recognises that the Imperator Elect may have survived. He may have somehow broken free of the cycle of worlds. Zuldamar does not want him followed. He wants the breach sealed. Otherwise the war will begin anew. On the other hand, Auganzar wants the Imperator pursued.'

'And you are with Zuldamar?'

Dessul nodded. 'Why should Men fare any better in another war? If any got away, let them build a new world elsewhere. Where they will be safe. Those of us who are left behind must make the best of things here. We are slaves as *moillum* but we have survived. Under Zuldamar, we might become something nobler.'

'You have no desire to pursue the man who betrayed us?' Pyramors said with apparent indifference. Had Vulporzol really not told Dessul that he, Pyramors, had been beyond the cycle? Had returned from it?

'I would cut him in half if I had the opportunity,' avowed Dessul. 'As would any of us here. But the freedom of the Imperator may be the price to pay for the survivors' freedom. They were not all betrayers.'

'No, perhaps not.'

Dessul walked to the pool in which Pyramors had been swimming, looking down into its waters as though they would reveal further truths to him. 'You, too, serve Zuldamar.'

'You think so?'

Dessul turned. 'Vulporzol told me I must trust you. You may be the instrument we have waited for. Already we have tried to prize a way into the system of the Supreme Sanguinary. Each time we have failed. We have lost a number of excellent men.' He suddenly drove a fist into his palm, his face colouring with anger. '*Good* men! Men I would have died to protect.'

Pyramors did not react. 'Can it be done?'

'The assassination?'

'The assassination.'

'It will be very difficult. And it will take time. That is the greatest of the obstacles.'

Pyramors knew they were in as private a place as they could be, at the heart of Zuldamar's warhall, but even so he felt vulnerable when speaking of the plot. He sat down on one of the carved marble benches and gestured for Dessul to sit with him. The latter did so.

'How must it be done?' said Pyramors. 'I have given it much thought, but there are many things I must know.'

Dessul nodded. 'While you are in this warhall, you will have the opportunity to win a place in the company that will be sent to the next Testament. Warhalls from all parts of the Empire will take part, each of the Garazenda being represented. All Zuldamar's *moillum* who have a chance of making the company have been gathered here.'

'All of them? Does that include any of the men from Skellunda?'

Dessul frowned. 'I don't think so.'

'There are men there who are as fine as any others I have ever fought with.'

'That's as may be, Pyras. But remember, to be part of the company that goes to the Testament, a man must be prepared to serve the company, to give his life for it, and thus to Zuldamar's cause. The men of Skellunda would spit at the very thought.'

Pyramors grunted, mildly amused. 'Perhaps so. Go on.'

'I have to warn you that every place in the company must be earned. No one will be included who has not won his place on merit. Even you.'

'Then I'll have to work hard.'

'And kill. You'll not be able to progress without killing our own kind,' said Dessul grimly.

Pyramors thought of those he had already killed, his jaw tightening. Dessul saw the coldness in the warrior beside him, the contained fury. 'Let us assume you win a place. You will then go to the Testament, and throughout its course, *moillum* will be eliminated. Most of them, the cream of our warriors, will die.'

Pyramors felt another stab of fury. He shook his head in disgust. 'And this is a better way for man? To die for the entertainment of our enemies?'

'I will not argue.'

'No, you can do nothing. Go on. The Testament.'

'Those who prove to be the finest will be reviewed by the Supreme Sanguinary. His own Swarm, known as Auganzar's Thousand (though it is said to be several times that size) consists of the best of the Csendook warriors. They are, for the most part, the official army of the Csendook nation, now that the wars are over. And they, too, have their own *moillum* serving them. Those who succeed in the Testament are likely to be selected for these ranks. Auganzar has a number of *moillum*, virtually free men, close to him, working in his own private estates. They are, as far as Auganzar is concerned, the ultimate proof that his *moillum* philosophy has been successful.'

'And none of them has ever attempted to assassinate Auganzar in the past?'

'Why should they? They have far better lives than they had in the days of Empire. They command respect, living almost on a par with the Csendook. They are like gods among their own kind. And of course, they have done much to teach the lower ranks that success reaps magnificent rewards. To be one of Auganzar's personal *moillum* is the highest honour a Man can win.'

'And, I imagine, many Men will kill ruthlessly and without scruples to achieve such a position.'

'Of course. Each time you go into the arena, you will face such men.'

'And if I become one of these *moillum*? One of Auganzar's chosen? How am I to kill him? Step up to him and drive my sword into him?'

'In the event, that may well be the way of it. But timing will be the key.'

Pyramors grinned mirthlessly. 'Particularly if I am to elude the wrath of Auganzar's Swarm. Or does Zuldamar think I am that much of a fanatic that I will merely do the necessary work and throw myself on my own sword? That I accept this as a suicide mission?'

'The detail of the assassination has not been organised. How could it? But once you are there, within the inner sanctum, you must plan accordingly. As I told you, it will take time. A year, maybe more. And there will be help from outside. Zuldamar will not abandon you. He will do what is necessary to get you away, and reward you.'

'You seem very sure of your new master.'

'I am. I know the intensity of his hatred for Auganzar. The Supreme Sanguinary is responsible for the deaths of many of Zuldamar's friends, though he has covered himself well.'

'Then Auganzar has much in common with Zellorian.'

'You think he is alive? Could they have survived? I know that Zuldamar thinks so.'

'Yes, he seems sure of it. Well, if he is, I would have an even greater incentive for escaping after the assassination.'

'You'd seek Zellorian?'

Pyramors nodded. 'I want his head. More than I want the death of Auganzar. But if I have to have the latter before I can reach Zellorian, then so be it. But I'll need a team, Dessul. If I am to win through to the Testament and succeed, I'll need a team.'

'You'll have to forge one here. There are men I'm sure would be willing to serve under you. But you and I alone know of Zuldamar's plan. We dare not let anyone else know. Auganzar has eyes and ears everywhere.'

'Even here?'

'It is possible.'

Dessul took Pyramors around the warhall, introducing him to some of the warriors. At first Pyramors was concerned that perhaps he might know some of them and that they might compromise his position, but in the event this did not happen. He met no one he had known on Eannor, though there were men of that world here. They were exceptional warriors, all of them, and Zuldamar's servants had chosen them well. Two thousand of them trained at this warhall alone, and every one of them knew that only a few hundred would go forward to the forthcoming Testament. They would be forced to kill each other, and yet they worked and trained together knowing this. Pyramors was amazed that their morale was so high.

'While you were on Skellunda,' Dessul told him when they were able to speak privately, sitting in the open and watching a group of *moillum* wrestling on a grass square, 'were you permitted pleasures?'

Pyramors saw the gleam in Dessul's eye. He guessed that his companion's good looks would have won the heart of many a woman in better times. 'Even on Skellunda we were permitted the sins of the flesh,' Pyramors smiled. 'Though I confess I found myself caught up in other matters.'

'The arrangements here are not as barbaric as you might think. Our women are treated with surprising respect by the Csendook.'

'Oh?'

'They are not all concubines. And they are never abused by the Csendook. In fact, much to my surprise, I find that the Csendook are oddly sentimental about our women. They treat them as gently as they would treat delicate porcelain. There is a degree of reverence that few men have. It is the most remarkable thing I have learned about the Csendook since coming to the Warhive.'

Pyramors did not hide his surprise. 'But surely they captured as many of our women as they could on Eannor and other such worlds. They herded them – '

'Never that. There were unscrupulous men who helped them gather the women. No doubt *they* herded the women, and treated them with the sort of scorn that such men have for women. They count for so much meat. But it is never that way with the Csendook.'

'Yet some are used as concubines. *Moillum* are serviced by them as any barracks might be serviced by city harlots – '

Again Dessul shook his head. 'Clearly you have never involved yourself in the system. It is not the way of things here. No woman is made to service *moillum*. The women are very particular about whom they, as you put it, service. They are given the opportunity to select *moillum* before the men ever see them! Ah, Pyras, we are the servants of the women!'

'The women accept this?'

'Some do. Those who refuse to accept the system are not forced into it. There is other work for them. And the Csendook encourage them in the arts. Did you know how greatly the Csendook admire the arts? They are as devoted to them as they are to war. Indeed, it may even supersede their love of war. In many cases, but not all. Zemoks are Zemoks. But they have been bred for such things, as we have been trained for it. Many of the women here are very content, having been shown a kindness they were not always shown before.'

'And may a man take a wife while he is here?'

'Not in the way that he used to. He may have a life-mate, as the Csendook call it. In fact, they prefer us to have life-mates rather than a number of mates. They do control our breeding. It is a selective process.'

Pyramors felt himself numbing at the words. 'Control?'

'To produce even finer *moillum*. There is a clinical logic to the Csendook doctrines on this matter.'

'I'm sure there is,' Pyramors snapped, getting to his feet. He indicated the *moillum* who were wrestling on the grass. 'We've spent enough time idling, Dessul.'

Dessul could see that he had probed a nerve with Pyras. The man was eager to work his sudden anger off in a bout or two. 'Will you wrestle?' he asked him.

Pyramors nodded. 'Select the best of those men there.'

Dessul's eyes narrowed as he scanned the group of about a dozen *moillum*. 'That'll be Osgundar. He's not tall, but very light on his feet and as slippery as an eel. And he's very good, Pyras. Are you sure you want to test yourself fully so soon?'

Pyramors turned to him with an unexpected glare. 'You'd better tell your *moillum* to look to their skills, Dessul. If *they* are ready, we'll begin.'

Dessul nodded, his smile gone. Very well, if this man wanted a true test, he would have one. He walked over to the wrestlers. 'Look out,' one snorted. 'Dessul has come to flex his muscles! Hey, Dessul, you want a bout? Wait till I tie an arm behind me.'

'No mask, Dessul?' grinned another. 'You want to risk bruising that handsome face?'

Dessul gave them an exaggerated bow. 'My dear fellows,' he said in a mock pompous rejoinder, 'I would not deign to insult your skill by testing my weak frame against it. But I have with me a newcomer who needs exercise. This is Pyras.'

Pyramors had already stripped off his shirt and tossed it aside. The wrestlers eyed him with interest.

'Is Osgundar here?' said Pyramors, his voice hardening.

The shortest of the men stepped forward. His hair was like wire, close cropped, his chest broad and his arms like the arms of an ape. He grinned through broken teeth. 'You the warrior from Skellunda?'

Pyramors nodded.

'They say the men of Skellunda are pretty good with their bare hands. But a rabble. Want to teach me different?' Osgundar flexed his arms and shoulders, the muscles leaping, the skin like burnished brass.

Pyramors ignored him and walked to a space on the field, turning, ready to begin. Osgundar followed. His companions cheered him on for a moment, surprised by the silence of the new man. It was how a Csendook might fight.

One of the wrestlers leaned close to Dessul. 'I've heard that the sun on Skellunda would fry the balls off a desert lizard. Has it scrambled this fellow's brains?'

'We're about to find out,' Dessul grinned.

Pyramors and Osgundar circled each other, and Pyramors guessed that if his opponent was an experienced wrestler he would not make the first move if he could help it. He may try a feint but Pyramors suspected that Osgundar would be too wily even for that. He would be very strong, having a perfect build, a perfect weight and height ratio. Close-in fighting would be dangerous, for Osgundar would use his superior strength to strangle any locks Pyramors attempted to apply. And he would probably use his dome of a skull to butt. Pyramors decided that of the two, he himself would be the faster. Victory would come from such speed.

Just as Osgundar was being evaluated, so he judged his opponent. The man had extreme confidence and so it must be justified. He had to be good. Fast, probably. And thus, elusive. Footwork would be important to him, so he would try to keep his distance. He wouldn't want to get in close. Crowding him in a room or bar would have been easy, but out here in the open it would be very hard. Osgundar was always happiest in a brawl, preferably a bar brawl, where he had made his name. These field battles were too formal for him. And this warrior had the looks of a disciplined fighter, one used to field tactics. It might give him the advantage. So this would have to be quick. He had to close in fast, apply one of a number of locks and threaten to break a limb, or even the man's back.

Pyramors made a few lunges that were designed to tempt Osgundar to attack, but the latter knew what he was doing and ignored them. But he was obviously looking for an opening, eager to get close. Pyramors made what appeared to be another false strike, then followed up at once with a punch that struck his opponent low down under the ribs. There was a loud smack as the fist struck home hard.

218

Osgundar rode the blow expertly, grinning. His belly was like beaten steel and he had not even been winded. Pyramors also grinned, the first time he had done so in this company. The blow would have rocked lesser men, even if only for an instant.

Pyramors landed two more such blows, with equal lack of result, and as he drove home a further blow, Osgundar took it and closed in with the speed of a striking serpent. Pyramors did not grapple with him or try to force Osgundar off. Instead he wrapped his arms about his back, dragged him in and swung backwards, using the momentum of the attack to throw them both. Twisting in mid-air, Pyramors swung Osgundar round and landed on top of him, a knee driving up into his belly.

Osgundar was not badly hurt but his grip was weakened enough for Pyramors to spring free. Most fighters would have untangled quickly and looked for the next opening, but Pyramors flung himself into a continued move which crashed his shoulder into the knees of Osgundar before he could use his arms. He had to reach for the ground to prevent himself from landing awkwardly, and as he did so he found Pyramors almost astride him, ready to drive his fist down at his temple.

The blow, had it landed, would have killed him.

But Pyramors released Osgundar as quickly as he had caught him and stood back. Osgundar was up in an instant but he knew what had happened. The men gathered around, stunned, their faces showing their surprise.

Suddenly Osgundar laughed, though it was a nervous, uncertain sound. 'Your inexperience here shows itself,' he said, taking a deep breath.

Dessul was nodding. 'They usually fight to the death in such a bout. There are rarely second chances.'

'I see,' said Pyramors. 'Then I will know next time.' He went over to his shirt and used it to towel himself, turning his back on the men and walking away.

Osgundar, to the surprise of his companions, was grinning. 'Next time you men want to learn something from me, be careful. I thought I was training you.'

No one laughed.

Someone nodded toward the retreating figure. 'No wonder the Csendook didn't want him stirring them up on Skellunda.'

'Dessul,' said another, 'you'd better keep an eye on that bastard.'

17

THE WAGER

'News, Zaru, that I think will please you.'

Auganzar waited, sitting perfectly still as though nothing could move him to excitement. Before him, standing stiffly to attention and wearing his armour as though he had just come straight from a field of battle was the recently promoted Zolutar, now named Zuarzol. He had taken his new name with pride and yet carried his pride with him.

'Very well, let me hear it. And relax a little, Zolutar.'

Zuarzol bowed and stood at ease, though the muscles of his face did not relax at all. 'Zaru, we have been able to trace the movements of the Man we have been looking for.'

Auganzar nodded slowly.

'As you know, Guntrazaal reported that he had been placed in the warhall on Eannor owned by Zuldamar. I have been tracking the Zolutar, Vulporzol, who serves Zuldamar, and I discovered that he's been in the warhall of Zuldamar here on the Warhive. He again left it and seems to move very freely about the worlds on the business of his master. Guntrazaal learned that Vulporzol had visited the warhall on Eannor where the Man had been secreted.

'Guntrazaal conducted another series of searches, and his tigerhounds found a fresh trail, one that led away from Rannor Tarul and along a neglected route to a small port, Harran Torsa.'

'The name is familiar,' said Auganzar. 'What does the port trade in?'

'Very little, Zaru. A small fishing fleet, larger grain ships. Quarried building stone. But it also serves supplies to the island of Skellunda, far out in the bay.'

Auganzar rose slowly, the trace of a smile playing on his lips as he listened. 'Skellunda. The last haven of the rebel *moillum*.'

'A dangerous breeding ground for dissent, Zaru.'

Auganzar's smile widened. 'You think so? The Garazenda were never sure that it was a good idea to use the place. They suggested that Men who would not accept the yoke of being *moillum* should be killed. You think the Garazenda were right? Come, give me your honest view.'

'Skellunda seems to me, Zaru, to impose a risk.'

'In a way it does. But it was my idea.'

'Zaru, I – '

Auganzar waved away what he knew would be an apology. 'No matter, Zuarzol. The Garazenda also argued with me, thinking of our safety, as you do. But imagine, if we could harness the anger and the skill of those rebels, they would make superb *moillum*. And they'd be superb examples to hold up to other would-be rebels.'

'I understand, Zaru.'

'But go on with your report.'

'Guntrazaal followed the trail of Vulporzol and the Man. It led him and his tigerhounds to Harran Torsa, and a study of the ships there quickly led him to the one that had taken prisoners over to Skellunda. Vulporzol had been with them. Guntrazaal also found the place where both Vulporzol and the Man had returned to the port, some weeks after they had left for the island.

'Before following the return trail, Guntrazaal thought it prudent to go to Skellunda to find out why Vulporzol and his charge should visit it for so short a period. Prisoners do not usually leave the island.'

'Very few are converted,' Auganzar agreed.

'Guntrazaal met Zolutull Karanzol, who is in charge of Skellunda. He confirmed that Vulporzol had brought the Man to him, together with other prisoners. Guntrazaal was able to deduce that the Man's name was Pyras. Little was known about him but Karanzol said he was given express orders by Vulporzol to keep an eye on him, as he was a particular trouble-maker. This proved to be true: the Man Pyras murdered one of the Zemoi.'

Auganzar's face clouded. 'How did this happen?'

'The Zemoi responded to a challenge. He met the Man

Pyras up on one of the peaks. There were no witnesses to the combat, but the Zemoi, Torruzem, told his fellows to keep away. He wanted to teach the Man a lesson in respect.'

'And this Man defeated him?'

'They found Torruzem's sword, but it had not been used. The Man seems to have killed him with a rock.'

'A Man killed a Zemoi in a fight with only stones for weapons,' murmured Auganzar. 'Extraordinary. What sort of Zemoi was this Torruzem?'

'Karanzol admits that he was not the best of his warriors. Not exactly slow or dull-witted, but he would have been no match for fitter Zemoi.'

'But the Man must be exceptional.'

'Karanzol grudgingly admitted that he is. In training on Skellunda, he showed more potential than any other Man Karanzol had ever seen.'

'Indeed?'

'Karanzol would have had the Man executed publicly for the killing of Torruzem, but was prevented by his instructions from Vulporzol, who had told him that Pyras must be imprisoned if he caused trouble, and under no circumstances must he be harmed. This was done, and Pyras was held for about a month.'

'So that Vulporzol could visit him?'

'Before that happened, Zaru, Karanzol had another visitor, who had heard of the incident. It seems that the Keeper of Eannor, Cmizen, concerned at the news, came to Skellunda personally.'

Auganzar laughed gently. 'Cmizen! Really? Do go on.'

'Cmizen confirmed that there would be no execution. The Man Pyras was to be removed. Shortly after his interview with Karanzol, Cmizen left and Vulporzol arrived. He took Pyras with him when he left.'

Auganzar was nodding as the Zolutar spoke. 'So the Keeper is part of this conspiracy, too. I should have guessed it, of course. It explains why it was so difficult to find out what had happened in the zone of sacrifice.' Cmizen is controlled by fear, and although he fears me, he fears Zuldamar more, which is a compliment to my adversary, Auganzar thought.

223

'Should I see that Cmizen's movements are recorded, Zaru?'

'That won't be necessary. Cmizen is not important. He would not be trusted with more than the minimum of information. It is the Man and his protective Zolutar that interest me most. You say Guntrazaal had found the place where they returned to the port?'

'The trail went up into some foothills, to a wasteland some distance from the city of Rannor Tarul. Vulporzol and the Man were travelling alone. No one reports having seen a lone Csendook and a Man, but a few people in the village spoke of two Zemoks travelling towards Rannor Tarul. Clearly the Man had been disguised.'

'Foothills?'

'For secrecy, I suppose, Zaru. They were met by a third party. An Opener.'

'Ah, and he brought them along a Path. Do your remarkable tigerhounds have the Opener's scent?'

Zuarzol permitted himself a brief, predatory smile. 'They do, Zaru. The Opener can be traced quite easily.'

'Like Cmizen, he may not be important. But find out if he serves anyone in particular. I presume it will be Zuldamar, but let us see. Now, they left Eannor. Did you find a fresh trail?'

'I cannot yet discover where they came to, Zaru. No assumptions are safe, of course, though they can guide us.'

'Where do you think it most likely they emerged?'

Zuarzol paused for only a moment, his gaze still level. 'Zaru, I think they came here, to the Warhive.'

'I think so, too, Zuarzol.'

'Vulporzol is here now.'

'In Zuldamar's warhall?'

Zuarzol nodded. 'Just so, Zaru. He visits it regularly, and so his trail is confused.'

Auganzar paced the room slowly, thoughtfully. 'They have come by a tortuous route. Why the time spent on Skellunda? Did Guntrazaal question any of the other prisoners there?'

'He did, Zaru. Few of the Men would speak. But there was

one, a Man by the name of Garrack, who gave Guntrazaal the most interesting news of all.'

Something in Zuarzol's tone brought Auganzar about to face him. He could see that the Zolutar had saved this information until now, proud of his discovery, eager to impress with it. 'And what was that?'

'Zaru, the Man is not named Pyras. He is no ordinary fighting soldier.'

'He killed a Zemoi. He could not be.'

'Zaru, he is a member of the Imperator Elect's Consulate. His name is Pyramors.'

Auganzar took a slow, satisfied breath. 'Ah. A clearer picture emerges. A Consul. But *why* has he come back? Did this Man, Garrack, tell Guntrazaal that?'

Zuarzol shook his head. 'Garrack and the other prisoners on Skellunda do not realise that the Imperator Elect has escaped us.'

'What did Pyramors tell them he wanted?'

'To achieve glory in the Testaments, Zaru. But the Men of Skellunda scorned him. They will neither cooperate with us, nor with the Consul.'

'How many of the Men on Skellunda know the true identity of the Consul?'

'Including Garrack, Zaru, twenty-two.'

Auganzar frowned. 'You have the exact detail?'

'Guntrazaal was most thorough, Zaru. He demanded of Garrack the names of all Men who knew the Consul's true rank.'

'And then?'

'Guntrazaal had them isolated, Zaru, awaiting orders. Karanzol has all twenty-two of them chained under the fortress on Skellunda. On instruction he will execute them swiftly.'

Auganzar looked out of the window at the gardens below him. He nodded. 'Very well. I want no further movement of prisoners to Skellunda. All traffic with the island must cease, apart from the supplies.'

'Zaru.'

'And have the Men executed.'

'I will send word at once, Zaru.' Zuarzol saluted, turned and was about to leave, when Auganzar called him back.

'On reflection, Zuarzol, that may be hasty. These prisoners. You say they refused to cooperate with the Consul? To support him in his so-called bid for glory in the Testaments?'

'So Guntrazaal reports, Zaru.'

'They have no love for the Consul?'

'The Man Garrack proclaimed his hatred for all members of the Consulate. He and his fellows on Skellunda see them as betrayers of their race. Cowards who either fled or attempted to abandon their posts.'

'An attitude they share with many of the *moillum* we have trained. And one which has facilitated their conversion.'

'You would rather the twenty-two on Skellunda were spared, Zaru?'

'Pick the best of them. Two will be adequate. Perhaps this Garrack ought to be included. Is he a notable warrior?'

'Karanzol confirms that he showed great potential but no will to become a *moillum*.'

'Then have Garrack and the best warrior from among the others removed from Skellunda. Take them as discreetly as possible to my warhall on Eannor. But find a way of letting Zuldamar know that I have them.'

'Zaru?' said Zuarzol, puzzled.

'If he knows I have them, he'll be concerned for the safety of the Man he is protecting. And he'll want them for himself. Very much.'

'You think he will offer to trade for them?'

'I'm sure he will. And he can have them with pleasure. But first we have to work on them. We will have to make it clear to them who they would do best to serve. I want them to end up in Zuldamar's warhall, here on the Warhive. Where they can watch this Consul for *me*.'

'And the others on Skellunda, Zaru?'

'Yes, they must be executed at once. Anyone there who has the slightest suspicion of the identity of the Consul must die.'

'I will have word with Karanzol with all speed, Zaru.'

'In the meantime I need to visit this warhall of Zuldamar's. I think it would be interesting to see how the Marozul will react to your tigerhounds. How many do we have now?'

'Fifty, Zaru, including those in the field.'

'Have Guntrazaal recalled. Like yourself, Zuarzol, he has conducted this business superbly. His efficiency is matched only by your own. Say nothing to him but I will confer upon him the rank of Zolutar.'

Zuarzol bowed, honoured by the promotion of his colleague.

'Prepare five tigerhounds for me. I will visit Zuldamar and offer three to him as gifts. During the demonstration, which will be at Zuldamar's warhall, we will have an opportunity to search out this Consul and note him.'

'Kill him, Zaru? An accident, the tigerhounds – '

'No. I want his presence confirmed, that's all. He must not be harmed. He will be more valuable to me than a dozen Swarms.'

Zuldamar and Horzumar sat comfortably in the huge chairs that overlooked the tiny lake. Birds were drifting across its waters and the trees on either side of it that made such a haven swayed in the merest hint of a breeze. The two Marozul sipped at their wine, relaxing, enjoying the tranquillity, affairs of state temporarily forgotten.

'He impresses you?' said Horzumar eventually.

Zuldamar nodded. 'I have watched him, discreetly, a number of times. As you would expect, he has all the qualities of one of their finest generals. Man chose well when promoting such warriors, as we do. We are not dealing with an ordinary soldier, by any standards. And already he is winning the respect of the *moillum* in the warhall.'

'Is he building the team he needs?'

'He knows what is expected of him. He is best left to it. But yes, I think it has begun. He is not an easy Man to please. Vulporzol tells me that he regretted not having the opportunity to win over some of the recalcitrants on Skellunda. Some of them, apparently, would have been ideal for his purposes. But if we had left him there we would have had to increase his protection. Even a Csendook as short on brain as Karanzol would have suspected something.'

'Can it succeed?' said Horzumar, not for the first time.

Zuldamar smiled. 'Who knows? Pyramors is the best chance we have yet had. But if he is to succeed in the Testament, he will need luck as well as skill. And we simply cannot engineer everything.'

Behind them they heard the soft footfall of one of the house guards, and presently he stood before them, saluting. 'A visitor requests an audience, Sire. I told him you would be available later this afternoon. But he asked me to let you know he was here.'

'Who is it?' said Zuldamar, only just keeping irritation from his voice.

'Sire, it is the Supreme Sanguinary.'

Zuldamar glanced at Horzumar, who nodded. 'Very well. Tell him to join us, and bring another glass.'

After the Zemok had left, Horzumar smiled wryly. 'I sometimes wonder if Auganzar has perfected the art of reading minds, my friend.'

'Who knows what arts he is tampering with? Ah, I would rather not have broken up the peace of so beautiful an afternoon, but it may be better to see him. It is not likely to be a trivial matter, however he dresses it.'

Shortly afterwards, Auganzar presented himself, bowing. He wore less formal dress than usual, as though he, too, had spent some of his day relaxing. He was known to be a great lover of gardens and his own estate was the envy of many of his colleagues. He sat, accepting the glass of wine offered to him, and he took in the vista with evident pleasure. 'I could never tire of such a view,' he said quite genuinely.

Zuldamar nodded. 'We had hoped to reflect on it a little longer, Auganzar but I have to assume your business is pressing.'

'Oh, nothing serious, Marozul. But something I would like to attend to fairly soon. As you know, the Testament is not far away.'

'It promises to be even more extravagant than usual,' observed Horzumar.

'I'm sure it will, Marozul. It will be the first time we are able to put so many *moillum* to the test. Competition for success among them will be fierce. Nothing short of true battle.'

'The people will be pleased,' said Zuldamar. 'Which will reflect well on you, Supreme Sanguinary.'

Auganzar smiled dismissively. 'I sincerely hope the Testament will be a success, Marozul. The entire structure of the *moillum* system of governing Man is under review.'

'Your own warhalls will doubtless provide some excellent warriors,' said Horzumar, hands clasped together across his chest. He seemed perfectly relaxed.

'They are eager to succeed. As I'm sure your own *moillum* will be.'

'The arrangements for the Testament seem to be satisfactory.' said Zuldamar. 'Are you content with them?'

'Indeed, Marozul. But there are constant developments. I am particularly interested in the Running Hunt. It will be the most exacting test of all, more so than ever before.'

'I enjoy the Running Hunt above all else,' said Horzumar, again studying the lake.

'I have been encouraging certain genetic experiments, Marozul,' Auganzar went on mildly. 'As you know, the hounds form a crucial part of any hunt but for some time now I have had engineers working on a new hybrid.'

'Tigerhounds?' said Zuldamar. 'Yes, I have had brief glimpses of them. Have you had much success with them?'

'They are almost perfected. I wish to use them in the Running Hunt at the Testament.'

Zuldamar and Horzumar glanced at one another. 'I think we would have to put this to the Garazenda,' said Zuldamar.

'Of course,' agreed Auganzar. 'And I am anxious not to have any advantage over my colleagues in the Testament.' He smiled, as if the anxieties of the others were unfounded. 'I would wish all of you to have an opportunity to use the tigerhounds. I assure you, you will be greatly impressed by them. They are able to do things which their predecessors could not. The perfect fighting beast, an ideal compliment to the Zemaal. Or perhaps I should say, the *moillum*.'

'You are training *moillum* to use these creatures?' said Horzumar. 'Is that not dangerous?'

'It's too early to let the *moillum* train with them. After the Testament, perhaps. But I would like to see Zemoks using them in the Testament. Just a few. If I could suggest a way forward?'

Zuldamar shrugged. 'Very well.'

'Primarily, Marozul, a demonstration. I have five new tigerhounds that I would like to show you.'

'Where should this demonstration be?' said Horzumar.

'In a warhall would be most appropriate.'

'What do you suggest?' Zuldamar asked the Supreme Sanguinary.

'A mock Hunt, on a small scale. Select a few of your *moillum*. I'll have the tigerhounds brought here. They'll be muzzled, naturally. And their claws will be sheathed. Provided you are happy with the outcome of the demonstration, I will be pleased to give the beasts to you, and to provide all those of our colleagues who are entering for the Testament with tigerhounds.'

Zuldamar did not look at Horzumar, instead watching the flight of geese across his lake. 'It's an interesting proposal. Give me a day to think about it, will you?'

'Of course, Marozul.'

Horzumar studied the Supreme Sanguinary for a moment, knowing that however casual and relaxed he could seem, his mind was never for a moment away from the things that interested him the most, the plots that he had drawn up, the ambition that spurred him. 'This regiment of *moillum* that will come out of this Testament, Supreme Sanguinary: how many of its members do you think will come from your own warhalls?'

Auganzar smiled. 'I am not, I trust, arrogant enough to assume that they will all come from my *moillum*. I have had my failures.'

'Oh? I am intrigued,' said Zuldamar.

'Yes. For instance, my plan for the recalcitrants of Skellunda does not seem likely to bear fruit. The prisoners there are more intent on killing one another than on bettering themselves as *moillum*. There has been something of a riot.'

Zuldamar pretended concern. 'Oh?'

'About a score of them dead.'

'You are treating Skellunda as a complete failure?' said Horzumar mildly.

'Not quite. I have a few of its rebels in one of my warhalls here. But I have to say I am beginning to despair of converting them. I cannot use them in the Testament. In time, I may win them over. I would like to, as they're extremely good warriors. But they are not ready. I may even have to execute them.'

'Your warhall cannot win them over?' said Zuldamar. 'That is interesting. But, of course, different warhalls use different methods. My own warhalls, for example, have been extremely successful in winning the loyalty of the *moillum*. I'll wager the best of my *moillum* are true warriors in the Csendook sense!'

Auganzar smiled. 'There will be much betting on the Testament.'

'I'll back my *moillum* heavily, it's no secret,' said Zuldamar, with amusement. 'In fact, what you have been saying has suggested a wager to me now.'

Auganzar looked at him with unfeigned interest. 'Oh?'

'Method is what counts in training. Preparing a warrior's mind as well as his body. Is that not so?'

'Assuredly,' nodded Auganzar.

'You say you've got Men that you cannot win over to the *moillum* code? Men of Skellunda, rabble?'

Auganzar nodded.

'If *I* were to have them trained in my warhall, and if they were won over and became *moillum* and fought for me at the Testament – '

Auganzar stiffened. 'With respect, Marozul, you do not know these Men, their stubborn resolve – '

231

'I'm prepared to take that chance.'

Horzumar cleared his throat, sensing that he had almost been forgotten. 'I think a little caution is called for here. Forgive me, but I do know your enthusiasm for a wager, Zuldamar. Are you sure you know what you are taking on?'

Zuldamar smiled. 'Yes, but I know the strengths of my warhalls. Well, Supreme Sanguinary? Will you wager with me?'

'That you can train the Men of Skellunda *and* have them ready to win honours in the Testament?'

'Yes. They will be alive at the end. Seeking a place in your elite corps of *moillum*.'

Slowly Auganzar nodded. 'An interesting wager. And far too tempting to resist, Marozul. Very well, I'll have the Men sent to whichever of your warhalls you nominate.'

'And if I win?'

Auganzar frowned. 'Marozul, you have taken me unawares. Give me time to consider the stakes, if you will. Although I am sure we can come to an agreement.'

'But the wager is accepted? Horzumar will witness it.'

Auganzar nodded slowly, as though unsure. Then he rose. 'I must leave now. If you would let me know about the arrangements for the tigerhound demonstration – '

Zuldamar also stood. 'Excellent. I look forward to it.'

Horzumar pretended to be absorbed by the lake. After Auganzar had gone, his face creased in a frown. 'I have evidently missed something.'

Zuldamar sat down, snorting. 'We must have those Men! There's been slaughter on Skellunda. Everyone who knew the identity of Pyramors has been put to death. They died in a riot, Karanzol's report says. But we know the truth of the matter. Two of the Men, however, have been taken off Eannor by Auganzar. They may have betrayed Pyramors but they are yet so full of hatred for the Csendook that they may not have said anything about the Consul. We must have them!'

'Could Auganzar have won their loyalty?'

'They hate Pyramors and all he stood for. But nothing could match their hatred for the Csendook. No compromise.'

'Then how can we hope to win them?'

'Only Pyramors can do that. Or try. If he fails, then they must die. But their secret will go with them. I'll meet Auganzar's wager. No price is too high to pay for these Men, especially if they have told him nothing.'

18

THE GIRL

'We'll split up here,' Pyramors told his group. They were all young men, so although they were experienced in battle, most of them having fought during the last years of the wars in various parts of the old Empire, and they still had enough spirit and enthusiasm to be able to adapt to their new roles as *moillum*. Few men accepted the role without complaints of one kind or another and the old bitterness sometimes welled up, causing a fight or an outburst of criticism. But it was more easily channelled in these young ones, Pyramors found. Though his own hatred of slavery, for he could see it no other way, was strong, he knew that the only real opportunity he had of striking a blow for his race, through the assassination of Auganzar, rested on his efforts to shape a weapon. Prepare it for use in the arenas of the Testament. And he was beginning to find excellent potential for his team among the *moillum* of Zuldamar's warhall. Those that had been brought here from various worlds were, indeed, superb warriors, and like Pyramors, they saw their best chances for survival in success at the Testament.

Today's exercise was a mock hunt. Pyramors and his group, about twenty men, all of whom he had picked, were the runners. It had been a challenge to the other *moillum*, for already Pyramors was proving to be an outstanding warrior, with all the qualities of a good leader and those who did not respect him, or were jealous of him, enjoyed an opportunity to put him through greater and more difficult tests. When he had agreed to be a runner, leading a group across the hunt area, there had been no shortage of volunteers to join him, and he had been able to pick a squad that he was sure would justify selection.

In the distance, across the wooded landscape in which the hunt took place, he could hear the roar of the xillatraal.

Although Men hunted Men, a small party of Zemoi super-vised the hunt, as they would in the Testament, where the hunt would be to a kill. Some of the Zemoi might even die in the real event but there were no penalties attached to such killings. The Running Hunt was the Running Hunt.

Pyramors had devised a plan which was intended to confuse the chase, based on tactics he had used successfully in the past, when the lives of his warriors had depended on such things, and in those days the pursuit had been composed entirely of Zemoks and their xillatraal. He watched as the men melted into the low trees. They were all aiming for a low peak that formed part of a range of foothills, the upper reaches of which were bare and open, where shelter would be hard to find. There were a number of pennants set up around the peak and the object of the hunt was to retrieve the pennants and get back to the perimeter of the warhall before being pulled down by the hunters.

Pyramors pushed his way through the undergrowth to the west, following a rough trail that looped around the foot of the hills, knowing where to find a particular stream. He had been shown it a few days before when he had been permitted to see the terrain on which the exercise would be carried out. At the Running Hunt, in the vast arena, all contestants were able to see the land before formulating their strategies. But Pyramors had been brought out here for another reason. While his men were engaged in following his tortuous instructions as to how they should retrieve the pennants, he moved further away from the likely area of activity to where the stream widened and ran down into a tiny valley. It was dense with trees, the canopy spreading overhead to form a dark ceiling. Pyramors paused, taking cover, but after a while he was certain that none of the men had doubled back to follow him. There was no need for any of them to do so, no need for them to suspect anything, but he was a man who took few chances.

Satisfied, he moved on down into the valley, away from the scene of the hunt. There was no time limit. The exercise ended when all the pennants had been retrieved, or the *moillum* had all been caught. It could be a matter of days – as the young warriors were likely to be elusive, particularly as they had found some of Pyramors's advice invaluable. He moved on down through the trees, avoiding the suggestion of a path and making as little noise as possible. The months he had spent in the Sculpted City on Innasmorn had almost made him forget what it was like to be in the field but now, after weeks of strict training, he felt himself tuning to his surroundings in that particular way of a warrior. It was something, he realised, that he had missed. War was an evil his people could do without, but Man had become a decadent creature, the rule of the Imperator a bleak one. For a moment, Pyramors let the thrill of the wild hold him. If he ever got back to Innasmorn he would visit its wild places, cast himself out from its would-be rulers and the evils that clung to them.

But he could not afford to linger. He moved on. Below him he could hear the splash of the stream as it dropped over a lip of rock into a small pool. He slid through the leaves and, satisfied that there was no one here, moved out on to the rocks and waited.

She would be here, they had told him. They had found Jannovar.

The moments slipped away as he watched the ripples spread out over the pool, away from the tiny fall. The sound of the water masked any footfalls that he might have detected in the woods, but Vulporzol had promised him that only the girl would be sent. There would be no guards, Zemoi; they would wait high up on the ridge overlooking the valley and they would prevent anyone from coming down here until the girl returned to them.

Pyramors felt his heart hammering. He told himself not to be foolish: he was no longer a boy, flushed with the first heat of romance. And yet he felt light-headed. The memories crowded him and he drew in his breath, steeling himself for the emotion of the meeting.

To his right the bushes swayed. There was very little breeze. Someone approached. They were circling the pool but keeping out of sight. They must have seen him: he had made himself prominent, sitting as he was on the rock that jutted over the pool. Like a cat he rose, ears straining for the slightest sound. Would she never come!

In a moment he knew that only a single bush separated him from the woman he had come so far to find.

'Pyramors,' came her soft voice.

He felt his throat drying out. Again he was the foolish youth, heart thumping. He smiled at his own foolishness.

And then she stepped out onto the rock, no more than six paces away.

'I am Jannovar,' she said.

His breath caught and he felt a gentle clenching inside his chest. She was a head shorter than he was, her hair cut very short, blonded by the sunlight and her features were finely cut, her lips curving in a way that suggested surprise and uncertainty. She was very slight, her figure beautifully balanced and in her there was a suggestion of litheness, of swiftness, like that in a young doe. Her eyes, a penetrating blue, were almond shaped, drowsy, though he could see it was an impression only. She held herself proudly but there was an unmistakable alertness about her, as though she might leap easily out of reach. Yes, she was very beautiful, with an aura and pride of bearing that could surely snare the heart of an army.

But she was not Jannovar.

He shook his head very slowly. She was very like Jannovar, but younger, less full of figure. Surely she did not think she could deceive him. 'Who are you?' he said, and the words came out in a whisper.

Even so, she had heard them. She stepped forward, her head turning from side to side as if to look for unwanted watchers. He, too, studied the verdure around the pool, but there was nothing to suggest an intrusion. Did she expect one? Was this a trap? Could Zuldamar have enemies here? Vulporzol had warned Pyramors that Auganzar had a remarkable spy network that no other Csendook had been able to duplicate.

'Who are you?' he said again. He tried to control the shock of disappointment, the cold shiver of realisation that he had fooled himself into expecting a miracle.

She held out her right wrist, which had been out of sight. On it was the bracelet that Pyramors had been given on Innasmorn, with the Csendook writing etched on it, the name, Jannovar. 'They made me wear this,' she said. 'After they found me.'

'Who gave it to you?'

'Zuldamar's agents. They took me to a Csendook called Vulporzol. He said you would recognise it.'

He lifted her wrist gently and studied the bracelet. If it was a copy, it was identical. But it did not make her Jannovar.

'I am Jannovar,' she repeated.

He looked past her to the trees beyond. 'You are not the woman I am searching for. I am sorry you have been troubled. You'd better go back.'

But she shook her head. 'You don't understand, Pyramors. I am Jannovar.'

'No – '

'I have become Jannovar. I have taken her place – '

'Taken her place – ?'

'I was her sister.'

He frowned. Sister? The resemblance to Jannovar was so marked, yes: it would explain so much. Jannovar had had a number of brothers and sisters, although Pyramors had actually met only her brothers, most of whom had served in the armies, under the Philostrons. Her father had been Mennon Philostron, a powerful member of that family. But Pyramors had conducted his affair with Jannovar in strict secrecy, so that meetings with her brothers had been by chance only, and on military terms. He had never had cause to meet her sisters. And the resemblance between this girl before him to Jannovar was painfully close.

'Where is she?' he asked, his voice roughening.

She stiffened under his gaze, but shook her head. 'You will never find her.'

'Is she dead?'

She looked down at the pool, as though something might shine on its surface, something to ease the sudden tension that gripped them both. 'I can't know for sure.'

'But you're almost certain?' She nodded.

'What is your name?'

She lifted her face, her mouth pouting. So like her sister! He felt a stab of regret.

'I am Jannovar. What I was, who I was, is not even a memory. I have erased it. The darkness has it, Pyramors. Just as it has my sister. I am Jannovar. I have become her.'

Was she mad? he asked himself. She must have been through ordeal after ordeal since the fall of Eannor. Had it turned her mind? But she did not have the manner, nor the look of a girl who had lost her reason. On the contrary, she seemed bright, assured. And he recognised only too well the determination that had burned equally as brightly in Jannovar.

'Tell me what happened.'

She nodded, sitting on the rock. He lowered himself gently, again watching the forest, but nothing stirred.

'My brother-in-law's lust for power was the undoing of us all.'

'Fromhal,' he said quietly. A name he had come to loathe, the name of the man he would have killed a hundred times had the opportunity arisen, and who had in the end fallen to the Csendook advance.

Again she nodded, her eyes locking with his for a moment, as though they had found common ground, their hatred of the Djorganist overlord. 'He was not a Consul,' she began, 'though he dreamed of nothing else. His support was for Gannatyne, and because of that, Zellorian ensured that he was never advanced to the Consulate. But in spite of Zellorian's antipathy, the Imperator Elect saw to it that Fromhal was chosen to go with him when the attempt was made to escape Eannor. Zellorian wanted an excuse for Fromhal to be left behind. To be stricken from the list. You know of this list?'

'My name was on it.'

'Yes. As were the names of all of Fromhal's family and many of the Philostrons. But my sister had a secret lover.' She did not look at him as she said this, though there was no suggestion of bitterness on her face, nor in her voice. 'Who could blame her? She was married to a man who abused her,

239

who treated her poorly, second to his ambitions. A man who was jealous of her father's position and prestige. A man who did not see his wife for weeks at a time.'

'You don't have to describe your brother-in-law to me,' he said coldly. 'I see him standing before us now.'

She turned to him, seeing the killing anger in his eyes. 'Fromhal was unworthy of my sister.'

'We went to great lengths to keep our affair secret. We were sure that only a very few, loyal friends, knew about it.'

'You deceived the court, and for a long time no one of any importance knew about the affair. But such secrets don't keep forever. You must have known that.'

'Our hope was that we would get away from Eannor before Fromhal learned the truth.'

She shook her head. 'Fromhal discovered the truth in the last days. I suspect that agents of the Prime Consul may have learned something.'

'Zellorian? What had he to do with it?'

'His agents knew before Fromhal that Jannovar had a lover, though they did not know who he was.'

Pyramors scowled, seeing the tapestry of the past more clearly, the hand of its weaver. 'Zellorian,' he breathed, and again the girl felt the iciness of his anger. But what she had seen in his eyes at the mention of Fromhal did not compare to this dark shadow, this power that was disturbing in its intensity.

'Fromhal found out, and although he didn't care for Jannovar,' she said, 'he made immediate plans to dishonour her, and all her family. His jealousy of my father, Mennon, burned anew. Here was an opportunity to discredit him.'

Pyramors was listening, hearing her words, but at the same time recalling the words of Garrack, the engineer he had met on Skellunda.

'Rannor Tarul was under siege,' said the girl. 'The Csendook were preparing to take Eannor's last city and destroy the Imperator and his last defenders. There were desperate men in the city – '

'Slavers,' murmured Pyramors.

Her brows rose. 'You know of them?'

'And their deals. They worked secretly for the Csendook. Harvesting our women.'

'Yes,' she said, her own eyes flashing with anger. 'Fromhal had had a number of slavers found and executed, but ironically, he used them to bring about our fall. He gave us into their hands. Jannovar and I and a number of our servants, our family, were sent to work in the gliderboat pens. At first we were told it was necessary. Many of the people in Rannor Tarul were working through the nights in whatever ways they could towards the escape from Eannor. Few knew about the list, the fact that only chosen ones would go. So when we were sent down to the gliderboat pens, we thought it was to be part of the drive to freedom. We did not have a chance to get messages back to our families.'

'Who did you work under?'

'We were assigned to Artificer Wyarne, who ran the pens.'

'What happened to Jannovar?'

She could not meet his gaze and looked away, into the distance. 'We had guessed that something was wrong. That perhaps Fromhal had found out about you. The pens were a terrible place. Those craft.' She drew in a breath, trying to compose herself. 'Then we heard about the slavers.'

'The man Crasnow?' he prompted.

Her eyes widened in surprise. 'How did you hear about him?'

'Never mind. Tell me about Crasnow.'

'He was selecting women for the Csendook, knowing that the city would fall. They paid him well for his treachery. He had these bracelets.' She held out her wrist. 'He used them to mark the chosen ones, the best of us. When the fighting began we were to be spared and taken away, to serve our captors.'

'And Jannovar?'

'She was chosen. But I thought if I could find a way of saving her, of getting her back to you, she would be able to leave Eannor.' She could not look at him as she said this, though he put it down to her distress at reliving the horror of the pens.

'You knew that Jannovar and I were on the original list?'

She nodded. 'We tricked the slaver. We look very much like one another. We made a false bracelet for me and she —'

He held her arm and his grip tightened slowly. 'So what became of her?'

'In the fighting, we were parted. It was chaos, Pyramors. Our plans were not well enough formed. We thought Jannovar would be able to go back up into the city but we had not reckoned on the depth of Fromhal's spite, nor on Zellorian's. Zellorian had secretly spoken to the Imperator, but the Imperator did not want a public scandal at that time, not with the siege about our ears. It was hushed up, this slight on the Djorganist household.'

'Which is why they never had my name. Why I was never accosted.'

'Yes. But Zellorian saw to it that Fromhal was given a difficult post to defend. He was killed in the fighting. And the Philostrons were scattered. None of us went with the Imperator Elect to the place beyond Rannor Tarul that we had heard of.'

After a long moment of silence, he leaned back. 'Then Jannovar might yet be alive?'

But she shook her head. 'There were many killed. In the last riots, as the Csendook ringed the city and trapped us, some died in the crushes, the awful pandemonium. Men went berserk, some of them killing each other. I saw women beaten, raped. You cannot imagine what it was like. Many of those who worked in the gliderboat pens were abused. The truth of the Imperator's betrayal caused fresh fury. The gliderboats had been taken beyond the city, engineers with them, and in its anger, the mob rose up against those of us who had helped create the machines. I did not see Jannovar die, but in that madness, she could not have lived very long, Pyramors. I am sorry, but I am certain she died.'

'While you wore the false bracelet?'

242

His remark angered her. 'You think it hasn't tormented me ever since! Knowing that if Crasnow had taken her, she would be alive, with me dead in her place! We did not plan that – '

He stilled her with a movement of his hand, gentle, soothing. 'You could not have known the outcome.'

His sudden tenderness surprised her. 'She is dead, I know it,' she said again, tears forming in her eyes. 'My sister is dead. And I have her name.'

'What is your true name?'

She lifted her chin, the proudness of her family, proudness that Pyramors knew so well, showing through her sorrow. 'I am Jannovar. I have taken her name. Her identity. It is how I am known. It is how I honour her. I will not speak of the past. I am Jannovar.'

He would have derided her but something in her manner prevented him from speaking. Instead he looked down, the coldness of the truth taking him. Dead. Now that she had confirmed it and he knew at that moment that it was useless to hope that it could be a mistake, he felt unable to give himself to the full grief. Perhaps the loss of Jannovar, the wrench he had felt when he had been parted from her before the Crossing, had already numbed him. He had been following a ghost, and part of his mind had already accepted that.

Something touched him. The girl had moved closer, her hand falling as light as a leaf on his shoulder. 'All that she was, I now am,' she said. Was she offering herself to him?

He frowned, getting up slowly, still not looking at her. 'Dead,' he murmured. 'I feared she would be.'

She could see that she could not reach him, not for the moment. 'What will you do now?'

'I promised the Csendook I would do something for them.'

'You, a Consul, helping the Csendook?'

'They offered me – ' But he did not finish.

She flushed. 'Jannovar.'

'Yes. But I am committed to what I promised them. And it will help our cause, what is left of it.'

Her eyes flashed. 'Cause? Then he is alive? The Imperator? He crossed?'

It occurred to him that all this might be an elaborate trap, set for him by the Csendook. Perhaps they wanted the Imperator after all. But he couldn't believe that. Cmizen's fear, Vulporzol's secrecy. Not a trap. They wanted their Supreme Sanguinary assassinated. The girl gripped him. 'Did he get across?'

'Many of us did. But I came back.'

'Who else came?'

'No one else.'

'But where did you go? Another region?'

'Yes. But many of the Csendook have no desire to follow. They want an end to the war. The last of our race left to their new, secret world.'

'You came back – for Jannovar?'

'So I thought. The Csendook helped me.'

'In exchange for what? Betrayal?' Her voice had dropped, the horror in her tone clear.

'No, not that. They want our people left alone. Sealed off. But the most powerful of their military rulers still seeks our people. The Csendook for whom I work want him killed.'

'By *you*? But how?'

He snorted. 'That is my problem.'

'And you will do this?'

'It is the only way I can get back to – the new world. The killing will not end here in these arenas. If I survive, I will go back. I will find those who have betrayed our race.'

She felt once more the extraordinary intensity of his inner fury, the blind will that must be driving him. 'You will need allies.'

He nodded. 'A team. There are good men here in this warhall.'

'And does your team comprise only of men?'

He glanced down at her, at the wry smile. So like that of Jannovar! But he must be careful with this girl. He knew nothing about her, her loyalties.

'We're killers, no more than that. It is an ugly trade.'

'Do you think that the women who were taken by men like Crasnow aren't used to ugly work?'

'I was talking of battle. The hunt, the Testament. Fighting is work for certain kinds of men only. It is not something to be proud of.'

'Then you've no use for anyone who cannot hunt with you, or use a sword as you do?'

For once he smiled. 'I am putting together a team of killers, girl. Professional butchers, assassins. It is not like an army. I've seen excellent swordswomen in the Empire that was. But this is something else. Once we reach the Testament, we'll be set loose in terrain like this and hunted down. Most of us will die. Some will make it to the last of the arenas and then it will be the survival of the hardest, strongest, stubbornest. Those with enough animal instinct, sheer bloodymindedness and perhaps a little madness in them. It is crude and brutal.'

'In the field, yes,' she agreed. 'But you'll need eyes and ears in other places. Not just Csendook.'

He looked at her, amused by her persistence. 'Go on.'

'There are many women like me in the warhalls. The Csendook have been very good to us, mostly. They treat us with surprising respect. We are not abused and not forced to do the things that rumour suggests. We are not concubines and we are never made to suffer indignities. We are slaves, I can't deny that. But we are part of the new thinking. You are right, the Csendook are not bent on the destruction of our race. They are using us to breed a new race of Men. Using the strongest and ablest of our warriors.'

Pyramors's smile vanished. 'They use us for breeding? Like horses?'

'Just as you select the best warriors, so the Csendook select the best brood mares. But we choose our own mates. None of us is forced to mate with a man of whom we do not approve. And we mate for life. It is a strict rule. The traditions are strictly preserved.'

Pyramors shook his head. 'It is obscene.'

'Perhaps it is,' she agreed. 'But it is better than death, or abuse, or concubinage such as practised by the Imperator

Elect and his court. And it has brought happiness to many of the women. Few would leave their warhalls.'

'And just how does this help me with my preparations?'

'If you are to kill one of the Garazenda, as you've implied you must, you'll need to get close to him. Have access to his household. Find ways to deceive his Zemoks, those who guard his side. A woman might find a path to him for you where a sword could not.'

Again he smiled. 'You could be right.'

'Then you'll consider it?'

'Using you?'

'I am well placed now. The Csendook respect me.'

'Who is your husband? Is he in this warhall?'

She made a moue, turning up her delicate nose. 'I have not yet selected a husband.'

'And what would you do if this man turns you down?'

She gave a snort of annoyance. 'In the Warhive, men do not turn down the women who select them.'

'They are executed if they do so?'

'You don't seem to understand, Consul,' she said, more than a hint of scorn in her tone. 'Men do *not* refuse. They are thankful.'

'I wonder if I will be thankful if one of the women of the Warhive chooses me.'

Again she snorted. 'You are presumptuous, I think. It is not every man who is chosen.' She turned on her heel and began to walk back to the trees.

'I'll think about your offer of help,' he called. 'How can I contact you if I need to?'

'When I find out something of interest for you, *I* will contact *you*,' she said, and with a final, slightly dramatic flounce, she disappeared.

He stood silently for a moment, and it was as though a ghost had passed before him and slipped away. 'Jannovar,' he whispered, then smiled. Dead and yet —

But he straightened. Perhaps he had told this girl too much. He looked up through the trees. There was a job to do up in the hills.

19

A DEMONSTRATION

Uldenzar bowed as he saw his Marozul step through the huge doors of the hall, the central building of the Csendook barracks at the warhall. The Zarull was dressed in full military gear, and on either side of him the twin ranks of Zemoi stood stiffly to attention, faces hidden behind their war helms. They looked as though they were about to join a Swarm and go forward to battle.

As Zuldamar approached, himself resplendently dressed, twin battle swords at his belt, he pulled off his own war helm and carried it at his side. A dozen of his own crack Zemoks were with him, although he had not brought any higher ranking officers. He reached his Zarull and bowed.

'An excellent turn out,' he said to Uldenzar.

'When the Zemoi heard that we were to be visited by the Supreme Sanguinary, Marozul, they rose before the sun in order to prepare.'

Zuldamar grunted, scanning the ranks. Probably, like most Zemoi and Zemoks, they were anxious to impress the legendary Auganzar. Most of them would not have been close to him before, and many would never have seen him.

An announcement from the doors heralded the arrival of the Supreme Sanguinary, and he marched in, his own war gear polished so that it dazzled the eye, swords at his side. He, too, removed his war helm as a sign of courtesy and bowed to both Zuldamar and Uldenzar. For the moment he was alone, but even so he was an impressive figure in the hall. He did not as much as glance at the rows of Zemoi, though he felt their eyes on him.

'Is everything in order for this demonstration?' said Zuldamar.

'It is, Marozul. I have brought five beasts and a small contingent of handlers, Zemaal. They are ready to begin

247

the hunt at any time convenient to you.'

Uldenzar nodded. 'Zaru, I have sent a dozen *moillum* out across the foothills as you asked in your communication. They have been told that they must avoid capture for ten hours.'

Auganzar smiled abruptly. 'Yes. No need to set them any other goal. Have you chosen the pick of your *moillum*?'

'I have chosen *moillum* who would, I feel sure, give any Zemoi a good run. Some of them have avoided capture on previous hunts for far longer than ten hours. Some have even brought back pennants.'

'This is to your satisfaction, Supreme Sanguinary?' asked Zuldamar.

Auganzar again bowed. 'Indeed, Marozul. I want you to be certain that the tigerhounds are capable of finding the wiliest of prey. Ten hours will be generous. Will you inspect the beasts?'

'Yes, I am intrigued,' said Zuldamar. He and Uldenzar walked to the great doors, which opened out on to a field lined with trees. Broad steps swept down to the field, and beyond their foot were a handful of the Supreme Sanguinary's retinue. Uldenzar's Zemoi filed out of the hall and lined themselves up on either side of the steps, waiting in silence.

Auganzar went down the steps. Zuarzol was waiting for him, holding on a leash the first of the tigerhounds. It was a huge creature, far larger than any normal hound, its shoulder reaching the Zolutar's waist. Its snout was muzzled with steel, but the eyes blazed as the head bobbed from side to side as if the beast was already eager to begin the hunt. Behind Zuarzol were four other Zemaal, and each of them held on their special leashes a tigerhound, though these were a fraction smaller than the monster that Zuarzol held in check. The Zemaal, like Zuarzol, were clad in tight fitting steel mesh and wore protective face masks that were lighter than the customary war helms. They carried lightweight swords, little longer than dirks, and no shields.

Zuldamar had noticed the collar about the necks of the beasts. From this, the lead ran to the large glove that the

248

handlers wore on their right hands, and from this wires ran along the underarm to the shoulder and up to the face masks. The tigerhounds were animals but how were they controlled? As machines were? How had Auganzar perfected his creation?

Auganzar pointed to the feet of the tigerhounds, which were sheathed in light material that belied its strength. 'They kill with their claws as well as their fangs,' he called up to the watching Zuldamar. 'But in today's hunt, no one need be killed.'

Zuldamar and Uldenzar went down the steps, examining the tigerhounds more closely. The beasts were restrained but there was a tautness in them, a lust to be about the business of the day, as though they could smell a hunt and knew precisely why they had been brought here.

'If I might ask, Zarull,' Auganzar said to Uldenzar, 'at what hour were the *moillum* released?'

Zuldamar answered before his Zarull could reply. 'We must treat this demonstration properly, Supreme Sanguinary. In real circumstances, we might not know at what hour the hunted escaped us. You would have to guess, or use your judgement.'

Auganzar smiled. 'Yes, of course. My tigerhounds will rise to such a challenge. They will be capable of seeking out the most recent trails, the movements of any *moillum*, and so we will take them beyond the perimeters of the warhall. They will scent all trails and select the most recent. If you have any other *moillum* on manoeuvres, Zarull, then let them look to their heels! The tigerhounds will find them. Each beast will select a number of targets and the scent will be followed, while the other beasts will ignore the scents that have not been chosen for them.'

'They are that selective?' said Zuldamar.

Auganzar nodded. 'It will be easy for them to find the trails, as they are fresh. These beasts can find trails that are much, much older.'

'The *moillum* have been warned that this is no ordinary hunt, Zaru,' said Uldenzar. 'They know that certain beasts are searching for them. They will put every conceivable object in the way, and will doubtless do what they can to corrupt any trail they might leave.'

Again Auganzar smiled. 'I sincerely trust that your *moillum* will be as inventive as Man can be. I want this to be as fine a test for my tigerhounds as possible. I have already tested them out on some of my ablest Zemoks.'

'Were the results interesting?' said Zuldamar.

'Extremely,' nodded Auganzar.

'Very well, let us begin.'

Uldenzar gestured towards the side of the building behind them. 'I have prepared xillatraal,' he said. 'Will you ride in the hunt, or watch from a distance?'

'Perhaps, Marozul, you would rather watch from the relative comfort of an overflier?' said Auganzar, referring to the light craft that skimmed the lower skies of the Warhive.

'I'd prefer to ride,' said Zuldamar, who like most of his race had no great love for the aerial machines, unstable as they were.

'I would be glad to ride beside you, Marozul,' said Auganzar. 'Do you wish to be part of the hunt?'

'No, I'll observe. But I will enjoy riding. You will ride with us, Uldenzar?'

'Of course, Marozul. I will have an escort put at your disposal if you require one.'

'Three of my own warriors will be sufficient, I think, otherwise the hunt might become a little cluttered.' He had already talked privately to Uldenzar about this, and although the Zarull would have been happier if his Marozul had agreed to a full escort and the protection one of his rank ought to have, Zuldamar had assured him that he had brought some of the best Zaru in his ranks to protect him, though they were disguised as Zemoks. Zuldamar had told Uldenzar that he really did not think Auganzar would be so foolish as to make an attempt on his life and disguise it as yet another of the notorious hunting accidents.

'My own company will wait here,' said Auganzar. 'If that meets with your approval?'

'Yes, that will be in order,' said Zuldamar.

Uldenzar took them to the waiting xillatraal and they mounted, while at some unseen signal, three of Zuldamar's warriors came down the steps and waited while xillatraal were prepared for them.

Auganzar brought his beast under control and goaded it gently forward until it stood before Zuarzol and his tigerhound. The latter had dropped to its belly and paid little attention to the snapping beast above it, but the xillatraal had to be brought under firm control, uneasy at the nearness of the tigerhound.

'You have your instructions,' Auganzar said softly to his Zolutar. 'You know what you are searching for. I am sure he is in this warhall.'

Zuarzol gave the merest hint of a nod. His tigerhound was fully prepared. Auganzar lifted his hand, turning to Zuldamar. 'Shall I begin the hunt?'

Zuldamar nodded and Auganzar dropped his arm. It was enough. The tigerhounds rose, hairs bristling like wire and the beasts began the surge that would take them out over the field. They pulled the Zemaal along with them, heading for the perimeter of the warhall.

'I follow you, Marozul,' said Auganzar, waiting.

Zuldamar stood up in the stirrups to get the best view he could of the land beyond the field. 'I have no idea where the *moillum* have gone. Nor would I wish to give anything away. But there is a ridge of low hills to the south. I suggest we start there.'

'The Zemaal will keep us informed of their successes,' Auganzar told him.

'Then let us ride,' said Zuldamar. He spurred his beast forward and it reacted at once, and moments later the six riders were racing across the long field, the wind racing past them.

Uldenzar tried to close out the thoughts that kept nudging his mind. Three of Zuldamar's finest warriors. Could they not cut Auganzar down in the hills? Assassinate him at a stroke and save all the planning, the risk, the doubt? But Zuldamar had forbidden it. He dare not be implicated in such a coup. It would bring him down. Uldenzar gritted his

251

teeth in frustration. It was a measure of Auganzar's power that he could ride so easily, knowing that he was in the hands of Csendook who wanted to kill him.

The *moillum* in the tiny arena cheered as they watched the two men with swords. One of them, Arquemand, was quicker than a serpent, excelling with the short stabbing weapon. His opponent, Nemund, was more defensive but used his imagination to keep himself out of trouble. This was no fight to the death, but to first blooding, designed to instruct the other warriors who were watching. Both Arquemand and Nemund were expected to go forward to the Testament.

Among the spectators sat Pyramors, though he was well back in the tiers, with only a few men near him. He rarely engaged in conversation if it was not concerned with tactics on instruction.

'They're good, yes?' said a voice beside him.

He kept his eyes on the fighting men in the arena, knowing that it was Dessul who addressed him. 'Yes. But Nemund's shortcomings will find him out. Perhaps not here. But in the Testament.'

Dessul grunted. Pyramors was often dour, although always practical. What he had said about Nemund was not meant unkindly or said out of spite. It was a balanced judgement. 'Will you fight today?' Dessul asked him. He had seen Pyramors with a sword; he was as dangerous as he had been with his bare hands. Several good *moillum* had taken wounds. But he had killed no one, as if the act disgusted him.

Pyramors shook his head.

In the arena, Nemund narrowly avoided a blow from the flat of Arquemand's sword that would have stretched him out but although he thrust through his opponent's guard, Arquemand turned and used his knee to wind Nemund. Amazingly Nemund slipped away from another strike that would have ended the contest, but he was struggling to get his breath. The warriors on the seats roared Arquemand on. But he turned to them and shouted abuse, taunting them.

'He should have knocked Nemund out,' said Pyramors.

'Still, it's only a practice, eh?' said Dessul.

'No. This is real. These men need to understand that.' Pyramors said nothing more, leaving abruptly. He went down into the shadows under the tiers, making his way back to his chambers. In the distance he heard the unfamiliar howl of a tigerhound. Uldenzar himself had summoned him yesterday and warned him that he must keep close to the warhall all day, and spend as much time as possible alone in his private chambers. Auganzar was coming, demonstrating these new beasts, and Uldenzar did not want Pyramors as much as glimpsed. He had told Pyramors of the hunt and that he was supposed to have provided the very best of the *moillum* for it, but Zuldamar himself had told him to shut away the best of the warriors, especially Pyramors.

'Auganzar will doubtless know that we have spared our best,' Uldenzar had growled. 'He would do the same. But there are good *moillum* I will send out who will test these creatures. And there will be no killings.'

Again Pyramors heard the howl. It sounded as though it had come from close to the edge of the warhall. Surely the tigerhounds would have moved off towards the hills by now. It was almost midday. They ought to have decided upon their course long ago if they were as effective as Uldenzar had said they would be.

Pyramors reached his quarters and settled back beside his pool, relaxing. He thought for a while of the girl, who now called herself Jannovar. How could she help him? What information would she have access to? Uldenzar had told him that he would be able to meet her as often as he liked, within reason, but for the moment Pyramors had not asked for her.

Uldenzar had been puzzled, assuming that Pyramors would be pleased at being reunited with his lover, the woman he had come so far to find, and for whom he had given up so much. Perhaps, Uldenzar had thought, the burden placed on Pyramors had dampened his ardour.

* * *

Zuarzol checked the tigerhound with a silent mental command. Something in the link with the beast enabled him to make it obey him. He had named his own beast Raal, and in its way it had responded to that with a kind of pride, a fierce hunger to please him. It would share blood with him if he desired it.

Today's hunt had gone as planned. The other tigerhounds had quickly picked up the most recent scents of *moillum* who had left the warhall and the trails led in varying directions. Raal, however, hunted carefully for the one human scent that it had been tracking for far longer than a day and on other terrain. The scent of the Man it had tracked on Eannor, first for Zuarzol and then for Guntrazaal. Now Raal was pleased to be back with its master and they moved as one unit.

Raal had doubled back towards the warhall. Zuarzol knew that they were being watched, both by Zuldamar's group and by others who had been posted to watch the hunt and to record the skills of the tigerhounds. But they had been told that no one would interfere with them unless there was any danger of a kill. As Zuarzol came to the perimeter of the warhall, he knew that Raal had found what it sought. It lifted its head and howled through its muzzle, a long, piercing sound of triumph. And Zuarzol knew that it had found the scent of the Man, the one who had returned from beyond the great Cycle. Just as Auganzar had suspected, that Man was here, in this warhall. 'How recent?' said Zuarzol aloud.

The beast understood. Zuarzol read its mind. This scent was very recent. The Man had returned here a few days ago, probably from a training exercise.

Zuarzol allowed the tigerhound more leash and it pulled him under the walls of the warhall. Up on them, Zemoi looked down, seeing the two beings below them, marvelling in the power of the beast, the potential of those great legs, those muzzled jaws. They passed under an open gate and Raal nosed at the ground, sure of its passage. Zuarzol looked back at the field beyond the walls. He had not been followed. Auganzar had managed to keep Zuldamar away, as he had said he would.

Zemoi in the streets of the warhall paused in their business as they saw the tigerhound and its handler, exchanging puzzled glances. Surely these two were well off the scent. None of the runaway *moillum* would have come back here. They would have had a far better chance of hiding out in the wilder tracts of country. But perhaps one of the Men had decided on deceit. If he had, he would soon be taken. Several of them, curious, followed Zuarzol at a discreet distance, eager to see what his beast would uncover. But they did not challenge the Zolutar. An error here would be acutely embarrassing in front of the Supreme Sanguinary and indeed, the Marozul Zuldamar.

Zuarzol threaded easily and with certainty through the narrow streets, coming at length to a small square. Beyond this was a group of stone buildings and a field for arms practice. Several *moillum* were exercising on the grass, they turned and stared with surprise at the ferocious monster that the Csendook had on its leash. But it ignored them and tugged its handler towards one of the houses. There was no door, and it went inside.

Down the polished corridor the tigerhound and the Zolutar moved, in absolute silence, their feet making no sound. They came to an open area, in the centre of which was a pool. There were towels laid out beside it, as if recently someone had been resting there.

Zuarzol held the beast in check, shortening the leash so that it was no more than inches long. The Man they were hunting was very close. Raal lifted its great head and growled, its anger at the muzzle suddenly flaring. But Zuarzol calmed it with his free hand, stroking the head as if the beast were a domestic pet. He could feel the bridled fury beneath his touch.

'Show yourself!' he barked, using Man's tongue. 'You will not be harmed.'

There was a pause, but from behind a pillar at the edge of the hall a single figure stepped. It was a Man, dressed only in a brief loin-cloth. He had recently been in the pool, his body still glistening. His muscles looked as though they had been beaten from bronze.

'Your name,' said the Csendook.

Pyramors watched the incredible beast that the Csendook was restraining. It was the most terrifying animal he had ever seen, a combination of huge wolf, tiger and something else, possibly a reptile, though that was, he thought, his own imagination at work. It was muzzled, but even so, its jaws looked enormously powerful, as did its feet, which were sheathed. 'I am Pyras,' he said. 'Your tigerhound would seem to be far off its trail. I was not sent out this morning with the others.'

The Csendook paid out a little more of the steel leash and the tigerhound tried to leap forward, restricted by the lead. Its eyes blazed, full of murderous hatred.

'Pyras? That is your name?'

Pyramors thought it an odd question. He nodded.

There was a commotion behind the Csendook and three huge Zemoi entered the hall, calling out to the handler. The tigerhound swung its head around and growled at them. 'With respect, Zolutar,' one of the Zemoi said. 'Your tigerhound is following a false trail.'

Zuarzol's eyes were visible through his mask. He never took them from Pyramors. But he nodded slowly. He snapped something to the huge beast and reluctantly it moved to his side. He spoke to the Zemoi, swung round, and led the tigerhound away with an effort.

One of the Zemoi came over to Pyramors. He had been assigned by Vulporzol to watch him and was never far from him. Pyramors could see that the Zemoi was embarrassed by Zuarzol's sudden and unexpected intrusion. If the tigerhound had been let loose, it would have ripped Pyramors to shreds in moments.

'You are unharmed?' said the Zemoi.

Pyramors nodded, puzzled. An accident? But as the Zemoi dismissed themselves, following the Zolutar and tigerhound out into the sunlight, he found himself growing more disturbed. Why had the beast sought him out? Its handler had acted as though it had been an error, but could it be mere coincidence?

* * *

'Apart from the one lapse,' said Zuldamar, pouring wine for his guest, 'the demonstration was fascinating. Excellent. Every one of the *moillum* taken well before the allotted time.'

Auganzar accepted the wine and sipped at it. He sat with Zuldamar and Uldenzar in private, the hunt having been concluded an hour before. No one had been harmed but the tigerhounds had brought to earth the runaway *moillum*.

'The *moillum* who somehow managed to switch scents with the warrior who was here in the barracks used considerable initiative,' said the Zaru. 'But in order to do it, he must have had the cooperation of the latter.'

Zuldamar nodded. He went along with the duplicity, not sure that it had worked. Auganzar surely realised that he, Zuldamar, knew that the tracking of the Man called Pyras had been deliberate and no mere accident.

'Well, it was a worthy try at getting the better of your beasts,' said the Marozul. 'Again, I have to say they were superb.'

'Then you will press for the sanction of their use at the Testament? I will of course, see that they are made available to all members of the Garazenda who are entering *moillum*.'

Zuldamar nodded. It would be difficult to refuse the request after such a successful demonstration. But he guessed that Pyramors had been marked. But *how* could Auganzar have known that Pyramors was here? A guess? But *how*? How could he have been so accurate?

'There is another matter, Marozul,' Auganzar went on.

'Yes, I have not forgotten. The Men from Skellunda.'

'Marozul?' said Uldenzar, his face creasing in a frown he could not hide.

Zuldamar smiled and it almost seemed genuine. 'The Supreme Sanguinary and I have a little wager. He has two Men that he cannot train, in spite of his best efforts. They defy all attempts to make *moillum* out of them. Is that not so, Auganzar?'

Auganzar inclined his head. 'I took the liberty of bringing them with me. They are under guard with my Zemoks. Have you considered the wager, Marozul?'

Uldenzar's frown deepened. 'You are to train these Men, Marozul? Here?'

Zuldamar sipped his wine, nodding. 'Yes.'

Auganzar set his own glass down steadily. 'I am eager to hear, Marozul. I hope that I can match your stakes.'

'I think you can. If I am able to train these Men from Skellunda, make them act as *moillum* should and win a place in my team to represent me at the Testament, I ask for this. I am to have the pick of the *moillum* after the Testament. Instead of joining your elite, Supreme Sanguinary, the two champions that I consider to be the most impressive will join mine.' And to confuse you, I will not choose the one Man you would expect me to choose, the Man Pyras. Thus removing suspicion from him.

Auganzar considered. It was a beautiful trap, of course. Zuldamar had guessed at once that the two Men would be spies and that they would have to serve him well in order to serve their true master, Auganzar. And at the end of the Testament, when they had shown themselves to be truly converted warriors, Zuldamar would win his bet. He would protect his own champions, including this enigmatic Man that Zuarzol had uncovered. But why? Still Auganzar did not know why the Man was here. He had tried to find out the truth from the two Men of Skellunda but neither could be trusted. They hated the Man and all those connected with the Imperator Elect, but even so, they were still reluctant to aid the Csendook in anything.

'I accept the wager,' said Auganzar. He could not refuse.

'And what would you have of me, if I should fail?' said Zuldamar.

It was possible, Auganzar thought. The two Men were very difficult. They may yet defy his attempts to win them over. 'I have been most impressed with this warhall, and with the way Uldenzar attends to it. If you lose, Marozul, give me free access to this warhall.'

Uldenzar hid his fury by looking away. Surely Zuldamar was not so foolish as to agree to this. It would make him more vulnerable than he had ever been previously.

But Zuldamar smiled. 'Yes, a fair wager. It matches my own demands. I agree. Have the two Men sent to the cells. I'll begin work on them as soon as it is convenient.'

'Who do we trust?' said Garrack. In the total darkness of the cell time dragged on, night and day merged into one long hot period. They were used to extreme hardship: Skellunda had toughened them beyond the resistance of most Men. But they had been taken in secret from the island, masked so they knew nothing of where they were going, their hands tied securely so they could not resist. But they knew that it had been Csendook who had moved and escorted them. All they had known at first was that they were no longer on Eannor.

They had been kept in darkness and ignorance for what must have been many days. At last they were questioned through a grille in their cell by another, nameless man. He had asked them what they knew of a man called Pyras. They had not answered.

Kajello growled in frustration. 'The Csendook want to find the Imperator, if the bastard's truly alive. And they believe he is. But *where* could he be?'

'This offer of freedom if we help – '

'Freedom!' Kajello spat in the dark. 'It no longer exists. Not for our race. But if the Imperator is alive, by my blood, I'd be glad enough to kill him, and all those who are with him.'

'Then maybe we should listen to the Csendook? Help them?'

'Only because we can use them as our instrument of revenge.' He spat again. 'This goes against everything we agreed on Skellunda.'

'If we don't, they'll kill us. Why not take the Imperator with us, if he is, as you say, alive.'

'When the voice next calls us, we'll tell it we'll listen to its master. This Supreme Sanguinary.'

20

CONSPIRACY

Pyramors watched the eyes of the three men who faced him. Like him, they wore the simple loin-cloth of the *moillum* and the sweat glistened on their bodies. The sun here in this part of the Warhive was remorseless, as though artificially controlled to ensure that the gladiators always trained under the most difficult conditions. The Csendook, however, were impervious to the heat, never disturbed by it, able to fight under the most atrocious of conditions. The three warriors all held short swords, the blades flat and wide, the ends pointed, so that a chop from either edge could be fatal, just as a stab could. Pyramors was an acknowledged expert in the use of the short killing sword, preferring it to the heavier long swords favoured by some of the warriors.

He was training the men in the use of the shorter weapon, teaching them the tricks of in-fighting, of avoiding being trapped, of getting under an opponent's guard. The three men he faced were all very good. They were not the best in the warhall, for even Pyramors could not take on three of them. But these were a little angered that they had been told to face Pyramors in a trio. Pyramors hoped it would sting their pride enough to lift their skill. He wanted to demonstrate his own. Since coming here he had won the grudging respect of many of the *moillum*, and now he was using it to put together the men he wanted for his squad.

The swords clashed in the sunlight. There were trees around the edge of the chosen arena, a hollow in the foothills where the *moillum* had come to train for the day after a long run. A score of the gladiators stretched out under the trees, watching eagerly. Some of them wanted to see Pyramors cut and one or two would have been glad to see him die. But they knew this was unlikely.

Although all three men were fast, Pyramors was faster,

260

using a defence that was new to them, his arm seeming to be in three places at once as he avoided all three blades that sought his flesh. The men did not at first realise it, but they were driving Pyramors backward, only to find that he had chosen his ground and was allowing them to force him to ground that he could use better for a defence. It was stony, pocked with holes and with a number of treacherously exposed tree roots running over it. The first of the attackers realised this far too late and, as he stumbled, Pyramors's blade smacked him loudly across the side of the face. Dazed, the man fell aside, and at once Pyramors used the brief consternation of the other two to disarm one of them.

The last of the three skipped back nimbly, sword before him.

'Now it would be my turn to drive you back,' Pyramors told him, but without emotion. He slipped his sword into its scabbard, motioning for the warrior to join the others on the grass. They were all sitting up, watching attentively. It had been a strikingly impressive performance.

Pyramors walked over to them. There were no Zemoi present, although they would be in the upper hills. They preferred to let the *moillum* train privately. This was the Warhive. There was nowhere a man could escape to, although no man would think about escaping once he had got this far, so the Csendook assumed.

'Always choose your ground with care,' Pyramors told the men. 'If you are outnumbered, let your opponents think you are panicking. Drop back to ground that disadvantages them, if you can.' He was about to say more, when the sound of xillatraal distracted him. He turned to see three of the creatures trotting down through the trees of the slope beyond the hollow. Zemoi in war gear rode them, and with them, on two smaller beasts, xillas, were two men.

Pyramors frowned. He recognised both. They were from Skellunda.

The xillatraal pulled up short of the *moillum*, showing their fangs in snarls, but the Zemoi dragged their heads away from the warriors. One of the Zemoi dismounted and waved Pyramors to him.

261

'All right, get on with your work,' Pyramors told the men, and they moved out into the hollow, some of them muttering. But moments later they were exercising, and the ring of steel filled the still air.

'Pyras,' said the Zemoi, lifting his visor to show his face. He was a warrior whom Pyramors recognised, one whom Vulporzol said could be trusted and who spent most of his time in the warhall.

'Ulzem,' Pyramors nodded. 'Have you brought me fresh *moillum*?'

'I think you know these Men.'

Pyramors glanced again at the two riders. 'Kajello,' he said to the larger of them. 'And Garrack. Late of Skellunda.' Kajello's beard bristled, but he inclined his head. Garrack's face was pulled in a tight frown.

'What brings you to the Warhive? A change of heart?'

Ulzem answered for them. 'These Men are the subject of great discussion amongst our rulers. They were sent from Skellunda to the warhall of the Supreme Sanguinary. He thought to make *moillum* of them, for the Testament. But, short of beating them to death, he has been unable to do anything with them.'

Pyramors grinned wryly. Again he looked up at Kajello. 'Stubborn to the end, eh, Kajello?'

'To the death,' the huge man spat.

Ulzem would normally have knocked a Man from his seat for such a retort, but he ignored it. 'Zuldamar agreed to accept both Men from Auganzar. He told the Supreme Sanguinary that this warhall is as fine as any other on the Warhive.'

'Ah, and he wants *me* to beat these idlers into shape, is that it?'

Ulzem showed his own bright teeth in a smile. 'Your reputation among the *moillum* is growing, Pyras.'

'Then you'd better leave them with me.'

Ulzem nodded. 'Dismount!' he snapped at Kajello and Garrack.

Slowly, faces like thunder, they climbed off the xillas and Ulzem's companions gathered their reins.

262

'I will visit you this evening,' Ulzem told Pyramors. 'Prepare a preliminary report for me then.'

Pyramors nodded, watching as the three Zemoi swung their xillatraal about. Minutes later they had ridden up through the trees and were gone from sight, the snarls of the beasts coming back faintly.

Some of the *moillum* were watching the newcomers, but as they saw Pyramors turn their way, they hastily continued with the training programme. Pyramors faced the two men from Skellunda. Why were they here?

'We wondered if you had survived,' growled Kajello. 'It seemed strange that you were not executed in front of us all on the island.'

'You have influence with these scum,' said Garrack. 'You speak their tongue as if born to it.'

'The Empire may be dead,' said Kajello, 'but rank still has its privileges, eh, Consul?'

Pyramors regarded him coldly. 'Do not use that title here. If you do, I'll kill you.'

For a moment Kajello looked as though he would lose control of his fury, but instead he turned away.

'I am Pyras. Just another *moillum*. Forget our differences. We have far more important things to do here.'

'Such as selling your sword to the Csendook,' said Garrack.

'I have my reasons.'

'You've done well enough out of it,' grunted Kajello.

'Yes, I have influence with the Csendook. The extent of that influence would surprise you.'

'Nothing would surprise me, *Pyras*,' said Kajello.

'Why do you think I was not executed on Skellunda for that killing? The Zolutull, Karanzol, was convinced that I had killed the Zemoi. You planned it well and fooled him.'

'Someone pulled you out,' said Garrack.

Pyramors nodded. 'Yes. I was sent to Skellunda to try and bring together a team. A team of the best, most effective killers I could find.'

'*Moillum* – '

'Not quite. Assassins. I told you once.'

Kajello's eyes narrowed. 'You still persist in that lunatic idea?'

'It's not something I would pursue without specific help.'

'The Zemoi – '

Pyramors shook his head. 'Far higher.'

Kajello and Garrack glanced at one another, but then focused their attention on the *moillum*. 'What do you expect of us?' said Kajello.

'What happened to you in Auganzar's warhall?'

Kajello snorted. 'Hah! They tried to rough us up a little. I broke a few heads and Garrack here split a few skulls himself. He'd match any of those swordsmen out there. Although I see talent among them.'

'Yes,' said Garrack, watching the contests. 'But there's talent in Auganzar's warhall, too.'

'Auganzar's heavies seemed to think if they could break the rebellious spirit of the rabble of Skellunda,' said Kajello, 'he could forge a team of *moillum* that would be second to none. But to do that, he had to win our respect.'

Garrack laughed grimly. 'He failed.'

'You saw no benefits in playing along – ' Pyramors began.

Again Kajello looked angry. 'We're lawless men. We spit on our old Empire and the bastards who ran it, who *betrayed* us. Just as we spit on the Csendook who harried us after the fall of our worlds and who would make slaves of us. We serve no one.'

'Then do you not welcome a chance to strike out at the things you despise?'

Kajello would not look at him. He thought for a moment. 'Tell me, why should we take sides in this private war between the Supreme Sanguinary and the Garazenda who oppose him? What difference does it make to any of us? I can see that someone like you, Pyras, would stand to gain a great deal. If Auganzar dies, your new masters will elevate you to some new post. You would be as favoured among Csendook as any of their own kind.'

'That's not why I'm doing it.'

Kajello laughed derisively. 'No? You were a man of the highest rank once. Yes, I'll not name your rank again if it means my head for it. But I've no respect for what you were. Now that you are a slave, how can you be content? Power is all your kind understand. It is what fuels you – '

'Is that how you see us?'

'It's the truth.'

Pyramors nodded slowly. Yes, this was the attitude the Imperator Elect had fostered through his cynical reign.

'In the death of Auganzar, you see power for yourself.'

'And we're not interested in being part of it,' added Garrack.

'You're wrong,' Pyramors told them. 'There are other reasons.' He knew they would never trust him unless he told them the truth.

'Whatever they are,' said Kajello, 'they won't sway us. We won't be part of your team. We will not serve Csendook.'

'If I were to ask you what you wanted most, what would it be?'

Both Kajello and Garrack looked surprised by the question.

Kajello answered at last. 'If you had been offering me a chance to join an assassination squad that intended to kill the Imperator Elect, and some of his vermin, *then* I'd have been with you. But as he was destroyed by his own sorcery – '

Pyramors shook his head. 'Perhaps not.'

'What do you mean?' said Garrack suspiciously.

'What if I were to tell you he is alive – '

Kajello's thick brows met like thunderheads. '*Alive?*' he breathed. 'Where?'

'Not on Eannor. Not on any of the worlds we know. Beyond them. Beyond the very cycle of worlds. With Zellorian. Alive and safe.'

'This is a trick,' said Garrack under his breath.

Pyramors shook his head. 'He found a way through. And *I* went through with him. I came back, alone.'

Kajello's eyes had narrowed to two tiny slits. 'So that you could kill Auganzar?'

Pyramors snorted. 'This will be the hardest part for you to believe. I came back for the simplest of reasons. To find a woman.'

Garrack's eyes widened. 'Ah, the woman you questioned me so hotly about. The Djorganist wife! Jannovar, Fromhal's woman. With whom you had an affair.'

'You know about this?' Kajello said to Garrack as if it surprised him.

'I told you he questioned me hard about Rannor Tarul and the fate of its women.'

'They've found her,' said Pyramors. 'And she is promised to me if I help them. But much more is promised to me.'

'Go on,' said Kajello.

'I will be sent back, with Jannovar. Back to the world where the Imperator Elect is hiding.'

'You still serve that bastard – '

Pyramors's face was cold, his eyes like ice. 'No. I am going back in search of his life. All those who betrayed you and so many others will be found out. But not by the Csendook. There are survivors who deserve to live. Whatever your feelings, Kajello, you are wrong to condemn them all.'

'But your masters here, the Garazenda you serve – do they *know* of this other world?' said Kajello incredulously.

Pyramors nodded. 'They knew of it soon after Zellorian's success. But they don't want the Crusade continued. They would be content to rule the worlds of this cycle without entering the new cycle Zellorian has found. Man can dwell there without the Csendook masses ever knowing.'

'And Auganzar?' said Garrack.

'He also knows, or suspects, that there is another world cycle. And *he* wants to enter it and continue the hunt, the enslavement of all Mankind. Not only would he kill Zellorian, the Imperator and all those you hate, but he would kill the others, the innocents. They must be allowed to survive.'

Kajello took a long slow breath and straightened. 'It is amazing,' he murmured. 'If it is true.'

'If Auganzar is assassinated, our race will have a better chance for survival,' said Pyramors.

'And if we help you?' said Garrack.

'I doubt that they will let me take many back to the new world. If I could, I would empty the Warhive of all *moillum*, and Eannor too, and other worlds. But I cannot. I can take

266

a few. The Csendook I serve will permit that. The assassins will come with me. It has been agreed. I will need them, if I am to succeed in the other killings.'

Kajello scratched at his beard, combing it for a long time, shaking his head. 'The chances of success in this venture are small. We may well succeed in the Testament, yet Auganzar chooses the best, I am told. But once we are part of his private host, what then? How could we kill him and escape? It sounds like suicide to me.'

'We'll have inside help. Never mind from where.'

Garrack grunted knowingly. 'The women? They also serve the Csendook houses – '

'Perhaps,' nodded Pyramors. 'But first we have to get to the Testament, and then be sure that as many of our team as possible live through it.' He stared into the faces of the two warriors, reading their confusion. 'What is it to be?'

'A quick death if we refuse,' said Kajello, grimacing.

'The chance to hunt our true prey if we succeed,' said Pyramors.

'You'd take us through?' said Kajello. 'You would promise us that?'

Pyramors nodded again. 'On my honour, and that is the most valuable thing I have, believe me. I was never the Imperator's toy, and never party to Zellorian's betrayal.'

Kajello sniffed. 'No, perhaps that's the truth.' He looked at Garrack. 'A chance to avenge our fellows, Garrack. Let us take it.'

'We'll train with you, Pyras,' Garrack agreed. 'But we'll keep up a pretence of being obdurate. We'll make it hard for you to win us over. It will look more convincing.'

Pyramors grinned. 'Come and meet some fine warriors.'

Auganzar watched the two gladiators with deep interest, his infatuation with the intricacies of combat something that no amount of such spectacle could wear down. The Men before him were very fast, probably as fast as any other Men he had seen. It was a mark in favour of his warhalls that the Men were trained up to new skills. Armies of Men such as these would be difficult to maintain. Rebellion on a large scale could cause the Csendook severe difficulties. But it was the price that they had to pay for control.

He felt movement beside him on the steep tiers and turned to see one of his Zolutull, Raduzol, waiting patiently. Auganzar waved him to him. This was one of the many private indoor arenas in Auganzar's warhall. There was absolute secrecy here.

Raduzol sat beside his master, watching the contest below with equal interest. 'Their speed is impressive,' he commented.

'They'll do well in the Testament,' agreed Auganzar.

'Our warhall will stand high among the victors.'

'You have news for me?'

'I do, Zaru. I fear you will lose your wager with Marozul Zuldamar.'

A trace of a smile crossed Auganzar's features. 'Ah, the two recalcitrants from Skellunda?'

'Indeed, Zaru. They are training hard with Zuldamar's *moillum*.'

'They have capitulated?'

'So it appears. They are part of the core unit that is being controlled by one of Zuldamar's finest *moillum*. It will not surprise you to learn his name.'

'I can guess it. I hope these Men were reasonably subtle about their so-called conversion?'

'The Man Pyras does not seem to be suspicious of them. I am told reliably that both Men were very convincing in their hatred of us and in their willingness to become part of his plans.'

'Ah, yes. His plans. And have we yet learned what these plans are?'

Raduzol frowned. 'We have, Zaru.'

'Then tell me, and do not spare me the worst of this conspiracy.'

'Very well, Zaru. The Man Pyras is preparing an assassination squad.'

'Is he now? I assume it is in my honour.'

'Zaru, you are to be the target.'

Auganzar smiled, watching another dazzling exchange below. 'Extraordinary ambition.'

'Should they succeed, Zaru, they plan to go further.'

'Further?'

'The Man Pyras seeks a way back to Innasmorn, with the survivors of his team.'

'Ah, he had to tell them the truth to win them. They hate their worthless Imperator as much as, if not more than they hate me,' Auganzar smiled. 'But what is more to the point, they hate this Man you call Pyras. They hate his rank, his past, what he did on Skellunda. Which is why they have elected to serve me. Now they will believe me when they hear Innasmorn exists. Pyras has confirmed it for them.'

'If I may be forward, Zaru, what did you promise them?'

'To win them? A chance to serve in my *moillum* when we go to Innasmorn. Pyras, Pyramors, may have offered them a chance to join him, but when the hunt for the Imperator begins, these Men know who will administer the kill.'

Raduzol bowed. 'How could they refuse? But since you have uncovered the detail of this foolish plot, Zaru, what would you wish me to do? I can arrange for the swift death of the Man Pyras.'

'Pyramors. The Consul. But no. I don't want him killed. He is far too valuable to me alive.'

'But, Zaru, even if you do not have him removed, there is the coming Testament in your honour. Clearly Pyramors will take part in the fighting, and in the Running Hunt – '

'No doubt he will survive them all. He'll be there, at the end. We may have to watch him, but he'll win through, along with the cream of his warriors.'

'And – you will select him?'

'Naturally. Then he will be mine to deal with. Zuldamar will no longer have control of him.' But the Supreme Sanguinary seemed to think of something and his smile became an ugly scowl. Unless Zuldamar protects him by choosing him for himself as part of the wager over the two Men of Skellunda!

'But the Man will plot your assassination from within – '

269

Auganzar's scowl dissolved as quickly as it had formed. Of course! Pyramors could *not* be chosen. He *must* stay with Auganzar if the assassination were to work. Then why had Zuldamar asked that his price should be the pick of the victorious *moillum*? But as he thought about this, it became obvious. Zuldamar would pick someone other than Pyramors, trying to draw suspicion away from him.

'I have other plans for Pyramors,' Auganzar told Raduzol.

The sound of water falling over the rocks hid the sound of her coming. Pyramors had bathed in the cold water of the pool after arriving here. It was late afternoon and again he had been training hard that day, driving himself and his men. Tomorrow they would go to the arenas for the beginning of the Testament. He had his team. Overall, a thousand *moillum* from this warhall would go, but fifty of them were Pyramors's assassins, among them Kajello and Garrack. They had been surly and difficult, just as promised: hard on those they trained with and fought, and there had been the inevitable deaths, but the two men of Skellunda had been convincing in their conversion. Pyramors would never be absolutely sure of them, they had hated what he stood for too much, but he needed their skills. If Auganzar was to die, he must have men like them when he reached the Supreme Sanguinary's inner halls.

'Dreaming of battle?' came a soft voice, almost at his ear.

He sat up with a jerk.

'I could have killed you,' said the girl.

She was right. He smiled in spite of himself. It was rare for him these days to be off his guard. 'Save that for later,' he told her. 'I may have to ask you to do such things.'

She grimaced. 'I suppose I'm ready for that. Not all the blood that is spilled will be spilled in the arenas.'

He looked down at her, again surprised by her likeness to Jannovar. She still refused to be called anything else. 'Can we succeed in this?'

'I don't know. It will take time. If you can be patient – '

'As you are patient with me?' he smiled.

She turned away from him, watching the play of the waterfall. 'There are things we must plan tonight.'

'For the Testament?'

'Yes. Tomorrow they open. It will be the eve of the fighting. By tradition, the women choose their men.'

'I see.'

She still had her back to him. 'If we are to go on planning as we have done, and if I am to be your contact within the system – '

He laughed softly. 'You will have to choose me, is that it?'

She turned, her cheeks burning. 'You think it's amusing?'

He stepped back, surprised by her annoyance, but he smiled again. 'Our masters would think it a bit suspicious if you chose someone else. Zuldamar himself would be curious.'

She pouted, and again he cursed inwardly, for she was at times the image of her sister. 'Pyramors,' she said, barely above the sound of the water.

'Pyras. Always call me Pyras.'

'Pyras. I will have to choose you. But there is something I must tell you.'

'Ah, you are already promised to another. As long as it is not Kajello.'

But she was neither amused nor angered as he had expected. 'It is not that. Zuldamar and all the others: they think that I *am* Jannovar. You are the only one who knows that I'm her sister.'

Now it was his turn for anger. 'What? Then they are no longer looking for her?'

She bowed her head. 'Pyras, I am sure she is dead.'

He came close to her and she could feel the fury in him, the coldness of his stare. 'You cannot be sure.'

She could not look at him. 'I am sure.'

'Why have you not told them?'

'They might kill me – '

He wrenched himself away. 'That's ridiculous! They know you are helping me – '

'If they found out I was not Jannovar, they would think they could no longer control you through me. They know how much you want her – '

He let out his breath slowly, his frustration difficult to control. 'Very well. We go on as planned. But while there is still a chance of her being found –' He broke off.

As he turned, she looked at him for a moment, tears in her eyes, but she turned away quickly. 'You think I miss her any less than you?'

He realised how the probable death of Jannovar must have wounded her. He put an arm about her. She clung to him. 'I'm sorry,' she whispered.

'No. Forgive me. We should comfort each other and not cause each other more grief. But I must be absolutely sure she is dead.'

She nodded. 'I understand. But I must remain Jannovar. And I must choose you. But understand that I will not hold you to any of the rules the Csendook have imposed on such things.'

Suddenly he laughed, lifted her from the ground easily and swung her round. 'Very well. Jannovar you are. And I had better accept.'

'Put me down, you fool,' she sniffed. 'There are many things you have to know and barely enough time.'

Ussemitus felt himself stretched almost beyond endurance as he sought to control the spectral he had sent so far beyond the World Splinter. He read its distant thoughts, saw through its eyes as the landscapes shifted below him.

Over Eannor the spectral soared and dipped, sifting from the thin, hot air clues to the whereabouts of the Man, Pyramors. He had been here, but the air of Eannor, its winds, were not as those of Innasmorn. They did not live and breathe in the same way. They hid their secrets. But the spectral learned through arts beyond Ussemitus's understanding that Pyramors had passed beyond Eannor. To the very Warhive itself.

In his darkness, the last dregs of his resolve thrust the spectral through the barrier to the world of the Csendook and in air that was even more arid and sterile than that of Eannor, the flickering spectral searched again with the last guttering flames of its powers.

BOOK FIVE

RUNNING HUNT

21

TESTAMENT

Pyramors watched the twilight beginning, the purple light fading swiftly beyond the huge superstructure of the amphitheatre above him. He turned from the narrow window. The hall he had been given here under the arenas was small, with only the most basic requirements. There were numerous such halls, built to house the *moillum* who were to fight in the Testament, and in these chambers they were permitted their final hours of privacy before seeing action.

Pyramors sat on the bench as the light faded. It had been a tedious day and one that had seemed to go on endlessly. Several thousand *moillum* had been presented to the Garazenda in the vast stadium above, which had been recently built for these games. The Testament was to be the first major event of its kind since the ending of the wars and promised to supersede any that had gone before. The Marozul themselves presided over it and every one of them had entered teams. It had been a remarkable sight, the procession of those warriors, but Pyramors could not hide the disgust he felt at the effective enslavement of his people. Honour and glory they may win, but their freedom was an illusion. And he knew that the *moillum* who survived, who became warriors in a new, subsidiary army, would have the task of searching out renegades, men on remote worlds who had so far avoided the sweep of the Csendook. Those of them who would not capitulate would be killed by their own kind, Man against Man. And it was Auganzar who had introduced this new system. The Testament was a tribute to it.

There had been no fighting today. The *moillum* had been able to feast, though they had all been cautious. Many of them had been subjected to the other ritual, the ritual that Pyramors had found even more humiliating. Women, also enslaved by the Csendook overlords, had chosen their men, men with whom they would couple and produce, it was hoped, finer warriors still. Tonight there would be many such couplings in the chambers, and many of them would be the last such acts of the warriors, who would die in the course of the next few days. The women who were widowed so swiftly would have a short time to recover themselves: those who were not impregnated would be able to choose another mate in time.

A knock sounded on the narrow door to the chamber. At first Pyramors hardly noticed, trying to smother the fury that had been mounting as he relived the day. But at length he rose and opened the door.

It was the girl.

She carried a tiny lamp, its flame flickering as if it would die at any moment, and as he motioned for her to come in, she set it down on the single slab that was the table. 'You are angry,' she said, her voice barely above a whisper. She was dressed in a plain white garment, the curve of her figure revealed beneath it. She waited, nervous as a bird. She seemed very small.

'I'm sorry you were put through that foolish ritual,' he said gruffly. In the heat of the arena, she had been one of the many women ordered to select her man, just as she had told him she would be. But she had kept very calm throughout the brief ceremony, and to the numerous eyes watching she must have seemed in complete control of herself, haughty and proud. He had been motionless, at attention throughout, his eyes locked on some distant point as if scorning the whole procedure.

'When you win through the Testament,' she told him, 'you will be permitted to take me to whatever halls you are given. If your plan works, that will be in the estate of Auganzar. I have friends there among the women. They will help us with the next phase of the plan.'

She had not moved, her hands by her side. He stepped toward her and lifted her right hand. She wore the bracelet with the Csendook lettering – her sister's name. 'When I came to Eannor,' he said, examining the bracelet carefully,

'I wore this. Zellorian gave it to me and I snapped it on my own wrist. It adjusts itself automatically. It is a remarkably fine piece of craftmanship.'

'It is made of gold,' she answered softly. 'A precious thing.'

'Once snapped into place on a human wrist, it cannot be removed by the wearer. It was removed from me, possibly by Vulporzol. He was the Csendook who first found me. Perhaps he had a key to such things. Who gave the bracelet to you?'

'Yes, it was Vulporzol. He said you would know me by it.'

'It belonged once to your sister.'

He felt her tightening, her eyes fixed on the bracelet. 'Yes.'

'It was made for her. Someone must have removed it from her wrist.'

Her eyes met his for a moment, then shied away.

'A slaver, perhaps. Whoever it was, they gave it to someone who in time put it into the hands of my enemy, Zellorian. He had not realised that the lover of Fromhal's wife was one of the very Consulate he sought to bring down. He was not even aware of the name of Fromhal's wife. But once he had the bracelet, the facts were given to him so that he could manipulate me.'

She frowned. 'I don't understand – '

'It is what took me back to Eannor.'

'Now that I wear it, I cannot remove it,' she whispered.

'That was once true of Jannovar. Perhaps you saw it on her wrist, marking her for the slaver, Crasnow, who was supposed to prepare her for sale to the Csendook when they overwhelmed Rannor Tarul.'

Again she nodded. His grip on her wrist tightened and she winced, standing on her toes as she felt the pressure increase. 'Someone took it from her wrist,' he went on, eyes fixed on her, a promise of further pain flaring in them.

'I don't know – ' She almost tumbled over, trying to keep her balance, eyes brimming with tears.

'A Csendook?'

She shook her head, the tears trickling down her face as she did so. He released her and she clasped her wrist to her chest.

'*Then who removed it?*'

'I told you, Pyramors, she is dead. She was killed in the riots. I did not see, but there would have been people there who recognised her as a member of the Djorganists. They would have – '

'Go on.'

She lowered her head. 'They would have pulled her limb from limb. The bracelet – oh, what do you think!'

Neither of them moved after she said it. She could not look into his fury, his anguish. He looked through her, imagining the horrors in the city when the Swarm had engulfed it.

Suddenly she looked up, anger in her own eyes. 'You think it does not pain me to think of it! My own sister! You think I loved her any less than you did? I, too, suffer.' She ran past him, bending to pick up the lamp.

As she reached the door, he called to her, more softly. She turned, her mouth set in a hard line. The shadows fled from the lamp and it was as though a ghost stood before him again.

Slowly he walked to her. 'I am sorry.'

She waited until he stood before her. 'If she were alive, we would have found her,' she whispered.

Again he lifted her wrist, this time stroking it. He could think of nothing more to say to her. In a moment she put down the lamp and took him in her arms, speaking softly to him as his own tears, held in abeyance for so long, fell, his body convulsed with the release of his sorrow.

Shortly after dawn, the Testament began.

The programme of events was simple: first there would be a number of contests to eliminate a great many of the contestants. The survivors would be let loose and hunted, and had a day to survive again. Those that did returned to the grand arena for the final contests, individual combat in the various types of weapons allowed, short sword, long or broad sword, pike, knife and bare hands. Three thousand *moillum* began the first day. It was expected that no more than two hundred would survive the last. The Supreme Sanguinary was to choose what he considered to be the finest fifty of these.

As Pyramors took to the arena on the first day, he was accompanied by a hundred of Zuldamar's best gladiators, chosen mostly from the warhall he had attended here on the Warhive. His own team of assassins consisted of twenty-five men, and every one among them knew that their chances of survival were slim. Pyramors knew that if he could get himself and four others through these contests, he would have an even chance of success. His team was good, and he was proud of the men he had trained. They would have made exceptional captains under him if he had yet been a general in the field against the Csendook. Among them were Kajello and Garrack whom he had known would be superlative warriors. Dessul was here also, being particularly good with a sword as well as a slippery opponent when it came to fighting with bare hands.

The first day began with contests with the short sword. The arena was gigantic, and Pyramors could not help but marvel at the architecture, the great sweep of tiers that rose up around the bowl, the engineering that must have produced such a building. Was this to be the future? A return to the secrets of the past, an age when it was known that technology flourished, racing headlong to unrecorded disasters that brought about such upheavals in the structure of the Empire? Where would such advances take the Csendook this time? Thousands of Csendook were seated in the stadium, the sound of their cheering deafening: they would all have bet on their favourites. Each warhall wore the colours of its owner, Zuldamar's warhall being a bright green, with a dark green slash down the front of the tunic. Auganzar's warhall wore scarlet.

For an hour Pyramors fought with the short sword, a weapon he favoured. The *moillum* he was forced to fight were all skilled and, like him, they knew that the only route to survival in this Testament was to kill. Twice Pyramors came close to death and somewhere in the huge circle of tiers above him, Zuldamar saw and felt the stab of defeat coming for him. But Pyramors recovered each time. He killed five men, men he had never seen before, men who could have served him well under different circumstances. Between each bout he was allowed to rest and clean himself in one of the wide troughs at the edge of the arena, but again he was called forward by the Zemoi who marshalled the fighting. After the seventh killing, he was pulled out of the sword fighting.

Again he rested, and an hour later the first of the bare handed contests began. It was some time before he was sent into the arena and the first opponent he faced wore Auganzar's scarlet. Again it was a man he had never known, and the fellow was very fast, very strong.

The crowd followed the fighting avidly, whole sections of it watching a particular contest. Pyramors sensed that several thousand Csendook were watching his own fight, and among them must be many of Auganzar's supporters. Each time his opponent landed a blow, they roared him on. But Pyramors closed the noise from his mind and concentrated on the work, using every technique, every trick he could find. At last he broke the defence of his opponent, damaging his leg. It slowed him just enough to give Pyramors the edge and when he finished him, it was with a clean punch to the heart, a killing blow.

Not all the fights ended in killings, but where *moillum* were beaten or had a limb damaged so they could not continue, the Zemoi moved in and despatched them with their swords. Again Pyramors was forced to choke back his fury, but it was another of the rules of survival in this place.

Later in the day, bruised and bloody, he fought with the pike, a weapon that he had never enjoyed using, the fighting technique being unique to it, but at the warhall he had worked hard on the deficiencies in his own skills. Fortunately he did not meet up with any warriors who specialised in its use and, having fought four times with opponents who were only marginally less skilled than he was, he was able to defeat them.

There was a longer break in the early afternoon, and for a long time the tiers were empty as the Csendook crowds left in search of food and to place still more wagers. The carnage in the arena had been grim, with countless *moillum* taken away to be burned on pyres beyond the city. Food and drink were brought into the arena for the surviving *moillum*. There were barely over a thousand of them left: they had been cut by a third. As Pyramors ate sparingly he moved slowly about the huge arena, permitted to do so during the lull. He found a number of his team were still alive. Kajello, Garrack and Dessul were among them, but they exchanged no more than brief nods of recognition. Tomorrow, in the Running Hunt, if they made it, they could work together. Teamwork was one of the essentials of the Running Hunt, and the Csendook expected to see it in operation.

Pyramors noted the large number of scarlet-clad warriors who had survived until now. Over a half of the survivors had been trained at Auganzar's warhalls.

The afternoon's bouts began, this time with the long sword, a weapon that demanded strength of arm. To fight with it for any length of time was exhausting, which is why it had been chosen as the last of the weapons. It would ensure that only the strongest would survive, those whose endurance was greatest. It would take sheer guts and dogged determination, a kind of madness, to come through the day's last taxing test.

Pyramors knew how to conserve energy when using one of these weapons. His first opponent did not and was already tired from the day's exertions. Pyramors had no desire to prolong any contest further than necessary. As soon as he saw the weakness of his opponent, he cut him down. His second opponent was stronger than the first and almost caught Pyramors with a sweeping strike, but he had gambled everything on maiming if not killing. Pyramors turned out to be the quicker of the two and used his own weapon to deadly effect.

The contest with the third swordsman looked as though it would be a more protracted affair, for the warrior was very fast and still strong enough to match Pyramors. Both of them had almost won vital openings when the long sword of his opponent suddenly caught Pyramors a glancing blow, knocking him sideways. He slipped to one knee. At once he knew that he was in real peril. The huge sword swung down at him and he managed to deflect it. But as it came at him again, he could not rise. The man above him knew how to finish a contest. Again the sword swung for his neck. It was very fast, but Pyramors saw his death in the blow, heard the rushing of blood in his own ears.

Something flashed, dazzling as sunlight, before his eyes, and the long sword seemed to rise in a strange arc, over his head. He felt the air of its passing. Sunlight? But it was behind his would-be killer. His bulk threw Pyramors into shadow. There was no more than a split second to act and Pyramors swung his own weapon sideways, chopping into the knee joint of the man above him. It brought him crashing to the ground. Pyramors recovered at once, leaping up and driving the haft of his long sword into the fallen man's temple. The man sank down, motionless.

Pyramors at once looked around, still puzzled by the sudden flash of light. Had someone in the sea of faces up on the tiers deliberately used some trick against the fallen warrior? But it was impossible. No one could hurl power, for it had been more than mere light. Something tangible had deflected the death blow.

Before he could think any more about it, the Zemoi stepped in and called a halt to the fighting. Enough of the *moillum* had been eliminated. The day of blood was at an end.

Pyramors, still bemused, was returned to his chambers, and after plunging himself into a piping bath, he cleaned his wounds. None of them troubled him, though he would carry several ugly bruises with him into the field tomorrow. The girl did not come to him that night, nor would she until the Testament was over. But he thought of her and the way she had comforted him. His emotions had become confused, and as he thought again of the dramatic last fight he had had, he drifted into sleep.

Alarms woke him, it seemed almost instantly, but the dawn was already seeping through the tiny window over his head. Outside in the corridor, he lined up with the other *moillum*. Today a thousand of them would go to another arena, a huge area beyond the city, where they would be hunted until the following dawn. The Csendook would use xillatraal and other beasts, such as the tigerhounds, to track them. Those that they found would be killed. The survivors would return for a final day, though there had been Running Hunts before where no survivors had come back.

Pyramors was permitted to join with other survivors from Zuldamar's warhall. Each contestant had been provided with fresh clothing, all in the colours of his warhall. Warhalls worked in teams now, though as the day wore on, there would be the inevitable lone-wolf, trying to resist capture through some wild gamble.

'Are any of you wounded badly?' Pyramors asked his team as they were prepared and given the weapons of their choice by the Zemoi in the plaza before the gates of the hunting grounds.

'I've a bruise the size of my head across my chest,' snorted Kajello. 'Some bastard caught me with the butt end of his pike. But I ripped it off him and broke his neck for his trouble.'

The others laughed.

'Is Dessul with us?' said Pyramors.

But his remaining group, about thirty of them, shook their heads. One of them, Suldarmon, a hardened veteran of many battles during the wars, spat into the dust. 'I saw him cut down near the end of the day. He was unlucky. One of the scarlets took him.'

Pyramors nodded slowly. 'Keep the deaths of all of them in your minds today. Let their faces be with you.' Of his original team, a dozen remained out of this thirty, but apart from Dessul, the best of them were yet alive.

The gates of the hunting ground were opened and the *moillum* were herded through by Zemoks astride xillatraal. They had four hours to find their first sanctuaries. After that they would be pursued without mercy. Pyramors and his group kept close together, hanging back from the main body of *moillum*, using its tracks to cover their own until they reached terrain they could study. They knew nothing of these lands, how far they extended, what sort of terrain there would be here, or whether there were hills, rivers, gorges. But they expected the land to be full of diverse features, for the Csendook had no intention of making the Running Hunt easy for themselves. They would have chosen land that would favour the *moillum*, eager for a difficult challenge.

'There's a river not far ahead,' said one of Pyramors's scouts. Most of the *moillum* groups would use it to cover their tracks.

Pyramors shook his head. 'Water won't cover our tracks. They're using a new beast. Tigerhounds. They don't track us in the usual way.'

'You know about them?' asked Suldarmon. 'I saw them in use at our warhall.'

'They are more machine than beast. They analyse trails in a way that no hound could. Water won't fool them. Nothing will erase our trail. And it's no use mingling it with other groups. They'll find it.'

'So whatever happens, they'll find us,' said Kajello gruffly.

'Yes, they'll find us,' said Pyramors.

'So how do we stay alive?' said Garrack.

'Avoid them as long as we can. Find ground that will be difficult for them. Make the Zemoks dismount. Then, when we can run no more, we make a fight of it.'

'A fight!' roared Kajello. 'You mean, a last stand?'

'We may not all survive. But we'll find a place we can defend as long as we need. And we'll keep them out. We have until dawn. Some of us will survive that long.'

As they trotted up through a shallow valley, they argued

286

over Pyramors's strategy, though they knew it was the best chance they had.

The ground became difficult to cross, stony and bare, rising up into the crags of a gorge. The river gushed down through it and other groups were still attempting to use the water to cover their trails. Pyramors pointed to a precipitous route that would take them upwards along the cliffs of the gorge. Kajello and Garrack used their climbing gifts that they had perfected so painfully on the exposed cliffs of Skellunda, helping less able colleagues, though by now the group were functioning automatically as a team. The climb was dangerous and one man was almost lost, but the group wedged itself high up in the gorge.

In the valley far below, they could hear the sound of the xillatraal snarling. The hunt had begun in earnest. Overhead a dark shape passed, an overflier, but the craft was being used by watching Garazenda only, and would not be used in the hunt itself.

Along the crumbling ledges Pyramors led his group. It was past midday and there was no sign of any immediate pursuit. Other groups had gone on up the gorge, while still others had fanned out around the base of the cliffs and moved away to the east and west, selecting terrain that was more easily crossed, having decided to put as much distance between themselves and the Zemoks as possible.

Pyramors pointed ahead. A huge column of rock rose up from the gorge. It seemed to have been sliced off from the cliff-sides, leaning at an angle that suggested it might topple into the gorge if pushed hard enough. Between it and the cliffs there was a gap. The group climbed to a point where the gap was narrowest, some thirty feet across.

'There's our fortress,' said Pyramors.

Kajello snorted. 'And will you also provide wings?'

For once Pyramors smiled. 'No. But I'll need the strength of your arm. That is, if the climb hasn't exhausted you?'

'Try me,' grunted Kajello.

Pyramors selected one of the tallest of the trees that clung by some miracle to the crest of the cliffs. His warriors set to work cutting into its trunk and it was inevitably the huge Kajello who finally brought it toppling down. The men almost lost it as it swung precariously over the lip of the gorge, but they cut vines and used them to drag the trunk into position. With great care they swung it out over the gap, dropping its end so that it wedged itself.

'There's our bridge,' said Pyramors.

'As our leader,' said Garrack, with a smirk, 'I think you should have the honour of crossing first.'

The others laughed but Pyramors wrapped a rope around himself and edged out on to the trunk. It moved as he dropped into a crouch. The others watched him, holding their breath, for they would all have to cross if they were to survive the day. Twice more the trunk threatened to roll, but Pyramors shuffled across, at last leaping down to the rock beyond. He secured the rope, and Garrack tied the other end to a trunk on the far side. The next warrior crossed, using the rope as a hand hold.

When they had all crossed, Pyramors cut the ropes and let them fall, dangling from the far side of the rock face. Then the trunk was levered free and sent toppling into the gorge.

'Lucky that you found such a spot,' said Kajello beside Pyramors.

Pyramors grinned. 'Zuldamar has to protect his investment as best he can.' But he would say no more about the matter, keeping to himself the fact that Vulporzol had got a message to him just before the day had begun, detailing this pinnacle, its potential for safety.

'They'll find a way over,' said Garrack.

'We'll be ready.' Pyramors had already planned his defence and had carefully checked the rock from across the gorge to ensure that there were enough saplings on it for his purpose, as Vulporzol had promised. He had the men cut several down and they spent the next hour shaping them into bows, using the vines that grew in profusion to string them. Two huge crossbows were also constructed, facing the opposite cliff wall.

By mid-afternoon the defence was finished and the

company faced the cliff, all of them armed with bows and a hundred arrows each. Kajello had made numerous coarse remarks about the weapons but he had never slackened his efforts to have them ready, and the company became used to his rough manner.

In the gorge, the sounds of the Running Hunt drew closer. The xillatraal howled at their successes, for it was clear that other *moillum* had been found. Garrack pointed to the cliff wall further down the valley, the ledge which he and the company had climbed. A tigerhound was wriggling its way along the ledge in a fashion that no ordinary hound would have been able to duplicate. It came on like a rippling, black lizard, sinuous and utterly at ease on the sheer rock. There were Zemoks with it. Before long they had reached a place opposite the rock where Pyramors and his companions were hidden, but Pyramors would not give the order to fire on them.

'Time serves us better than the Zemoks,' he whispered.

At first the Zemoks and the tigerhound were puzzled, for the trail ended. When the Zemoks found the ropes that hung down into the gorge, they were even more puzzled, but when they hauled up the ropes and found them cut, they reached the obvious conclusion and stared over at the rock. After that they climbed upwards to the highest ridge, disappearing over it with the tigerhound.

Three hours of daylight remained when they returned. There were some fifty Zemoks with them, all armed. And they had ropes. They climbed down to the ledge that faced the rock. 'As soon as they attempt to use their ropes, use your bows,' said Pyramors.

His men waited. Several of the Zemoks flung their ropes across the gap. There were hooks tied to the end of the ropes, and these dragged at the rock for purchase. Most of them failed to attach at first, the rock crumbling, or the irons sliding off. But a few gripped. The archers on the rock released their first arrows. Two Zemoks were knocked off the ledge by the impact. Others were wounded, most protected by their light armour. They became instantly more careful. They launched more ropes, and soon had several attached. Once they had secured them on their side of the gorge, they began climbing out across the span, swinging dangerously, swords gripped in their teeth.

Some of Pyramors's men were excellent bowmen and they sent their arrows into the hands and wrists of the Csendook, dropping two more to their death on the rocks far below.

It was half an hour before the first of the Zemoks was able to get on to the rock but as he climbed upward, spider-like, he was dislodged by a huge chunk of rock tossed at him by Kajello. Other Zemoks tried to cross without success. Three fell to their doom when the ropes holding them pulled free of the rocks, and others died with arrows in them. The defenders had seen the success of Kajello's tactic with the boulder and they were prepared, a wall of stone readied to be flung down on any other Zemoks who got over.

Dusk fell, and twilight was brief, as it always was on the Warhive. For the moment the Zemoks had given up trying to cross by ropes. Pyramors had given the order that his men were not to light fires. Instead they found pockets of dark loam among the rocks and smeared themselves with it, using it as camouflage so that the Zemoks would not be able to see them. The latter, by contrast, had brought torches and could be seen clearly on the opposite wall.

'They'll have found the trunk of the tree we cut down by now,' said Pyramors. 'They're bound to try a similar trick. If not, we'll pick them off easily throughout the night.'

His prediction proved correct. Less than an hour later the Zemoks had brought down a massive trunk and they dragged it over to the gorge, using the same tactic with ropes that Pyramors and his men had employed. The trunk swung into position, but as the Zemoks prepared to let it fall, Pyramors had his men release a thick arrow from one of the big crossbows. It tore across the narrow gap and ripped through two of the Zemoks holding the ropes of the trunk. Both were flung aside, and the trunk veered out into darkness. It swung for a moment, then the sheer weight of it pulled it into the void, taking with it six more of the Zemoks who became tangled in the ropes, unable to release themselves.

But the Csendook were renowned for their persistence. An hour later they had brought another trunk. Again the crossbow was used to harry them but they were more cautious. They finally managed to get the trunk into place, and had their bridge.

The first of their warriors who came across was knocked from it by an arrow from the crossbow. Then a group of three Zemoks tried to cross together. Arrows rained on them, their shields, and one fell to his death. But the other two reached the rock, only to find their way impeded by a row of sharpened spears. They chopped at them but Pyramors's men had time to kill them before they could break through the defence.

And so the battle of attrition wore on. Pyramors at last had fires lit, using ignited arrows to set light to the underside of the bridge. As the Zemoks crossed, more arrows tore into them. They could not find a way past the boulders or the spears. By the time they had made any impact at all, the end of the trunk bridge was ablaze and had to be abandoned.

Another was brought. The crossing began afresh. More Zemoks fell to their death. Pyramors's men cut more arrows, keeping their supplies fresh. 'One night,' he said to his men. 'At any other time, we would fall to them. But we have to survive only until dawn.'

As the Zolutar leading the pursuit prepared to send a dozen more of his Zemoks in yet another desperate bid to gain a foothold, the first rays of dawn spread across the skies almost unnoticed. The tigerhound, which had waited so patiently for its chance to kill, let out a howl that had in it a note of defeat, almost of despair.

22

EXECUTIONS

The pain had receded at last. But with it went contact.

Ussemitus gasped as he realised that his link with the spectral had somehow been severed. The striking sword, deflected by the spectral, had snapped the tenuous chain.

Beyond Eannor the spectral had journeyed, draining the last of Ussemitus's powers as he fought to draw even more deeply on the forces within the World Splinter for help. He had closed out everything around him, just seeing the one point of light before him like a man in a fever, and in that dim halo of light he had watched the progress of the spectral as it came at last out into the fresh light of the Warhive. Again the search had begun, until at last, following clues, the scent of blood, of killings, the spectral had come to the huge arena. Far down within it, Pyramors fought.

The spectral had hovered in the air, unnoticed by the multitudes, disguised by its very nature, unseen in the searing heat of the day. Almost too late it had watched the battle, had seen Pyramors stumble. The sword fell, the death blow imminent. In a blur the spectral had swept in, using most of the remaining power it had to deflect the blow.

Ussemitus had seen the flash of light, a silent explosion. Then the darkness closed in as if he had been snatched out of a dream. One that he could not recall.

But he knew that he must. Pyramors had been found, possibly saved. He must be found again. Another spectral must be sent. Again he dived with his mind into the endless depths of the powers about him. They answered him. Pyramors must be found. But Ussemitus knew that his own strength was waning, the length of time he could control a spectral at such a fantastic distance was not infinite.

* * *

They faced each other in the full knowledge that this would be for both of them the ultimate test, their last contest. Dust swirled about them. It was another blistering day and the arena had been turned into a dust bowl by the fighting that morning. Up in the tiers, now filled to absolute capacity, the Csendook waited excitedly, the last massive wagers made, a final opportunity to win back losses on the Testament, or compound successes so far made. Some fifty *moillum* had won through this last day's contests. The two warriors who faced each other were to be the last contest.

Pyramors had fought twice today, both of the contests exhausting, both men who had been his opponents determined to beat him, and as skilful as any opponents he had yet met, on or off a battlefield. But the warrior before him, Gastarmon, from the warhall of Auganzar, was, he knew, his match. He had watched him fight twice today as well, and the superb control he executed over his blade had won him victory against deadly opposition. Now he stood between Pyramors and success, a place with the inner *moillum* of the Supreme Sanguinary.

Garrack and Kajello had already fought their last contests in this arena, and they had won them, though Garrack had been badly wounded in his last fight. The corpses of the dead had already been removed. Many of Zuldamar's last warriors had perished. But if Pyramors could now win this last contest, he would have the core of a team to follow through with the assassination plot.

Gastarmon did not seem to be tired but Pyramors knew it would be part of his skill to hide any such exhaustion. They circled, the crowd cheering, the noise becoming deafening. Auganzar's supporters drowned out any others and Gastarmon's name could be heard clearly. The Csendook wanted his victory. He had become a popular killer for them.

The circling was over: the exchanges began. They were fast, quick thrusts, stabs. In and away. Sparks flickered as the blades clashed, but neither warrior could find an opening. Gastarmon decided to attempt a prolonged attack, using speed, and pressed home for as long as he could. Pyramors was forced to weave a defence, and three times it was almost beaten. His footwork saved him and the crowd screamed for his blood, sensing that Gastarmon had the advantage. Neither warrior spoke. They watched each others' eyes but read only concentration. No emotion, no hatred, no anger, and no fear. If either felt the closeness of death, it did not show.

Gastarmon switched to a more defensive style and Pyramors guessed that he would invite attack, only to renew the power of his own, so he did not take the bait. He allowed Gastarmon the advantage and again the Csendook thousands roared for his death.

Pyramors chose an unlikely moment to mount a brief attack, and although Gastarmon's defence was superb, extra-ordinarily fast, Pyramors scored a deep furrow along his sword arm. Blood ran from it, mingling with the scarlet of his tunic, silencing whole sections of the crowd. The warrior knew that the wound would weaken him if Pyramors could prolong the contest. He also knew that he could win it, could break down Pyramors's defence given time, but Pyramors had robbed him of that advantage. At last he began to attack with a shade less caution. Although he maintained the initiative, Pyramors took control and would not surrender an opening.

When at last Gastarmon saw an opening, he went for it, knowing that it would not kill, but would wound his opponent so badly that he could finish him. He struck, but realised too late that he had been set up. Pyramors twisted, riding the slicing blow, which slit his skin, no more. But in turning, he chopped upwards with his blade and it dug deep under the arm of Gastarmon. Blood ran thickly from the wound and as he tried to turn his sword for another attack, Gastarmon found that his arm would not obey. He switched hands, standing groggily, knowing that he now faced not a warrior, but death itself.

Pyramors continued to watch him carefully. Neither man had said a word during the contest. But Pyramors spoke now, softly. 'This is no way for men to end their days. It should be Csendook blood in this arena.'

'Aye. Forgive me, warrior, for all those brothers I have killed on this bitter world. And kill me quickly. You will be Auganzar's toy now. Perhaps it is better that I die.'

Pyramors cut through the weakened defence and gave Gastarmon the clean death he had asked for. He pulled the sword from under his ribs and turned to face the crowd. The silence erupted in roars of appreciation. Even Auganzar's supporters howled their pleasure at the victory, a magnificent fight. But Pyramors was deaf to the sounds, thinking of Gastarmon's words, of the countless men who had died to provide this spectacle of horrors.

The remaining fifty *moillum* were lined up in the centre of the vast arena. Around them in the burning afternoon sun, the crowds had at last fallen silent. Members of the Garazenda approached, surrounded by twin lines of Zemoks, carrying tall pikes. All other weapons had been removed from the scene of the fighting. There was always the possibility that one of the surviving warriors would lose his head and attack, though for these victors there would be a new life, a prize that all *moillum* throughout the worlds would envy. Auganzar himself headed the Garazenda, as honorary master of the Testament. At his right hand was Xeltagar, the renowned war veteran of his race, and he looked grimly at the *moillum*, as if in spite of their valour he would rather have had them put to death. On Auganzar's other flank was Zuldamar. The latter did not look at Pyramors as he approached.

The Supreme Sanguinary turned to Zuldamar and they spoke in their own tongue, quietly, so that most of the words were lost to the *moillum*. But Pyramors heard them.

'I am forced to bow to the superb skills of your warhall,' Auganzar told Zuldamar, a thin smile on his face. It was a face that Pyramors marked well, now that he had seen it for the first time. It was not a cruel face, not like the hideous mask of anger that Xeltagar wore, with all the scorn and loathing of a Csendook killer of men. Auganzar's face had the stamp of Csendook hardness, grim determination, but there was intelligence in it, even humour. It made him appear even more dangerous. 'The two recalcitrants from Skellunda,' Auganzar went on, 'not only served you as *moillum* should, they are here, among the victors. I have to congratulate you, Zuldamar.'

The latter looked down the line to where Garrack breathed deeply. If he had had to fight again, he would have died quickly. Beside him Kajello stood proudly, chest matted with blood. His awesome strength had seen him through the last of his fights, but he, too, was spent.

'I promised you the very best of the warriors,' Auganzar told Zuldamar. 'Since you have won your wager, perhaps you will choose them before I make arrangements for the others.'

'Thank you, Supreme Sanguinary. But it will not be easy. I could pick ten of these and still not be satisfied that I had the best of them. A mark, I am sure, of the success of the *moillum* system.' Zuldamar had raised his voice deliberately so that it carried clearly.

Auganzar bowed to the public compliment. 'Even so, Marozul, I must offer you the first choice. Though I will be sorry not to have them all for my stable.'

Zuldamar inspected the *moillum*, walking down the line, Zemoks at his side, pikes dropped, ready to kill. Zuldamar stopped before a number of them, including Pyramors, and studied them, turning them, inspecting wounds. Had he chosen Pyramors, the crowd would not have been surprised, for he had fought as well as any.

Pyramors glanced at him only briefly. So this was the Csendook for whom he had fought, for whose plans he laboured so painfully. Like Auganzar, he had an intelligent face, although he was yet a warrior, a creature of great strength.

In the end, Zuldamar settled for two of the other warriors, both of whom had acquitted themselves excellently.

Auganzar saluted Zuldamar's choice. 'You surprise me, Marozul,' he said. 'I would have thought at least one of the recalcitrants, that huge fellow. And Pyras, from your own warhall.'

Zuldamar smiled indulgently. 'Ah, the man Kajello responded well, but he needs great discipline. You may have the pleasure of controlling him from now on. And the man Pyras is also headstrong. No, I think I have made a good choice. I am content.'

'Then I, too, am satisfied, Marozul.' Auganzar now moved down the line of *moillum* himself. He could have had them all transferred to his *moillum*, but instead he touched those he wanted on the shoulder, missing a few of them. These would be sent to other warhalls, but their futures were made.

Auganzar stopped before Pyramors. The two warriors looked directly at one another, Auganzar a head taller. It was the first time either had seen each other properly, and Pyramors was stunned by the size and evident power of the Supreme Sanguinary. He was a war machine, a beast primed for battle, the fusion of speed, power and resolve. He had everything that the Csendook race craved and respected. There could be no more dangerous creature in any world cycle.

'I admire your technique,' said the Csendook. He spoke the language of Man as naturally as he spoke his own.

'You honour me, Zaru,' replied Pyramors, using the Csendook speech. He had always instructed his warriors, to learn the Csendook speech as it could be a valuable weapon.

'And would you honour me further? You have fought and killed my people in the wars. Clearly you were a warrior of high rank. I would restore it, within my own army. We are no longer at war.'

'I will serve you, Zaru,' nodded Pyramors, all emotion masked.

Auganzar was silent for a moment, as though weighing a decision. But then he grunted. 'Very well. Go with my Zemoks.' He walked on down the line, choosing the last of his personal *moillum*. Both Kajello and Garrack were among them.

* * *

Something cool across his forehead woke him. He tried to sit up but soft hands pushed him back on to thee couch. He felt as though any number of bones had been broken, and a dozen bruises protested at the movement, as did aching muscles.

Slowly he opened his eyes. The girl was looking down at him, her face anxious. In her hand was a cloth, beside her a bowl of cold water. 'It's over,' she told him.

Briefly he glanced about him at the room. It was new, quite large and, although it was by no means extravagant, it looked as though it must belong to one of the Csendook. There were crossed pikes on the wall by the door, and vases filled with plants, a strange contrast, so typical of the Csendook.

'Your new quarters,' said Jannovar, reading the questions in his eyes.

'In Auganzar's warhall? I don't recall much after the Testament.'

'Most of you were exhausted, and some of you collapsed. You were brought here. It is the garrison of his Thousand. Barracks where his particular *moillum* are housed. Your plan has been successful this far.' She dabbed at him and he was grateful for the ease it brought him. It would be a day or two before he had properly recovered from the rigours of the arena.

'Garrack and Kajello?'

She gave a little frown. 'Here somewhere.'

'We are the only three,' he said. 'As I feared.'

Her frown deepened. 'And I?'

His severe expression suddenly melted. He took her hand gently. 'Where are you housed?'

'With the women. Those of you who have been brought here have had your women transferred. We are not permitted to live with you as a wife would in our own worlds. You are warriors first. But we are close by, and can be summoned.'

'Our captors are generous,' he snorted. 'Tell me, did Kajello and Garrack have women? Women who chose them as you chose me? If they did, they were secretive about it. It never occurred to me to ask them.'

Again she seemed puzzled. 'Yes, they were both chosen. Garrack is reputed to be as promiscuous as a hound, but in Beleenis he seems to have found a mate to tie him. She and Frenulda, Kajello's mate, are both in the women's quarters.'

'How well do you know these women?'

'Not well at all. But I am beginning to. Frenulda is remarkable. She has the will power of ten, and the resolve of a hundred. Nothing moves her if she will not be moved. I have seen Zemoks shudder under her gaze! But she worships Kajello, even though she curses him every time she mentions his name. Beleenis is more quiet, more thoughtful. I think she may be ambitious.'

'Can both be trusted? Will they serve our plan?'

'I have not spoken of it to them. I won't until I'm more certain of them. I'm not sure that Garrack and Kajello have said anything either. They'll be guided by you, won't they?'

Pyramors nodded, sitting up with a groan at his injuries. 'That's the plan. When will I be able to talk to the others?'

'I'm not sure.'

'I must talk to them soon. I have to know where they are housed, what plans Auganzar has for us. Will we all be kept here, or will we be dispersed, sent to different warhalls?'

She shook her head. 'No, as elite *moillum*, you will be kept together. Your training will continue here, and you'll work as a team. You all have your own private quarters. Everything you want, in fact.'

'Access to each other?'

She nodded.

'Then I must see Kajello and Garrack soon. Where can I find them? Close by, sleeping off the Testament?'

He could see that something troubled her and his grip tightened on her hand. 'They are the last to arrive,' she told him. 'Frenulda has been hurling abuse at the Zemoks for the last few hours, saying that Kajello deserves to be allowed some time with her. But they have said nothing of his whereabouts.'

'And Garrack?'

'We have not seen him either, but he was wounded. Even so, we're not usually refused permission to see our men. It is one of the first rules of this garrison. The Csendook have always been insistent that the *moillum* here are treated with great respect.'

A germ of suspicion began to spread in his mind. Was this, after all, a betrayal? Had Garrack and Kajello been conditioned by Auganzar, before coming to Zuldamar's warhall? But they hated the Csendook, perhaps even more passionately than other men did.

'Something's wrong, isn't it?' said Jannovar.

'I don't know. But I must see those men.'

'Do you want me to look for them?'

'What freedom do you have in this place?'

'You'd be surprised,' she smiled. 'I'm no one's slave. And the Zemoks are most courteous.'

'Then find out where they are. If you can talk to them, bring word to me. I must know what their movements are. If I can trust them.'

Her eyes widened. 'Pyramors, you don't think they can be your enemies?'

'They know what I was. It may be that they hate me more than they hate the Csendook. If that is so, Auganzar himself will know why I am here, and who I am.'

She gasped. 'But – '

He put his hand over her mouth. 'We don't know that. Find the two men. Talk to them, if you can.'

She took his hand in hers. 'Rest, then.'

He felt her shaking, as though her mission filled her with a fresh trepidation. 'Be very careful.'

'I – saw you in the arena. Those last moments – '

His smile dissolved. 'Killing my own people. Like rats trapped in a culvert. For these savages.'

'I thought you would die.'

He pulled her to him. 'Perhaps it would have been better.'

She shook her head and he felt the warm tears on his shoulder.

* * *

'If they don't release him soon, there'll be *more* blood spilled!' snarled the woman, stalking up and down the chamber, fists clenching and unclenching, eyes blazing.

Jannovar watched, mildly amused. Few women lost their tempers the way Frenulda did. A good many men would have preferred the arena to meeting her fury. And some of the Zemoks were wary of her, too.

'What's keeping them?' Frenulda snapped. 'It's been almost a day since the last contest. Kajello isn't that exhausted. Garrack I can understand. But Kajello should be *here*. With me.' She bunched her fists as if she would strike out, and the other women moved back as Frenulda's considerable bulk moved up and down, a human storm about to break.

'Do you know where he is?' ventured Jannovar.

'If I did, do you think I'd be here!'

'Perhaps a few discreet inquiries – '

Frenulda put her hands on her hips and laughed derisively. 'Discreet! Hah! When did you know me to be discreet, my dear!'

'Then let me see what I can find out.'

Frenulda suddenly softened. 'Would you? The Zemoks are fond of you, Jannovar. They'll tell you what's going on.'

'Well, I'll see.'

She left the chamber, glad to be away from the storm that was again mounting there. But Frenulda was right: it was unusual and unfair for her to have been kept apart from Kajello for so long. As she slipped down through the corridors to the lower quarters of the barracks, she saw two Zemoks escorting one of the other women along a parallel corridor. Normally this would have meant nothing, but her curiosity was aroused. It had been Beleenis.

As silently as a cat, Jannovar followed, hugging the shadows of the wall. Ahead of her she could see the three figures clearly. Beleenis, who normally held her head up high, almost haughtily, whenever the Zemoks were near, was slumped forward, her head down, eyes on the stone flags as if in deep thought. The company reached a door and one of the Zemoks unlocked it. Jannovar watched the three silent figures enter and she moved as close to the

301

door as she could. Slowly she peered around it. In the room beyond there was a bright lamp which illuminated a slab of stone. Jannovar crept to the door and flattened herself against the wall. Again she looked.

Beleenis had fallen to her knees before the slab, the two Zemoks towering over her like colossal statues, their size exaggerated by the light in the chamber. Stretched out on the slab, covered by a thin sheet of material, was a body. Jannovar could just see its head. It was Garrack.

'We are sorry, my lady,' said one of the Zemoks in a rough accent. His voice echoed in the stone confines. 'His wounds were worse then we realised. He lost too much blood.'

Beleenis rose, turning, her face streaked with tears. One of the Zemoks guided her to the door and again Jannovar made for the shadows. There were narrow arches in the corridor where brands were sometimes set and she pressed herself under one in the hope that she would not be seen.

Beleenis came out of the room, rushing past her, and one of the Zemoks followed her, his attention focused on her as he quickened his pace to ensure that she got back to her chambers. He did not see Jannovar.

The two figures disappeared and Jannovar waited. There was movement in the chamber, but she dared not risk looking in again. She heard the sudden ring of steel, as though the Zemok had slipped one of his blades from its scabbard. There was a single thud, and then silence. After a while, Jannovar heard another door within the room being opened. 'Take it away and have it burned,' she heard the Zemok growl. She knew the Csendook tongue well enough to understand. Someone was being asked to dispose of the body of Garrack. It would be a secret, ignoble funeral.

Presently the first Zemok came out of the room and put something down on the floor of the corridor. It was wrapped in a piece of cloth. The Zemok locked the door, looking casually up and down the corridor. Then he retrieved the cloth-wrapped object, turned and walked further down the corridor. Jannovar waited until he had rounded a bend in it and then followed. These corridors led under the chambers of the *moillum* and seemed to be seldom used, remnants perhaps of earlier chambers which had been superseded by the better buildings above.

The Zemok had no reason to suspect anyone of following him, and did not look back. Jannovar was able to keep close, hardly making a sound. There were doors on either side but they were bolted shut and looked as though no one had used them for a long time. Dust was heaped against them, and the bolts were wrapped in spider web.

Ahead, a single lamp burned. The Zemok again put down the object and pulled another key from his belt. He unlocked the door before him, picked up his burden, and went in. This time he shut the door behind him, but there was a small grille set in it at head height. It had rusted solid in a partially open position.

Jannovar couldn't reach it and looked for something to stand on, but there was nothing. Frustrated, she listened.

'How much longer are you bastards going to keep me locked up here?' snarled a voice.

Jannovar did not recognise it but when the Zemok replied, she caught her breath.

'Not much longer, Kajello, if you do as you are told.'

'Where's Garrack?'

'You'll know soon enough.'

'I thought we had a bargain. I should have expected treachery. You Csendook are all the same. Your master is no better than the rest of you – '

'Be silent!' shouted the Zemok and Kajello began to swear obscenely. The sound of a hand smacking hard across flesh came to Jannovar.

'So beat me to death. It won't help you.'

'You asked about Garrack,' said the Zemok. 'I ask you for the last time to do as you have been asked. Give me the names of all those who serve Consul Pyramors.'

Jannovar felt a cold knife of terror slide into her gut. She staggered, pressing herself against the wall. They knew! All this had been a sham.

'There are no others!' shouted Kajello. 'Garrack and I were the only ones left. All the others were killed in the Testament. Every last one of them.'

The Zemok did not answer but he must have shown something to Kajello. There was a brief moment of silence, a void in which Jannovar pictured something to herself, something horrible. The object that the Zemok had taken into the room —

Kajello began cursing once more, but his voice died down. There was a trace of horror in it.

Jannovar heard again the sound of steel being drawn.

'Since you have nothing else to say on the matter,' said the Zemok, 'we will conclude our business.'

Jannovar heard Kajello gasp as the Zemok must have driven the blade into him. She did not wait to hear any more, but turning, fled back up the passage. She was careful to pass the cell where Garrack's body had been seen by Beleenis, but the door was locked. It was as though no one had been here for days.

But they knew! They knew who Pyramors was and they must know why he was here. The thought kept flashing through her mind. She must get to Pyramors quickly to warn him. But what could he do?

She went back up to the *moillum* quarters, turning along the corridor to the chambers where she had left Pyramors. As she did so, she almost bumped into a trio of *moillum* who had swung into the corridor from another branch, a branch that led up towards the Zemok barracks. The three *moillum* were dressed in light mail, swords belted to their waists. They had been absorbed into Auganzar's elite corps some months before the Testament. Their eyes were cold, their smiles false. Their leader, Intenza, bowed to Jannovar.

'Forgive me, my lady, but we have orders to visit your husband on behalf of the Supreme Sanguinary. It would be prudent of you to withdraw for a time.'

'What do you want with him?' she gasped. 'He's still resting after his ordeal. Surely you understand that.'

'But of course, my lady. The Supreme Sanguinary merely wants to honour him for his success. Privately. Which is to say, honour indeed. We are to escort him. He will be well provided for. And tonight you shall have him to yourself.'

Jannovar could read nothing in the steel gaze. 'I — I see.'

304

Intenza nodded to his companions and they marched stiffly to the door of Pyramors's chambers.

'May I be permitted to wish him well on such an auspicious occasion?' Jannovar faltered.

Intenza gazed at her for a moment longer as though he would dismiss her irritably. But he nodded. 'Of course. If you'll come with us.'

They stood at the door and Intenza knocked loudly upon it. Jannovar tried to bring her crawling fears under control as it opened. In her mind's eye she saw the cloth-bound object of the Zemok below, and she heard again the falling steel in the cell, the single thump.

23

ESCORT

Pyramors opened the door. Beyond it were three *moillum*, dressed in armour as though about to take to the field. Over each heart were twin circles, the Eyes of Auganzar. These men were from his elite corps. Their leader bowed. 'I am Intenza, of the third corps,' he said. 'May I have a word with you, Pyras?'

Pyramors was about to reply, when he saw Jannovar beside the other two guards. She tried to smile but he read something else in her expression, a warning, perhaps. Instantly he was on his guard, though he had no sword to hand and wore little more than a towel. But he would have to admit the trio of guards.

With a nod, he stepped back. 'Of course. Come in.'

Intenza strode into the room, his two guards allowing Jannovar to go before them. Pyramors closed the door and turned to face them.

'I apologise for this formal visit, especially after your exhausting service in the Testament,' Intenza went on, his voice level, his expression fixed. 'But I am here at the behest of our lord, Auganzar.'

Pyramors hid the unease he felt at the title, so easily accepted by these men. They had made the transition from warriors to slaves very easily, too easily. 'I am honoured to receive you. What can I do for you?'

'We are to escort you to the Supreme Sanguinary. He will address all his new *moillum*, all the victors at the Testament. It will be the first of many rewards.'

'We are to go now?'

'If you would dress, Pyras. No need for ceremonial clothes. No need for arms.' Intenza almost smiled, as if the conversation was of little real interest.

'Is my wife to accompany us?'

306

Intenza studied Jannovar for a moment, but then nodded. 'Yes, I am sure that would be appropriate, if you wish it. If she would not mind waiting with us, while you prepare yourself.'

Pyramors felt himself tense. They did not want Jannovar to speak to him. Why should that be? But his expression did not change. 'Very well. I'll be a moment.' He smiled as reassuringly at Jannovar as he could, leaving the room.

'You have picked a fine warrior for a mate,' said Intenza to Jannovar. 'He will do well under his new lord.'

'I'm sure you are right, Intenza.'

'A wise choice. Life under Auganzar can be very rewarding. For the wife of a warrior, too. There are few things you will lack.'

She could not meet his gaze, unsure what he meant. But her fears were racing. The trap was closing. Somehow she would have to alert Pyramors. They dare not go before Auganzar.

It seemed to take a protracted time for Pyramors to dress, but when he finally emerged, Intenza bowed once more. Pyramors went to Jannovar. 'I take it my fellows will be present at this address?'

Jannovar smiled sweetly. 'Will their wives be there, too?'

Intenza nodded. 'Of course. Most will bring them – '

'You haven't had an opportunity to talk to Kajello, or Garrack, have you, Pyras?' Jannovar said, again smiling with feigned innocence.

Pyras looked directly at Intenza. 'No. They fought well. Garrack was injured. Will they be present?'

'Indeed they will,' said Intenza. 'They look forward to the reunion.'

Jannovar felt herself going cold. They meant to take Pyramors out and slaughter him, before he even got near Auganzar. Before anyone realised what she was doing, she ran to the door and turning, pressed her back to it. 'Wait,' she laughed, her cheeks flushing.

Intenza scowled, glancing at his two warriors. 'What is it?'

'You permitted Pyras a chance to get ready. Must I go to this audience with the Supreme Sanguinary dressed in these rags? Let me find something more suitable. Pyras, I appeal to you – '

'There's no time,' snapped Intenza.

Jannovar's hands worked behind her, sliding home the bolt to the door. She used her pretended embarrassment to cover the action. 'But, Intenza – '

'I'm sorry, but we have no time to waste – '

Pyras waited, his every muscle tensed. Jannovar knew something but dared not speak with these three armed men in the room. He needed a weapon. The only ones available were the two pikes, crossed on the wall. But he would never get to them before the warriors. Jannovar was watching his face closely, as though seeking a clue. What should she do? said her eyes.

'Come, Jannovar,' said Intenza, trying to sound good-natured. 'Stand away from the door.' He made to move towards her, and as he did so, Pyramors used his eyes to indicate the pikes.

Jannovar skipped aside lightly, moving along the wall, under the weapons. One of the other guards went to pull the door open but grunted as he found it bolted. Both Intenza and the third guard were staring at him. Jannovar spun round and pulled one of the pikes free.

As the guard by the door unslid the bolt, cursing, he turned. Jannovar rushed forward, driving with the point of the pike. It caught the guard under the ribs and sank easily into him. He shrieked, trying to fling himself back to avoid the thrust.

Pyramors used the few seconds he had to elbow Intenza aside and rush at the remaining guard. The latter was pulling out his short sword, but at close quarters he was unable to free it before Pyramors crashed into him. Pyramors used his head like a ram, driving it down on the guard's nose. He had acted so fast that the guard could not prevent his nose being smashed in the impact.

While the first guard rolled over on the floor, gasping in agony, hand trying to drag the pike from his ribs, Jannovar bent over him and pulled out his short sword. She leapt away from his clawing fingers.

Intenza swore crudely, his own blade free. 'Cut his arms off!' he snarled. 'And gut the bitch!'

Pyramors had jumped clear of the guard he had struck. The man shook his head, blood gushing over his chest from his nose. Now he had freed his sword and came forward with murder in his eyes.

'Alive!' shouted Intenza. 'He wants this bastard alive!'

Jannovar slipped Pyramors the sword and he pushed her behind him, close to the wall. 'They're dead,' she told him, and he could feel her shaking. 'Kajello and Garrack. The Zemoks murdered them. They know who you are.'

'Get the other pike,' he told her softly.

Intenza was coming forward, moving very cautiously, and the wounded guard had gone into a defensive crouch. Pyramors knew that both these men would be dangerous, picked for their skill with the sword. They did not want him dead, for all their fury, but they intended to maim him.

'The door is unlocked,' Pyramors said softly to the girl after she had taken the other pike from the wall. 'Get away from here. I don't know where you can go, but I'll keep these two busy – '

She shook her head. Again she stepped to the door, again slid its bolt. She turned, holding out the pike.

Intenza laughed, a short, derisive snarl. 'We'll place your corpse beside the other scum,' he told her.

'Intenza,' gasped the man on the floor. A pool of blood widened about him. His face was white, his hands twitching helplessly. 'For pity's sake, help me.' Blood began to run from his mouth.

Pyramors watched Intenza, but the warrior did not as much as glance at his fallen colleague. He looked only at Pyramors.

'Is that a fitting way for a man to die?' Pyramors asked him. 'Gutted like a fish, here on the Warhive? A slave to these creatures we have fought for so long?'

Intenza spat. 'Save your breath! You're not talking to one of your thick-headed rebels from Skellunda.' As he spoke, his companion moved in, chopping at Jannovar. She met

309

the sword stroke with the pike but the blow almost took it from her fingers.

Pyramors swept his own blade in an arc that would have opened the man's chest, but the latter sprang back. In spite of his wounded face, he was going to be difficult to kill.

'To me, Intenza, you are vermin,' said Pyramors. 'The worst kind of man. You would never have succeeded in man's true armies. Only here, serving the Csendook, as a slave, could you hope for rank. What were you, a foot soldier?'

Intenza's face clouded with fury. '*Never mind what I was,*' he said, his anger livid.

'It does not matter to me,' said Pyramors coldly. 'You are beneath contempt.'

'We shall see, *Consul.*' Intenza spoke the word with sheer venom. Again it came to Pyramors just how many of his people hated the Imperator Elect and what he had stood for. Perhaps the division among his supporters had been such that it had weakened man's resolve to beat back the Csendook.

Intenza pressed his attack, though his fury did not make him as careless as Pyramors had hoped it would. He met the blade and parried it. They cut at each other, testing, and both knew they were well matched. Intenza's companion watched closely, looking for a chance to stab at Pyramors. There would be no scruples here, no etiquette. They wanted him maimed and it did not matter how they achieved it.

As Intenza attacked hard again, his companion stepped in, shifting sideways, but Jannovar thrust the pike out at him. She was careful not to get separated from Pyramors, knowing that if she did, she was dead. The man facing her sidestepped her lunges, chopping at the steel pike, but she clung to it tenaciously.

Intenza drew blood on Pyramors's arm but his smile was wiped away as Pyramors caught him across the chest, staggering him. Suddenly he had to defend himself, but he was too good a swordsman to be beaten this easily. His companion swung round, still intending to concentrate on

Pyramors rather than the girl, though he watched the pike as she raised it for another thrust. He felt something grip his leg, as if he had stepped into a trap. His fallen companion again gasped for help, the life gushing out of him. But he held on to the man in a final desperate plea. The man stumbled, cursing. Jannovar rushed at him, driving hard with the pike. It slid up over his thin breastplate, but the point caught him under the chin. He tumbled backwards, avoiding the worst of the strike.

Intenza saw what had happened from the corner of his eye and swung round to cut at Jannovar before she could kill his companion. But Intenza's blow never landed. Pyramors brought his own blade down hard into Intenza's wrist, and he felt bone and gristle part like threads. Intenza's sword clattered to the floor.

Jannovar leapt back. She had wounded her opponent but not killed him. He cut down at the hand that still tried to grip him, freeing himself. As he straightened, he was too late to prevent the upward thrust of Pyramors's sword. It dug deep into his vitals, and he gasped as the searing pain tore through him.

Pyramors pulled his blade free and swung round lithely. Intenza had staggered back, his sword arm useless. But he had pulled another short sword from his belt with his left hand. White-faced, he prepared to defend himself. His companion fell to his knees, bent forward, vomiting, then toppled over beside the other fallen guard. They died together.

Intenza's chest heaved, his teeth gritting with the sheer agony of the wound in his right arm. It leaked blood as he tried to hold it against himself. Pyramors stepped towards him coldly, a killing machine, face devoid of emotion. 'I cannot let you live.'

'There's nowhere to run, Consul,' breathed Intenza, his face greying. 'This is the Warhive. There's nowhere. The Csendook will find you. The tigerhounds will drag you before Auganzar yet.'

Pyramors did not reply. He finished it as quickly as he could, the death blow swift and clean. Afterwards he slipped a short sword into his belt and carried the sword he had used.

Jannovar was shaking almost uncontrollably, letting the pike fall. Her face was pale, tears streaking it. Pyramors put his arms about her, stroking her hair, talking softly to her, trying to encourage her. But the butchery before her threatened to snap her nerves.

'We cannot stay here,' he said. 'But where do we go?' He thought of the tigerhounds. Once unleashed, they would indeed find him. And there would be no mercy for the girl. The orders from Auganzar would be to kill her on sight.

'Down,' she whispered.

'Down? To where?'

'There are rumours of a few people who have found life on the Warhive intolerable, or who have offended the Csendook in some way. They went down, into the hollow regions.'

'There are caves?'

She shrugged. 'I've never talked to anyone who's been there. It may just be folklore. But nowhere else is safe. It will be a matter of time before we are caught.'

And now that I am found out, thought Pyramors, Zuldamar's agents will want me dead. They will not want the Marozul implicated in this plot. 'Can you find the way?'

'I think so – '

'Bring a pike. We may have to fight as we have fought here.'

She shuddered, wiping at her tears. 'What about Auganzar?'

He looked at her closely, their eyes holding for a long moment. But he turned away. 'If he knows why I am here, he will be invulnerable. He will surround himself. I cannot try for his life. If there is any kind of sanctuary to be found below the Warhive, then take me there.'

They slipped out of the chamber of death, she leading the way along the corridor. At its far end she saw a warrior coming towards her. He did not seem to be on business, but he would inevitably meet Pyramors. She warned him and he ducked back into a doorway. They had become ruthless. It was a silent kill, the man dropping to the floor without resistance. Pyramors had never seen him before. But one word from anyone and he would be taken. Jannovar tried to close her mind to the coldness of their acts, but she knew what it would mean if they were caught.

On their way down through yet more corridors, Pyramors called a halt. 'Where is the chamber where the Crossings are made?'

'The Paths to the other worlds of the cycle?'

'Yes. I was brought through a large chamber, one which must be used for the Swarms as well as individual travellers. Is it the only one on the Warhive?'

'I don't know. I came the same way. But won't it be heavily guarded?'

'If we could get back to Eannor, there may be a chance for us.'

'Perhaps if we could capture an Opener.'

His eyes widened. 'Yes, an Opener would suit us well. Where are they to be found?'

But again she looked perplexed. 'I've never seen them in our part of the Warhive. Their movements are very carefully controlled. Most of them are assigned. Very few of them are permitted to open Paths to Eannor.'

'Could any Opener create such a Path?'

'To Eannor? Yes. But we dare not get too close to the chamber of Crossings, Pyramors. Death waits for us there.' She turned as she spoke, listening. She had heard the tread of warriors somewhere beyond them. 'Let's keep going down, at least for a while.'

He was forced to agree. Whatever course of action they took from now on, it would need planning carefully.

Jannovar led him down through another maze of corridors with care. There did not seem to be a particular pattern to them, and they did not, as far as he could tell, serve any useful function. There were no longer any doors, no open chambers, and the light was poor. She commented on this, saying they would have to get brands if they were to see their way further below.

'How do people survive down here?' he asked her, as they paused at a junction between corridors. The walls were made of steel as far as he could tell, slightly warm to the touch as if there must be power of some kind behind them.

'It is an endless maze,' she answered. 'No one knows how far down it goes, or where it leads.'

'Who made these passages? Csendook?'

'They don't know. This is an area that goes back beyond their remembered past.'

'Why has it never been sealed off?'

'There are too many passages. They run under the entire city and far beyond it. It's said that you can go down anywhere under the Warhive and find such a maze as this.'

He shook his head in bewilderment. 'These walls are made of steel. Is that local, or part of the mystery of the mazes, too?'

'I don't know,' she answered.

'The Warhive has a strange history,' he told her. 'Some say it's an artificial world. I've always treated such talk as foolish. A world? Imagine the technology that would be needed to build such a thing. And sustain it. There were reputedly great wonders in the past, but an entire world?'

'No one knows how large it is,' she agreed. 'Or how small.'

'But it is part of the world cycle. The Openers use it. Therefore it must be linked to the other worlds physically. They are like the parts of a huge body, a network of arteries. I cannot believe that anyone could *construct* a world and incorporate it into such a system. Even at its height, our Empire never knew such skills.'

'Weren't there stories, though? Legends about the far past? Magic, power. The power that first led our race to open the door to the Csendook regions.'

He shook his head in bafflement. 'Contemplation of such things leads to madness, I should think. Better to think of our present dilemma,' he grinned.

She held his hand tightly. 'I cannot believe we are alive. The Testament, and that fight above – '

314

Again he held her. 'Don't think about that. Think about fire, and light. Without light, we will go mad down here.'

'Perhaps,' she said, 'we could move along the same level for as long as the light holds. Eventually we'd be bound to come under the lands beyond the cities. Maybe we could go back up.'

'And live as hermits in the wilds?' he chuckled.

'It might not be so bad,' she smiled. He could just discern her features in the glow of distant light. 'You might even learn to . . . love me a little.'

'Is that what you want?'

She put her hand against his face. 'Yes. I cannot replace what you have lost. I have her name, but – ' He put his own fingers over her mouth, silencing her. 'The deepest wounds trouble a man longest. And you must not think that I could not love you.'

'My sister spoke of you, secretly. It was almost as if I knew you.'

'Did I object when you chose me?'

She laughed softly, the sound muffled in the confines of the corridor. 'Should I release you from that vow, now that you are a free man?'

'Are you that anxious, now that you are a free woman, to look around you for a better choice?'

She made the pout that so reminded him of Jannovar. 'Well, I am no longer sure that I made such a good choice. After all, you have no fire to light the way. How can I be sure that you will provide for me?'

He laughed, suddenly lifting her from the ground as easily as he would have lifted a child. Something went out of him as he did it, a deep sorrow, a dark cloud. He swung her round.

'How dare you!' she laughed back at him. 'This is abduction! How dare you take me from the safety of the palace!' But he pulled her to him and kissed her, holding her in the embrace for a long time. Her hands dug into him, and she was aware of his hunger for her, of her own fierce desire.

'I will go with you,' she whispered into his ear as she broke from him. 'But not as your companion.'

His face became serious for a moment.

She read the inevitable sorrow behind his eyes. 'I'm sorry. I should not make demands – '

He was about to say something, when she felt his body tensing. His face had changed once more, his brows knitting in a frown of concentration. She did not speak but her eyes demanded an answer. He shook his head. He had heard the distant baying of a tigerhound. Then something else moved, much nearer to them.

'Keep very still,' he told her softly. 'We are no longer alone.'

Carefully he released her, then with stunning speed had slipped out his sword and spun round, facing the dark wall opposite. There was a movement in the shadows, a gasp of indrawn breath. Pyramors lurched forward: a figure broke from cover and started to run down the corridor. But Pyramors moved too quickly for it. In a few short paces he had caught up with it and gripped it by its skinny arm. He swung the figure around. It growled abuse, trying to shake itself loose, but he held it, lifting the blade.

'Spare me! Spare me!' it howled in an atrocious dialect.

Jannovar came up to them, squinting in the poor light. 'What is it, a child?'

'Speak up,' Pyramors told his captive. 'Who are you?'

The creature he held was a man, not a child, but what seemed to be an old man, bent and wizened, the face crinkled and lined, the hair sparse, but the eyes alive, staring almost comically as if they would pop from their sockets.

'I Ungertel. Let me go. Mean no harm. Let me go back. Won't come up again. Let me go, master. I Ungertel. Worthless.'

But Pyramors would not release him. 'Ungertel. And where are you from, Ungertel. From below?'

'Yes, yes,' hissed the strange being. 'No need to fear Ungertel. I weak.'

'I'm not interested in what you're doing here, Ungertel,' Pyramors told him. 'But you may be able to help us.'

Ungertel was staring at Jannovar. Even in this light his curious eyes sparkled.

'We mean you no harm,' she told him.

'You *moillum*?' he asked Pyramors.

'I was.'

'Other *moillum* with Girder Folk.'

'Who are they?' said Pyramors, darting a look at Jannovar, but she shrugged.

Ungertel seemed to clam up. 'You bring Zemoks?'

'No, we're trying to get away from them,' said Jannovar.

'Not hunt Girder Folk?' Ungertel said, with deep suspicion.

'We've never heard of them,' said Jannovar. She gently prized Pyramors's fingers loose. 'But if they'll help us, we'll be glad of it. The Zemoks are looking for us.'

'Why?'

'To kill us,' said Pyramors. 'We've killed their servants.'

Ungertel snorted, stamping his bare foot. He screwed up his face, adding to its incalculable lines. 'Filth! Warlords over us! Won't find us. Can't take the deep darkness. Won't harm Girder Folk.'

'If you are enemies of the Zemoks, Ungertel, we need your protection,' Jannovar said again.

'Blood on you both. I smell it. Human blood. Sword is thick with blood. And this other.' Ungertel indicated the pike.

'*Moillum* who tried to prevent our flight,' said Pyramors.

Ungertel looked back up the corridor. He lifted his nose and sniffed at the air like a huge rodent. 'Yes. Not far behind. Zemoks come. I smell them. They bring steel.'

'Will you help us?' said Pyramors.

Suddenly there was another howl, the sound of a tigerhound that has found a fresh trail. It seemed to come from very close. Ungertel leapt back as if he had been bitten. 'What monster comes!' he gasped.

'Tigerhounds,' said Pyramors.

'Follow me,' grunted Ungertel. He swung round, loping off, now more like a tiny wolf than a rodent, and Pyramors and Jannovar followed him at a slow trot, exchanging puzzled glances. They could hear nothing immediately behind them but they knew the tigerhound would be

317

racing down upon them quickly. If Ungertel knew of a sanctuary, they would be glad of it, however dark and forbidding a place it might be.

The spectral hovered over the huge bowl, the arena where so many had died during the Testament. Darkness shrouded it now. There were no guards here, no signs of life, as if this part of the Csendook city had been totally abandoned. Ussemitus watched from his dreams as the shape of the spectral slipped downwards to the heart of the arena, searching, always searching. Now its search was twofold. To find the Man, but also to see if there was anything left of its forerunner, the spectral that had saved Pyramors from the death blow of the sword.

There was a trace of Pyramors, signs that he had been here. He had left, alive, but it would mean a fresh search within this alien city to locate him.

Something else stirred in the night, itself like a faint dream, a hint of light. Ussemitus guided the spectral slowly, until at last, in the starlit skies over the city, he found the first spectral he had sent. Moved listlessly by the breezes of the Warhive's atmosphere, it drifted, like a tiny craft without a rudder. Gently the spectral drew it to itself, discharging what little power it could spare into repairing it.

Ussemitus shuddered, striving to hold on to the far visions. Around him he felt the darkness uncoiling, heard the unmistakable susurrations of his enemies, their pleasure at his suffering.

24

THE GIRDER FOLK

Ungertel stopped, the darkness beginning to close in around him and the two refugees. He lifted his head, cocking his ears, his eyes widening as he caught something, some subtle sound that seemed to surprise him.

'What can you hear?' asked Jannovar.

'Those creatures,' he murmured. 'No need of light. They hear us move. Taste our breath. Very close.'

Pyramors felt Jannovar's hand tighten in his. 'Find sanctuary soon, Ungertel. If those beasts come upon us, they'll tear us to pieces. Auganzar himself sent them.' He didn't say that his life would be spared, that Auganzar would still want him alive.

Ungertel's face was an ugly grimace. 'Auganzar! He seeks you?'

Pyramors nodded.

It seemed to be the final confirmation Ungertel needed that he should help these people. He grunted, walking a little further down the corridor, stopping in the centre of it. He bent down, his claw-like hands scrabbling in the dirt until his fingers had revealed something. In the poor light it seemed to be a rectangular design, inlaid with a circle of steel. Ungertel dug under the rim of the circle and pulled, remarkably strong for such a deformed being.

It was a section of steel and it came away in a cloud of dust. Pyramors helped Ungertel manhandle it to one side. A square of darkness was revealed, and a current of warm air drifted from it.

'Who's down there?' said Jannovar, eyes wide with fear.

'Girders,' said Ungertel. 'Tread carefully. Ladder.' He pointed to rungs that dropped away into the pitch dark.

Pyramors went down through the hole and climbed on to the first of the black steel rungs. He could see nothing, only the hole of faint light above him, but he raised his hands for Jannovar to follow him. She hovered at the edge of the drop, Ungertel behind her, watching for movement up the corridor.

'I'm afraid,' Jannovar whispered.

In answer, there came a frightful howl, almost on top of them, the sound echoing round the corridors, magnified. It was enough to motivate her. She reached out for his fingers, then his hand, and he helped her on to the ladder. She had dropped the pike without realising, but Ungertel had picked up it easily, carrying it as if it were no burden to him at all. He followed her, dragging the trap door with him. As Pyramors and Jannovar descended, Ungertel slid the trap back into place, just as something crashed into the metal. There were steel bolts on the underside of the door, and Ungertel slammed them into place. Mercifully the trap door held, muffling the frightful sounds above, the roars and the scratching as the claws of the beast tore at the metal.

Ungertel began the climb downwards. The only sound down here was the sound of their feet on the steel. At first they could see only the dark, thinking they must be in a wide well. But as Pyramors went down, his arms about Jannovar, light began to seep through the shadows, his eyes becoming accustomed to it.

This was no well. It was a gargantuan chamber, or possibly a linked series of them, the steel ladder attached to a thick spoke of steel that rose up from the depths like a part of a wheel. In the network of chambers there were other such steel spokes, some thin, some as thick around as a dozen men, all forming an angled forest. Some of them were linked by curving girders, so that the overall impression was one of countless steel webs woven by unimaginably huge spiders, machines that defied the mind. The girders bent away into the distance on all sides, steel nerves of this inner world.

Pyramors paused in his descent. He could feel Jannovar shaking like a bird. There were sounds above, but the trap door seemed proof against the monsters beyond it. 'Who built this place?' he called softly to Ungertel.

'Who knows?' came the gruff response.

'Where is he taking us?' Jannovar whispered.

'How far down does this construction go?' Pyramors called.

'No one been all way down. Hub there,' said Ungertel. He was hanging on to the ladder with one hand, swinging out over the void as he spoke. Like a child, he was completely at home here, totally devoid of fear.

'What is the Hub?' said Pyramors.

'Centre of Warhive. Place of Conceptors.'

'And who are they?'

But Ungertel would say no more on the matter for the time being. He pointed to a thick girder some yards below Pyramors. 'Climb to that.'

Pyramors did so, finding himself on steel that vibrated very slightly as though it fed into machinery somewhere. He had to help Jannovar on to the beam. She was almost rigid with terror. Ungertel dropped beside them like a spider, sure-footed as if he were walking over a field.

'Follow. Scuttlers about. You may need sword.' He was waving the pike about, delighted at being in possession of such a weapon.

Pyramors did not ask what these Scuttlers might be, knowing that it would do nothing to help Jannovar overcome her fear of these intricate heights. Instead he guided her along the curve of a girder. Around them the light pulsed softly, and from somewhere below they could hear the rhythmic throb of something huge and powerful, as though they were in the heart of an immense ship.

Ungertel took them down yet more ladders and across further girders. To Pyramors they all seemed identical but Ungertel clearly knew every girder, every rung.

Jannovar drew in a sharp breath, pointing across to a girder some twenty yards away that ran parallel to the one they were on. Several humped shapes had gathered on it. They moved along it, and from their movements, Pyramors guessed them to be the creatures that Ungertel had mentioned.

'Scuttlers!' Ungertel confirmed. 'Keep to ladders.'

As if they had heard him, the creatures shifted down the girder to an intersection, coming across. Jannovar looked away, biting off a scream, but Pyramors got her to another ladder and again they went down. The Scuttlers, the size of small dogs but with the erratic movements of crabs, seemed to avoid the ladders, but they wove their way backwards and forwards along the girders, dropping ever lower, seeking a place which would bring them face to face with the fugitives.

Lower and lower they went, until Ungertel, now on the loweer rungs, stopped. 'Go up,' he called. Below him there were yet more shapes, more of the Scuttlers.

Pyramors held on to the rungs with one hand, his sword in the other. How many of these creatures would there be? Suddenly he felt something swing through the air not many feet behind him. He turned, twisting dangerously, his sword ready to cut into anything that attacked. From a girder high above, a number of strands hung down, and swinging from these were more beings like Ungertel, about a dozen of them. Silently they dropped down towards the girder below. They carried weapons in their teeth, lengths of metal, steel bars.

On the lower girder, a grim and silent battle began, as these Girder Folk went for the Scuttlers. They beat at them furiously, and a score of the spider-like creatures swarmed up on to the girder, joining the fray.

Pyramors would have dropped down and engaged them as well but Ungertel was urging him upwards. 'Away! Girder Folk cover us.'

Jannovar needed no second bidding, leading the way up the ladder. She went out on to the next girder and with Pyramors and Ungertel, quickly moved away from the sounds of the battle below.

When they came to a halt, some distance away, Ungertel was grinning, his face like that of a demon in the weird light of this subterranean world. 'Thought to devour us, but many will end up in bellies of Girder Folk.'

'You eat them?' gasped Jannovar, appalled.

Ungertel nodded. 'Of course! Good meat.'

Jannovar's face twisted in an expression of disgust and Pyramors laughed softly. She would have to learn about being in the field. They felt some of the tension easing, but were glad to begin their flight again.

Below them they could see another peculiar feature of this strange realm. Like a dark hive, it clung to the sides of one of the thicker steel spokes, light radiating out from a number of perforations in its sides. As they climbed down to it, Pyramors realised that it was deceptively large, a vast nest, woven from broken sections of steel and bands of metal, twisted fibres, all scavenged from this realm. He was also aware of movement along the girder network on all sides, and looking around him saw other people like Ungertel converging on the place below. Some of them carried spikes from which dangled the dripping carcasses of Scuttlers.

'Good hunt,' muttered Ungertel. He took them down to the nest, climbing on to a wide girder than ran across to it. A curved arch opened into it. A dozen of the Girder Folk lined this doorway, each of them armed with one of the crude weapons.

The first of them jabbed his towards Ungertel, eyeing the pike that the latter carried with evident envy. 'Who are these?' he snapped. 'Your business at Hive Six?'

'Runaways from Csendook. To see Gehennon.'

'*Moillum*?' said the guard. He was no bigger than Ungertel, his hands like great hams, his eyes huge. He and his compannions all stared with interest at the outsiders.

Pyramors nodded. 'We escaped from a Running Hunt.'

The guard suddenly nodded, as if in sympathy. 'And the woman? Few women brave the Girder Folks' world.'

'She is under my protection,' Pyramors told him, with a look that he could not meet.

The guard grunted again, sending one of the others within. They waited. Jannovar turned to Ungertel, asking him quietly, 'how did you people come to be here?' She gazed up at the jumbled building clinging so precariously to the steel spoke.

'Like you. Runaways,' said Ungertel. 'Our race goes back far in time. To the days of the building. Before Warhive was complete. We were different then. But Csendook tried to enslave us. We hid. Now we help those who come down to us. Join us.'

'The building?' said Pyramors. 'You mean the entire Warhive is a constructed world?'

'The Csendook built it?' asked Jannovar.

Ungertel shook his head. 'The Conceptors. Wove it from the Hub, where they dwell.'

'What are they?' said Pyramors. 'Engineers?'

'Some say gods. But who knows? No one goes there. Death waits. You ask Gehennon, our ruler. He knows. He has travelled much.'

The guard returned and after a brief conversation with the others, it was agreed that Ungertel could take his companions within. Pyramors and Jannovar followed him and the leading guard, Urmezzin, into the hive-like building. They were taken through the narrowest of corridors to a central room, lit by metal lamps that intrigued Pyramors. The quality of their workmanship suggested lost arts, powers that had once been known to mankind but on most worlds had become forgotten.

A single being sat in the room, and by the light, Pyramors recognised him for what he was with a start. It was one of the bloated creatures used by the Csendook for creating Paths between worlds. It was an Opener. They, too, it seemed, had their renegades.

'I am Gehennon,' he said in his deep voice after the guard had withdrawn. 'As you see, I am an Opener. Or was. I, too, am a runaway. Perhaps that surprises you?'

Pyramors nodded. 'As does this whole realm.'

Ungertel bowed. 'Found them in lower passages of the city, Gehennon. Csendook pursued them. Using new creatures. Very bad.'

Gehennon's mouth dropped, his thick jowels sagging. 'Tigerhounds?' he asked. 'Word of them had reached me. The Csendook do not like losing *moillum*. Least of all if they have been in a Running Hunt. The Csendook like to dissuade belief in the Girder Realm. Few of your kind are aware of its existence,' he told Pyramors. He turned to Ungertel. 'You may leave us. My guards will see to it that you eat well.'

Ungertel bowed once more, glancing at Pyramors.

'Our thanks, Ungertel.'

The little being nodded, silently putting down the pike, as though reluctant to leave it. He left without another word.

'There are other gladiators here?' said Pyramors.

'Further afield. The Girder Realm stretches under the whole of the Warhive. Our communities are mostly centred under the cities, although we do little scavenging up there. If the Csendook found a way to us, they would eradicate us.'

'What plans do these people have?'

Gehennon's eyes sank into his thick face as he frowned. 'Plans? You mean for rebellion? There's no such plan here. The Girder Folk have only one aim. Survival. It is hardly the best of lives. But it is, for us, better than life among the Csendook.'

'But who were these people?' said Jannovar. 'Were they once men?'

'Perhaps in the remote past. Their ancestors must have been engineers. Working for the Conceptors, who themselves designed and built this world for their masters. The Csendook.'

'And what are the Conceptors?' said Pyramors.

Gehennon smiled, his face creasing. 'I have glimpsed them, or at least, the power that they wield. They are vast beings, unlike anything you could imagine, a life form that is very different from your own, though they have more in common with my race. Openers, you understand, were genetically constructed by the Csendook.'

Jannovar felt herself shiver at the words, standing closer to Pyramors, her hand reaching for his.

If Gehennon saw her revulsion, he ignored it. 'You understand the principles of the world cycle? How each world is linked, how we Openers create paths between worlds?'

'Yes,' nodded Pyramors.

'It is an organic thing, this linking,' Gehennon went on. 'There are those who hold that each world is an organism, a living being. To some, a god. It is the common bond of life which enables Paths to be made. Blood is the life force that unites the worlds of the cycle. But the Warhive is a false world, a constructed one.'

'Yet it is part of the world cycle,' said Pyramors.

Gehennon nodded his huge head and sweat ran in rivulets from his brow. 'Oh yes. That is because the Conceptors at its heart, the Hub, are organic beings, huge creatures rich in power. In blood. They are the source of the power of all Openers. We are their offspring. We were moulded from them.'

'But where are they *from*?' gasped Pyramors, stunned by the revelation.

Gehennon laughed, but it was a hollow sound. 'I've spoken too much already. Though I am a rebel and have left my own kind, there are secrets that are not open.' He looked away for a moment, almost sleepily, but then his gaze returned to his guests. 'But you must tell me something about yourselves. I can see you are a gladiator. Why has the life of a *moillum* become impossible for you? Is it, as I suspect, something to do with the beautiful lady who clings to you so? An abduction?'

Pyramors's grip on Jannovar's fingers tightened. 'It is. I had gained some distinction among the *moillum*, and was due to serve under Auganzar – '

'The Supreme Sanguinary! An honour, at least, for *moillum* – '

'Jannovar was – '

'I was the slave of one of the Zolutars,' she cut in quickly. 'I was promised to Pyras, but the Zolutar refused to part with me.'

'I killed the Zolutar,' said Pyramors. 'And together Jannovar and I fled.'

'Where had you intended to go? Did you know of the Girder Folk?'

Pyramors shook his head. 'No. We went under the city, hoping to find a way out of it, back to one of the warhalls. In time we might have left the Warhive.'

'If you have killed one of Auganzar's Zolutars,' snorted Gehennon, 'you will never leave the Warhive. He will see that every Opener is warned. Even his secret enemies will have nothing to do with you. It is far too dangerous.'

Pyramors nodded, making a showing of being humbled. 'It was a blind and reckless flight – '

Gehennon's great bulk quivered as he shrugged. 'It always is. Flight is often irrational, speculative. But you've found a sanctuary. Not what you might have expected. So, what do you intend now?'

'I must get off the Warhive.'

'As simply as that?' said Gehennon, with a smirk.

Pyramors shook his head. 'There are those who will help me.'

'Who might they be?'

Pyramors stared at the gross Opener for a moment, masking his mistrust. 'Forgive me, Gehennon, but I would rather not share the knowledge. Not yet.'

'You do not trust me. Of course, why should you? You know nothing of my own history. Perhaps if I shared some of it with you, you might.'

'It seems strange for one of your kind to be here,' said Pyramors.

'It should be. But you see, unlike my kind, I developed a thirst for things I could not have. Knowledge, a deeper understanding of the powers the Openers use. A desire to know what lies beyond. Such thoughts led me into trouble with my superiors. More than once I was disciplined for experimenting.'

'With what?'

Gehennon sat back and emitted a massive sigh. 'I am no longer young. I hesitate to accept, as it were, defeat, and yet I'm no longer sure that I'll ever have my theories proved. Not now.'

'Theories? About what?'

'Your masters, Man's scientists, once believed in such theories, too. Zellorian, Prime Consul of your race. He thought he could take the Imperator Elect beyond the cycle of worlds to another.'

'You believe in that?' said Pyramors softly, aware that Jannovar was watching him.

'I think it is possible. My kind, the Openers, shun such thoughts, seeing them as madness, full of danger, a threat to our existence. A number of Openers have died investigating these theories, although this is kept very quiet. The Consummate Order, highest of the Openers, has decreed that no one is to attempt to open a Path beyond our world cycle. It is utterly forbidden.'

'You tried?'

Slowly Gehennon nodded. 'And failed. But still I wonder –'

'They punished you?'

'They would have dismembered me, made a Path to the emptiness beyond the cycle and cast me down it. The Consummate Order would have unmade me. Thus, like you, I fled.'

'To the Girder Folk. And do you . . . still experiment with your theories?'

Gehennon's massive chest heaved as he gave another great sigh. 'No. Not physically. I dream of such things.'

'Can you still create Paths?'

Gehennon smiled. 'You want me to open a Path for you, away from the Warhive? Well, other *moillum* have gone before you. We here among the girders rely heavily on our bargaining powers, you know. We have very few weapons. So little that we need.'

'Then you have sent men from here – to other worlds in the cycle?'

'Yes. Though they will never be truly safe. I thought of such flight myself but I can think of nowhere that I would be safer than down here. And in this wretched realm, I am a king of sorts. I control everything that goes on. I gather news as well as anyone can. Life could be far worse for me.'

'But will you help us?' said Jannovar. 'Get us away from here?'

Pyramors squeezed her hand, a gentle warning that she recognised.

'Why not? What do you want? Do you have friends that will hide you from the Eyes of Auganzar?'

'What must we pay you? We have very little,' said Pyramors.

'As for that, why, your weapons will do nicely. We have so few.'

'Is that all?'

Gehennon's smile turned into a long yawn, as if none of this mattered greatly to him. 'Once I would have demanded something grander. For you to go out and hunt down a pack of Scuttlers or to destroy some of the more unpleasant mutations that dwell in the lower girders. But I've servants enough for all that now. And I'm tired of such things. Life will not change for me. Give me your weapons. They are excellent tools. The Girder Folk need such things.'

'Very well,' nodded Pyramors.

'Where do you want to go?'

Pyramors looked down at Jannovar. There was no time to talk to her privately. 'We wish to go to the world of Eannor,' he said quietly.

'Eannor?' said Gehennon. 'But this is an odd choice.'

'It is where many of our loved ones perished,' said Pyramors, turning again to the Opener. He was aware of the deep-set eyes scrutinising him, trying, perhaps, to pry into his mind.

'Also where Zellorian and his scientists performed their final rituals,' said the Opener. 'I have never been to Eannor. As you may know, it is highly restricted. I was told more than once that it is a blasted realm, full of death, choked with it. They say that only a fool would go there. Yet you, Pyras, are no fool, I think.'

'I've been there,' Pyramors said quickly. 'Eannor is not a blasted world. There are warhalls there. Auganzar develops them, seeing in Eannor, a perfect place to develop *moillum*.'

'Ah, under cover of the ban.'

'There are also pockets of resistance there still. Some of our families,' he added, looking at Jannovar.

She nodded at his cue.

'Eannor,' mused Gehennon. 'Probably the most dangerous world you could have picked. I hear the Garazenda are most particular about which Openers they allow to go there.'

'Will you take us?' said Pyramors.

'Interesting,' muttered Gehennon. 'You have stirred up a host of old emotions within me. Eannor. All those ideas I had about experimenting. Tell me, since you have been on Eannor, was there ever anything to suggest that Zellorian might have succeeded?'

Pyramors held his gaze, unflinching. 'We would like to have believed, Gehennon, but if you had seen the bones, the heaped skulls – '

Gehennon sucked in a long breath, nodding slowly. 'Yes, perhaps you are right. It was an act born of desperation.'

'Will you take us?'

The Opener rose, and his true girth became evident. He was exceptionally large, his legs as thick around as small trees. He moved sluggishly across the room, thinking over the request, shaking his head, but then raising his brows as if an inner voice were telling him that he should agree. At last he spoke. 'I should say no. Eannor is bound to be protected. If I am discovered, I will be taken to the Consummate Order.'

Pyramors nodded.

Jannovar felt her heart lurch in her chest. If the Opener refused, their chances of getting to Eannor would almost certainly be ruined. Pyramors knew that, if he had to, he would tell the Opener the truth of the Path beyond Eannor. Surely that would entice him.

But Gehennon was nodding again. 'Very well. Where, exactly, do you wish to enter? There are limited points of access.'

Pyramors smiled grimly. 'There is one place where no one would ever expect us to emerge. The zone of sacrifice itself. At its heart.'

Gehennon looked momentarily appalled, but then appeared to control himself. 'A ghastly concept. But yes, how apt!' He pointed to the weapons. 'In that case, you had better keep your sword until we get there. I can bring it back with me, assuming we survive at all!'

* * *

330

Ussemitus felt himself drifting dangerously close to exhaustion. The spectral, burdened with its damaged companion, was still unable to find Pyramors. Somewhere under the city of the Csendook where the great Testament had been held, the trail had disappeared, far too dangerous to probe further with so many enemies about. Reluctantly, the spectrals were forced to withdraw from the Warhive, and Ussemitus barely managed to rally his powers to begin the complex task of guiding them back through the complex phases of their journey to the World Splinter.

25

DEATH ZONE

Jannovar almost passed out as she and Pyramors felt the tunnel of darkness closing around them like a throat. It was stifling, the air thick, and her head whirled. She felt Pyramors's arms about her waist, supporting her, and her fingers tightened on the sword he had given her. Somewhere ahead of them, in the swirling shadows, Gehennon moved on down the Path he had created for them like a giant slug, his bulk swallowed by the vortex. Jannovar could hear distorted sound and thought it must be Pyramors saying something to her, but the words were sucked into the torrent of noise. She had never been used to gate travel but this journey seemed particularly strenuous, as though Gehennon was at fault, no longer used to the rituals involved.

Light finally blotted out the whirling confusion. Jannovar did not fall, but Pyramors was holding her up, stroking her hair, encouraging her. For a moment she thought she would be sick but she recovered, sitting up and gazing about her. They were no longer in the grim confines of the world of girders. Sunlight glared, a few clouds streaking overhead in an azure vault. They had arrived in a wide open area, paved with stones that were cracked and in places angled. Gehennon stood nearby, watching the surroundings for signs of movement. Although it was hot, he had his robe pulled about him. His face was a sheen of sweat.

Pyramors helped Jannovar to her feet. She gasped as the shapes in this huge plaza took form. They were bones, countless thousands of them. Some were individual ones, others whole rib-cages, while some almost complete skeletons still littered the place. And there were skulls, singly and in heaps. In all there must have been the remains of thousands of people. To her amazement, Jannovar noticed that some of them were Csendook bones.

'The place of sacrifice,' breathed Pyramors. It was his first sight of it since leaving Innasmorn. The debris sent shudders through him, the testament to enormous loss of life. The handiwork of Zellorian, the price of his own safety.

Jannovar stood very still as Pyramors gazed about him, walking slowly towards Gehennon, who himself did not seem moved.

'So this is Eannor,' said the Opener. 'Zellorian's grave.'

Pyramors nodded, his eyes turning to the raised area in the centre of the plaza. The skulls were thickest there, although many had been disturbed. Pyramors knew that Csendook had been here and attempted a Crossing to Innasmorn. The Accrual had assured him that a small group of them had succeeded. They would have to be found.

The Accrual. Pyramors thought of the monstrous thing now. There would be a reckoning with it. A price to pay for his own safety. For his and Jannovar's journey back to Innasmorn. The Accrual was hungry, greedy. It expected him to deliver up to it life in plenty.

Jannovar watched Pyramors as he walked slowly towards the raised area. Gehennon, too, did not move, face blank, glistening. Why is he indifferent to this terrible carnage? Jannovar asked herself.

As Pyramors mounted the first of the long steps, something rattled among the bones above. He held his sword before him, as if about to be confronted by a ghost. But it was no ghost that came from beyond the top of the dais, sun behind it, casting its huge shadow down the steps like a finger singling out a fresh victim.

Jannovar heard sounds around the rim of the plaza, the sudden snarling. Spinning about her, she saw the tigerhounds. There were a dozen of them, crawling forward on their bellies, long metal leashes taut behind them, linked to the wrists of their handlers, the armoured Zemaal.

The plaza was ringed. Up on the dais, a single figure rose up and there was no mistaking it for what it was. It was the Supreme Sanguinary, Auganzar himself.

Pyramors faced him, as he had done in the great arena.

Auganzar lifted his visor, then removed his war helm completely, setting it down on the marble slab. There were two swords in his belt, the traditional Csendook swords of combat. He waited, as if this meeting had been prearranged.

Pyramors took in events around him. He saw the circle of Zemaal, the slow encroachment of the tigerhounds. This was a trap from which there would be no escape. He had no time to think about how it had been set. But Gehennon stood apart, not moving, his face blank, almost disinterested. His doing, then! How easy it had been for him to lure his prey here.

Jannovar, who was rooted to the spot by a different emotion, overcame some of her terror and shouted.

'Well met, Consul,' came the deep voice of the Csendook warlord above Pyramors. He was forced to turn and meet the steady gaze. The game was over, the time of deceit past. 'I almost lost you.' Auganzar paused at the edge of the dais. His size seemed even greater in this empty place, his power limitless. If he chose to use his sword, Pyramors knew that he would at least die swiftly.

Abruptly Pyramors swung round, about to make a dash to Jannovar's side. He suspected they would not harm her. The strange Csendook respect for Man's mate would preserve her. But even as Pyramors moved, a tigerhound sprang from the circle, unleashed, cutting off his route back to the girl. Jannovar screamed as Pyramors raised his blade to meet its spring. But the tigerhound dropped to a crouch, fangs barred, saliva running in loops from them. Its eyes blazed hatefully at him, but behind it one of the Zemaal came forward, talking to it gruffly, commanding it to be still. He bent down and fitted the leash to its collar.

'Keep away from the girl,' came the imperious voice of Auganzar. It suggested that she would be killed if he disobeyed.

Pyramors locked eyes with Jannovar. He read the terror in her. 'Keep absolutely still,' he told her. But he saw other Zemaal moving towards her. She lifted her sword, but there would be no point in resisting them. They grouped close by her, as if waiting for word from the huge figure up on the dais. Mercifully the tigerhounds were kept at bay. He turned back to Auganzar, though he spared one swift and contemptuous glance at Gehennon. 'I presume we thank you for this?'

Gehennon smiled blandly. 'I told you I was cast out by my own kind. It is true, I am a refugee. But I serve Auganzar.'

Pyramors did not reply. He waited, face like stone, though his eyes were full of frustrated fury.

'They tell me,' Auganzar went on, his voice dropping as he came closer, 'that you came to Eannor for one reason. To find the woman, your lover.' He looked across at Jannovar, saw the tears on her face. 'She is very beautiful. A worthy prize for a warrior of such stature.'

Still Pyramors did not speak but his eyes never left the face of his enemy. He read the power in it, the strange humanity as well as the hint of cruelty, of willingness to destroy.

'You gave up the sanctuary of another realm, a realm beyond this cycle of worlds, to return for her. You must love her and desire her very much to have taken such a risk.'

It was only then that the truth came to Pyramors. They still did not know that this was not Jannovar! Her deceit had fooled them.

Pyramors nodded. 'Yes,' he said. 'I came for her.'

'From Innasmorn.'

'Yes, from Innasmorn.'

'I am glad that we do not have to maintain the structure of lies, Consul. I have known for some time of the existence of this world.' Auganzar stepped closer to his enemy. He had still not drawn a weapon.

'You will never visit it,' Pyramors told him quietly.

Auganzar smiled, and again, Pyramors was struck by how human it made him seem. 'Surely you wish to return there, with the girl?'

'I would rather die than give you what you want.'

'Still loyal to your Imperator Elect? I assume he is alive?'

Pyramors said nothing.

'And Zellorian?' Auganzar added, his eyes momentarily narrowing. He gestured at the heaped skulls and the destruction about them. 'The architect of this slaughter. I presume *he* is alive?'

All warmth left Auganzar's face at that. He was again the warlord, the bringer of destruction, the focus of destruction for mankind. 'And you, Consul, possess the key to Innasmorn.'

Pyramors nodded slowly. Throughout the exchange he had been thinking frantically. *The Accrual.* How could he use it? How could he lead Auganzar and his creatures to destruction, feeding them to the Accrual? It was waiting, so eagerly. It had given him the means to summon it.

'Jannovar can be yours, and you can both have your freedom.'

'You think I would betray my people that easily?'

'Would you protect your Imperator?'

Pyramors scowled. 'He's a fool. We both know it. Weak and self-indulgent. No one who knows him respects him.'

'But he's a symbol,' nodded Auganzar. 'A rallying cry for your scattered race. Yes, I know that. Yet he betrayed your people. He and his Prime Consul. How many of them know?'

'The Men of this world cycle know. Few of them would rally to him now, nor his Consulate.'

'And Zellorian?' Auganzar persisted. He had moved very close, no more than a few feet away. Only Pyramors heard him, the hunger in his voice.

The Consul snorted, a short, derisive laugh. 'There's irony in this. You seek Zellorian's head. I tell you, I would cut it from him myself and present it to you, had I the chance.'

Auganzar straightened slowly. 'There is much to be admired in your race, Consul. I am sure that all Men worthy of the name would condone your thoughts.'

'You have subjugated us, all but exterminated us. You use our slave army to continue the purging of the world cycle. When that's done, when you have brought the last of us under your heel, what then? Will you destroy our race, even though you find things to admire in us?'

336

'Genocide?' said Auganzar. But he shook his head. 'It is not what I want, not if I am truthful. But truth is something I guard very carefully. I have many enemies, Consul. The worst of them is Zellorian. The truth is that I seek him. Above all others. There is no price I would not pay to have him. No price.'

'And the rest of mankind? What is the truth about them? You would let us go?'

'If you give me what I want, yes.'

Pyramors snorted. 'It is easily said.'

'Yes, I acknowledge that. But we should be able to conduct this affair sensibly, without resorting to barbaric measures.'

'What do you mean?'

Auganzar indicated Jannovar. She was standing rigidly, the sword hanging limply in her fingers. 'You do not want to see her tormented before you. This beautiful creature you have travelled so far to find. You must care deeply for her. You have made such sacrifices for her. I am moved by such things.'

Not for her, Pyramors thought. Not for this girl. And yet, as he looked at her, he felt a sudden stab of fear. She had offered him her love, as deep a love as Jannovar herself had shared with him. He had sensed that, touched it, and the realisation that within him a response waited, shook him. Her pain will not hurt me as Jannovar's would have, he had thought. If she must suffer. But as he looked across at the girl now, a great coldness took him. Death was a step away from her but first there would be torment. He shook his head. No, it must not happen.

'Kill us both,' he whispered.

Auganzar shook his head. 'I fear that would achieve nothing. We would all fail.'

'You are not savages!' Pyramors snapped. Below him he heard a tigerhound growl low in its throat.

'No, we are not savages. But unless you give me the key to the gate of Innasmorn, I will bring before you as many of your people as I must, and they will suffer and die. And I will have Marozul Zuldamar exposed. He and all those who support him, who *know* that a Path to Innasmorn exists.

337

The Garazenda will have no alternative but to agree to a renewed search for the Path. And if *they* find it, I cannot be responsible for what happens. There *are* Csendook who would commit genocide.'

'I don't understand.'

'There are members of the Garazenda who would welcome the genocide of your race. Xeltagar, for one. An old military genius who would sweep every living Man before him.'

Pyramors nodded slowly. He knew of Xeltagar, and Csendook like him. They had been the scourge of Man on many worlds.

'If they find Innasmorn, and they will, Consul, there will be no bargaining. No peace.'

'You'd prevent this?'

Auganzar nodded. 'Give me the key and only I will use it. With my personal Swarm, my Thousand. For this, you and the girl will have your freedom, on Innasmorn if you wish it. The killings here will stop. And your people on Innasmorn will be spared, save those I have named.'

Pyramors looked away, his mind trying to close out his surroundings. If he could believe this! But Auganzar had him trapped. If he refused to help, he and Jannovar and many others would die. Auganzar was utterly ruthless: he would go to any lengths to take from Pyramors what he wanted. But if he exposed Zuldamar and the Garazenda changed their view about searching for Innasmorn, it could be disastrous. Dare he trust Auganzar?

'There would be terms,' Pyramors said at last. His eyes fell on Jannovar. He began to realise how much he longed for her, to give in to his needs. Her sister was dead. He could go on pursuing her ghost but that would lead him to madness. He had to look away.

'Let me hear them,' said Auganzar. He called out to the Zemaal guarding the girl. 'Take her to the steps.'

Jannovar made only a token protest as the Zemaal prodded her to the foot of the dais. Auganzar called to Gehennon, and he, too, went to the steps.

'We all must talk,' Auganzar told Pyramors. He went down a few of the steps, Pyramors following. Jannovar looked searchingly at him and he tried to give her some comfort with a smile. Her eyes were filled with questions, doubts.

They were now standing in a semi-circle. Pyramors reached out with his fingers and touched those of Jannovar.

'You came here for this woman,' said Auganzar.

'Yes,' nodded Pyramors.

'But you had another purpose.' Auganzar tapped his breast plate, the twin circles. 'To take my life. Zuldamar's assassination plot.'

'You can understand my reasons.'

Auganzar smiled. 'Of course. You saw me as the prime threat to your race. Perhaps you still do. But we will achieve nothing without mutual trust.' He drew out one of the swords and set it down on the steps. The other he freed from its scabbard more slowly, holding it up to the light. It was a superb piece of craftmanship. As Auganzar went to set it down beside its mate, the sunlight seemed to catch its blade, dazzling them all for a moment so that Pyramors's hand tightened on his own weapon. Even Auganzar looked momentarily puzzled, as though the weapon had threatened for a second to come to life. Overhead there was a whisper of air and they looked up, expecting to see something in flight, but there was nothing, only the glare of the sun. Carefully Auganzar set down the sword.

Then he turned and began the climb. Somewhere out among his Zemaal there were murmurs of disapproval, but Auganzar turned, his face clouded.

'Be silent! No one is to move without my order. Not one pace.'

Absolute silence fell among the Csendook, but every eye was on the Supreme Sanguinary.

'Come to the dais. The three of you. Bring your sword, Consul.'

'Is he mad?' whispered Jannovar. Her own weapon had fallen to the stones but Pyramors retained his.

'Climb,' he said. Beside them, silently, Gehennon also climbed the steps.

The top of the dais had been cleared of the bulk of the debris that had covered it and was now in full view of the circle of warriors below. Auganzar turned, Gehennon beside him.

'You have your sword. The opportunity to use it on me,' said the Csendook to Pyramors. 'You'll die quickly if you do and will have achieved nothing. Others will follow me. But I am prepared to show you that I act in good faith, Consul. So tell me, what are your terms?'

'You can't bargain with him!' protested Jannovar, real-ising what the Csendook meant. 'Not for me, not for our freedom!'

'Be quiet,' Pyramors told her.

But she shook her head. 'Pyramors! You cannot give him what he wants!'

'We have already discussed the matter,' said Auganzar.

Jannovar gripped Pyramors's arm. 'This is insane! You know what he'll do! If you let him have the key – '

Pyramors stared directly at Auganzar, the Csendook tow-ering over him, even though they were some distance apart. Although the Zaru had no weapon, he would be a terrifying opponent. 'These are my terms. Jannovar! Witness them.'

She gaped at him, shaking her head in disbelief.

Gehennon bowed. 'I, too, witness them, Consul.'

'My terms are these,' said Pyramors. 'That I will give you the means to enter Innasmorn, on the understanding that you will not come for one year.'

Auganzar's eyes narrowed. 'A year?'

'In that time I will have the chance to let my people know you are coming, with your Swarm. The enemies of the Imperator and the Prime Consul will be warned. When you come, they must be spared.'

Jannovar gaped. Pyramors was *bargaining*? Believing that Auganzar would be willing to destroy only certain men?

'Six months,' said Auganzar.

'I need a year.'

Auganzar shook his head. 'I dare not delay my own plans beyond six months.'

Pyramors closed his mind to Jannovar's reactions. 'Six months. Very well.'

'What else?' said Auganzar.

340

'Immunity for my people afterwards. An end to persecution. You must leave Innasmorn once it's done. You will give the key to Innasmorn to none other.'

'That will mean those of your race who live in this world cycle will never find their way back to you,' said Auganzar. 'The door will be closed forever to them.'

'As it will for the Csendook.'

'Yes. There must be no contact. I agree. What else?'

'Just you, Supreme Sanguinary. You and your Thousand. No *moillum*. No other members of the Garazenda. No word of this must go to any of them.'

Auganzar nodded. 'I agree. And where is Zellorian?'

'In a mountain city, the Sculpted City.'

'In six months I will come to Innasmorn and I will level it. I will kill all those I find there. If Zellorian escapes me, I will pursue him, with every means at my disposal. All those who aid him will perish. He belongs to me. *That must be clear.*' The Supreme Sanguinary spoke this with real venom.

What is it that drives him to this? Pyramors wondered. What is there between these two masters of power? But he had no time to consider it now. 'I agree.'

Again Jannovar gripped his arm. 'Pyramors,' she said softly. 'You cannot mean to go through with this! He is a Csendook. He will destroy us all – '

He shook his head. 'No. We have to trust him.'

'If there is ever to be peace between our races,' said Auganzar, 'it will have to begin with trust. Are we agreed to the terms?'

Pyramors nodded. 'We are.'

'Then we must discuss the Path.' Auganzar turned to Gehennon. 'You know something of my Opener, but the truth of his past is more complex. What do you know of the Consummate Order?'

'Very little,' conceded Pyramors.

'Gehennon is an Ultimate, one of the most exalted positions attainable by an Opener. He has far greater powers than most other Openers. Through using these powers, through exercising far more discretion than the Consummate Order approved, he was cast out, as he told you. I recognised his potential. And I assume you will need an Opener?'

Pyramors masked his emotions. Trust. They would trust him. And yet, when he summoned the Accrual, it would demand a terrible price for the work it would do. It would create a Path back to Innasmorn, but it would feed on countless lives as a reward. An entire Swarm? Would it wait six months for such a feast? Would time matter to such a being? And would it trust Pyramors?

He stared at Auganzar. Amazingly, the Csendook was at his mercy. After all this time, these years of killing, the Testament, the Running Hunt, he could betray his nemesis, and with him his army. Feed them to the Accrual, the all-devouring horror with which he had already made his bargain.

'How is it done?' said Gehennon, suddenly much closer to him, as if trying to sift his thoughts.

'It is very dangerous,' answered Pyramors, hearing his own voice as if from a great distance.

'I'm sure it is,' nodded Auganzar.

'There must be sacrifice — '

'The giving of blood,' said Gehennon.

'Of life. Such a Path needs much life,' said Pyramors, his mind seeing again the shape of the Accrual, its frightful feasting.

He could feel Jannovar gripping him. 'Don't seal this bargain,' she begged him a last time.

Pyramors snapped out of the reverie. Suddenly he saw Auganzar more clearly, the eagerness, the vulnerability. Yes, he could destroy him and his Swarm. He could betray him, just as Zellorian had betrayed Man.

'It's not that simple,' he said. 'There are hazards.'

Gehennon stared at him even more intently. 'Such as?'

'There is a creature that has to be appeased,' Pyramors told him. 'A guardian. It is the key to the Paths between world cycles. And it must be satisfied.'

'Does it have a name?' said Gehennon.

The warrior looked directly at Auganzar. Trust. It, too, was a key. Though a gamble. 'It is called an Accrual. I have already spoken to this thing. As I came here. I promised it what it wanted.'

'Life,' said Gehennon. 'Sacrifice.'

Auganzar stepped forward. 'Csendook life. How many?'

'The Accrual has an insatiable lust for sacrifice. If you led a Swarm to it, it would devour every member,' said Pyramors.

Jannovar's eyes widened. Pyramors, she realised, could have *led* them to this thing, to disaster, tricked them all.

Gehennon was nodding. He drew back, turning to Auganzar with a surprised expression. 'Zaru, I think this Man can, after all, be trusted.'

Auganzar looked more formidable than ever. 'So you chose not to betray us.' He nodded to himself, deliberating. 'We know of the Accruals,' he told Pyramors grimly. 'Gehennon learned of them and their appetites. They do indeed guard the world cycles and prevent Crossings from one to another.'

'They are mutations,' said Gehennon. 'In the past they sprang from the Conceptors, the binders of the world cycles.'

'The Conceptors?' murmured Pyramors. 'In the Warhive?'

'They are the offspring of the Conceptors of world cycles. Just as the Accruals are. But the Accruals are rogue, outlawed. They serve nothing but their own lust for blood. In them it has become unnatural, a disease.'

'It promised to return Jannovar and me to Innasmorn,' said Pyramors. 'But in exchange, it seeks life, and an excess of it.'

'We knew of its existence,' said Auganzar. 'Through Gehennon's careful experiments in the realm of the Girders. But all our attempts to contact it have led to disaster. Ipsellin, an Opener who, like Gehennon, was an Ultimate, summoned it, as far as we know. He attempted to lead an army through the gate between world cycles.'

Pyramors nodded. 'A mere handful got through.'

'You know of them? Of Vorenzar?' said Auganzar.

'The Accrual told me a few had got through to Innasmorn. I don't know if Vorenzar was one of them.'

Gehennon again studied Pyramors. 'You can summon the Accrual?'

Pyramors nodded. 'Yes, I have the means. But as I have said, there will be a price.'

Auganzar looked out across the plaza. His Zemaal were still, the tigerhounds as silent as their masters. 'It will be met.'

When he finally looked away from his warriors, it was to find Pyramors standing at his side. 'There is no other way through,' said the Consul.

'Sacrifice,' breathed Auganzar. 'So many must die.'

'Who will you use?'

Auganzar looked down at his Zemaal. 'I admire your honesty, Consul. Because of that, I promise you that I will not use *moillum*.'

'You are committed?'

Auganzar nodded. 'All that I have said, I will do. You have six months. You must teach Gehennon what he must do to summon the Accrual.' Six months, he reflected, in which many Csendook will breathe their last, enjoy their last training, dream of final victories. Before they return here, to feed the hunger of the creature that straddles this dark gateway.

Pyramors and Jannovar watched Auganzar and Gehennon descend the steps, waving to the Zemaal to prepare to leave. Auganzar picked up his twin swords, pausing briefly to examine the second of them before he sheathed it. Pyramors was not certain, but he thought the Csendook was listening to the blade, almost as if it had spoken to him.

'Try to understand,' he told Jannovar as she put her arm about his waist. 'I have bought our people time.'

'You trust Auganzar?'

'I thought I had the means to destroy him, though Gehennon knew of the Accrual. But I chose to warn him. He is not without honour. If man is to survive, ironically, we have to trust Auganzar.'

She turned to the emptiness behind them, the open dais. 'And for us?'

'We go back and prepare.' He watched as the Csendook mounted their xillatraal beyond the plaza, and in moments they had gone from sight.

'I am not the one you came for.'

He put his fingers on her cheek. 'I came for Jannovar.'

'Perhaps you've found her.'

He nodded. 'Yes. I have found her.'

EPILOGUE

EPILOGUE

Pyramors gripped Jannovar tightly. He had warned her what would come, of the danger of facing the Accrual and its bizarre hunger. Alone on the dais, they held each other as Pyramors prepared to speak the words of the incantation that would begin the unlocking of the Path back to Innasmorn.

Something flickered in the air about them, light glancing from a drawn blade, perhaps, and they both watched the plaza around them for signs of treachery from the Csendook. But there was no movement. The air was utterly still.

Pyramors drew a thin line over his lower arm, letting a small amount of blood flow from it and he made a similar incision on Jannovar's arm. It was painless: she watched as their blood mingled, a few drops falling on to the stone floor.

Again there was a flash of something near them. It seemed to swoop down like an invisible hawk towards the blood. Presently Jannovar drew in her breath as she saw the blood bubble, as if it had been heated on the stone, and wisps of mist trailed up from it.

The mist thickened and within it something took shape. Pyramors drew back, holding his sword as if unsure of himself.

Far beyond him, on another world, Ussemitus felt a final surge of power. At last! He had given Pyramors up for lost, a victim of the Warhive, until now, pulling the spectral back through the Paths, about to quit Eannor, he had found him. Down in the zone of sacrifice, he was with the girl.

He had sent the spectral downwards, but had had to pause. There were Csendook here! Would he bring them to Innasmorn? Ussemitus felt the Mother within him stirring, urging him to speak to Pyramors through the spectral. Bring them! Bring them that the work may be done.

The spectral, burdened as it was with its injured companion, felt the abrupt flow of power as one of the Czendook drew a weapon which *called* to the elements. The elements of Eannor were stunted things, lacking the awesome power of those of Innasmorṇ. But the sword pulled, its will powerful. The spectral had to struggle to resist, realising that it would be sucked into the sword's power.

Too late the spectral felt its companion being sucked like a leaf into a whirlpool. There was a flicker of light, a brief turning of heads below as the watchers sensed something in the skies. Then the sword had taken its prey. The spectral hovered, careful. Below it, on the stones, the sword gleamed. It had trapped the injured spectral. It could not be freed. Not yet.

Ussemitus saw this. The Mother understood. *Bring them. You must bring them.*

The spectral waited for a long time then, listening to the words of the people below, the Man Pyramors, the huge Csendook, and the Opener. It dared not interfere. Pyramors was not in danger, not if he came to terms with his enemy. Ussemitus felt the will of the Mother urging him to force the spectral to act, but he would not. Events must be allowed to unfold. They would yet favour Pyramors, his freedom. But the Csendook could not come, not yet. In six months . . .

The spectral waited until it was over, watching as the Csendook and his followers moved away over the stones and beyond to the silence.

Soon afterwards Pyramors and the girl shed a little blood, and in horror the spectral realised that Pyramors was about to summon the Accrual, to attempt to bargain with it. Quickly the spectral swept down, using the power of the blood. As it reformed, it saw the confusion of the Man, the suspicion.

'Pyramors,' the spectral called, faintly.

'Who calls?' said the warrior. Jannovar drew back in alarm.

'One who will guide you safely through to Innasmorn. You must trust me. Do not summon the Accrual. It will destroy you.'

Pyramors looked no less dubious. He could see the shape of the ghost-like figure more clearly but he did not recognise it. It was not human, though it was vaguely familiar. 'Who are you from?'

'Allies of Aru Casruel sent me.'

'Aru! Is she alive?' he gasped.

'Yes. She escaped the Sculpted City and came to the Innasmornians. I will take you to her allies. Quickly.'

Pyramors turned to Jannovar, and he saw her puzzling over the strange words.

'Casruel?' she said. 'They are a family of nobles – '

He nodded. 'Some of the finest knights to survive the Crossing. I thought Aru was dead.'

'Come with me,' said the spectral. Already its form was shifting as the mist weakened. Beyond it the air moved, a line of darkness starting to open. 'I will guide you through and will not cross the path of the Accrual. You have cheated it of its prize. Dare you risk its fury?'

Pyramors frowned. It was true, he had nothing with which to appease the Accrual.

'Perhaps we should trust it,' whispered Jannovar.

Pyramors took her by the hand. He nodded. Time fled away from them mercilessly. They could afford no more for debate. Behind them the stones of the plaza were silent, and if there were watching eyes somewhere out beyond the perimeter, Pyramors was not aware of them. He knew he could not afford to refuse the strange hand of this guide.

'Very well. Take us.'

'Well?'

The word was like the twist of a knife. Jubaia slumped down in the prow of the gliderboat, shaking his head. Beyond him, eyes blazing, Aru had begun to look more like the warrior woman she must once have been during her days as a commander among her knights. Inactivity was wearing her nerves very thin.

'Jubaia,' she hissed, 'if we hear nothing from Ussemitus soon, we'll have to take action ourselves. Pyramors may be lost, but there are many people in the city we have to help. Vittargattus draws closer every day. Are you sure?'

Jubaia straightened. 'Yes, my lady. I've sought Ussemitus, but he is locked in his working. The World Splinter is like a tomb. Impenetrable. Nothing will stir its powers. Ussemitus cannot be reached.'

'How long dare we wait?'

'In three days Vittargattus will be in the valley. His shamen and those of his allies will want to unleash their powers soon after that. Unless Fomond has persuaded them otherwise, which I doubt.' For once his humour had entirely deserted him. He had the feeling that something malign watched over them, manipulated them. Drawing them into an inexorable darkness.

Aru's next words did nothing to allay his fears. 'Then we go into the city soon. Very soon.'

'Ah – you have a plan?'

She snorted. 'I'll let you know the details as we go along.'

He shuddered, and beneath him he felt Circu stir, echoing his misgivings.

Another dawn crept warily up over the mountains. Armestor pretended he had not seen it, nor heard the stirring of the armies around him. But Fomond's foot nudged him roughly.

'Prepare!' hissed his voice. 'We only have a few more days.'

'What's keeping them?'

'Ussemitus must know the dangers of delay. Vittargattus has gathered real power to him. If Aru wants to save her people, she is leaving it perilously close.'

'Perhaps we should leave this camp.'

'Vittargattus would not trust us to do that.'

'But you've seen his warriors. One word and they'll hang us up for the hawks.'

Fomond grimaced in the early light. Armestor's pessimism was unrelenting. But this time it was well-founded. Where were the others? The skies here were filled with silent menace, as though something far more ominous hid behind their clouds.

A storm was coming, but what terrible countenance would it wear? And who, if any, would prosper in its flood?

APPENDIX A

THE CSENDOOK MILITARY REGIME

The Csendook are governed by the Garazenda, a body comprised of all the principal generals, the foremost of which form an inner council, the Marozul.

Subordinate to the generals are the military commanders, the Zaru, who have control of a unit of the army, or Swarm. Each Zaru would have under him a number of captains or Zolutars, this number varying from Swarm to Swarm, dependent on the honorary standing of the Zaru, which would usually be calculated by victories in the field. The rank and file warriors of the Swarms are the Zemoks.

With the introduction of the gladiatorial system by the Supreme Sanguinary, Auganzar, who uses Men, or *moillum* as warriors to hasten the subjugation of rebels, new titles have been introduced. The *moillum* are trained in special schools, known as warhalls. Warhalls are put under the command of a Zaru acting for the owner of the warhall, who would be one of the Garazenda, and these Zaru are renamed Zarull. Their Zolutars serving specifically at the warhalls become Zolutulls.

The Zemoks are also renamed where they have specific duties in a warhall, or relating to *moillum*. Zemoks with a responsibility for training *moillum* are called Zemoi, while the Zemoks with particular responsibilities for animals are called Zemaal.

There are periodic Games held, the principal of which are at the stadia on the Warhive, although all warhalls have their arenas. There are also the Hunts, which are held over a designated area of land surrounding the warhalls, which are built away from the city areas for just this reason. The principal Games are known as Testaments, the Hunts as Running Hunts.

APPENDIX B

CSENDOOK NAMES

Csendook names are generally family names, with rank or title built into the name, usually as a suffix. Thus a member of the Marozul would have a name ending in -mar, such as Zuldamar; a member of the Garazenda who was not one of the Marozul, would have a name ending in -gar, such as Xeltagar; a Zaru would have a name ending in -zar, such as Auganzar, and so on.

Certain Csendook who have not earned enough battle honours to give them the right to their full title do not have part of the title suffixed to their name, such as Cmizen, the Keeper of Eannor, although this tends to be something peculiar to the Zemoks as promotion through the ranks almost always depends on battle honours.

Apart from the Zemoks, Csendook are usually addressed by subordinates by their rank or title rather than name: thus Uldenzar is addressed by his warriors as 'Zaru' and less often by his name. Auganzar, the Supreme Sanguinary (a title unique to him) is also a Zaru, and is most commonly addressed by this title by his contemporaries.

In *Star Requiem*, loyalties among the Csendook are divided, chiefly between the followers of the two Marozul, Zuldamar and Horzumar, and those of Auganzar. The principal characters are as follows:

ZULDAMAR – HORZUMAR

ULDENZAR   a Zarull with responsibility for Zuldamar's warhalls, both on the Warhive and on Eannor

GADRUZAR	a Zaru, some of whose Zemoks have been seconded to the Bone Watch on Eannor
VULPORZOL	a Zolutull, Uldenzar's agent on Eannor and the Warhive
DAGRAZEM	a Zemok at the Bone Watch, under Vulporzol
XINNAC	a Zemok at the Bone Watch, under Dagrazem's command
HUURZEM	a Zemok at the Bone Watch, under Dagrazem's command
THAGRAN	a Zemok at the Bone Watch, under Dagrazem's command
ULZEM	a Zemoi on the Warhive
CMIZEN	the Keeper of Eannor
ETRASCU	an Opener, assigned to Cmizen

AUGANZAR

KURDUZAR	a Zaru, keeper of the Bone Watch
UKRAZOL	a Zolutar, under Kurduzar
ZUARZAAL	a Zemaal, chief handler of the tiger-hounds, promoted to rank of Zolutar, re-named ZUARZOL
GUNTRAZAAL	Zemaal, subordinate to Zuarzaal
ANNUZAAL	subordinate to Guntrazaal
IMMARZOL	a Zolutar on the Warhive
QUENZOL	a Zolutar on the Warhive
HOZERMAAK	a scientist on the Warhive
XIMOZER	subordinate to Hozermaak
TORRUZEM	a Zemoi on Skellunda
KARANZOL	Zolutull, Keeper of Skellunda
RADUZOL	Zolutar on Warhive in Auganzar's warhall